BACK FROM THE DEAD

ANDRÉ SPITERI

 MAVERICK WORDS

First published by Maverick Words Ltd 2024

This novel is entirely a work of fiction. The names, characters and incidents portrayed in it are the work of the author's imagination. Any resemblance to actual persons, living or dead, events or localities is entirely coincidental.

André Spiteri asserts the moral right to be identified as the author of this work.

First edition

ISBN: 978-1-7384480-1-2

PART ONE

CORNERED

CHAPTER 1

I'm rubbing the sleep from my eyes, cursing myself for having that sixth pint even though I knew it was a shite idea, when I spot the dead bloke.

He's lying on the left side of my bed. Dressed to the nines in a black tux, red bowtie, and immaculate iron-grey pompadour. A Rolex peeks out ostentatiously from beneath his left shirt cuff. And his black brogues are so shiny they reflect the weak light that's seeping through a crack in the blackout curtains, making it pool on my white and blue checked duvet.

He looks relaxed. Peaceful.

Except for one tiny problem. He isn't fucking breathing. And, judging by the iciness radiating from his skin, it seems unlikely that his lungs are going to magically fill up with air and get back to doing their job.

I jump out of bed like I've been scalded, my face contorted in fear and disgust, and stagger backwards until I bump into the sofa across the room. In the twelve or so paces it takes me to do this, the alcohol-induced tendrils of pain that were toying with my temples mere seconds ago have turned into a full-on rager. My head's throbbing in time with my heart, which, through some freakish feat of biology, seems to have split into two parts that have lodged themselves in my eardrums.

The familiar itchy warmth expands across my chest, like flames swallowing up a nest of dry twigs.

My breath quickens.

The four corners of my studio flat close in on me.

Oh my fucking god. Who is this bloke? What's he doing in my bed?

What in the name of fuck?

I reach for the pile of clothes lying next to my bed and snatch my phone from the back pocket of my jeans. My fingers are trembling so badly it takes me four attempts to dial 999. But with my thumb millimetres away from the big green button, the image of a dank, dark prison cell fills my mind's eye, and I fling the phone away like it's a live grenade, sending it clattering onto the floor.

How do I explain a dead man to the police? In my bloody bed?

How did he get here?

They're going to think I had something to do with this, aren't they? It would be just my fucking...

Luck.

I double over, gasping for breath. The room. It's...

It's like there isn't enough air to go around. My lungs feel like they're collapsing inwards and my stomach's on fire.

'Good god, man. Get a grip,' I mutter unsteadily, doing my best not to give in to the increasingly overwhelming sense that I'm drowning. 'Of course they won't arrest you. You had nothing to do with this. At all.'

But I might as well be talking to a brick wall for all the

good it's doing me. Telling an anxious person not to panic is like telling somebody with a cataclysmic case of the runs to stop shiteing.

I sit down on the edge of the sofa and focus on my breathing like my therapist taught me.

Breathe in. Breathe out.

In.

Out.

In.

Out.

With every outbreath, my heart rate slows down ever so slightly. When it reaches a more reasonable tempo, I walk to the kitchenette, where I turn the tap and splash my face. The cold water jolts me, and the brain fog eases.

Come on, Bertie, bud. You'll get through this.

I walk towards the bed and force myself to give the bloke a proper look.

He's lying on his back with his eyes closed and his arms by his sides. His suit looks expensive. Tailored. Possibly bespoke. His face meticulously shaved. The skin clear. Unbroken. There are no obvious signs of violence. At least, not that I can see. No bruising. No blood.

For all I know, he had a fucking heart attack.

But why is he here?

Surely, there must be a reasonable explanation for that.

Right?

I close my eyes and think back to last night, squeezing my brain cells for all they're worth. Willing myself to remember.

Memories come back in brief flashes.

Joan telling us something Phillip did. Something typically idiotic of him, but which I can't quite put my finger on.

Shawn being reliably crass.

Me feeling decidedly worse for wear. Cutting my night short. Coming back home to an empty flat.

Yes, empty. I'm sure of it.

Whatever happened here must've happened after I checked out for dreamland.

That's all I can tell the police. And if they don't believe me... well... they're welcome to dig into my miserable excuse for a life as much as they like.

I bend down and reach for the phone, which has landed face down next to a stray sock. The thin, white arm stretching out before me looks like a dead fish. Or an alien appendage.

Boom. Boom. Boom.

The knocking — three sharp raps of the knuckles — reverberates around the walls, and I almost lose my balance and fall flat on my face.

'Holy mother of god!'

My heart seems to have lodged itself in my throat, and the words come out in a half-choked croak.

Is this it? Could it be the police?

I stand up on unsteady legs and stare at the dead bloke. A wave of nausea sweeps my body. I swallow down what feels like a big chunk of rotten apple.

Oh fucking hell.

Who is it?

What do I do?

I creep towards the hallway, feeling like the character in a horror movie who's walking blissfully towards their death.

'You're not home. Don't answer. Step away you blithering idiot,' my inner voice screams at me.

But the panic I'd just about managed to hold at bay is back in full force, gripping me in its steel claws. I'm just an outside observer, watching myself put one wrong foot in front of the other.

My eye is level with the peephole. As if on cue, my visitor knocks again, making me jump out of my skin. My breathing's too loud. Can they hear it through the door?

I risk a quick peek. When I see the granny glasses, fluffy pink sweater, and steel-grey bun on the other side of the door, I recoil for the second time this morning.

Dear god. Of all the people who could've darkened my doorstep.

I back away. Break into a run. She knocks again, louder.

'Bertie! Are you there?' she says. 'I need to speak with you.'

'Just a minute!' I shout hoarsely.

Fuck. Why'd I do that?

Operating purely on autopilot, I pull on my jeans and a striped Gap t-shirt. Then I cover the dead bloke as best as I can, pulling the duvet up as far as it can go and rumpling it in a fruitless attempt to conceal the obviously human-shaped bulge underneath.

This is the last thing I fucking need. Morag getting involved. I can see her, pushing her chest out, a twinkle in her eye. Our building's self-appointed keeper and the world's biggest busybody, feeling completely in her element.

More knocking.

'Aye, five seconds!'

Steeling myself, I crack the door open, hoping my dishevelled appearance will discourage her from going on one of her endless diatribes about whoever the fuck's bothering her this week.

'Hiya Morag, what can I do for you?' I say, making my tone as bright and neighbourly as I can muster.

'Oh Bertie, hi,' she replies, casual as can be, as if she'd bumped into me at the cafe down the road, not almost banged down my fucking door at 9:45am on a Saturday morning. 'Have you noticed any water in your bathroom, by any chance?'

This throws me for a loop.

'Water? How do you mean?'

'I noticed water pooling around my sink while I was brushing my teeth this morning.'

I want to facepalm myself. But through an astonishing feat of self-control, I don't. What do I care about her oral hygiene? Dear god.

'...it's seeping from between the tiles,' she continues.

'Sorry, come again?' I say.

'I said at first I thought I'd splashed the water when I rinsed,' she repeats, more slowly. 'But it's seeping from between the tiles.'

'Right,' I reply.

We stand there for a second, the silence hanging awkwardly between us. She looks at me expectantly, her hands resting on her considerable hips.

'Err... as far as I know my bathroom's fine. I'm not sure what to tell you...' I stammer, taking an involuntary step backwards.

'Perhaps it's nothing. The gutters might've clogged and the rainwater could be trickling down through the wall,' she says. 'Anyway my plumber's taking a look just now. Maybe he can come up and check your bathroom when he's done with mine?'

My stomach feels like somebody forced a can of petrol down my throat and chased it with a lit match. It takes every ounce of mental energy I have to keep an outward appearance of what I hope comes across as nonchalance.

'It's really not a good time,' I say.

'Oh I don't think it will take too long. I'm sure it's the gutters. But you never know. It might be a leak, so we'd better get it checked out.'

I will myself not to look behind me at the bed and scream. Christ on a monocycle with a flat tyre.

'Err I'm fairly certain I don't have a leak. My bathroom's fine. Anyway, I'd rather get my own plumber and, as I said, it's not the best time.'

I can hear a hint of desperation creeping into my voice as I repeat what must be the biggest understatement in the history of understatements.

'Let me see what the plumber says,' Morag insists. 'Water damage can turn nasty if you don't get on top of it straight away. Better safe than sorry, right?'

I could honestly throttle her, but decide arguing the point isn't going to get me anywhere.

'Fine, but it depends what time he's coming,' I say in a last-ditch attempt to buy myself some breathing space. 'Err... someone's coming over so I can't really have him here.'

'He'll come up in the next ten minutes or so.'

'Right. Send him over and I'll see where I'm at.' I bluster.

And with that, I slam the door without waiting for her reply.

Shite! Hellfire!

Fuuuuuuckkkkkk!

I need to do something. Fast. Before that bloody plumber comes knocking.

'Think, man. Think,' I tell myself in between shallow, gasping breaths.

But it's just.

Too.

Hard to focus.

I'm paralysed.

This is a nightmare, isn't it? My alcohol-pickled brain playing nasty tricks.

Has to be.

I grab the fleshy part of my thigh with my thumb and forefinger and twist sharply to the left. A jolt of pain radiates outward.

'Ow. Fuck!'

Nope. Not a nightmare.

I scan the room frantically as the walls loom closer, threatening to bury me. My studio's not exactly palatial, so there isn't much to look at. The double bed takes up most of one wall, the sofa takes up the wall opposite, and the longer wall facing the bathroom and entryway is shared between the five-unit kitchenette and the closet.

The closet!

I race towards it, sweeping all the clothes hangers to one side and sizing up the space — a rectangular box around one foot wide by two feet deep.

Can I pop him in here for now, until the plumber leaves and my head's screwed back on straight?

No, it's too tight. I don't want to risk him falling into the plumber's lap while he's walking by.

What about under the bed?

Aye, that's probably better. Safer. It might be snug, but I'm sure he's past minding about that.

Running purely on adrenaline, I pull out the storage boxes, some of which I haven't touched in aeons. Fine dust fills my airways, and a fit of sneezing doubles me up.

I wait for it to pass, eyes closed, chest bucking in anticipation of a sneeze that never quite makes it out. Sniffling, I finish clearing the space under the bed, set the covers aside, and size up the bloke.

He's about five foot eight, average build. Not a hefty guy, thank god for small favours. Admittedly, my exercise routine mainly involves lifting sandwiches off the table and moving them towards my mouth. But seeing as he's of similar build to me it seems doable. It's not like he's going to thrash about.

I wipe my nose absently with the back of my hand, grab him under the arms, and pull him towards me. The weight takes me by surprise and I drop him. His arms hang loosely over the bed, grazing the floor.

I take a few deep breaths and try again. This time I put my back into it, and manage to move him half off the bed before I have to let go. His head bangs against the floor with a sickeningly loud thud.

10:15, proclaims the clock on my side table.

How long has it been since Morag came up? Five? Ten minutes?

That blasted plumber's going to knock any minute.

I brace myself, place my hands under the body's armpits, and give a mighty heave. He slips off the bed, unbalancing me in the process, and his head bangs the floor. Good thing he's past worrying about concussions. My arms hurt. I think I might've pulled a muscle. But he's off the bed. Half the battle.

I squat next to the body, move it parallel to the bed, and try pushing it into the space I've made underneath. The legs slot in like the final missing piece of a jigsaw puzzle and disappear from view. But the head won't budge. Something's blocking the way.

Right on cue, the door knocks. I push the bloke frantically with both hands. Willing his head to get under the bed.

'Come on. Please. Fucking move it,' I plead.

But the dead bloke stubbornly refuses to cooperate.

I peer underneath the bed and immediately see what's wrong. There are two shoe boxes lying at an angle, stuck between one of the bed's legs and a large plastic box. I move them out of the way to the sounds of more door-knocking and give the body a good shove. The head disappears from view.

The bloke behind the door is tall and gangly, with an expanding forehead and a scruff of white-speckled beard.

'Hiya bud, can I help you?' I tell him, hoping I don't look too flushed from the exertion.

'Alright bud? Morag sent me,' he replies, brandishing his paint and grime-splattered toolbox like a weapon. 'Said I should take a look at your bathroom.'

'Did she? Does it look like a leak then?' I ask him, hoping my voice doesn't sound as shaky to him as it does to me. 'Honestly, my bathroom's bone dry. If there's a leak I don't think it's coming from here.'

'Doesn't matter if your bathroom's dry or not, bud,' he fires back. 'The leak could still be coming from here, even if it's not affecting you. Just let me check and I'll be out of your hair as soon as I can.'

'OK then,' I say.

I swallow nervously and let him in.

He gives my studio a long, appraising look I find unnerving. Has he gazed just a tad too long at my bed?

I scan the small gap between the edge of the duvet and the floorboards, but nothing jumps out at me. If I didn't know about the body, I wouldn't be able to tell something's amiss. But, for some reason, I don't find this the least bit reassuring.

'Err, bathroom's this way,' I say, resisting the urge to grab him by the arm and drag him away.

'Right.'

I usher him into the room. He puts down his toolbox and takes another look around.

'So Morag's saying her leak's coming from here?' I say, compelled to fill the silence and eager for him to do what he's here to do and get the fuck out double quick.

I wave a finger at the area around my pedestal sink.

'See,' I say hopefully, giving the tiles a few tentative swipes with my right hand, 'Bone dry.'

The plumber looks at the tiles, cocks his left ear, and raps a few places with his knuckles. Seemingly satisfied, he squats in front of his toolbox and takes out a small device that reminds me of the PKE meter the ghostbusters use to detect ectoplasm. Seems apt.

'Just looking for wet spots inside your walls,' he explains. 'This is a thermal imaging camera. If there's a leak, I should be able to see it.'

'You mean that camera shows you differences in temperature?' I ask, unconsciously moving between the plumber and the bathroom door to block his view of the bed.

Do dead blokes in tuxes show up on thermal imaging cameras? I suppress the urge to run my hands through my hair.

'Kind of. The difference in temperature is quite subtle, but moisture spreads in a very distinctive pattern. It's easy to recognise it if you know what you're doing. And this camera's quite powerful.'

Fabulous. Just what I want to hear.

He scans the whole room, taking his time. My heart skips a beat as he hovers over the bathroom door, into my studio's main room and the bed beyond. Then he stops abruptly.

What the fuck? Has he just seen a human-shaped cold pocket? Is this it?

Something sharp twists in my stomach.

'There you go. There's a bunch of water pooled there,' he says, pointing the camera towards the bath, 'It's probably where the pipes from your sink go.'

He squats in front of his toolbox and produces a Phillips screwdriver.

'Let me take a look, see what's going on,' he mutters to himself.

He gets to work unscrewing my bath's plastic front panel, whistling a tune that sounds familiar but which I can't for the life of me seem to recognise. I shuffle my feet like I need to pee and scratch the back of my head absently with my right hand.

'Had a good one last night, by the looks of you, eh?' he says conversationally, his eyes never leaving the bath.

So he hasn't seen anything, has he?

No, surely not. He pointed that blasted thing in the bed's general direction for barely half a second, and I was in the way.

'Err aye, not too bad,' I say. 'Could've done with an extra hour of sleep to be honest, but apparently my plumbing had other ideas.'

'There it is,' he grunts. 'This pipe's wet to the touch. Do you have some towels? This is going to get messy.'

'Aye, sure.'

I'm reluctant to leave him alone, because the edge of the bed is in his line of sight.

Would it be weird if I told him to feel free to make as big of a mess as he wants?

Who'd bloody say that? Of course it would be weird. Jesus Christ.

I step out of the bathroom and walk towards the closet, but not before stealing a quick glance. The plumber's lying flat on his back, unscrewing something with an adjustable wrench.

Feeling thankful I decided against stuffing the dead bloke in the closet after all, I turn the knob, open the closet door wide, and survey the array of towels on the upper shelf. I pull two blue ones with frayed edges out from the middle of the pile, placing them in the crook of my left arm, and get ready to go back to the bathroom. But, just as I'm about to turn around, I hear a noise that freezes my blood.

I've never been near a gun in my entire life, but there's no mistaking the click of the safety being released. I've watched enough gangster films to recognise the sound.

'Turn around, very slowly. And don't try anything funny, bud.'

The previously laid back voice has acquired a distinctly steely edge. The tone of a man who doesn't take shite from anyone. Especially not from the likes of me.

But, why? What the hell just happened? Who is this bloke?

'OK, OK. Don't shoot,' I say, hating the tremble in my voice.

I lift my hands chest high, palms open, and keep them shoulder-width apart, letting the towels tumble soundlessly to the floor. I turn around slowly, taking great care to show him I'm not going to try and be a hero.

'Alright bud,' the plumber says, the barrel of his gun aimed straight at my chest, his arm rock-steady. 'We need to have a chat, you and I. Why don't you sit down?'

My stomach drops and my arsehole clenches. The troublesome itchiness in my chest is back with a vengeance. I tiptoe my way to the sofa and sit down.

'That's good,' he says. 'Nice and easy.' He walks closer, pulls up a chair, and sits astride it, his gun trained on me the entire time, not moving a fraction of an inch.

'Now, tell me, Bertie,' he says, his voice positively over-flowing with quiet menace, 'what have you done with that prick?'

CHAPTER 2

So, you may be wondering at this point. How the hell did I end up with a dead bloke in my bed, a gun in my face, and no recollection of what must've been a pretty eventful night?

Well, it's... complicated. But I can explain.

Or, at least, I can tell you what I've managed to piece together.

My city — let's call it Strathburgh, that's close enough — is unofficially divided into four sections. And when I say unofficially, I mean the drug gangs divvied things up between them without any input from the local authorities. South of the river Strath, which bisects the city into more or less equally-sized semi-circular zones, the Billy Boys and the Strike Team coexist in relative harmony. But north of the river, where I live, the Company and the Red Hand have been on the brink of all-out war for years, though the tension has never quite boiled over.

Nobody's really sure what caused the rift between the Chairman and Boaby Kiernan, the leaders of the Company and the Red Hand. But, whatever happened, it must've been serious, because, growing up, I remember them — at the time, the Chairman was more simply known by his given name, Franco Guthrie, and Kiernan was... well, he was always Boaby to everyone — being as thick as thieves. Getting themselves into all sorts of trouble and laughing all the way to the local police station. Then, at some indeterminate point, they went from being best buddies to a high-stakes dick-measuring contest, and formed two separate gangs that, by proxy, were also at loggerheads. Which is why, on a blustery September afternoon around twelve months before my appointment with a gun-wielding plumber, Al and Jonno, two long-standing members of Guthrie's crew, were about to come to blows with two blokes from the Red Hand who had had the audacity of loitering in the car park of The Sentinel, a graffiti-riddled pebbledash box with a flat roof where Company men whiled away the time drinking beer, playing pool, and, occasionally, talking shop.

'What the fuck do you think you're doing here, you pair of shrivelled up bawbags?' Jonno said, spreading his legs and squaring his shoulders. 'Yer mothers will be waiting to tuck you in. Move along.'

Tall and heavy, with a shaved head and deep-set brown eyes that bored into you from under bushy black eyebrows, Jonno looked formidable even in his usual stance — shoulders slumped, back sloping forward, staring intensely in the distance at something only he could see. The kind of bloke you'd cross the road to avoid even if it added twenty minutes to your journey. But when he stood to his full six feet three, his black t-shirt billowing behind him like a pirate ship's sail, he looked positively terrifying. A giant in a land of five year-olds.

'You heard him,' Al said, nodding at the two blokes.

'Unless you want me to rearrange those two sorry excuses for faces into something more presentable.'

At five feet five, skinny almost to the point of emaciation, and snappily dressed in light blue skinny jeans, white Nike trainers, and a paisley shirt, Al couldn't have looked more different to Jonno if he'd tried. The twins, they called them, in reference to the film with Arnie and Danny DeVito, strictly behind their backs. But nobody who'd spent any time on the streets of north Strathburgh would dare underestimate him. Not if they were in their right minds.

Fingering his left shirt cuff, where he kept a razor blade handy for situations just like these, he took a step forward, the chib scar snaking its way up his right cheek looking unnervingly pale in the flat light of the overcast sky. One of his two adversaries — a short, pimply bloke who couldn't have been a day over eighteen and had the same expression a deer would get if it were caught in an oncoming lorry's headlights — took an involuntary step backwards. But the other bloke, a seasoned veteran of the street at twenty-five, stood his ground and sneered.

'What's so funny? Eh?' Al asked, taking another step forward. 'Did I stutter?'

Even though it was four on a Friday afternoon, the car park was mostly empty. But a small crowd of Company blokes had congregated on The Sentinel's front steps, pint glasses in hand, looking on like this was a cage match on the telly. The distant sounds of car engines, the beep, beep, beep of traffic lights, and semi-regular gusts of wind punctuated the silence.

The four blokes sized each other up, each considering their chances. Jonno balled his meaty hands into fists. Al took another step forward. Pimple guy took a step back.

And the sneering bloke, whose Ma had christened him Ritchie, sneered on, not conceding a single inch.

'Keep the head, bud. We're leaving,' Ritchie said, breaking the tension, casual as can be. 'We're only here to deliver a message, not to step on any toes.'

'That joke Boaby Kiernan can deliver any messages to the Chairman in person,' Al growled. 'If he has the balls to do so.'

'Och, the message isn't for the Chairman,' Ritchie said, spitting the word 'Chairman' out like he'd found a hair in his porridge, and digging his hands deeper into the pockets of his dark blue Adidas trackies. 'It's for you.'

Al and Jonno moved forward in lockstep, staring Ritchie down. Ritchie held eye contact. His chin, which was covered with a scraggly patchwork of pubic hairs that just barely approximated a goatee, jutted outward. Behind him, the other bloke was pointedly studying the tops of his black Vans trainers like they were an interesting new specimen.

'Mr Kiernan says Mrs Edwards won't be getting any special treatment,' Ritchie continued.

At the mention of his Ma, Al's knuckles went ghostly white, his lips pressed themselves into a barely perceptible line, and his eyes turned to slits. In a flash, he was on Ritchie, snatching him by his tracksuit top and lifting him several inches off the ground. Ritchie looked straight at him, unperturbed.

'What's that supposed to mean, you fucking prick?' Al hissed, giving Ritchie a noseful of his lager-flavoured breath.

Ritchie curled his lips in distaste. His buddy took another step backwards, his face the sickly pale of some-body who's just had a crippling stomach cramp and realised they're miles away from a working toilet. Jonno moved closer, staring both blokes down, but not before he'd given Al a subtle warning look. They were under strict orders not to take things too far. The Chairman was keen for business to keep flowing steadily no matter what, and giving the Red Hand a pretext to up the ante would be very bad for that.

'Ask her. She'll tell you herself,' Ritchie said from around his sneer.

Al sized him up, his eyes scanning him from the top of his bowl cut to the tips of his Vans — unlike his jumpy companion's, his were an impossibly bright shade of red. Then he let go of him.

Ritchie landed with a soft thud of rubber soles on gravel, scoffed, and smoothed down his top. Seconds later, he was flat on his arse, blood gushing from his nose. Al's fist had come out of nowhere, connecting with a crunch of cartilage on bone.

'You fucking prick,' Ritchie said, his voice sounding like a foghorn. 'You're going to regret that.'

But there was a note of petulance in his voice, and the sneer was gone. Al took another step forward, looming over him.

'Consider that a friendly warning,' he said, nodding at the bright red blood that had covered Ritchie's chin and chest. 'I won't be so gentle next time round. Understood?'

He spat on the ground, and the bright green glob of coagulated snot just about missed one of Ritchie's immaculate trainers.

'Now fuck off.'

Ritchie, not so sneery anymore, got to his feet and beckoned his buddy with a jerk of his head. They backed away slowly, not wanting to turn their backs on Al and Jonno while they were still within striking distance.

'I said, am I clear?' Al repeated.

'We'll see each other again soon, I'm sure,' Ritchie replied.

With several feet between them and Al and Jonno, the two blokes turned around and walked out of the car park as briskly as they could without breaking into a run.

'What the fuck was that about?' Jonno asked Al when the two blokes were out of view.

'I've no fucking clue and I don't care,' Al replied. 'I'm not about to ruin my afternoon by talking to Ma.'

'Fair enough,' Jonno said.

'Pint?'

'Aye, OK.'

They strolled towards The Sentinel. The crowd had dispersed the minute they'd realised the action wouldn't go further than a single punch. So when they stepped into the cave-like interior of the pub, it was abuzz with chatter and the sounds of billiard balls clicking against each other. The air reeked of stale beer and the sweetly aromatic smell of good weed. On the stereo system Struan, The Sentinel's landlord, kept behind the bar, David Coverdale was lamenting having to go again on his own.

'Hey Al, what did those two poor sods want?' said Mel, a short, stout guy who was sitting in one of the booths nursing a whisky.

'None of your fucking business,' Al said.

'Och, don't tell me. They were asking you where you got that shirt from weren't they? D'you tell them it's your grannie's leftover wallpaper?'

'It's called fashion, you tasteless prick. Look it up.' Al retorted.

Mel burst into low, trollish laughter that turned into a ripe cough deep in his chest. Jonno and Al walked up to the bar, and Struan, a gangly forty-something who looked like he'd been teleported from 1983, wordlessly pulled two pints and handed them over.

'Ta,' Al said.

'What the fuck's this, bud?' Jonno said. 'That's way too much head.'

He looked around the room, made a show of winking at Al, then lobbed the glass lazily at Struan, spilling beer and foam all over the bar top. Struan ducked just in time, and the glass shattered behind him, soaking his wispy, mouse-coloured skullet and the back of his denim jacket.

'Whoops,' Jonno said, the ghost of a smile playing on his lips.

The pub erupted into more trollish laughter. Struan, who knew better than to protest, laughed along, then pulled another pint and scurried off in search of cleaning supplies

'That's better. Good man,' Jonno said, taking a long pull from his beer.

He eased himself onto a bar stool. It creaked ominously, but held. Al took the stool to his right, and looked down at his untouched beer, turning the glass around and around between his palms.

'What's the matter?' Jonno asked.

'Fucking disgrace is what's the matter,' Al said. 'Absolute state of it. Those bastards are getting bolder by the second.'

'Och, aye. I think you're spot on,' Jonno said, draining the rest of his beer and snapping his fingers at Struan, who was on his knees, mopping up the puddle of beer with blue roll. 'We've been far too soft on those pricks, if you ask me.'

Struan got up, threw a sopping wad of blue roll into the bin, and pulled another pint. Jonno gulped half of it down and belched gingerly, covering his mouth. A jarringly dainty gesture for such a big man.

'Orders are orders,' he said with a shrug.

'Well, tell you what,' Al said. There was venom in his voice, but he'd pitched it low so only Jonno would hear, even though Struan had disappeared round the back and they were alone at the bar. 'He should come spend the day. Do some actual work for a change, instead of trousering most of the money we bust our balls to earn and brown-nosing bankers and politicians.'

Jonno kept his face neutral and said nothing.

'Och, you're a fucking softie, you know that?' Al said, clapping him on the back.

He took another small sip of beer.

'How'd you get on with Neil, anyway? Did it take long to restock?'

'Och, what an eejit,' Jonno said, giving Al a contemptuous look. 'I had to get the bus down to Wee Dave's.'

Al snorted laughter.

'What? Why?'

'His bloody motor wouldn't start.'

'Well, you're the one who recruited him, weren't you? Maybe you need to tighten up your HR and whatnot.'

'Fuck off, won't you?' Jonno said.

They fell into a companionable silence. Jonno staring ahead and Al toying with his beer glass while the noise around them got louder and more raucous.

'So are you going to-'

Al's phone buzzed in his pocket, cutting him off. The number was a local landline, but not one he recognised. In his line of work, most calls came from numbers he didn't recognise, so he swiped right, wondering whether he'd have to forgo his evening plans before said evening even started because some high roller felt like partying.

'Aye?' he said.

'Mr Allan Edwards?' the voice on the other end — a woman with a hoarse voice — asked.

'Aye?' he said warily.

'I'm calling from the Royal Infirmary. I have you down as Mrs Jane Edwards' next of kin?'

The ball of lead he invariably felt whenever Ma was the topic of conversation made its presence felt. He gripped his phone tighter, pressing it to his ear.

'What's she done now?' he snapped.

'Mrs Edwards was admitted about an hour ago,' the woman on the other end replied. 'She's been assaulted.'

He could hear her frown in disapproval at his reaction. The lead in his stomach became more substantial.

'I see,' he said, trying to feign concern. 'Is she alright?'

'Aye, she's going to be fine,' the woman said. 'But she's asked us to call you.'

Al sighed. Of course she'd do that. She knew he wouldn't answer if it was her number on the caller ID.

'When are the visiting hours over?' he asked, getting up off the stool.

'10pm,' she replied.

'I'll get there as soon as I can.'

CHAPTER 3

Originally housed in an 18th century neoclassical building south of the Strath, the Royal Infirmary was moved to a sprawling, modern campus about ten miles northwest of the city proper in 2010. The new hospital's grounds were surrounded by rolling hills, a nest of narrow B-roads in dire need of resurfacing, and little else. So they were of very little interest to the Company, the Red Hand, or any other gang. It was a dead spot. Neutral ground.

Al followed the signs to the visitor's car park, stepped out of his black Discovery, and made his way to the hospital's big glass double doors, passing next to a scrawny older patient who was puffing away at a cigarette despite being hooked to a drip. Wading through the thick crowd of visitors, patients, and staff that thronged the lobby, he took the lift to the second floor, then followed the signs to the orthopaedic ward, rang the bell, and waited for someone to admit him, tapping an erratic rhythm with his fingers against his thigh as he did so.

The fact he'd got a call from Ma so soon after the

confrontation outside The Sentinel was nagging at him, though he wasn't sure what the connection was yet — if there was one. But, more than that, the prospect of spending any length of time with her in the confined space of a hospital ward cubicle had set him on edge, heightening his senses to the point where they were almost about to overload. The fluorescent lights were too bright. The sounds of the hospital too loud. The faintly medicinal smells of bleach and disinfectant too pungent.

He ran through the conversation he was about to have with her, trying to anticipate how she'd make out whatever had happened to be his fault and thinking of ways he could respond without escalating, as their conversations tended to do. But it was no use. Every run through had a worse outcome than the previous one, which made his body flush with heat and the bile rise in his throat.

The door opened with a harsh electronic buzz, and he inhaled sharply. With his hands in his pockets, feeling the comforting weight of his car key in his palm and the razor blade in his shirt cuff pressed against his wrist, he walked in towards the nurses' station, and nodded at the bloke on duty.

'Jane Edwards, please,' he said.

'Room 209, bed F,' the nurse answered in a pleasant baritone.

'Ta,' Al replied.

He walked down the corridor, eyes fixed on the grey aluminium plates with the blue room numbers printed on them. When he reached 209, he stopped in front of the door and steeled himself, pushing away his angry inner voice and clearing his mind.

'Are you alright?' a voice said from behind him.

'Fuck!' he muttered, jumping and turning around to

see a woman in blue scrubs and a surgical mask peering at him from behind chunky black glasses.

'Och, sorry, didn't mean to startle you,' she said.

'It's fine,' he replied, feeling decidedly not fine. 'Just about to go in.'

'Och, OK,' the woman replied. 'Just go to the desk if you need any help.'

He walked through the open door into the room. Bed F was the last one on his right, by a window overlooking the landscaped gardens below. From his vantage point, he could see a pair of matchstick legs covered in a hospital-issue blanket, and the edge of a light blue armchair's seat.

He took a deep breath, walked down the aisle to the bed, then surveyed the scene. At fifty-seven, Jane Edwards' hard-partying lifestyle had left its mark. Deep wrinkles spread out from the corners of her eyes and the folds around her mouth. Her skin was sallow despite the considerable amount of makeup she'd slathered on. And her frizzy hair, which she'd dyed dirty blonde, hung lifelessly down to her shoulders. She was sitting up in bed, her phone in her immaculately manicured left hand, her right hand resting in a sling. A puffy, purplish black bruise covered her eye and most of the left side of her face.

'Ma, what the hell happened?' Al said, easing into the armchair and crossing his legs tightly, an involuntarily defensive gesture. The nagging at the back of his mind grew louder.

Jane didn't reply. The talon-like red nail of her index finger clicked on her phone screen. When she finished what she was doing, she swiped away the app, placed the phone on the bed next to her, and looked Al up and down.

'Took you long enough to come,' she said by way of

welcome. 'The nurse said she called you almost an hour ago.'

Al's crossed legs tightened. He breathed and counted to ten. It wouldn't do to snap at your injured mother in a ward full of people.

'I got stuck in traffic,' he said, struggling to keep his tone even and just about managing. 'I came as soon as I could.'

'Busy day at work?' she said, more a statement than a question.

'It was, aye,' Al said.

'But you wouldn't know much about work, would you?' he bit back. Instead, he focused on his breathing, his face impassive.

They looked at each other like two pro wrestlers circling the ring, each waiting for the other's move. Jane straightened her gown with her good hand. Al uncrossed his legs, shifted in the chair to ward off the pins and needles that were creeping up his left thigh, then recrossed them.

'So are you going to tell me what happened? Who did this to you, Ma?' Al said, hoping her answer wouldn't confirm his worst fears.

She clenched her jaw and fidgeted nervously with her phone. Al leant forward, looking at her expectantly.

'Promise you won't be angry,' she said.

'What?' Al replied, nonplussed. 'Why would I be angry?'

'Because-'

She put her face in her hand and shuddered. Then she wiped her eyes gingerly with her thumb, careful not to smear her makeup, and looked back at him.

'It was one of Boaby Kiernan's guys,' she said. 'I-'

'How'd you get involved with him?' Al shouted,

shooting up from his chair, which squeaked on the vinyl flooring. Ritchie's words rang in his ears. So this was what he'd been going on about. Fuck.

The volume of the chatter that filled the ward lowered noticeably, as if somebody had turned the knob on a stereo system. An overweight woman in a flowery blouse stared at him openly from the cubicle across the room, where, until a few minutes before, she'd been busy chattering away to a patient who was almost her carbon copy. Al glared at her until she turned back around, then drew the dark blue hospital curtain for more privacy.

'Tell me what happened,' he said, his voice an ominous whisper, his fists curled into tight balls.

'Don't look at me like that Allan,' she said. You're one to talk.'

As soon as the words left her mouth, he was eight years old again, standing in front of their tiny flat's threshold, silent tears streaming down his face, while she flitted across the hallway, black leather handbag tucked under her arm and ready for a night on the town, her flowery perfume filling the air.

'Don't be selfish, Allan,' she'd say. 'Your Ma needs her R&R. Now go watch telly and be in bed by nine.'

He pushed the memory away.

'Tell me. What happened?' he repeated.

His chest felt like it was being crushed by a vice. His stomach roiled. His breath was coming out in angry rasps through flared nostrils.

'I borrowed some money, OK?' she blurted. 'In case you haven't noticed, I'm not exactly rolling in it.'

'What the fuck, Ma?' he said, any pretence of civility gone. 'How could you? Why didn't you come to me?'

'Och, so you're going to make this about you?' she shot back with a snort. 'Typical.'

She crossed her arms and looked straight ahead at the blue curtain.

'Of course it's about me!' he hissed. 'Do you have any idea how this looks? The position you've put me in? My Ma in hock to those pricks?'

His face had reddened. Spittle flew from his mouth. Behind him, somebody cleared their throat. The nurse who'd asked him if he was feeling all right had entered the cubicle.

'Is everything OK here, Mrs Edwards?' she said.

'Everything's fine,' Al butted in. 'I'm going to be leaving shortly.'

The nurse ignored him.

'Are you OK, Ms Edwards?' she repeated. 'I can call security if he's bothering you.'

'It's fine,' Jane said, meek as can be. 'We were just having a heated discussion. I'm sorry about the noise.'

'Are you sure?'

'You heard the woman,' Al said.

Jane nodded, her eyes downcast, a picture of vulnerability. The nurse looked at him and scoffed, her eyes full of contempt.

'Please keep it down. You're disturbing the other patients. Ring the bell if you need anything, Mrs Edwards.'

She looked at Al, shook her head, and walked out, tutting under her breath. Around them, the chatter had resumed. But, in their cubicle, the silence was so thick it weighed heavy on Al's eardrums.

'How much?' he growled.

Jane didn't look up. A small tear spilled over the corner of her eye and trickled down her cheek.

'How much, Ma?'

'With interest, it's twenty-five grand.'

'Twenty-five... Jesus fucking Christ, Ma.'

He sat back down in the armchair mechanically, his mind whirring. Looked at Jane, who'd leaned into the pile of pillows that were propping her up and shut her eyes so tight they'd sunk into their sockets.

'And when were you planning on telling me?' he asked.

'I wasn't,' she replied absently, her eyes still closed. 'It was meant to be an advance. I had a line on a sure thing.'

The sure thing in question was a consignment of contraband cigarettes that never made it through border patrol because her bumbling friend Angela's shifty behaviour betrayed her. As it turned out, Al would never find out about this. But he knew his Ma well enough to guess it must've been some hare-brained scheme, which made the rage sink deeper into his muscles, making them thrum like live wires.

He stood up, his breathing barely under control, and looked at Ma

'I'll set up a meet. See if I can fix this,' he told her. 'But you've got to promise me you won't do something this stupid again.'

He stepped back from the armchair and banged his arse cheek against the sill so hard it would leave a bruise. But he barely noticed.

'Fucking hell, Ma,' he said.

She looked up at him and her gaze hardened.

'Don't you dare patronise me, Allan,' she told him.

'Fine, Ma. Then how about I let you sort it by yourself? What do you say, eh?' he retorted, making as if to leave. He got as far as placing his hand on the curtain when she replied.

'So you're going to leave your Ma in this predicament?' she said quietly. 'You were always an ungrateful brat.'

The last bit stabbed him through the heart, and he felt his face flush with shame.

'I'll see what I can do,' he relented. 'But don't pull this shite again. You need money, you come to me. Are we clear?'

'Crystal,' she said through pursed lips.

'Anything else you should tell me?' he asked.

Her eyes shot daggers at him.

'Now's the time,' he pressed.

When she didn't reply, he glanced at the clock on his phone's screen.

'If you'll excuse me, I've got a steaming pile of shite to clean up,' he snapped. 'Try not to fuck anything else up in the meantime.'

CHAPTER 4

Al stormed out of the ward in a daze, light-headed with fury. How could that bloody cow have done this to him? How could she have been so fucking stupid?

More importantly, how was he going to get them both out of this mess?

If Boaby Kiernan was half as smart as he thought he was, he'd milk this for all it was worth. At least, that's what Al would do in his position.

'He must be jumping for joy,' he muttered, as he power-walked down the stairs. 'The fucking prick.'

He screamed, a guttural sound that started deep in his throat and echoed around the stairwell, and hit the wall so hard he knocked a hole in the plasterboard.

'Shite!' he shouted. 'Fuck!'

He blazed through the lobby and raced towards his car, barely registering the chilly air and the wind blowing through the neatly manicured trees. Before he knew it, he was taking the onramp to the city bypass, which was chock-a-block with rush-hour traffic.

He pushed the Discovery as hard as he could, revving the engine, braking at the last possible minute, and banging on the steering wheel with his open palms when the Hyundai Tucson in front of him stopped on the orange light.

'Och, come on you fucking twat!' he screamed, switching lanes without indicating and eliciting a squeal of tyres and a stream of strident honking from behind him.

He pulled down the window, flashed his middle finger, and inched his car forward despite the red light. An Audi that was crossing the intersection braked, managing to stop less than half an inch away from his front bumper. The driver glared at Al, who glared back. The driver dropped his gaze faster than you could say 'right of way'.

Thirty minutes later, feeling like his stomach had been boiled in its own juices, he drove the Discovery into a free parking bay next to The Green Lady, almost running over a bloke in filthy trousers and an army surplus coat in the process.

'Hey, who taught you to drive?' the bloke shouted at Al, who had just climbed down from the Discovery and slammed the door shut.

'Get the fuck out of my way, jakey,' Al replied.

He kicked a stray half-empty bottle of Lucozade, missing the bloke's face by an inch, and kept walking without looking back.

'Prick,' the bloke muttered.

But Al was too preoccupied with what he was going to do to Kiernan when he got his hands on him to hear what the bloke had said. Or to notice he'd pulled out a phone from his coat's front pocket and snapped several pics, including one where Al's face was clearly visible.

The Green Lady was a pebbledash box in the vein of

The Sentinel, but even dodgier. A feat of this particular type of architecture which you'd have thought impossible. A crack in the plasterwork snaked its way down the front of the building like a scar. On the peeling red door that led inside, some wit had scribbled 'I suck monstercocks, call me Nessie,' in silver marker.

Except for who he assumed was the landlady and four punters nursing their pints around a well-worn wooden table three feet across from the bar, the pub was empty. At the sound of the door slamming shut, their conversation stopped and the punters turned towards him, scanning him from top to toe. Thrusting his chest and chin outwards, Al walked to the bar, the soles of his trainers squeaking on the worn vinyl flooring, which was sticky with beer and fuck knew what else.

'Where's your boss?' Al asked the landlady, a voluptuous thirty-something with brown, curly hair, heavy makeup, and a faded infinity symbol tattooed on the outer side of her left hand.

'Who?' she asked.

She winked at him and smiled, exposing a set of nicotine-stained but even teeth, then crossed her arms beneath her considerable breasts, which her tight black tank top was displaying to the best advantage, and leaned back against the bar shelves.

'You know exactly who I'm talking about,' Al said, holding her gaze. 'Where's Kiernan?'

'What's going on here, Sinéad?' a familiar voice said from behind him.

Al turned and spotted Ritchie in the archway that led to the loos, feet shoulder-width apart, chest puffed out. He'd changed out of his blood-stained clothes into fresh tracksuit bottoms and a crisp white t-shirt. Somebody had splinted his nose, which had swollen to twice its usual size.

'Look what the cat dragged in,' he said, taking a step towards him. 'How's Mrs Edwards? I hope you gave her my regards?'

'How's your nose?' Al retorted. 'Broken, I hope.'

He dug his nails into the soft flesh of his palms, focusing on the stinging pain to quell his racing mind.

'So, what can I do for you, Al?' Ritchie said after they'd stared at each other for a few seconds. 'What brings you here?'

'Where's your boss?' Al growled, taking another step forward. 'I need to speak with him.'

Ritchie laughed. A short, sharp bark, as if to say, 'Can you believe this bloke?'

'Mr Kiernan isn't here,' he said, walking to the bar and snapping his fingers at Sinéad so she'd pour him a drink. 'But you're in luck. He told me I could deal with you on his behalf.'

The implied insult of having to deal with a bloke who was barely old enough to shave wasn't lost on Al. The rage he'd managed to turn down to a low simmer bubbled up, threatening to boil over.

'Right. So let's get this over with,' he said, fighting for control of his temper and feeling the battle slip from his grasp. 'Tell me how much she owes you, I'll pay it, and we'll call it quits. Sound fair?'

Ritchie looked him in the eye, sipped his drink, and broke into a wide sunny grin that changed his face completely, giving him an aura of boyish innocence.

'D'you hear that, boys?' he said to the blokes on the table, who were looking on, rapt. 'He's gonna pay.'

This elicited a wave of low chuckles. The tips of Al's

ears flushed red. He lunged towards the bar, snatching Ritchie by the front of his t-shirt, and made as if to punch him. His fist stopped a fraction of an inch from Ritchie's injured nose, and Ritchie flinched involuntarily.

'Now, listen here you little gobshite,' he said, 'we're going to sort this out like men. Or I'm going to beat the living shite out of you. Your choice.'

A safety clicked behind him and he felt the cold, hard steel of a gun against the nape of his neck.

'Simmer down, prick,' a voice growled from behind him.

Al's bowels turned to water. He clenched his buttocks and let Ritchie go.

'Is that how you do it, you big fucking jessie?' he said, steeling his voice. 'Look me in the eye while you shoot. If you have the balls.'

The bloke behind him pressed the gun harder into the soft flesh of Al's neck.

'Don't test me, prick,' he said.

Ritchie smoothed his t-shirt, dug his hands into his pockets, and moved so close Al could smell the foul mix of whisky, fags, and hunger on his breath.

'Let me explain something to you, Al,' he told him, his grin widening. 'The thing about negotiating successfully, is that you need leverage.'

Al straightened, his fists squeezed tighter than ever. An explosive cocktail of rage, hatred, and fear coursing through his veins.

'And you don't have any,' Ritchie continued.

'Cut the shite, prick. What the fuck do you want?' Al said through clenched teeth.

'What makes you think we want anything?' Ritchie retorted.

'Obviously, you want something. Or your buddy back here would've killed me by now.'

'Ah, did you hear that, boys? Not just a pretty face.'

More chuckling.

'Stop wasting my time,' Al said. 'Out with it.'

Without warning, Ritchie backhanded him across the face. A loud crack exploded in Al's head and he saw stars. He doubled over, his cheek stinging, uttered a scream of rage, and lunged at Ritchie. The bloke behind him grabbed him around the waist with one meaty forearm and held him tight before Al could do any damage. The smell of Lynx Africa mixed with body odour was overwhelming.

'Are you going to behave yourself or what?' he whispered into Al's ear.

Overpowered, Al nodded imperceptibly in between rasping breaths.

'Good man.'

The bloke's grip on Al loosened, but the gun dug deeper into his neck

Ritchie put his hand in his pocket and brought out a crumpled yellow post-it note he'd folded in half.

'Mr Kiernan would like you to obtain a package for him and deliver it to this address,' he told Al, handing him the paper.

Al unfolded the post-it, read the scrawled note inside, and his eyes widened.

'What if I refuse?' he said.

'Well, poor Mrs Edwards might get more than a black eye and a sprained shoulder next time we call on her,' Ritchie replied with mock regret. 'And you'll join her. She'll enjoy the company. I'm told being six feet under can get a wee bit boring after a while.'

Al felt his gorge rise.

'One time. Once. And we're done.'

Ritchie's grin stretched impossibly, almost bisecting his face into two.

'You're done when Mr Kiernan says you're done,' he said.

'What?' Al sputtered. 'What do you take me for, your fucking errand boy?'

'Aye,' Ritchie said. 'Something like that.'

CHAPTER 5

Saturday morning. 8:30 am.

Jonno lifted two wooden crates with Alisur stamped across their sides in red lettering off the bed of an articulated lorry, and handed them to Al with a grunt.

Al, his eyes bloodshot and bruised from lack of sleep, held on to the heavy crates just barely, his back tightening uncomfortably. He crossed the warehouse floor, dropped them on a growing stack of similarly-sized Alisur crates, and walked back to the lorry, ready for Jonno to hand him more.

The warehouse, which was located ten miles to the northwest of Strathburgh in an abandoned industrial complex, belonged to the Nisbeth Food Company, a corporation which, officially, was in the import and export business, supplying high-end restaurants across the central belt with Wagyu beef, game, and other premium meats, as well as hard-to-find produce like truffles and exotic fruits. But while this line of business was lucrative, it was a sideline. Nisbeth Foods made most of their money from one particular crop, imported from the hinterlands of Peru via the Caribbean.

Aside from the small stack of crates Jonno and Al had unloaded so far, the warehouse was mostly empty. The lorry took up half the floor space. A stack of three cardboard boxes with the Marvel powdered milk logo stamped on them stood in one corner, looking like a budget caricature of the leaning tower of Pisa. Next to them, there was a rickety picnic table on which somebody had laid out a knife and battery-operated scales.

After spending the night in his armchair, sucking down one herbal tea after another like it was oxygen and alternating between cursing Ma and fruitlessly trying to figure out a way to turn the tables on the Red Hand, this was the last place Al wanted to be. He was spoiling for a fight. Willing someone — anyone — to say the wrong thing so he could beat them to a pulp. Not the right mood to be in on a job. But he'd known about the delivery for several days, so he'd had to come. Except for his two-year stretch at Bar-L, the country's finest retreat for people of a certain criminal persuasion, Al had never missed work. It would've been weird if he'd begged off at the last minute.

'Slow down, bud,' he growled, absently flexing his arms to get the blood flowing. 'Just give me one at a time. My back's killing me.'

'Och, come on,' Jonno said half-jokingly, grunting with effort, sweat filming his stubbly head, 'The exercise'll do you good.'

'Look who's fucking talking,' Al snapped, nodding at Jonno's considerable gut, which was peeking out from underneath his black t-shirt, and rolling his eyes. His voice was harsh. His expression stern.

Jonno let it pass. He armed sweat off his forehead,

walked back into the bed of the truck, and picked up a single crate.

'We've still got a bunch of them,' Jonno complained, looking at the three, four-foot high stacks of crates inside the truck bed. 'We're never going to finish at this rate.'

'Who's moaning now?' Al muttered, dumping another crate on the pile and returning to the lorry.

'Hey what happened to you there?' Jonno said, nodding towards Al's cheek.

The spot where Ritchie had backhanded him the previous evening was faintly bluish yellow.

'Mind your own business, will you?' Al said, hoping the exertion was camouflaging the flush of heat Jonno's question had elicited.

'Jesus, who crawled up your arse?' Jonno replied.

They carried on in silence. Jonno's breathing whistling softly like a kettle about to boil, and Al grunting like he was trying and failing to excrete a particularly dry jobby. Forty-five minutes later, they'd offloaded all the crates. It was time to empty them of their precious cargo. A crew would go in later to cut it and pack it so it would be ready for the street.

Jonno picked up a crowbar from the grimy floor and pried the first crate open, revealing neatly stacked blue boxes. He lifted them out two at a time, dropping them carelessly on the floor. Two rows deep, the boxes became noticeably heavier. He took four of these boxes in his meaty hands, walked to the picnic table, and opened them. Inside each box, instead of the reddish brown quinoa grains the packaging promised, there was a single, white brick wrapped in cellophane and sealed with duct tape.

Jonno placed a brick on the scales. One kilo. He grunted, satisfied, and repeated the process with the next brick and the next. In the meantime, Al worked the crates, prying them open and emptying them of boxes until he got to the good stuff.

'What time's Harry's crew coming in?' he asked.

'In an hour or so,' Jonno replied, still absorbed in his task. 'Why?'

'Somebody needs to take the lorry back to Wee Dave's before they're here.'

'Right,' Jonno said. 'I can take it after we're done.'

'Why don't you go now? Get it over with?' Al said, driving the crowbar beneath a stubborn crate lid with both hands. 'I'll finish up.'

He applied pressure with his bodyweight, and the wooden lid made a whip-like cracking sound that echoed around the warehouse. He threw the crowbar to the floor and attacked the lid, ripping the wood open with his hands like it was cardboard.

'Are you sure?' Jonno asked, looking doubtfully at the two three-foot stacks. 'There's a lot to get through.'

'Aye, I'll be fine,' Al replied.

He'd already moved onto the next crate.

'Just go, bud. Don't worry about me. The sooner that lorry's off the street, the better I'll feel.'

This was another sticking point. The Chairman believed it was easier to get away with something if you were blatant about it, so he insisted on deliveries being done in the morning, rather than under cover of night. Al thought this was total BS. The Chairman wouldn't be the one up for a holiday in His Majesty's facilities if the shite hit the fan. At least, not unless someone dared turn grass. So, as far as he was concerned, the Chairman believed it because he could afford to.

Jonno tended to agree with Al. But you wouldn't have got this out of him if you'd strapped him down on a bed of nails and pulled his fingernails one by one with red hot pliers. Luckily, there was no need for either of them to say anything. They exchanged a meaningful look, and Jonno nodded and lumbered towards the truck.

'See you at the pub later?' Jonno said as he climbed into the cab.

'Not sure,' Al said. 'I'll bell you.'

He got back to work, attacking the next crate with gusto. Behind him, Jonno fired up the lorry. The engine's booming rumble and the rich smell of exhaust filled the warehouse.

'I'm off,' Jonno said, waving a hand out the driver's side window. He edged the lorry out of the warehouse in a cloud of smoke and trundled towards the road.

Al dropped the crowbar and walked outside to survey the scene. When the lorry had disappeared over the hill, he walked to his Discovery, which he'd parked behind the warehouse, and fetched a black gym bag from the boot.

He stood over the pile of bricks on the picnic table, the gym bag open in his hands, his heart thumping loudly in his ears, conscious that, if he did this, there was no turning back. He'd be setting fire to the only life he'd known since he was a pimply fourteen year-old.

Then he pictured Ma in her hospital bed, the black bruise spreading across her cheek. And that smug prick Ritchie, sneering at him. Begging to be punched in the face.

He curled his hand into a fist and banged on the picnic table. Once. Twice. Three times.

On the third blow, the table's legs gave way and it toppled over, sending the knife, the scales, and the bricks of cocaine clattering to the floor.

'Fuck!' he screamed, kicking the table.

It banged against the wall and rebounded. A crack had

formed in one of the corners and snaked its way across the table's surface in a semi-circular arc.

He squatted down, the black bag between his legs, breathing hard and racking his brain. There had to be a way for him to get back on the front foot. And the solution was probably right under his nose. But the situation felt inescapable. Just too fucking complex. Unless he wanted to join Ma in the hospital, or worse, he was going to have to play along, at least for now, and hope for his sake that he didn't make a wrong move and get on the Chairman's radar.

Aye, that was the only play he had.

He put the table back right. Then, working quickly, his hands trembling, his mouth dry, he put three bricks of cocaine in the bag, debated taking another one, then packed two more for good measure. If he was going to risk it all, he might as well have something extra stashed aside. Insurance.

Walking on feet that felt like rubber, he stowed the bag away in the Discovery and went back inside to finish unpacking the crates.

The day was still relatively young, but he had a shit tonne of work left to do.

CHAPTER 6

While Al was wrestling with his conscience and losing miserably, I was on my way home from the Co-Op, still reeling from an absolutely brutal session with my therapist, Serena, the previous afternoon.

Most people who go to therapy sell it as this magical balm that'll 'heal your soul' and 'transform your life'. Whatever the fuck that means. What nobody tells you is that you'll feel like shite for days. Possibly even wish you'd never been born.

Early on, Serena told me it's because therapy's like reopening your wounds so all the pus can come out and they can heal properly. But, on this particular morning, I was tempted to take my chances living with the pus.

Shrouded in this cloud of negativity, a cloth tote bag containing a pack of four jam doughnuts and a carton of chocolate milk in my left hand, I stuck my key into my building's main door, opened it, and almost crashed head-on into Graeme, my neighbour across the hall, only managing to avoid him by crushing myself against the wall.

In typical fashion, the self-absorbed prick ignored me.

'Exactly. There won't be anything to go back to,' he was saying into his phone, which was permanently glued to his right ear.

He lifted his shoulder to hold the phone in place and sat astride his motorcycle, listening intently to whatever the person on the other end was saying and scratching at his luxurious beard. I'd already climbed the first three steps before doing a double-take, almost losing my balance and falling flat on my arse in the process.

What the fuck was a motorcycle doing in the bloody hallway?

Right on cue, I heard a door crack open, and the shuffling of slippers on the landing.

'Graeme?' Morag called. 'Can you wait a second? I need to speak with you.'

'Aye, that's sensible,' Graeme said to whoever he was talking to, oblivious.

Morag appeared at the top of the stairs and descended them slowly and painstakingly, one shaky leg at a time, her right hand gripping the banister like her life depended on it.

'Graeme!' she said, louder.

Her voice had schoolteacher vibes, and my head involuntarily rose to attention.

'Oh, Bertie,' she said, looking at me. 'How fortunate for you to be here too. Let's get this sorted.'

Good lord, what did I just walk into?

'Wha-' I was about to ask.

But Morag had finished coming down the stairs and hobbled up to Graeme, waving her hand in his face to attract his attention. It took thirty seconds for Graeme to look at her.

'I'm going to have to call you back,' he said.

He ended the call, trousered his phone, then looked up at Morag like he'd just found a dead fly in his pint.

'Morag, what's the matter?' he told her.

'I should say the same,' she said, her voice indignant. 'What's all this?'

She waved her hand over the motorcycle.

'It's a Kawasaki Vulcan 500 series,' he said. 'This is the 2008 model with a six-speed transmission and a belt drive. I hadn't pegged you for a motorcycle enthusiast.'

'Don't get smart with me, young man,' she told him, absently massaging the base of her left thumb with her right hand. 'You know exactly what I mean.'

'I... don't?' he shot back, looking at her evenly, his hands curled around the motorcycle's handlebars.

'Is this an appropriate place to park?' she said, placing her hands on her hips and peering at him over the rims of her granny glasses.

She might've been seventy and verging on decrepit, but at that moment she looked formidable.

'Where would you have me park then?' he said. 'In the street? It won't last a night. They'll steal it.'

'Well you should've thought of that before you bought this... contraption,' she spat. 'Shouldn't you? You can't park here.'

'Says who? You?' he said. 'Who put you in charge?'

There was a note of challenge in his voice, but no menace or aggression. This was a game to him. Red splotches crept from under the lacy collar of Morag's white blouse and up her neck. She squared her shoulders, which made her look all of her five feet and two inches.

'It's a residential hallway, not a garage,' she said. 'I think we might even have issues with the insurance cover.

Keeping that thing here's dangerous, and I'm sure everyone else in the building would agree.'

She turned to me, her eyebrows arched, expecting me to jump in and back her up. I kept my face neutral — or, at least, I hoped it looked that way — and clutched my shopping, wishing I could disappear. I wasn't keen on him parking the motorcycle here, of course. Who would be? It was dirty, it was in the way, and it was characteristically inconsiderate of him. But I also wanted a peaceful life, and I wasn't about to get dragged into a feud with my next door neighbour if I could help it.

'Well?' she said.

'Morag, I-' I stammered.

'Look I'm going to sell it anyway,' Graeme said. 'So there's no need to get all worked up.'

He lifted the kickstand, and started duck-walking the motorcycle out of the door.

'Wait a minute,' Morag said, taking a step forward. 'Graeme, I'm not finished. You can't park here.'

Graeme fired up the engine and drove away. But not before giving Morag the finger. Morag's mouth gaped open, a scandalised expression on her face.

I took this as my cue. I crept up the stairs as quickly and quietly as I could, before she could corner me and start ranting, jabbed the key into the lock, and shut the door behind me. Hopefully, she wouldn't come up to 'make me see sense', because then I'd have nowhere to go.

Which got me thinking. Perhaps I should ditch my plan to scoff doughnuts in front of the telly and go somewhere until she calmed down. Getting out of the flat might even do me some good.

I glanced at my shopping, then reluctantly at the front door. Listened intently. It was quiet. I couldn't hear the telltale shuffling of slippers on my landing, so maybe she wasn't coming up after all.

Och, what the hell. I was feeling more rubbish than rubbish. I needed a morning to loaf about. Deserved it. Why should bloody Morag make me feel like a prisoner in my own home?

I stepped into the main room and made a beeline for the sofa. Caught something from the corner of my eye. Turned to see what it was.

There it was again. The curtain fluttering.

I walked to the window.

I'd made roasties the previous evening and cracked it open so my ageing oven wouldn't set off the smoke alarm. But I was pretty sure I'd closed it all the way before I went to bed.

Huh.

I pulled the handle. The window didn't budge. So that was it. I must've been so tired I didn't realise it was stuck.

I put my shopping on the floor and grabbed the handle with both hands. Gave it a mighty pull. The window shut with a loud thump. There, you bastard.

One of these days, I'd have to hire somebody to take a look. Not just at this one. At all four windows in my flat. In the meantime, I'd have to be more careful. Or maybe some WD40 might do the trick, if I could be arsed to buy some.

CHAPTER 7

The stereotypical Hollywood drop house is a decrepit, graffiti-riddled building with broken windows, peeling paint, and junkies lying in dirt-crusted stairwells, moaning with pleasure in the throes of their highs. But while that makes for great visual drama, it wouldn't be practical in the real world. Reality is frighteningly mundane. It has to be. Because, otherwise, it would be all too easy for the police to catch on, and much harder for criminals to get away with what they do for as long as many of them manage to.

No. Real-world drop houses can't be obvious. They have to blend in. Hiding in plain sight. Looking like a million and one other houses in a million and one other neighbourhoods across the country.

The drop house Al drove to that Saturday evening was in the part of the city north of the Strath that the Red Hand had carved out for themselves through years of attrition. But despite being unofficially within gang territory, it wasn't the frontline. There were no teens sporting bowl cuts, Lonsdale or Adidas trackies, and heavy chains around their necks loitering about on the corners. No dishevelled customers trudging towards them, looking to score. And no police cruisers driving by on a regular basis to make sure the situation didn't get out of control. This was a respectable neighbourhood of cookie-cutter but well-kept terraces, tree-lined streets, and cycle paths in a great catchment area, where people wished their neighbours a good morning before getting into their Volvos, Volkswagens, and Hyundais to drive to work, and had trampolines and barbe-cues they fired up maybe once a year in their back gardens.

Now that he was so close, not to crossing the line — he'd done that in the morning when he'd taken the Chair-man's drugs — but to obliterating it, dousing the ground on which it had been drawn with petrol, and aiming a flamethrower at it, his heart was thumping in his chest and his mind was screaming at him to stop and take a breath. He attempted to parallel park his Discovery and completely misjudged it, so the left rear wheel ended up on the pave-ment and the front of the car jutted out into the middle of the narrow street, blocking the way. He tried again, to no avail, swore through gritted teeth, and inched forward until he found a space that was big enough for him to drive into from the front.

He killed the engine, unbuckled his seatbelt, and leaned back with his eyes closed, feeling the leather stick uncom-fortably to the back of his neck despite the cool, wet weather. The second hand on his Tissot wristwatch edged forward, bringing him inexorably closer to the moment when he'd be expected to show up and hand over the pack-age. But not a single muscle responded to his brain's commands. He was paralysed, his mind full to bursting with images of the possible repercussions of what he was about to do.

He ran through his options once more, but they brought him back to the same inevitable conclusion.

He could call Kiernan's bluff. Refuse to go along with it. But while he might be able to evade the consequences for some time, and put up one hell of a fight when they eventually caught up with him, they'd get him in the end. Ambush him some time when he was alone. Probably on the night when he'd finally let his guard down and have one too many drinks.

More to the point, Ma wouldn't stand a chance. Which was something that, the more he thought about, the harder he found to stomach. As angry as he was at her for putting him in this position — and for the constant emotional rollercoaster he'd had to endure since the day she'd told him Da wasn't away for work, after all, and would never be coming back — he felt he owed her. That was the thing about parents. You might know, rationally, that they don't have your best interests at heart. That, in fact, their effect on you is completely toxic. But that doesn't make the pill any easier to swallow. Or the guilt of not being a good enough son go away.

And then there was option two. Give Kiernan what he wanted, at least for the time being. And, more importantly, make sure the Chairman didn't get wind of it. Because if he did...

'What a fucking shiteshow,' he murmured, pinching the bridge of his nose with his thumb and index finger. 'Fucking hell.'

The second hand had made two revolutions around his wristwatch's dial. It was almost time. This was it. The point of no return.

His hand hovered over the gym bag in the front passenger side footwell, which contained three of the five bricks he'd taken that morning — he'd stashed the other two in a storage locker on Waterfront Gait, three minutes' walk from the bridge that connected northwest Strathburgh to the south side.

He grabbed the handles. The cloth felt rough under his palms.

He lifted.

Dropped the bag back into the footwell like he'd just touched a red-hot poker. Ran his hands across his face, feeling the ridged edges of his chib scar, where it hadn't healed quite cleanly.

'Whichever way you cut this, I'm fucked,' he muttered.

A memory popped up unbidden. Ma in a bright yellow summer dress. Him, eight years old, wearing a brand new herringbone shirt — one of the very few items of clothing he'd owned as a child that hadn't been a hand-me-down — and his best jeans. Walking down the high street two towns over, looking at the menus outside the restaurants and picking the poshest one. Dashing away after they'd eaten their fill, Ma's careless laughter filling the air as one of the waiters, a fifty-something bloke with an obvious combover ran after them, shouting.

'Excuse me, ma'am. Your bill. Excuse me!'

When it came to his childhood, he could count the good memories on the fingers of one hand. And this wasn't just a good one. It was a great one.

How happy he'd been, walking down that high street, his hand in Ma's, a spring in his step. How he'd looked in wonder at all those families gathered together, eating, chattering, and laughing away, and feeling like, for once, he and Ma were like them, too.

That's all he'd ever wanted growing up.

To be normal.

To have some sense of agency over his life.

He was walking up the street now. Through some process he didn't understand, he'd made the decision. The Discovery, parked and locked, was several yards away. The bag was in his hand. His eyes fixed on the house numbers, on the lookout for thirty-two.

There it was. An end-of-terrace with a bright red door, windows that refracted the light from the lamppost on the street corner, and a meticulously manicured front garden. In between the rose bushes, the rear of a dark blue Renault Kadjar peered out from the flagstone driveway.

The gate swung inwards soundlessly. He walked up the path to the front door, pressed the doorbell, and heard the faint ringing from within, followed by the sound of shuffling slippers.

'Aye?'

One of the most nondescript men he'd ever seen in his life looked at him from behind the door, which he'd left on its chain. He wore a brown jumper over a blue checked shirt and had a droopy moustache. His head was bald except for two tufts of salt-and-pepper hair, very heavy on the salt, on each side.

'Delivery,' Al said in the practised voice of somebody who'd done this a million times before, even though never for the wrong side.

The bloke shut the door, and Al heard the chain rattle. The door reopened, wider.

'Give me it,' the bloke said.

Al did as he was asked.

'I trust it's all there,' the bloke said, scanning the street to make sure it was empty. 'Anything missing, somebody'll be in touch. Now get off my porch and fuck off.'

The door slammed shut. That was that. After all the

nervous energy he'd spent since that prick Ritchie had handed him the post-it the previous evening, the build up, this felt like the softest of whimpers. Hardly the momentous event he'd pictured.

He walked back to the Discovery, his trainers thudding faintly on the pavement, feeling wrung out but also a strange sense of equanimity.

It was done. The decision made. The task performed.

And the sky hadn't fallen on him.

Not yet.

CHAPTER 8

'She actually said that?' Kris asked, incensed. 'What a useless eejit.'

She was sitting at the breakfast bar, still in her charcoal grey trouser suit, her straight, blonde hair tied in a careless ponytail. A steaming mug of chamomile lay untouched in front of her.

Despite having just got home from a twelve-hour shift, she was wired, partly from all the coffee she'd drunk at work, and partly because leading the Strathburgh police's gang task force gave her an adrenaline rush she found very hard to shake off, especially on a Saturday night, when the action tended to be heaviest. But while her reaction was a bit over the top, she did have a point, as her husband Neville, who was standing across from her, his head in his hands, a white t-shirt hanging off his gaunt frame, acknowledged. His conversation with the head at their seven year-old son Jason's school the previous Friday had taken a rather disappointing turn.

'Aye. He's going to need to be re-assessed,' he said

quietly, repeating the phrase that had provoked her ire word for word.

'But this is mad. What was the point of him doing all those tests, then? And what are we supposed to do in the meantime?' she replied.

Her voice had dropped several decibels. But it wouldn't have mattered if she'd said it at normal volume. Jason was on the sofa at the other end of the large, open plan kitchen-living-dining room, completely absorbed in the train documentary he was watching on his iPad.

Neville winced at the edge in Kris' voice. He'd expected this reaction, which was why he hadn't told her the previous day before she'd left for her shift. Bad decision. Jason had had a difficult night. And now he was having to have the conversation while he was completely knackered and she was jacked up on coffee and a post-work high.

'The tests weren't for nothing,' he said, making a placating gesture. 'We have an official diagnosis. We wouldn't even be able to have the conversation about getting him extra help without it.'

'That makes me feel better,' Kris huffed.

'We'll get there,' Neville said, with an optimism he didn't feel. 'It's obvious he needs help, if only so he doesn't disrupt the other weans in his class.'

She took a small sip of chamomile, put the mug down, then stood up from the breakfast bar and walked to the window overlooking their garden. The sunshine that had threatened to break through the clouds that morning was gone, replaced by a drab grey. A squirrel scurried down the apple tree that, in what seemed like another life, had been her pride and joy, picked up a stray piece of dried bark and gave it a tentative nibble. It must not have been to its satisfaction, because it discarded it and scurried back up the tree, disappearing between the branches.

Neville grabbed a tea towel and began fastidiously drying the few dishes in the drying rack — a blue and white mug with World's Best Lover emblazoned on it in a loud yellow font, two plates, and a large saucepan. The remnants of the tea he'd shared with Jason. A train whistled through the iPad's tinny speakers, punctuating the silence.

Ever since they'd started suspecting Jason's tantrums might be a sign of something more serious than him just doing what toddlers do, things had changed. Neville was a practical man. He liked tackling problems head on. But Kris had had a harder time with it. It had been easier for her to throw herself into her work. Gangsters, she could understand. Eventually, they always did what you expected of them. The distance had now grown to the point that every conversation was a minefield. A single misplaced word could blow their tempers to smithereens.

'How's the new book coming along?' Kris said, moving on to safer territory.

'It's... coming. One word at a time,' Neville said.

He grabbed a plate and wiped it carefully, starting from the middle and moving outwards, studying its surface intently to make sure there wasn't a speck of dirt left. He placed it in the crockery drawer and turned around.

'Are you going to drink that?' he asked, pointing at the mug.

'I don't think so,' she said, wrinkling her nose. 'It's worse than that pish we have at the station.'

Neville gave a light chuckle. He emptied the mug in the sink, rinsed and dried it.

'God I need a shower,' Kris said. 'How about I change

and we can do something together? Watch a film or play with Lego? Maybe share some wine later?'

'That sounds nice,' Neville said.

He walked around the breakfast bar and kissed her lightly on the cheek. Something — an emotion he'd once taken for granted but wasn't sure he recognised anymore — stirred inside him, and he wrapped his arms tenderly around her. She leaned in briefly, enough for him to get a whiff of her crisp perfume mixed with a not unpleasant undertone of body odour, then gently pushed him away.

'I stink,' she said. 'I'll be right back.'

She walked out of the room, barely glancing at Jason, her sensible, kitten heel shoes clicking on the wooden floor, and climbed upstairs to the bathroom. She switched on the electric shower and turned up the heat. Then she went into the bedroom, sat down on the edge of the bed with a sigh, and took off her shoes. Her calves ached. She massaged the right one and winced. It was tight. Hard to the touch.

The sound of her phone vibrating made her look up.

'DI Hendrie,' she said, reaching for it and swiping right without looking at the display.

'Kris, it's me.'

'Doug, what's going on?' she said.

'Are you sitting down?' her colleague DI Doug Lennox replied.

'I am. Why?'

'You won't believe this,' he said, his voice laced with excitement.

'I won't believe what?' Kris asked.

She worried absently at her pinky fingernail with her right molar, then caught herself.

'Guess who was at The Green Lady Friday afternoon?' Doug said, doing his best quiz-master impression.

'Who?'

'Greasy hair. Chib scar. Proclivity for wearing hideous shirts. I'll give you three guesses,' he replied.

'What? For real?' she said.

'Aye. Allan fucking Edwards. Deep in Red Hand territory.'

'Are you sure? How reliable is the info?'

'Very. We have pics of him going in and out.'

'We do? From who?'

'A long-term informant. I'm told their info always checks out.'

She got up, padded to the bathroom, which had filled with steam, turned the electric shower off, and went back to the bedroom. She sat heavily on the bed, eyes staring fixedly at the closet door, her mind spinning.

'What the hell was he doing there?' she asked.

'That's the first question I asked myself. We're not sure. But whatever it is, I doubt it's good for his career prospects at the Company.'

'What makes you say so?' Kris asked.

Her fingernail was back between her teeth, and she forced her hand into her lap.

'For one, he was alone. The informant said he was pretty agitated when he went in, and the meeting lasted for over half an hour.'

Kris considered this.

'And, get this,' Doug continued.

She could hear the self-satisfied smile in his voice.

'I did some digging, and it turns out Ma Edwards is in the hospital. Sprained shoulder. Pretty bad bruising all over. She says she slipped and fell.'

'You don't think the Chairman had anything to do with it?'

'I don't know. But she has a history of getting herself into trouble with the wrong crowd, doesn't she?'

A pause.

'Anyway,' Doug continued, 'Whatever happened, I'd say there's a good chance it's something our friend Edwards wouldn't want the Chairman to know about, or he wouldn't have gone alone, would he?'

'No. It does seem foolish of him to go there without backup,' Kris agreed. 'That's great work, Doug. Absolutely smashing,'

She switched the phone from her right ear to her left, and picked up her shoes from the cream-coloured, low-pile carpet, her promise to spend the afternoon with Neville and Jason forgotten.

'Are you still at the station?' she asked.

'I was about to leave, why?'

'Wait for me, I'm coming in,' she said. 'Can we get more out of this informant? Perhaps he'll give us something we can use to put the squeeze on Edwards.'

CHAPTER 9

A l woke up at 2pm feeling mildly hungover but surprisingly cool and collected.

When he'd entered The Sentinel the previous evening after delivering the package, it had felt like every person he'd nodded his hellos to was giving him a knowing look. Their eyes *boring into him*. And his stomach had clenched with unease.

'Jesus fucking Christ,' he'd thought to himself. 'They know. How could they find out so soon? Who saw me?'

Then, Jonno, who'd been parked in his usual spot by the bar, nursing a pint and ribbing Struan about his skullet, had looked him up and down and grinned.

'Look what the cat dragged in,' he'd said. 'Still going through your time of the month?'

The laughter had been loud enough to drown out the music, and thank fucking Christ for that. Saturday evening was Power Ballad Night, which meant enduring *Home Sweet Home*, *November Rain*, *Poison*, plus a slew of deep cuts from the backwash of the hair metal scene on repeat until someone got aggressively drunk enough to unplug the stereo system or threaten Struan with bodily harm if he didn't 'turn that shite off.' Usually both.

Al had raised his fist and stuck out his middle finger, which got everyone going again. Inwardly, he'd sighed with relief and cursed himself for being such a paranoid eejit. If he wasn't careful, he'd admonished himself, he'd be his own bloody undoing. Nobody suspected a thing. And if anyone realised some of the drugs had gone missing, he'd be the last person they'd point their finger at. Nobody would fucking dare.

Struan had handed him a pint, and the cold liquid going down his throat had made any residual tightness melt away. By his third pint, he'd been himself again. He'd even helped Jonno tip Struan into one the bins behind the pub — to wild and raucous applause — for having had the audacity to play *Honestly* by Stryper a fifth time, before screeching out of the car park and heading home.

He yawned loudly, stretching his arms, threw on his fleece robe, and padded downstairs to the kitchen for a cup of coffee and two paracetamol — the breakfast of champions. He fished out a mug from the stacked dishwasher, slotted a coffee pod into the Nespresso machine, and let it do its thing while he fetched the pills.

The cupboard where he kept his medicines was over-stuffed and badly organised, and a bunch of boxes and bottles — paracetamol, ibuprofen, Rennie, wind settlers, Imodium, and assorted vitamins and supplements — rained down on the quartz countertop.

'Och, for fuck's sake!' he muttered.

He pushed two paracetamol out of a blister pack and set them aside, then picked up the boxes and bottles and stuffed them haphazardly into the cupboard. The door wouldn't close properly, despite several attempts. He opened it again, causing three or four boxes to fall back out, and rearranged the mess into some semblance of order.

'There, you fucking bastard,' he said, looking smug. 'You're not getting your way.'

Mission accomplished, he popped the paracetamol into his mouth, swallowed them with some water straight from the tap, and grabbed his coffee from the Nespresso machine.

In Al's line of work, you could never really let your guard down, especially when there was constant trouble brewing with a rival gang. But now that the stress of the previous two days was behind him, he felt like he could treat himself to a quiet one. Coffee. A good book. Maybe some telly and a nice plate of spag bol later, once his stomach settled. The distance would do him good. A more permanent solution to his issues with the Red Hand might even drop into his lap while his mind was focused on other things.

He walked into his living room, which was tastefully decorated, but messy. His camel-coloured leather sofa and the cowhide rug beneath it were littered with crisps crumbs and stray roasted corn nuts, and the cushions were all piled on top of each other to one side. On the round, steel and glass coffee table, there were four mugs in various stages of emptiness, a wine glass, the TV remote, and an inch-long, reddish smear that looked suspiciously like dried tomato sauce.

The wall-to-wall bookshelf behind the sofa was impeccably organised, though. A stark contrast to the rest of the room, and to most of the other shelves, cupboards, and drawers around the house. Al had sorted his extensive book collection — which, in the company he kept, was somewhat a guilty pleasure — alphabetically by author and by date of publication. A few months prior, he'd debated sorting them by colour, to turn his bookshelf into a feature. But he owned so many books doing so would've eaten a big chunk out of a rare day off, so he'd decided it wasn't worth the trouble. Besides, it would make the job of finding a book to read painfully inconvenient.

Setting his mug on the table, he walked to the shelf and gravitated to the F section, where his eye fell on Ken Follett's *Edge of Eternity* — a book he'd read four times and could quote whole chunks of by heart. For some reason, stories that took place during the Cold War captivated him. Made his skin break out in gooseflesh, even. He suspected they triggered memories of growing up in the eighties. But it wasn't something he'd freely admit, not even to himself. Except for what surfaced on the frequent occasions Ma riled him up, his childhood was a box he liked to keep locked and padlocked.

But who wanted to think about Ma when they didn't have to, especially on their day off?

He pulled out the thick, heavy hardback with his index finger and leafed through it lazily, remembering his favourite bits. The construction of the Berlin Wall, and how it split up and trapped some of the characters. Rebecca's discovery that her husband was a Stasi agent. Walli's thrilling and heartbreaking escape from East Germany, where he left his pregnant girlfriend behind.

Aye, this would do. He hadn't read it in a while, anyway.

His eyes never leaving the page, he settled down on the sofa, absently reaching for a cushion and placing it behind his neck for support. Then he leaned back, crossed his legs, and got lost in the pages of the novel.

The shrill ring of the doorbell jolted him back to the present.

He put the book down and cocked his ear, wondering who the hell this was and waiting to see if they'd leave.

His colleagues called. And so did VIP clients. Nobody dropped by unannounced. Ever.

Which made him think that perhaps…

More ringing.

He shut the book with a thump, got up, and opened the closet under the stairs, where he kept an aluminium baseball bat — lightweight but fucking deadly. Gripping the handle, he headed to the door and looked through the peephole.

It took a second for what he saw to register. And when it did, shock doused him like a cold shower. One of his visitors leaned into the doorbell. The ringing went on for several seconds.

'Mr Edwards,' a gravelly voice called. 'Open up. It's the police.'

Worried they'd attract the neighbours' attention, he cracked the door open, leaving it on the chain.

'What's this about?' he snapped.

'Mr Edwards?' the owner of the gravelly voice — a forty-something constable with an acne-scarred face and a no-nonsense black ponytail — said.

'You know I am.'

She and her sidekick, a young, blonde bloke who looked like he'd only graduated from the academy a few hours before hitting Al's doorstep, flashed their warrant cards.

'We need you to come down to the station,' the older officer — Adamson, her warrant card proclaimed — told him.

'Why? Am I under arrest?' Al snapped back, tightening his grip on the baseball bat.

'No, we'd just like to have a quick chat,' Adamson said.

'And can't we do that here?' Al said.

'We'd prefer to do it at the station,' Adamson said, straightening her back and looking him in the eye.

Al straightened himself too, even though the officers could only see part of his face through the crack in the door.

'And if I refuse?' he said.

'We'd have to come back,' Adamson said without missing a beat. 'But then we wouldn't be so friendly.'

She smiled, revealing her nicotine-stained front teeth.

'And the neighbours might get the wrong impression,' she added, almost as an afterthought.

Al sighed, and laid the baseball bat next to the umbrella stand in the corner.

'Fine. Let me put some clothes on and I'll come. But make it quick,' he said, shutting the door and unhooking the chain. 'I'm busy.'

'I'm sure you'll be back home in no time, Mr Edwards,' Adamson said.

CHAPTER 10

‘So, let's recap,’ Kris said, getting up from her chair and standing across from the interview table, her piercing blue eyes never leaving Al's.

‘We've got photos and CCTV footage placing you in a known Red Hand hangout for close to forty-five minutes. A witness who'll confirm as much, including the time you arrived, the time you left, and your state of mind. "*Very agitated*," they said. And yet you're insisting you were "just passing by"? That you didn't go in? Is that the long and short of it?'

She punctuated each bit of information with one of the fingers of her right hand, extending her thumb to the photos, her index finger for the CCTV, and her middle finger for the witness. Which, to be fair, was how Al felt about that jakey rat bastard. It had to be the jakey in the car park, didn't it?

DI Doug Lennox was sitting back in his chair with his legs crossed, giving Al the death stare and making short work of a piece of chewing gum while she laid things out. Both looked extraordinarily pleased with themselves. Two cats that knew the mouse was kidding itself if it thought it was home free. That, even if it managed to scurry away to safety, it was only a matter of time before they sunk their claws into it.

Al pointedly ignored their smug faces and stared impassively at the interview room's grey door, which was peeling and covered in years of grime, his hands clasped in front of him on the chipped melamine.

'That's exactly what happened,' he said. 'Since when is it a crime to walk by a pub?'

'I don't know Al,' she continued. 'Not to get technical, but I'd say we've got you dead to rights.'

The 'quick chat' constable Adamson had promised had turned into a three-hour ordeal, and Al was starting to get hungry and irritable. But he laughed at her comment in spite of himself. Hearty guffaws starting deep in his belly.

'Want to know what I think, Inspector?' Al said when he'd composed himself, a wide smile still plastered on his face. 'I think you're fishing. You have nothing. Fuck all. Zilch. Even a first-year law student could shut this down faster than you can say bogus rap.'

He downed the dregs of the coffee they'd brought him what felt like an eternity before, grimaced, and leaned forward.

'But, sure, Inspector, let's play along,' he continued, looking her straight in the eye. 'Say I went in there, had a long heart-to-heart with that bunch of pricks. And say you really have something up your sleeve you're not letting on and I get charged and tried. Let's even say, for the sake of argument, that I'm convicted of whatever it is you think I'm guilty of. Do you honestly believe I'd worry about doing a stretch? Do you think it would scare me?'

He leaned back in the chair, his eyes darting from Kris to Doug and back to Kris.

'It would be great to get away from it all, actually. Have some peace and quiet for a change,' he continued. 'Fuck. Here. Why don't you lock me up right now?'

He offered his wrists in mock surrender.

'Och, I think you *will* be scared if the Chairman hears you're hanging about with the enemy,' Kris replied without missing a beat. 'This has something to do with your Ma, doesn't it? You've had to come to some arrangement with them.'

Al's smile faltered.

'He wouldn't like it if he found out about what you were doing, would he?' she pressed. 'No. He wouldn't like it one bit.'

Al's mind went to the drugs he'd lifted the previous morning. He'd rented the locker where he'd stashed two of the five bricks under a false name. But if they dug deep enough...

He caught himself rubbing his chib scar, and placed his hand back in his lap.

How did they know about Ma? Suddenly, the room felt much smaller.

Kris and Doug exchanged a look.

'You're bluffing,' Al sneered. 'Now, unless you're going to arrest me, I've got places to be and stuff to do. So, if you'll excuse me, inspectors.'

Al sat up. Kris gestured for him to stop.

'You know what? You're right,' she said, walking back towards the table and planting both palms on it. 'We aren't sure why you were at The Green Lady. But it doesn't matter. Whatever you were doing, you didn't have your boss' blessing. The look on your face gave it away.'

'Did it?' Al said.

He hardened his gaze and squared his shoulders. But his heartbeat had kicked up a notch.

'Fine. Perhaps we got it all wrong. You've been a loyal soldier and that bloke in the photos is an Al Edwards looka-like who's out there sullying your good name,' she contin-ued, implacable. 'But do you honestly believe that will matter to the Chairman? That the whiff of a rumour won't be enough? I bet people have been forced into "retirement" for less.'

She moved her face closer to his, close enough that he could smell spearmint toothpaste mixed with the lingering aftertaste of the station's coffee on her breath.

'And, here's the thing, Al,' she said, her voice a conspira-torial whisper, 'it took us less than two days to find out what you've been up to. How long do you think it'll take the Chairman?'

Al sat back down, looking at the two inspectors intently, the corner of his mouth quivering into a snarl. Kris fixed him with another one of her piercing stares.

'So the real question is,' she resumed, 'do you want to take your chances, Al? Or can we persuade you to look at the bigger picture? It's really up to you. We only have your best interests at heart.'

She was right. If the Chairman got a bee in his bonnet he'd be done for. And that wasn't a hypothetical. In the unlikely event the Chairman woke up on the right side of the bed and decided to check Al out before doing anything drastic, it would only delay the inevitable.

Kris sat down and watched the internal battle play out on Al's face. His brow furrowed. His eyes darted across the room, like those of a cornered animal desperately searching for an escape route it might've overlooked. He nibbled the inside of his cheek.

'What do you want?' he growled, at last. 'And what's in it for me?'

'We want you to tell us everything you know, Al,' she said without hesitation. 'We want names, places, routes. We want the Chairman's head on a silver platter. In return, we'll make sure your mates don't find you. Give you a fresh start, so to speak. How does that sound?'

'Are you daft?' Al said, feeling the bile rise in his throat. 'Do you think the Chairman gets his hands dirty? That's what guys like me are for. It would be my word against his. I barely ever see him, anyway. We talk a few times a year, at most.'

'Well then, we're going to have to find a way to get you more face time with the big man, won't we?' she said, flashing a smile that reminded Al of a freakishly large, man-eating shark. 'You seem like a smart guy, Al. I'm sure you'll figure something out.'

CHAPTER 11

Half an hour of back-and-forth later, they reached an impasse, so they cut him loose.

'Have a good night,' Kris said, as Al staggered out of the interview room, his arse numb from sitting in one of those cheap plastic chairs that seemed to be a mainstay of every government building up and down the country. 'We'll be in touch again soon, I'm sure.'

If, before reaching the station, he'd began feeling the first tentative hunger pangs, food was now the furthest thing from his mind. His stomach was churning. His mouth was dry. And despite the exhaustion that had set in, sleep was out of the question. He'd never be able to quiet his mind enough to drift off. His brain was a thousand-strong crowd of people, all talking at once. Clamouring for his attention.

'Some fucking predicament I'm in,' he thought as he climbed out of his Uber, which he'd been careful to order several blocks away from the police station, and walked up to his front door.

If he played ball with the police, he'd live out the rest of his days in some shite burgh in the middle of nowhere. And that was the best case scenario. The worst case scenario was being hunted down like a wounded animal. Gunned down on the pavement on his way to Gregg's for a steak bake. Or having his brains scrambled with a tyre iron.

Or he could call their bluff. Keep his head down. Juggle the Red Hand and the Chairman until he figured out a way to extricate himself that wouldn't raise suspicion or get him killed. Except managing the situation was going to be even more complicated now, with the police watching him. Waiting for a reason to tighten the screws. He wasn't just between a rock and a hard place. There was the rock, the hard place, and a giant fucking meteorite hovering over his head, ready to drop from a great height.

He patted his trousers for his house key and felt his phone vibrate. The sensation jerked him upright, and he fumbled for a few seconds before he managed to slide this phone out of his front pocket.

Jonno.

He debated letting it ring out. But that might give the wrong idea.

Or would it?

The paranoia was back in full swing. Everybody knew. All eyes were on him. He wasn't thinking straight.

The phone continued to vibrate, so he swiped right, put it to his ear, and braced himself.

'Jonno,' he said. 'What's up?'

'Al,' Jonno replied, sounding flustered. 'Where the fuck have you been all afternoon? I must've called you half a dozen times.'

Al sat down on his doorstep, letting the cool evening air wash over him. A stray reddish brown leaf drifted lazily towards a gutter, oblivious of Al's racing thoughts. He closed his eyes and focused on the two points of light behind his eyelids to centre himself.

'Settle down, bud,' he replied, his eyes still shut. 'I've been doing some work around the house and I wasn't checking my phone. What's so urgent?'

'The Chairman wants to see us,' Jonno said.

The news was a slap in the face. This was either a devastatingly large coincidence or a total catastrophe.

'The Chairman?' Al said, unsure how to play this. 'Our quarterly catch up isn't due for another week. Do you know what this is about?'

'Maybe he wants to give us a gold star. Pat us on the back and thank us for all our hard work and suchlike,' Jonno said. 'How the fuck should I know, bud? I don't ask stupid questions. The Chairman says jump, I say, "Is this high enough?"'

'OK. Keep the head,' Al said.

'Where are you right now? At home? I'll come pick you up.'

'No, no, no,' Al replied.

There was no way he was going to get in Jonno's car willingly until he took the Chairman's temperature and got a sense of what he might know. But he also regretted how frantic that sounded.

'I'm covered in paint and I reek. I've got to make myself presentable,' he said, making an effort to slow down. 'How about *I* pick you up. Say in about an hour? That work?'

'Aye, that should be fine,' Jonno said.

Was that a slight hesitation? Al wasn't sure. Not three hours in the bloody nick and his instincts had gone haywire.

'Smashing,' he said.

He raced inside. Peeled off his clothes. Jumped into the

shower. Turned up the heat as high as he could bear it and scrubbed himself raw to get rid of the rank police station smell that had stuck to his skin. Then he towelled dry and padded to his bedroom to change, his mind still going at a hundred miles an hour.

Why had the Chairman called this meeting?

Could he possibly have found out?

No. No.

No.

Maybe he just wanted to discuss a sensitive job. That had happened before.

Whatever it was, he needed to pull himself together. If he seemed jumpy, it would give the game away. But he was still brooding when he stopped the car next to the Ladbrokes on Gulf Square, a flag-stoned rectangle in Kelty Brig, an unsavoury part of west Strathburgh five miles due south of Al's house, almost bordering Billy Boy territory.

Jonno was sitting on a bench beneath a lamppost, scrolling his phone. To his right, near a pigeon shite-infested bronze statue of John Cawood, a 16th century Strathburgh physician who'd founded one of the city's first free clinics for the indigent, three teens in grey trackies were trying ollies on their skateboards, with varying degrees of success. One of them, a tall, pimply bloke with a bleached afro, careened towards the steps that led to the statue, jumped onto the railing, and promptly lost his balance, landing flat on his arse. His black skateboard clattered face-down next to him.

'Fuck!' he shouted.

He lifted himself up with his hands, jumped to his feet, and picked up the skateboard, tucking it under his arm.

'Och, you eejit,' one of his mates called.

'Fuck off,' the bloke replied.

All three burst into shrill laughter.

Jonno eased his considerable bulk into the passenger seat of Al's Discovery with a grunt.

'Alright Al?' he said.

'All good,' Al replied.

Al put the car into first gear and joined the sparse traffic. He turned right into Old Orchard Road, which would take them into town and then back up northwest.

'So what were you so busy with this afternoon?' Jonno asked, breaking the silence that had settled between them like a thick blanket.

'Eh?' Al said, his eyes on the road, his hands gripping the steering wheel at ten and two.

'Where were you painting?'

For a moment, Al wasn't sure what the hell Jonno was talking about. Then he remembered his excuse for not answering his phone. He indicated right, and made a show of carefully changing lanes and navigating the roundabout to buy himself a few more seconds.

'The living room,' Al replied, saying the first room that came to mind. 'It needed a makeover.'

'What colour did you paint it?' Jonno asked.

Al stopped at the lights. A woman in a nicotine-stained white pixie cut and skin like crumpled crepe paper crossed at an excruciating pace, hunched over her rollator.

'What's with the third degree?' Al said, more snappily than he'd intended. 'I don't suppose you want to come check if I did a good job?'

'Jesus Christ, bud. What's with you lately?' Jonno tutted. 'I'm interested because my living room's a dump. Thought I'd get some inspiration.'

The woman reached the other side of the crossing several seconds after the light had turned green. Al drove forward, his heartbeat pulsing in his ears. Christ, had he put his foot in it?

'Since when do you care about interior design?' he said, trying to keep things light. 'Anyway, I thought you rented.'

'So?' Jonno said defensively. 'Am I not allowed to make my flat look nice?'

Al scoffed.

'Who are you and what've you done with Jonno?' he said.

Jonno rolled his eyes, thumbed his phone's screen, and googled living room colour scheme ideas. They drove into town in silence. Jonno scrolled aimlessly through the images of living rooms Google had turned up, his breath whistling softly. Al kept his eyes glued to the road, his internal voice screaming at him to calm the fuck down.

It was dusk, and the looming darkness had changed the atmosphere. The light from the streetlamps reflected off the tenement windows, creating ethereal, otherworldly haloes on the flagstoned pavements. The crowds were thinning out. And with most of the office drones leaving or about to leave for the day, and only a few handfuls of scarf, puffer coat, and backpack-clad tourists out and about, there was an air of mystery. Of menace. Of secrets best kept locked behind the centuries-old front doors.

Al navigated a maze of cobbled alleyways, then took Strathburgh Way, the traffic light-spotted thoroughfare that slashed through the old town. The unbroken rows of storied stone buildings began slowly being replaced by soulless pebbledash turned dirty grey by years of exposure to the exhaust fumes. Al signalled a left, turned into a tree-lined avenue, and parked right next to a Soviet-looking three-storey monstrosity with a flat roof.

'Right,' he said, hoping Jonno didn't detect the shakiness in his voice. 'Let's see what the big man wants.'

They got out of the car and made their way towards the building, which was divided into four blocks of six flats each, all with identical layouts. This had been the Chairman's base of operations, where he gave important orders and took meetings, for as long as Al could remember, and the setting never failed to impress him. While the building was clean and reasonably well-maintained, it was dated and unremarkable. A far cry from the buildings Franco Guthrie typically favoured. Buildings with concierges, marble floors, solid oak and leather furniture, and open views across the city. Love him or loathe him, you had to admire his ability to restrain his flashier tendencies. It was probably why the location had remained a secret — and the police hadn't been able to make much of a dent in the Company's operations — for such a long time.

Feeling his muscles tense, Al pressed the buzzer. The aluminium and glass door clicked open seconds later, and he and Jonno climbed the two flights of stairs to a soundtrack of evening telly coming out of the other flats.

Jonno knocked. It was code. Two slow knocks with a three-second pause between them, then three sharp raps in quick succession.

'Come in,' the Chairman commanded from the other side of the door.

Jonno and Al nodded to each other and walked inside.

The flat was small. But because it was perfectly rectangular and expertly furnished, it was deceptively roomy.

A large picture window overlooking the burn took up most of one wall. Across the entryway, there was a double bed with one of those Ikea storage units in front of it. The kind with eight square shelves stacked two by two. The unit separated the sleeping area from the main living space, where there was a five-unit kitchen in glossy grey melamine, a round table with four bright yellow chairs, and a well-worn, but comfortable sectional sofa.

The Chairman, dressed in light grey slacks, spotless black oxfords, and a crisp white shirt, was standing at the picture window, looking out at the burn and tapping his nails rhythmically against a Glencairn glass containing a finger of amber liquid.

He turned around and sized Al and Jonno up.

Al made himself hold the Chairman's gaze for a few seconds before looking away. Jonno instinctively dropped his eyes to the floor. Suddenly, he wasn't a grown man anymore, but a ten year-old who'd been summoned to the prefect of discipline's office.

'Al. Jonno,' the Chairman nodded. 'Can I offer youse a dram?'

'Aye,' Jonno said softly, loath to turn down a drink, especially from the Chairman's stash, despite his nervousness.

'Al?' the Chairman said.

'No, I'm good. Ta.' Al croaked.

He was parched. But his throat was so constricted he worried the liquid wouldn't go down.

'Well, go on then, Jonno. Help yourself,' the Chairman said.

Jonno walked towards the old-fashioned drinks trolley next to the dining table, on which five whisky bottles were lined up next to each other. It was an impressive selection by any yardstick. 200 years of combined ageing in fine casks. He debated the selection. Then he unscrewed a bottle of thirty year-old Lagavulin, poured himself a generous measure, and drained it in one swallow.

Al sat down on the edge of the sofa, ready to spring to his feet and leg it if the situation called for it. The Chairman seemed relaxed. Friendly.

Too fucking friendly.

Al's misgivings were increasingly difficult to ignore.

Jonno rinsed the glass in the kitchen sink, and placed it carefully on the drying rack. He walked back to the living area and stood across from the sofa.

Was he blocking the way to the door?

Al shifted.

'Stop being so fucking paranoid, god,' he told himself.

'So,' the Chairman said 'How are things going, boys? Anything I should know about?'

His black, beady eyes slithered from Al to Jonno.

Jonno squirmed.

Al's heart drummed in his chest. These meetings always made him nervous. But his ordeal at the nick had taken things to a whole other level. The more he thought about it, the clearer it seemed to him that this wasn't a coincidence. It couldn't be.

'I had a spot of bother with one of them Red Hand pieces of shite today,' Jonno offered. 'Fucking prick must've taken a wrong turn, so I sorted him out. We really should do something about them. Teach them a lesson they won't forget.'

'I didn't ask for your opinion, Jonno,' the Chairman said quietly. 'I asked if there's anything I should know about. Is there?'

'No,' Jonno replied.

His eyes were downcast, and Al was impressed at how well he was hiding his anger at the putdown. This was a bloke who'd put a sixteen year-old wean in the hospital for smiling at him the wrong way.

'Otherwise things are going well, aye,' Jonno continued. 'Quality product. And business is up.'

'Just what I like to hear,' the Chairman said. 'And you Al? Anything I need to know?'

The Chairman took a few steps towards him. Al returned his gaze.

'No, no issues so far,' he said, in a voice he hoped was steady. 'I've got nothing to report.'

'Smashing,' the Chairman said, taking another sip of whiskey. 'So no bother with the Red Hand then?'

'No,' Al said, fighting the urge to lick his lips.

The Chairman took a step back, eyeing Al like a tiger about to pounce on a lame antelope. Then he looked down at his glass, lifted it to his lips, and drained it.

'Ah, that's good whiskey, ain't it Jonno?' he sighed.

'Och, aye,' Jonno replied.

'It's a rare one,' he continued. 'Very little stock left. A gift from Russ.'

Russ Bidmead was a young tech whiz. One of the two founders of the Mango Bank, one of the country's biggest financial startups. The Chairman didn't just enjoy bumping shoulders with the business elite. He also name-dropped them whenever he could. Made them out to be his best friends.

The tension in Al's shoulders eased.

So was this it? Just a quick status update? He almost felt stupid for worrying so much.

'How about one for the road, boys?' the Chairman asked.

'Probably better not,' Jonno said reluctantly.

'You sure?' the Chairman said.

Jonno nodded.

'And you, Al?' the Chairman asked.

'Och, no I-'

Al's head exploded with pain, and wetness dribbled down the left side of his cheek. His hand went to his head, but before it could reach halfway, the Chairman was on him. Grabbing him by the shirt. Pulling him to his feet.

Fabric ripped.

'YOU LYING PRICK BASTARD!' the Chairman screamed, spittle flying from between his lips. 'Did you think I wouldn't find out you're dealing with that scum on the side? EH?'

The room spun. Al's mind scrambled to catch up with what had just happened. But he was still disoriented from the blow to his head. A shard of the Chairman's Glencairn glass stuck out of his scalp like a lone cat's ear.

'You were nothing. NOTHING, when I picked you off the street. And this is how you thank me?' the Chairman seethed.

Al could feel the Chairman's arms thrumming with naked anger, like electrical cables about to overload. He shook him violently. The sound of more ripping fabric filled the room.

'Why the fuck did you get into bed with them, you ungrateful prick! Why? Tell me, you bastard!'

Al inhaled the sour tang of whisky on the Chairman's breath. Saw his thick, hairy hands gripping his shirt. His brain screamed at him to do something. Anything. But his body didn't respond. Everything felt like it was happening in slow motion. Even the Chairman's voice had dropped an octave. Jonno pulled a gun and aimed it at Al's head, his eyes swimming in betrayal.

'I should've taken Hendrie up on her offer when I had the chance,' Al thought.

He emitted a bray of laughter, cut short when the Chairman kneed him in the balls. Exquisite pain filled his stomach, and he doubled up, retching dryly.

'YOU THINK THIS IS FUNNY?' the Chairman screamed, his face the colour of dark clay.

Another knee connected with Al's eye. He saw more stars and fell to the floor helpless. Not just cornered, but captured. Fucked. Dead meat.

'Is this funny?' the Chairman screamed over and over again. 'Is it? Is it?'

Powerful kicks came thick and fast, like machine gun fire. Hitting Al's stomach. His lower back. His face. His kidneys.

'Why, you bastard? Why?' the Chairman continued in between gasps for breath.

But what could Al say? That Ma had dragged him into this? Brought trouble to his doorstep as usual? That he'd felt like he had no choice but to get involved? That, secretly, he'd hoped helping her would finally win him her approval? Make him feel like a good son? Even though all she'd ever cared about was herself?

He opened his mouth. Tried to explain. But all he could manage was a strangled croak. The kicks eventually subsided, getting fewer and farther between until they stopped altogether. Every single cell in Al's body was crying out in pain. His balls throbbed dully. His eye was swollen shut. His face sticky with blood.

'I'm disappointed in you Al. You should've come to me if something was bothering you, and we'd have sorted it. But instead, you go behind my back?'

The voice sounded disembodied. Like it could be coming from anywhere. Quiet. Icy.

Al made another attempt to say something. To explain himself. But he began coughing uncontrollably. The pain in his ribs flared. And his coughing descended into shallow gasps.

This was it, then. The end of the line. And it was everything he'd ever inflicted on others and worse. Karma had punched him in the solar plexus. The Chairman hawked, a gurgling sound deep in his throat, and spit. Al felt more wetness on his neck: a dark grey glob of snot mixed with blood from his head wound.

'Get him out of my fucking sight,' the Chairman growled in between ragged breaths.

Footsteps moved away from him. The front door slammed shut.

Jonno leaned over Al, grabbed his limp wrists.

'Jonno,' Al pleaded. 'Jonno what are you doing, bud?'

Jonno averted his eyes, busying himself tying Al's wrists behind his back with cable ties. The sharp edge of the plastic dug into the tender skin.

'Jonno, come on bud. We go back, don't we?' Al said, his voice taking on a frantic edge

He squirmed, trying to free himself, but Jonno placed his knee on his chest to keep him still. The weight felt as heavy as a two tonne lorry. It was hard to breathe.

'Jonno,' he squeaked.

Jonno pulled his gun arm back. The last thing Al saw before the world went black was a hunk of dark grey metal rushing towards his face.

CHAPTER 12

A cross from the flats, a dark figure stood in the shadow of a copse of trees, toying idly with his vape and waiting. His nicotine centre was screaming for a hit. But the cloud of vapour, redolent of the mixed berry flavour he favoured, would give him away. And his employer wouldn't be pleased if that happened.

No. His employer wouldn't be pleased at all. The instructions were clear and specific: observe, report back, and stay under the fucking radar.

So he waited in the gathering darkness, turning the vape over and over in his hand. Trying to ignore the hunger pangs that weren't really hunger pangs, but his lungs begging for a hit of poison.

Half an hour in, his patience was rewarded.

The Chairman walked out of the building. He stood in the doorway looking around the deserted street, absently tucking in his shirt and readjusting his thick curls. He lit a thin cigar with a silver Zippo lighter, exhaled a cloud of blue grey smoke — the dark figure unconsciously took a deep breath, hoping his nostrils could catch a few stray nicotine particles, even though he was hidden at least eight feet away — and sauntered towards a white Vauxhall Astra that was parked over the rise.

Dim lighting still shone out of one of the building's top floor windows. So the dark figure stayed put. A cool gust of wind rustled between the branches. He shuddered lightly, zipped up his jacket, and stamped his feet on the soft grass to get the blood flowing.

He glanced at his phone.

Fifteen more uneventful minutes passed. Twenty.

Then, at long last, Jonno appeared in the building's doorway. His forehead glistened in the streetlight, despite the brisk air. His breath wheezed softly. Across his shoulder, like a sack of potatoes, was a limp, human-shaped form, the hands secured behind the back with white, plastic cable ties.

The dark figure smiled. It had worked.

Jonno hurried towards a black Discovery, trying to look everywhere at once. He pressed the fob, unloaded his burden into the boot, then eased himself into the driver's seat and started the car.

The headlights splashed over the row of bins that were arrayed on the pavement outside the flats like soldiers on parade day. The car performed a drunken three point turn, then headed up over the rise with a crunch of gravel.

The dark figure fired up the call app on his phone and pressed the number at the top of his call log. The person on the other end answered on the first ring.

'What's going on?' they asked without preamble.

'One of his men — the big one — just left the building with the other one all trussed up. So he must've seen the photos.'

'Excellent.'

'Now what?' asked the dark figure. 'Do we need to do anything else?'

'No, not yet. Now, we wait.'

'Och?' muttered the dark figure, slightly nonplussed.

'We let the pot simmer a bit,' his boss said. '*Then* we swoop in.'

Chapter 13

When Al came back to his senses, it was pitch black and he was curled in a foetal position with his hands tied behind his back. His shoulders burned. His wrists were raw. His head felt like a broken egg. But other than the sense he was in a cramped, confined space, he couldn't make out where he was. The darkness was disorienting.

He tried to stretch, but couldn't. His feet bumped against a hard, unyielding, weirdly curved surface that emitted a muffled metallic thud when his trainers connected with it.

'What the fuck's going on,' he thought. 'Where am I? What's happening?'

He opened his mouth to shout, but it was duct-taped shut. A wad of what felt like flannel was lodged in his throat. The fabric, soggy with saliva and blood, made him dry-heave.

He focused on his breathing, but it was a losing battle. Panic had him in its steel jaws. His stomach lurched. Sour acid flooded his taste buds. The urge to scream and struggle was overwhelming.

No. No. No. No. No.

If he wanted to have a fighting chance of getting out of whatever this was, he needed to keep his head.

He closed his eyes. Tried to clear his mind. Heard a low hum. He couldn't pinpoint exactly where it was coming from. And he felt slightly dizzy for some reason. Was it because of the blows he'd suffered to his head?

No this was-

His body jerked violently forward, and he banged his forehead against something hard. Bright white spots flashed in front of his field of vision.

'Ungh,' he moaned from around a mouthful of duct tape and flannel. 'fkneeeelllll.'

He pressed his forehead down against the rough fabric beneath him, waiting for the pain to subside. Tears leaked from the corners of his eyes.

The smell of the fabric and the vibrations jogged his memory. It clicked. He was in the Discovery.

'What a fucking bastard,' he thought, his body white hot with fear. 'He's driving me to my death in my own fucking car.'

The rising tide of panic felt tangible. Solid. A fist that had punched the air out of him. The fabric in his mouth was making him salivate uncontrollably, and he swallowed instinctively. The flannel slid deeper down his throat. He gagged. Tasted more sourness.

'Unghhh,' he moaned.

He shook his head. Closed his eyes. Physically pushed the fear down. If he didn't do something, that prick wouldn't even have to finish the job. He'd choke on his own vomit.

'No,' the voice inside him said. 'I'm not spending eternity in a shallow grave on the side of a B road.'

He took a deep, shuddering breath through his nose. Then let it out slowly through flared nostrils. Then one more. And one more.

His thudding heart slowed imperceptibly. Progress.

'Good. Breathe,' he told himself. 'Breathe. Nice and slow.'

One more breath followed another. And another. When he felt confident he wasn't going to dry heave, he bent his right wrist experimentally. It couldn't quite reach his left shirt cuff and the razor blade stashed away inside it.

'Shite,' he thought. 'Fuck.'

He pulled his wrists apart to create some give. The skin burned. Sticky wetness pooled under the plastic of the cable ties that were binding his hands together, and dripped down onto the Discovery's carpet. A thin runnel of snot seeped out of his right nostril. He gave a mighty snort, to get it all out. Then wiped his face on the carpet, giving himself a friction burn. One more injury for his growing collection.

When he flexed his right wrist, he could almost touch his shirt cuff.

Almost. But not quite. It was a fraction of an inch. But it might as well have been several yards.

'Come on, you beautiful bastard,' his internal voice said.

He pulled his wrists as far apart as the cable ties allowed. It was agony. Sweat mixed with blood and dirt stung his eyes. He blinked it away.

Was his shirt cuff within reach?

He wasn't sure. But he had to keep going. If doubt

crept in, he might as well be the one to dig the hole where Jonno would bury him.

The car swerved, jerking him sideways and sending shockwaves up his shoulders. He waited for the vibrations to even out, every second feeling like an eternity. Then he pulled his wrists apart with a moan of pain and frustration.

This time, when he flexed his wrist, he could touch his shirt cuff. Sort of. Well, OK, just barely. With the tips of his fingers.

But that was all he needed.

'Aye! Aye!' his internal voice shouted, exultant.

He gripped the tip of his shirt cuff with his thumbnail and tugged. Worried at the loose thread on the seam. The car jolted forward and his shirt cuff almost slipped through his fingers. He grasped the fabric, and his thumbnail bent backwards, sending a bolt of exquisite pain up his finger. He bit the inside of his cheek and held on. The blade was coming out of his shirt cuff and he was going to cut himself loose, if it was the last thing he ever did.

He inserted his thumbnail into the seam. The fabric ripped. He gripped the razor blade between his thumbnail and forefinger.

'There, I've fucking got you!'

Another jolt. The razor blade sliced the pad of his finger, but he was too wired to feel it. Too focused on pulling the blade out of the shirt cuff. The pain. The burning in his shoulders. The flannel in his throat. They felt distant. Pushed into a dark corner of his subconscious. All that mattered was slicing the cable ties open. Cutting himself free.

He made the first cut. His hand was slick with blood, and the blade almost slipped through his fingers. The car was jostling him, making the job even harder.

The low hum of the engine was replaced by crunching tyres. They'd left the road for a dirt track. His window was shrinking. He flashed the blade in an arc and felt more pain. More blood welled out. The car lurched forward. He braced himself for another impact, and managed to avoid it just barely. But he lost his grip on the blade.

'Fuck, fuck, fuck, fuck,' he thought frantically.

He hadn't heard it drop. But would it have made a sound when it landed on the carpet?

His mind flashed. The muzzle of a gun, like an enormous black eye, bearing down on him. Jonno pulling the trigger. The heat was suddenly unbearable. His shirt and jacket were plastered to his back. The air in his lungs felt like liquid fire.

'No. I'm not going to be worm food because of Ma's stupidity,' he said. 'It can't happen. I won't let it.'

He eased his palm gently down on the carpet, probing it with his fingertips. He was holding his breath but didn't notice. He moved his hands slowly, deliberately.

'Where the fuck have you gone?' he thought to himself. 'Come on, you stupid fucking thing.'

The car slowed down. His heart rate shot up.

'Where are you? WHERE??'

He felt a stinging pain in the soft flesh of his inner forearm. The razor blade had never made it to the boot's floor. It had been trapped in the tangle of plastic that was keeping his wrists locked behind his back.

He fished around and gripped it, holding it almost by its edge, his thumbnail hooked into one of its holes. His wrist cramped. Numbness spread down his pinky finger and up the side of his right hand. He ground his teeth and sliced. Blindly. Not caring if he cut himself to ribbons.

The cable ties tightened, constricting his wrists. Then

they loosened. He pulled his wrists apart and they gave way like old paper. In the meantime, the car had slowed to a crawl. Not long before it stopped.

Moving as quickly as he could in the cramped quarters of the Discovery's boot, he ripped the duct tape off his mouth, spat out the gag, and gasped for breath. The air was stuffy. Cloying. But it felt as fresh as if he were at the top of a mountain, and he gulped it in gratefully, relishing the sensation of it filling his lungs.

The car stopped. The sound of the handbrake being pulled cut through the silence. Then the weight shifted as Jonno opened the door and got out.

Al moved as close to the boot door as he could, and pulled his foot back, ready to strike. He was in an extremely vulnerable position, but there were no other options. No weapon he could use aside from the razor blade, which required him to be at close quarters. All he had going for him was the element of surprise.

The minutes ticked by. Jonno's footsteps were barely audible on the soft grass. Al heard him fiddle with the boot door. He tensed.

A huge orb of light — Jonno's smartphone torch — filled Al's vision. Blinding him. He kicked out with his eyes shut against the glare, praying he'd land at least a glancing blow.

It went better than he'd hoped. There was a meaty thud as his trainer connected with Jonno's jaw. Jonno staggered backwards, dropping his phone and the shovel he'd been holding. Scrabbling blindly, Al pulled himself out of the trunk, landing on unsteady feet. He lunged for the shovel, keen to get the upper hand while he still could.

The sound of a whip crack filled the air. A bullet whizzed past Al's ear, grazing the skin. A high pitched buzzing like a swarm of angry bees filled his head. He felt wetness trickle down his neck from behind his ear.

'In your face, you prick!' he screamed, lunging forward with the shovel above his head.

The edge of the shovel's blade hit Jonno square in the face, bringing him to his knees. The gun fell to the ground. Jonno's hands flew to his face, which was a mess of blood, snot, and saliva. Al took another swing at Jonno's head. The blow landed with a sickening thud. Jonno was senseless before his body hit the grass. Blood seeped from a deep gash in his right temple.

Al dropped the shovel and rushed towards the car. The key was still in the ignition. He got in. Fired up the engine. Performed a three point turn with the driver's side door still open. Then he braked hard, almost smashing his head into the steering wheel in the process.

'Where the fuck am I?' he said, his voice a croaky grunt.

He'd no idea how much time had passed since Jonno had knocked him out. They could be in Ireland or France at this point, for all he knew. He patted down his pockets, but his phone wasn't there.

'Fuck. Fuck. Fuck,' he shouted.

He was jacked up on adrenaline, and the sound of his voice energised him. He screamed his throat raw. Hearing the primal sound reverberate through the clearing was like being plugged into a 24,000-volt socket.

He raced behind the car and spotted Jonno's phone straight away. It was lying face down next to the rear back tyre. It was an old model. One of those you unlocked with your fingerprint, not with Face ID, so Al didn't have to play around with Jonno's face to get the angle right. He squatted next to him, grabbed his limp hand, and placed his thumb on the scanner. Then he navigated to Settings and turned Touch ID off.

He fired up the Maps app, but there was no service. He let out a growl of frustration. Never mind. He was going to have to hack it.

He could see nothing but trees, with the full moon shining above them like a freshly-peeled Babybel. But he climbed into the Discovery and drove straight ahead anyway, checking his phone every few minutes to see if he had service.

Ten minutes of aimless driving later, the 3G icon appeared.

'Thank fuck,' Al sighed.

The tension in his shoulders eased, but only slightly. Once he found his way back to civilisation, he was going to have to do what he should've done in the first place.

Chapter 14

When Jonno regained his senses, it was because his clothes were soaked with dew. The cold had settled into his bones and he was numb all over. His groin felt so tight he was sure his balls had climbed back up into his stomach.

He tried to get up, pushing himself into a sitting position with a grunt, and his head exploded with sickening pain. The world spun alarmingly, and he sat motionless until it stopped, fighting the urge to boak.

He touched his head with his fingertips and they came back sticky with blood.

'That fucking bastard,' he muttered to himself, shaking his head in disgust. 'That traitor.'

He looked around him in a semi-daze, trying to remember the exact sequence of events that had ended with him flat on his arse with his head split open. That prick Al had managed to free himself somehow. He'd caught him on the wrong foot. And now the car was gone and he was stranded in Nowhere, West Arsehole. Ah what a piece of fucking shite. He needed to find him and fix this before the

Chairman got wind of what had happened, or it would be *his* head on the chopping block.

He reached for his phone. Then he remembered he'd dropped it when that bastard, that fucking traitor, had socked him in the puss. He got up on all fours, slowly, painstakingly, so he wouldn't get dizzy again, and crawled towards the spot where he'd parked the car, feeling every inch of the tyre-flattened grass with his hands. He clocked the shovel almost immediately. It was too big to miss. But the phone was gone. He went through the area once, twice, three times. Each time, he searched more slowly, starting in the middle and working his way outwards. But it was gone. Vanished. Al had taken it. That was the only explanation.

'Shite,' he growled, slamming his fist into the grass.

The ground yielded, and his fist buried itself into the mud with an unpleasant squelch. He pulled his hand out and wiped it on the seat of his jeans, not caring about the suspiciously sulphur-smelling brown goo it left behind.

So what now? He had to get back to Strathburgh and figure out where that prick could've gone. That was what. And forget about a gun to the head. He'd wrap his hands around Al's scrawny neck and squeeze until his face turned blue. He could already feel the tendons creaking. The Adam's apple bobbing helplessly up and down beneath his grip.

'Och, you traitor. You're going to regret switching sides,' he growled.

Jonno grabbed the shovel, planted it into the soft earth, and held on to it to get to his feet. Bright white spots of light flashed briefly in front of his eyes. He stood still, waiting for them to clear. Then he made his way to the B road, shovel in hand, his mind a jumble of contradictory thoughts.

His anger at Al was red hot. A burning fire in his belly. All the hours they'd spent together. All the times they'd got into scrapes, fighting shoulder to shoulder. This line of work wasn't conducive to friendships, but they'd been as close as you could reasonably expect. Which was to say he'd trusted the bloke. Even helped him move house, carrying pile after pile of those stupid books he read into his living room. How could he have turned against them, just like that? Made a deal with their sworn fucking enemies? It beggared belief.

But Jonno was also angry at himself, for letting Al catch him by surprise. He should've anticipated it. Al was a streetwise bloke, not some lamb who'd go willingly to slaughter, nuzzling him as he prepared to slit its throat.

His mind kept going round and round in circles, wrestling with whose fault this was — Al's or his — as he walked on the edge of the road. Stewing. Getting nowhere. A pair of headlights appeared on the horizon. He considered stopping the car. Then another car appeared behind it. Its headlights illuminated the first car, revealing the unmistakable shape of beacon lights on its roof.

Jonno ducked behind the bushes, crouching down so they wouldn't see him, and peered through a gap in the foliage. He was just in time to see another pair of headlights appear over the horizon. They illuminated the second car, revealing it too had beacon lights on its roof.

What the actual fuck? What was going on here?

The beacon lights were off, but the cars blazed past him, in a hurry to get somewhere. As the third car whizzed by, he saw it also had beacon lights on its roof. But why would not one, not two, but three police cars be speeding through a B road at this time of night? And with their beacon lights off?

It was like they were after somebody and didn't want to alert them of their...

Unless...

Could it?

A knot formed in Jonno's stomach.

No. Al wouldn't do that, would he? That couldn't be possible.

And yet, he'd turned against them. Got into bed with the Red Hand. The bloke was capable of betrayal.

But the polis?

Jonno's hand made a fist. Squeezed. Then relaxed. Squeezed. Relaxed.

It was inconceivable. But now that he'd had the thought, he couldn't unthink it. It grew in his mind like blood on white carpet. Spreading out beyond its epicentre. Staining every fibre it could reach deep red.

His gut urged him to get a move on. Maybe he was wrong. Maybe he was right. But wherever the polis where headed, it was too fucking close for his liking. More importantly, he needed to turn this bloody mess around. ASAP. Especially now that doubt had sunk its teeth into his brain and began secreting its deadly poison.

'You incompetent eejit!' the Chairman's voice boomed in his mind. 'How could you possibly have fucked this up?'

A hand flew towards his face. His cheeks stung in anticipation of the blow. The nerve-endings had built muscle memory even before he'd got in with the Company. Long, long before.

He tramped through the shrubs, swatting away the thick branches out of the way with the shovel so he wouldn't get a punctured eye to go with his split skull. His damp clothes clung uncomfortably to his skin, making it hard to manoeuvre.

A fresh pair of headlights appeared over a rise. The tree cover was much lighter here, and the Moon had come back out from behind the clouds. In its weak glow, he saw there were no beacon lights. This was a civilian car. The break he sorely needed.

He got out of the bushes and stood astride the B road. Legs spread. His left hand, palm open, stretched out in front of him. The shovel hidden behind his back. This wasn't what he'd usually do on a job, but circumstances had changed his priorities. Discretion was going to have to take a back seat to speed.

The driver was doing thirty miles an hour at most, but the hulking mess of blood and dirt standing in the middle of the road startled him. Tyres squealed. The car's rear end skidded ominously before regaining traction. It stopped a bawhair away from Jonno, jerking the stunned driver forward. The smell of burning rubber filled the air.

The driver — an older bloke with a wimpy mouse-brown moustache — lowered his window.

'Hey! What do you think you're doing?' he said weakly, his voice trembling with shock.

He'd leant out of his seat ever so slightly. Rookie mistake.

In three strides, Jonno was on him. The shovel met the driver's nose. The driver's hands flew towards his face with a cry of mingled pain and surprise. Blood fountained out from between his fingers.

Jonno swung the door open and slammed the driver's face against the steering wheel with one fluid, practised movement. Then he leaned in, unbuckled the seatbelt, and dragged the driver out of the car by the hair, ripping it out of his scalp in clumps.

The driver was a sobbing, powerless mess, crumpled on

the tarmac. Job done. But his pathetic, breathless whimpering enraged Jonno. Before he could stop himself, he was kicking him in the face.

'Shut up. Shut up. Shut up,' he shouted over and over again, like a mantra, unaware he was doing it.

His trainer connected again and again. The driver's whimpering petered out. His body went limp.

Eventually, all Jonno could hear was his own heavy breathing, and he stopped. His mind was blank. The nervous energy exhausted. He grabbed the driver under the armpits and dragged him into the tall shrubs so he wouldn't be visible from the road. The longer it took for somebody to find him, the more time it would buy him. And he needed every spare second he could get.

He slid into the driver's seat, slammed the door shut, and drove off.

'Och Al, you messed with the wrong fucking bloke,' he said to himself as he headed towards the onramp to the city bypass. 'You're going to be really fucking sorry. And that's a promise.'

Chapter 15

Kris walked back into the interview room, shut the door, and plopped a thick sheaf of papers down on the table. Al looked at them and squirmed in his chair. It was the same instrument of torture he'd been sitting in barely six hours before. Except that, instead of his own clothes — their blood-and-dirt-caked remains had been bagged and tagged as evidence of the Chairman's assault — he was wearing a prisoner's uniform: grey track-suit bottoms and a grey jumper over a white t-shirt.

After swabbing his wounds, picking a whole pub's worth of glass shards out of his hair and face, and taking photos of the damage, the custody nurse had stitched him up and given him two paracetamol he'd washed down with tap water. The plastic cup they'd brought the water in was still in his hands. As he sipped from it, he contemplated what awaited him now that he'd managed to dodge his appointment with an early grave.

So much had happened, it seemed like a lifetime ago that he'd strode out of this very interview room. He'd been approaching a crossroads back then. Now, he'd blazed through it at 100 miles per hour and the road had caved behind him.

How the fuck had it come to this?

Kris snapped him out of his reverie.

'Your buddy Jonno's in the wind,' she said. 'We combed every inch of the field you told us he took you to with sniffer dogs, and he's nowhere to be found. We don't know how he managed to disappear so fast if you got him as bad as you say you did. Any idea where he might've gone?'

Al shrugged and sipped his water. The Sentinel? Wee Dave's? Out of the city to lie low until the heat died down?

Who knew? The prick had always been a sneaky bastard.

'The good news is that your preliminary paperwork has come through.' She pointed at the papers on the table. 'There's your way out.'

Al wanted to say he was relieved, satisfied... whatever positive emotions one was supposed to feel in a situation like this. But Kris' words had left a bad taste in his mouth. Here he was, about to do the worst thing anyone in his position could possibly do. And the fact he had no other choice was cold comfort.

'So what's going to happen next?' he asked.

'Your solicitor's on his way. He needs to OK the deal before you agree to it and sign,' she says. 'But I'll give you the highlights. You'll need to admit to your role in the Company's operations. We'll charge you, and you'll appear before a judge and admit to those charges.'

Al was about to protest, but Kris raised her hand to silence him.

'That's non-negotiable. We can't just let you off the hook. It would send out the wrong message. But, in return for your evidence against the Chairman, you won't do any prison time. We'll relocate you. You'll have a new identity. A chance to start over.'

'Where am I going?' Al asked.

'I've no idea, I'm afraid,' Kris replied. She sucked in her teeth and crossed her arms. 'That's above my pay grade. The fewer people know about your new arrangements the better, you understand.'

Al nodded slowly.

'Me and inspector Lennox here,' she nodded at Doug, who was looking at him impassively from his chair across the table, 'will see you in court for your testimony. But that's about it. Somebody from the UKPPS is going to take over from here.'

So it was happening for real. Once he signed those papers he'd be officially the worst of the worst. The lowest of the low. The scum of the earth.

A grass.

He looked around the interview room, taking it in, suddenly aware he was about to take a big leap into the unknown.

'Do I go home and pack?'

Al wasn't a sentimental bloke, but he was overcome with the urge to walk through his house one last time. Maybe visit a few of his old haunts from before his life choices had swallowed him whole. It was mad how quickly you started getting nostalgic for things you took for granted when they were ripped away from you.

'No. It's not safe,' Kris replied. 'We don't know who your buddy Jonno might've managed to get in touch with and what he's told them. This is it.'

'And what about Ma?'

'They'll expect you to get in touch with her, but it's better not to. For her sake as much as yours.'

Al felt the familiar relief, followed by an intense guilt that flushed his chest, neck, and temples. She was a difficult woman to love. And now, any hope of him having the kind of relationship with her he secretly wished was possible had been extinguished for good.

'Of course, we can't stop you from contacting her,' Kris continued, 'but I strongly suggest you keep your distance. Don't text. Don't call. And most definitely don't visit.'

Al dropped his gaze to the floor and sipped his water. It had a faint plastic aftertaste. What was it he was feeling? Sorrow? Grief?

No, more like emptiness. A numbness that was hard to explain had set in.

'I know it's difficult,' Kris said, not unkindly, 'but this is the right choice. You do understand this is for the best, don't you?'

'I don't know,' Al shrugged, draining the last of his water and crushing the cup.

It was the honest truth. He genuinely didn't know.

CHAPTER 16

J onno's foot was itching to slam down on the gas pedal, but he forced himself to stay under the speed limit. In the twenty minutes or so he'd been weaving his way through the maze of B roads that cut through Stratburgh's green belt, he hadn't crossed paths with a single other car. But he didn't want to risk it. He'd already done more than enough damage for one night, and he didn't want to attract more of the wrong kind of attention if he could help it.

The priority was to find Al. Finish the job. Then ditch the car. He'd worry about the fallout from beating the shit out of that pathetic old sod later. His brain might be too scrambled to remember what hit him, anyway.

He glanced at the clock on the dashboard. Five past midnight. How far could Al have possibly gone? He was probably still somewhere in the city. The question was where.

When he could no longer avoid it, Jonno put on his indicator, slowed down, and did a textbook right turn onto the onramp to the city bypass. Miles of deserted tarmac stretched ahead of him, but he didn't accelerate. The speedometer hovered at a sensible and legal sixty-eight miles per hour while he mulled over his options.

Where to go? Where to look?

If it were him — not that he'd ever consider stabbing the Company in the back — he'd pack a bag and leg it. Get the fuck out of Strathburgh double quick.

Aye, that was the best starting point. Al's house. Even if he missed him, it was still worth going. He'd probably be able to uncover a few clues to where he might be headed next.

Jonno negotiated a roundabout and turned northwest towards Al's neighbourhood. Except for the streetlights and a few signs — a Co-op to his right, a Tanz almost right across from it, and a chippy several blocks up — the buildings were pitch dark. The denizens of this part of Strathburgh were sleeping the sleep of the righteous, oblivious to the secret life the city lived at night. In a rickety playground across the street from a tower block, a figure in a torn hoodie passed a Bic lighter to a similarly attired figure. The second figure sniffed and flicked the lighter with a scabbed hand, placing the flame under a crusty spoon.

The graffiti and the rubbish slowly gave way to manicured front gardens and freshly-waxed middle class cars. Jonno shifted down to second gear, turned left then right, and stopped on a tree-lined street. He parallel parked between a blue T-Cross and a black Vitara, hoping their bigger sizes would take the attention off his stolen car.

The sound of the driver's side door closing was impossibly loud in the dead of night. Jonno scanned the street, but nothing moved. Not a single window was alight. The wind gusted and he wrapped his jacket around him. It was still damp to the touch and ice-cold. Head down, he strode towards Al's house, then kept walking. He turned left and made his way around the block until he reached the fence that demarcated the sizeable garden at the rear of Al's house.

Another look to make sure the coast was clear. It was. His hand reached over the fence, found the latch, slid the bolt free. The fence swung soundlessly open, and Jonno walked in. So far, so good.

On the wall above the patio door, a wireless camera fixed him like a dead eye. A pinprick of blue light flashed. A motion sensor. Jonno reached up and unscrewed the camera from its holder. He banged it twice on the edge of the single concrete step that led up to the patio door and the living room beyond. The lens broke with a crunch of glass. No more prying.

He tried to slide the patio door open.

Locked. No surprise there, but it was worth a try.

He debated what to do next.

The glass panel was thick. Double glazed. If he hit it with the shovel's metal handle he probably wouldn't even scratch it, and the noise was bound to wake somebody up. The door also had a Yale, key-operated lock. The question was, was it a multi-point system, or one of the flimsier top-and-bottom types?

He fished his debit card out of his wallet and slid it between the door and the door frame. He tilted the card toward the door handle, jiggling it around very gently, until he felt it slide in front of the latch with a soft click. Then he bent it the other way.

The plastic bent, but the lock didn't budge.

'Shite,' Jonno muttered.

He hadn't expected his evening to involve breaking and entering, so he didn't have any other tools of the trade with him except for the gun and the shovel. Shooting the lock would be idiotic. He surveyed the door. Perhaps if he slid the blade of the shovel underneath it, he might be able to pull it open.

Swinging the fence shut, he half-walked, half-jogged back to the car, trying to keep to the shadows. He fetched the shovel from the passenger seat. Then, an idea struck him. He opened the boot of the car.

What he found was an absolute mess. A half-empty bottle of wiper fluid. Several bottles of Autoglym and balled-up microfibre cloths, most of them filthy. A yellow bag for life full of empty wine bottles. But no toolbox.

'Christ alive,' Jonno thought, tossing away a resealable lunchbox that was empty except for a couple of slices of cucumber that had turned white and mushy.

It was like an episode of Hoarders. Smelled like it too.

He lifted the boot's bottom panel to expose the spare tyre. At first, he couldn't find what he was looking for. Then he spotted it next to the jack. A single tyre iron with a flattened end like a screw-driver's.

Back in Al's garden, he squatted down, forced the blade end of the tyre iron underneath the door, and pushed down, the tendons in his neck creaking.

Nothing.

'Fuck's sake,' he grunted. 'I don't have time for this.'

He fiddled with the tyre iron, moving it closer to the door jamb, then further away, trying to find the sweet spot. The door jiggled tantalisingly in its frame, but the lock stayed in place.

Frustration mounting, he got to his feet, squeezed his fists together, and took a deep breath. The clock was ticking. The longer it took him to find Al, the greater the likelihood the Chairman would learn about his fuck up. And he couldn't afford that.

He stepped on the tyre iron, using all his body weight. The door moved up in its frame, leaving a sliver of a gap underneath. With his foot still on the tyre iron, Jonno used both hands to pull the sliding door towards him. The veins in his temples popped.

'Move you little shite,' he growled, pulling.

There was a loud click. His fingers slipped and he shambled backwards three steps before coming to a doddering halt with the backs of his knees against a wood planter. The door had cracked open.

'Thank fucking Christ,' Jonno said.

And now for the matter of nailing that bastard.

Wielding the shovel in front of him like a cricket bat, he stepped inside. The house was pitch dark, and, other than the faint hum of the fridge coming from the kitchen, eerily quiet. He tiptoed from one room to the other, making sure the coast was clear before going in and inspecting shelves, opening cupboards, and rifling through drawers for some clue to where Al might have run off.

In the kitchen, there was a small assortment of dishes, plates, and cutlery, and a meagre collection of bachelor staples. A couple of bottles of pasta sauce, one half-empty pack of store-brand spaghetti, six tins of tuna, half a loaf of bread, and one banana blackening in the fruit bowl on the quartz countertop. The fridge was even more depressing. One mouldy plate of leftover rice, a block of cheddar, and a few slices of ham. Not exactly Jamie Oliver, was Al. The pile of papers next to the fruit bowl was all junk. A flyer for gutter cleaning, a torn Farmfoods catalogue, and a flyer for home insurance. No bills. No postcards.

The living room didn't give Jonno much more to work

with. The bookmark in the Ken Follett novel on the marble coffee table was a page from a Farmfoods catalogue, probably ripped out of the one on the kitchen counter. And the framed photos that punctuated the anally-organised books were all of Al. No relatives anywhere to be seen.

Al in full fishing garb, posing with a trout in front of the loch.

Al in a dark blue suit, standing in front of a lighted fountain with his hands cupping his balls like a defender waiting for the opposing team to take a free kick.

A much younger Al standing proud, his hand draped over the bonnet of that ridiculous red Honda CRX Del Sol he never used to shut up about.

Jonno padded down the hallway, pressed his back against the staircase with the shovel aloft, and opened the cupboard door. The fucker wasn't hiding in there, waiting to pounce. Ditto the downstairs bog. Empty, and untouched.

He snuck his way upstairs, where there were two bedrooms, one of them with an ensuite, and a family bathroom. The beds were made in both bedrooms. And in what he guessed was the master, the built-in closet and chest of drawers were stuffed to the brim with clothes, all neatly folded and organised.

He stepped into the ensuite. A single dark blue towel was folded over the rail. The toothbrush and a tube of Colgate were in a glass on the pedestal sink, next to a bottle of purple Listerine. His shoulders sagged. If Al had made a pit stop here — and that seemed like a very big if at this point — he wouldn't be able to find out much about where he was headed from here.

The front door clicked shut.

Jonno was on high alert, but he didn't move. Then he

realised he'd switched on the ensuite light. He crossed the room, flicked it off, and closed the door as quietly as he could manage.

'Aye, I told him a million times that nobody gives a shit about Knight Rider. Who even remembers it at this point? But it's all he ever bloody talks about. Drives *me* up the wall, and he's my brother. I can't bear to think what it must be like going on a date with him.'

It was a female voice with the distinctive hoarseness of somebody who indulged in one too many fags.

'Knight Rider? What the hell's that?' the other voice said.

This one belonged to a bloke. Young. Definitely not Al.

For a second, Jonno questioned whether he was in the right house. But that wasn't possible. He'd seen the books. The photos. The loud clothes.

'It's an eighties show about a talking car. With David Hasselhoff. The bloke in Baywatch,' continued the female voice.

She coughed. A ripe, two-pack-a-day hack.

'No shit, a talking car?' replied the bloke, like this was the most gob-smacking thing he'd ever heard. 'What's Baywatch?'

'Do you not know anything at all? Why do I even bother talking to you?'

'Hey, it's not my fault you're ancient, fam.'

'Fuck you very much.'

The stairs creaked as Al's two mystery visitors made their way up to the second floor. They were headed straight towards Jonno. He cracked the ensuite door a hair and peered into the bedroom, gripping the shovel.

The light went on, revealing two hi-vis jackets, black shirts, and black trousers. The shorter of the two turned their back to the ensuite. POLICE was emblazoned in white lettering over a blue background on their hi-vis.

A chill shot up Jonno's spine. What the fuck was going on here?

'Nice house,' the short one — the bloke — said. 'And they say crime doesn't pay.'

The two uniforms walked out of Jonno's line of vision. A drawer opened with a high-pitched squeak.

'What are we getting him?' the bloke continued.

'Nothing fancy,' replied the woman. 'A few shirts, a couple of pairs of trousers, and some pants should be enough to tide him over. The UKPSS will get him whatever else he needs. He's their problem now anyway. They'll handle him until he testifies.'

'Do you have the bag?'

'Here. Catch.'

There was a rustle of fabric and a zipper slid open.

The bloke changed the subject, and the two officers continued chatting in friendly tones as they packed. But Jonno didn't hear any of it. One word the bloke had said — testify — was ringing in his ears. Blotting everything else out.

So those three police cars weren't racing along that B road by accident. Al must've told them where to find him. He'd come to and left in the nick of time.

He pressed his back against the bathroom tiles, and shut his eyes. His gut was on fire. He squeezed the shovel so tight every single vein and tendon in the back of the hand stood out.

It was even worse than they'd thought then. Not just a traitor, but a fucking rat.

Dealing with the Red Hand was bad enough. But grassing?

He had two thoughts in quick succession.

The first was that he needed to tell the Chairman about this as soon as possible, or they were all going to be completely and utterly fucked.

The second was that if he told him Al had gone and grassed, he'd still be completely and utterly fucked. The Chairman would put the blame squarely on him for letting Al get away.

And what would his punishment be?

As he slumped against the wall and slid slowly onto the floor, all he could think was that he desperately didn't want to find out.

CHAPTER 17

U nlike Jonno's, my Monday started reasonably well. My commute to work was uneventful, and I reached the office early, which was always good. With no emails pinging me out of the zone every few minutes, and no inane chatter about who had designs on who around the office or what had happened on bloody Love Island or whatever the fuck it was poisoning my ears, I managed to put in a solid hour of deep work. By the time the first stragglers powered up their laptops, I'd finished a tax return, crossed several admin tasks off my to-do list, and began work on a presentation for a big new client. The client, a financial conglomerate with offices across the UK, Ireland, and mainland Europe, was looking to reorganise their business to lower their tax exposure. It was my job to figure out the best way to achieve this.

You might think poring over tax laws, technical manuals, and HMRC guidance notes is mind-numbing stuff. But I love it. It's like speaking a secret language. Or being the only one who can confidently make their way through a maze because you've got a map that guides you from A to

B. And I get a kick out of making connections others can't see. Getting the system to work to my advantage.

By 11am, I'd made a fair amount of progress. I'd put together a proposed organisational chart, double-checked a few things in the law, and started making a few tentative handwritten notes ahead of working out whether the maths made sense. Then I heard a knock at my door and looked up to see Phillip, as ruddy-complexioned as ever, standing straight in the doorway and studying me.

Phillip McAllister was one third of Kinnock, Fraser, and McAllister Financial, and my direct boss. A fifty-six-year old dandy with a bald spot that was increasingly difficult to hide (not from lack of trying, mind), who'd spent most of his career running Daddy's business into the ground while everyone else worked overtime to pick up his slack. Not to put too fine a point on it, but he was the bane of my existence. And that was on a good day. When he really put his mind to it, he made me totter on the edge of doing something I'd almost certainly regret.

This project was one of those instances. For once, he'd got off his arse and brought in a valuable client. But instead of congratulating himself on a job well done and letting somebody — how shall I put this delicately? — who actually had half an idea what they were doing take it from there, he'd decided to get involved. That meant dropping in on me to 'check progress' and lengthy status meetings where I had to listen to him spouting inanities with a straight face.

'Good morning, Mr Haig,' he said.

His voice was a cross between a prepubescent Alan Rickman and a strangled otter.

'Phillip, good morning,' I replied cheerfully, not lifting my gaze from my notepad, hoping I looked suitably busy.

Well, at least busy enough to put him off any further conversation.

'Did you have a good weekend?' he replied.

Phillip attacked every conversation like a man who had all the time in the world. He never scrimped on the small talk.

'It was good, thank you,' I said, swallowing down my annoyance.

It was actually horrible. I'd spent most of Saturday and Sunday brooding about what had happened in therapy in front of the telly while trying to ignore the sounds of Graeme talking loudly on his phone at all hours and slamming his front door whenever he popped out. Which was at least twenty fucking times a day.

'What are you working on?' Phillip continued, stepping into my office with his hands in the trouser pockets of his impeccably tailored, conservative suit.

The man had good taste, I could give him that. But then, he could probably afford it.

'Is it Carruthers Capital?'

'Err... aye,' I said, reluctantly. 'I've made good progress on the restructure.'

'Excellent. Excellent,' Phillip said, helping himself to one of the chairs in front of my desk.

A delicate chiming sound filled the room.

'If you'll excuse me a moment,' Phillip said, making a show of sliding his leather-encased iPhone out of the inside pocket of his suit jacket and checking the caller ID. He rejected the call, placed the phone back in his pocket, and crossed his legs.

'Right,' he said, tilting his head at an angle. It made him look bird-like. A particularly pink species of pigeon, perhaps. 'Why don't you catch me up?'

Doing my best not to roll my eyes, I let go of my pen and leaned back in my chair — a rather weak attempt at marking the office as my territory.

'This is only preliminary, OK?' I prefaced, which in retrospect was an invitation for him to make suggestions and, so, a terrible mistake. 'I'll need to validate.'

'Go on,' Phillip prodded.

'So here's what I was thinking. We'd move the holding company to Ireland, to benefit from the 12.5% corporation tax rate. Then have subsidiaries in the UK, and key EU countries that also have favourable tax treatment — Luxembourg, Hungary, Estonia, perhaps.'

As I outlined my plan, laying out the broad strokes and explaining the reasoning behind each decision, I could see Phillip's eyes glaze over, and this boosted my confidence. I knew exactly what I was saying. And hearing it out loud made me more convinced that it was a sensible way forward. I just needed to work up a few scenarios to show the client. But I had good reason to believe they'd consider it sound too.

'And, of course,' I concluded, while Phillip fidgeted with his mother of pearl cufflinks, 'we'd issue preference shares to the big shareholders, to hit two birds with one stone. It would allow us to-'

And there it was. Phillip shoved his palm in my face to shut me up. It was inches away. So close I could see a small squiggle of a scar in the crease where his pinky finger connected to the rest of his hand.

'Mr Haig, this is all well and good,' Phillip said. 'But what about the international implications?'

For a minute, I wasn't sure what the fuck he was on about, and I stared back at him blankly.

'The different regimes in Ireland, Luxembourg, and... was it Latvia you said?'

'Estonia.'

He waved a hand dismissively. 'Wherever. It would be all very complex to navigate wouldn't it? It might put us in an awkward position.'

'You mean it'll put you in an awkward position,' I thought. 'Expose you as the incompetent fraud you are.'

'Well, err, obviously we'll have our network of partners in these jurisdictions to assist with the technical detail,' I stammered. 'But since Carruthers has operations in multiple jurisdictions anyway, surely we should be using that to our advantage. Plus, as I was about to say, with the preference shares we could max out the tax benefit without diluting voting rights too much.'

'But, Mr Haig,' Phillip's usually pink colouring was going a shade of purple. 'wouldn't all the dividends be taxed the same way? How is it more tax-efficient?'

If you're an accountant, you don't need me to tell you that what Phillip had just said was, at best, disingenuous and, at worst, completely clueless. If you're not an accountant, trust me. He was talking absolute bollocks.

I didn't tell him this, of course. Nor did I tell him he wouldn't know a tax loophole if it fucked him up the arse with a chilli-covered dildo. A display of self-control I was quite proud of. Instead, I let him ramble on and on about his ideas. Some of which were nonsense. And some of which had been taken off the statute books back when I was too busy playing Super Mario on my Game Boy to care.

Fifteen minutes of polite nodding later, he seemed to have run out of steam, like a toy robot that had exhausted its batteries. He glanced at his wristwatch, stood up abruptly, and said his goodbyes.

'Time for a long lunch, old boy, eh?' I thought.

'Keep working on it. See if you can structure it like I told you,' he said, stopping in my office doorway.

'I'll certainly look into it,' I replied, folding my hands in front of me on my desk.

'Good man,' Phillip said.

As soon as he left, I sagged in my chair. My mouth was dry and there was a faint tremble in my fingers. Honestly. Why did dangerously incompetent fucks like Phillip McAllister have to ruin everything?

In case you hadn't realised, there wasn't much going on in my life at this point, so a lot of my self-worth was tied to my work. OK, I cared far more than was reasonable or healthy. And I resented Phillip coming in and pissing all over my efforts. More importantly, this was looking like a case of having to indulge him every step of the way, until he realised his ideas were unworkable on his own. A prospect I found painful and exhausting in equal measure.

I tried to get back to it but I was too worked up to concentrate. The numbers on my notepad could've been scribblings in an alien language, and I stared at them until they blurred together. My colleague — and perhaps one day, I hoped, something more — Joan, who worked in tax, on the other side of the building, dropped by my office to say hi, looking heart-stopping in a charcoal grey trouser suit and blood red silk blouse. But even chatting with her about this and that couldn't lift my spirits.

'Wow, Bertie,' she remarked. 'Where have all your happy thoughts gone?'

I smiled grimly back and said nothing.

By lunchtime, I'd accepted the day was a write-off, so I made up a stomach ache and caught the bus home.

Walking up to my building, I kept running my conversation with Phillip over and over in my head, kicking myself for coming up with eight different ways to diplomatically nip him in the bud only now, when it was far too late to deploy them. My head was so far up my own arse I only realised there was a gaggle of people outside our building when I bumped into Blair from flat two.

'Och, excuse me,' I told her. 'Are you all right?'

'Aye, aye, don't worry about it,' she said, without turning.

Then I realised everybody who wasn't at work was either outside or looking on out of their windows. Graeme was in the doorway, his phone glued to his bloody ear, as per. And Morag had picked a spot where the road inclined upwards, giving her a better visual. She was saying something to an older bloke I'd seen walking his Labrador a few times, but her eyes were fixed on the scene. The Labrador was sprawled at its master's feet, tongue lolling happily and tail thumping on the pavement.

I stood on my tiptoes to get a better view. Four squad cars and an ARV were parked haphazardly on the kerb. Several uniformed police officers were coming out of the door two down from the one leading up to my flat, carrying cardboard boxes, stacking them in the trunk of the ARV, and walking back in. They looked like a line of ants storing food for winter

'What the hell's going on?' I whispered to Blair. 'Did somebody die?'

'I'm not sure,' she said.

She was unable to tear her gaze away. But, in all fairness, neither was I. While we were technically in gang territory, it was a quiet neighbourhood, and this was the most excitement I'd experienced since moving here five years earlier.

'From what I gather,' a bloke whose breath reeked of

raw onions butted in, 'there was gang activity in one of the flats.'

'Is that so?' I asked, alarmed.

An image of young blokes in trackies hanging around our building, brandishing knives, flashed in front of me. Dealing with Phillip seemed trivial in comparison. Maybe I should've stayed in the office. Powered through.

'But I've never seen anything untoward going on for as long as I've lived here,' I stammered. 'It's so quiet.'

'Aye,' onion-breath continued. 'maybe that's why. They look for places where they can fly under the radar, you know.'

This bit of information had spread through the whole street like wildfire. But the exact nature of the goings on in the flat depended on who you talked to.

Onion-breath assured me they'd been cutting and packing heroin in there. Lizzie, an older lady with a penchant for tie-dyed harem trousers who lived in one of the terraces across our building, insisted it was a shooting gallery. The kind where the shooting was done with heroin-filled needles, not guns. Blair, who'd gone off somewhere, then re-appeared out of nowhere, said she'd just learned from John from the flats next door, who had a cousin on the force, that it was a meeting place where the gang's head honcho discussed business.

Whatever it was being used for, people eventually started losing interest and trickling away. There was only so long you could watch boxes being stacked inside a van, even if said van belonged to the police and the boxes were evidence of a serious crime. From the corner of my eye, I saw Morag coming towards me, inching forward with her halting gait. I made a beeline to the front door, determined to reach the safety of my flat before she could engage me in conversation, but even though the small crowd was thinning, it slowed me down, and she caught up to me.

'Hiya Morag,' I nodded, resigned, pasting on a smile.

To my astonishment, she gave me the most cursory of glances and kept walking towards our building, her brow furrowed. Part of me was glad. The last thing I was in the mood for was a one-sided conversation I couldn't get out of. But I also couldn't help wondering whether she was annoyed with me for not backing her up on that business with Graeme's motorcycle.

Aye, that's me. I can never bloody win, can I?

CHAPTER 18

Father Baker paced in front of the teacher's desk, his arms crossed behind his back, his breviary clutched in his left hand so tightly the finger marks on the black leather cover were clearly visible even from the back of the long, narrow classroom.

'You should all be ashamed of yourselves,' he said, his voice unnervingly quiet, the vein in the middle of his forehead pulsing rhythmically. 'This is mediocrity. Do you know what mediocrity is?'

He paused, making eye contact with each student in turn, challenging them not to look away. The classroom was so silent you could hear a pin drop on the threadbare carpet.

'Mediocrity,' he continued, his voice rising a notch, 'is being satisfied with enough.'

He brought his right hand in front of his chest long enough to make violent air quotes, then returned it behind his back, where it clamped down on his left wrist in a death grip, tendons bulging.

'You. Are mediocre. All of you.'

It was a beautiful June day, warm, but with an occasional breeze that took the edge off. The sky was bright blue as far as the eye could see, unmarred by a single cloud. Jonno wished he could be anywhere except there, in that stuffy, overbearing atmosphere, but the afternoon stretched interminably before him. He was looking at a double English lesson, followed by maths, followed by prayers, homework, tea, more prayers, and lights out.

Jonno stared out of the classroom window, and his mind drifted. Father Baker's ranting faded into the background, a meaningless drone. He pictured himself running across the open fields that surrounded the school grounds. He felt the cool breeze in his hair. The grass was soft and inviting under his bare feet. Nothing and nobody could touch him. He was invincible. Free.

His eyelids were getting heavier by the second, drowsiness descending on his brain like fog on a cold winter morning. The grass looked greener. Brighter. The smell of lavender blossoms filled his nostrils. Then a sound like a thunderclap jolted him to attention.

'Wallace,' Father Baker seethed, his fist hammering Jonno's desk, spittle flying from his lips.

His face was the colour of fired clay. If he didn't calm down, the bloke was going to have a stroke right there in the classroom, someday.

'I'm boring you, am I now?' Father Baker said.

'Err... I,' Jonno stammered, knowing he'd been caught red-handed and unsure what to say.

'Get out of my sight, before you make me do something I'll regret.'

Jonno got up to leave, and it just happened. He hadn't planned on it. The words slipped out of his mouth of their own accord.

'Thank you, Father.'

There was a chorus of nervous laughter, and Jonno rushed out of the classroom before he could see Father Baker's reaction.

There was an alcove with a bench and a few chairs in the middle of the corridor. He made his way there, planning to chill for the rest of Father Baker's double lesson and try not to think about the world of trouble he was probably in. Then a door slammed shut behind him, and footsteps thundered towards him.

'Wallace!' Father Baker roared, his voice echoing around the empty corridor. 'Wallace, freeze. Come back here, you arrogant brat.'

Jonno turned to face him. He'd had his fair share of run-ins with Father Baker at this point, and he was used to his temper. But he'd never seen him this worked up. His pale blue eyes were blazing with fury. His large, strong hands balled into tight fists.

A pang of fear wormed its way into Jonno's chest, and he took several involuntary steps backwards. The cool solidity of the corridor wall stopped his retreat. He was cornered.

Father Baker lunged forward, up in his face, every blackhead on his nose and a spot of stubble he'd missed in stark relief.

'I'm sick of your posturing, Wallace,' he shouted, his voice deafening at this range.

Warm spittle showered Jonno's face.

'You think you can pull one on me and get away with it, do you? You think you're cool? Keep this up, and I promise I will make your life a living hell!'

Father Baker's face grew bigger. Enormous. Blotting out everything else. Jonno looked to the right and to the left, weighing his options. How could he get away from this deranged priest?

It was impossible. There was nowhere to go.

And he couldn't move. His neck was stiff. His feet were numb. The wall was digging uncomfortably into his back.

Except.

Was it really a wall?

It felt strange. Not the smooth, plastered surface he remembered from his boarding school days. But soft. Yielding.

He opened his eyes. Saw Al smiling at him from a brass frame on a wooden shelf. Light seeped in from the crack between light grey satin curtains.

For a minute, the disorientation was overwhelming.

Where the fuck was he? What had happened?

Then he remembered.

He was no longer a twelve-year-old wean. And this wasn't St Patrick's Home for Troubled Boys. No. He was a grown man, covered in the cold, sickly sweat only a twenty-year old nightmare could bring on.

Jonno's back was murder from having passed out in a sitting position, slumped on Al's living room sofa. His head throbbed dully, and his mouth tasted like a dragon had gorged on curry and taken a cataclysmic shite in the middle of his tongue.

He stood up and stretched, trying to work the kinks out of his sore muscles.

As the fog lifted, the memories came flooding back.

Al's foot coming towards his face.

Waking up soaked in dew.

Police cars. Looking for him.

Uniformed officers in Al's house. Packing his bags.

Making sure they'd left. Scouring the house for a phone he could call the Chairman from. To warn him.

Because Al had turned grass.

Even scum was better than that disgusting piece of shite. That rat.

He remembered sitting on the sofa for a second, to collect his racing thoughts. Then, at some point, perhaps while resting his eyes, exhaustion must've set in, because he'd fallen into the troubled sleep he'd just woken up from.

Every thought was a slap in the face. Jonno's gut said it was every man for himself. But the Chairman had taken him in when he'd been new to the city. An eighteen-year-old wean fresh from ten years of hell in a Catholic orphanage. He'd given him money and a purpose. He couldn't skip town without at least trying to warn him. He owed him that much.

He grabbed the shovel, which was lying on the floor next to him, and tiptoed into the hall. He stopped, shovel aloft, ears straining for the faintest sound that might indicate he wasn't alone. He heard nothing but silence.

Slowly, he stepped forward, counted to five, and opened the closet under the stairs.

A plastic bucket crashed to the floor. Jonno jumped.

'Motherfucker!' he growled.

He kicked it back into the closet and shut the door. Then checked the downstairs loo and the kitchen. Both unoccupied. Everything looked the same as he'd found it the previous night.

Satisfied, he headed upstairs, checked the bedrooms and the bathroom, then headed into the ensuite and stood in front of the mirror above the sink. The man staring back at him looked like Freddie Krueger from the nightmare on Elm Street. His head and the left side of his face were caked with dried blood, and a greenish yellow bruise had blossomed on his right cheek.

Jonno needed to hustle. He had to find the Chairman as soon as possible. But the polis were probably looking for him, so he couldn't afford to walk around looking like he'd been tied to a car and dragged thirty miles.

He stripped off his grass-and mud-caked clothes, wincing as pain flared up his shoulder, and cleaned himself up in the sink as best as he could, dousing the cut on his head with TCP and applying the largest sticking plaster he could find in Al's medicine cabinet. When he was done, he pulled on his jeans and the baggiest hoodie he could find in Al's closet. It made him look like a badly stuffed sausage, but his own jumper was a write off. It was going to have to do.

He headed downstairs to the kitchen and rustled up a sandwich out of Al's meagre supplies. It was bland and tasteless, but it was better than nothing. He hadn't eaten in over twelve hours and he needed the sustenance.

Feeling better, he let himself out of Al's house the way he'd entered the previous night — through his patio door — and walked towards his car, head down, shoulders squared.

He wasn't sure what he was going to tell the Chairman. If he could even get in touch, that was. But now that he'd cleaned himself up and put some food in his belly, he felt much more optimistic about his prospects.

The Chairman was an unpredictable man, but he valued loyalty. Perhaps he'd even appreciate the fact Jonno had brought him information that might save his skin.

Well, the whole team's skin.

CHAPTER 19

Doug unscrewed the thermos, refilled Kris' travel mug and handed it back to her.

'Are we sure this is it?' he asked.

'No, but it's the only place that makes sense.' Kris replied, feeling as frustrated as Doug sounded.

She took a small sip of coffee. It was tepid and bitter, but when you're so deep into overtime it's more accurate to call it a double shift, any coffee's better than no coffee.

'The house is owned by a corporation registered in Germany,' Kris told Doug, who, judging by the grimace his face had just rearranged itself into, wasn't particularly keen on the coffee either. 'Doesn't that strike you as odd? Why would a foreign business buy an investment property right here of all places, in a sleepy suburb forty miles away from any sort of action?'

'Aye, that's a good point,' Doug said, shifting in his seat.

'And one of the shareholders is a known associate of Guthrie's. He's a partner in one of his legitimate businesses. That's too much of a coincidence. This has to be it.'

Plus, they both thought but didn't say, they weren't

exactly drowning in leads. High-ranking informant or not, tracking the Chairman down had proved much trickier than they'd anticipated. The bloke was a slippery fellow.

They'd been sitting in Doug's blue Insignia, strategically parked on a street right across from the house, since four in the morning. But except for the occasional car passing through, nothing had happened. No movement at all. Unless they had this terribly wrong and Guthrie was already in the wind, he was yet to make an appearance. So they'd continue to wait until central command decided enough was enough and pulled the plug. The glamour of the job.

Kris took another pull from her travel mug. The coffee sat like battery acid in her stomach, and she was so wired she was grinding her teeth. Her thoughts drifted to Neville and Jason, probably just about to start their day, and she felt a wave of longing mixed with guilt. On the one hand, she wished she hadn't spent the wee hours stuck in a car, her arse halfway numb, drinking police-issue coffee from a thermos with a dodgy valve. On the other, being with Neville and Jason was a constant reminder of her shortcomings as a wife, mother, and human being.

The house was a four-bedroom bungalow that looked exactly like the four other bungalows on either side of it. You had to give the bloke credit. It was the ideal place to blend in. Affluent but nondescript. Unremarkable. Boring.

Kris' travel mug made its way towards her lips for another hit of caffeine, when a black Range Rover appeared from around the corner, trundled towards the house, and parked in the driveway.

Kris' and Doug's walkies crackled into life.

'Unit Fourteen do you copy? This is Alpha. Did you see that?'

Kris and Doug had a squad of armed police with them, split into two teams. The plan was for Alpha to arrest the Chairman on his doorstep. Meanwhile, Bravo had set up a perimeter around the block in case he tried to leg it. It seemed like a lot of bother for just one bloke. But when you were dealing with somebody like the Chairman, you had to be prepared in case he tried something funny. The bloke took great pains to seem like a legitimate and affable businessman. But he hadn't got to where he was by being meek and compliant.

Kris hoped fervently that everything would go to plan. She'd been working on bringing down the Company too long for it all to go tits up when the Chairman was so close she could smell his posh aftershave.

A short, barrel-chested man climbed out of the Range Rover, picked his black slacks out of the crack of his arse, and shut the door. He locked the car with his key fob and ambled towards the front door.

Kris looked at him through the binoculars and recognised him immediately. There was no mistaking the beaky nose, the slicked back black curls, and the arrogant thrust of his lips. She'd seen them way too many times to count. But, this time round, his photo wasn't going in the business section of the local rag. And it wouldn't be showing him shaking hands with some two-bit politician, all smiles, playing the grateful citizen giving back to the community he'd actually been ruining.

No. If Kris had any say, this time he was going to be glaring straight ahead at the camera, with a white backdrop behind him.

"Alpha, this is Unit Fourteen. Target confirmed. That's definitely Guthrie,' Doug whispered into his walkie.

'Copy. Bravo, are you in position?'

'Yes, confirmed.'

'OK, we're moving in. Wish us luck.'

The walkies fell silent. Kris was so amped up she could almost hear the sound of the Chairman's oxfords crunching on the gravel as he made his way towards his front door, oblivious of the mayhem that was about to be unleashed on him. Her stomach did a backflip, and she regretted every single drop of coffee she'd drunk over the previous twelve hours.

Doug tapped his fingers rhythmically on the dashboard.

'Can you stop that?' Kris hissed. 'It's setting my teeth on edge.'

'Sorry.'

He took his hand off the dashboard, reached mechanically into the front pocket of his trousers, and produced a crumpled packet of chewing gum. It was empty. He huffed, balled it, and began rolling it silently between his thumb and forefinger.

From her vantage point, Kris could see the Alpha team, in full gear, weapons at the ready, edging cautiously towards the Chairman in a pincer movement, cutting off his escape routes.

The Chairman had almost reached his front door when sergeant Hamilton, who was leading the Alpha team, barked out the order.

Kris and Doug were several feet away, but they heard him loud and clear: 'Armed police, lift your hands up where we can see them.'

The Chairman hesitated, his right hand frozen mid-way between his chest and the front pocket of his slacks.

'Whatever you're thinking, don't,' sergeant Hamilton said. 'You're surrounded. Put your hands up.'

The Chairman heard the steel in sergeant Hamilton's voice.

'I was just about to fetch my house key from my pocket, that's all,' he said, lifting his hands up. 'I'm not armed... officer.'

He spat out the last word, an unmistakable note of contempt in his voice.

That was Kris and Doug's cue. They walked towards the gaggle of police officers with the Chairman at their centre. In the house to the right of the Chairman's bungalow, a window opened and an older man with his hair still standing in sleep-induced corkscrews peered out.

'Let's wrap this up before it turns into a circus,' Kris told Doug.

They took out their warrant cards and flashed them at the Chairman.

'Franco Albert Guthrie?' Kris said in her most commanding voice.

'Who's asking?'

'I'm DI Kris Hendrie and this is DI Doug Lennox.'

'You could've just given me a bell, hen,' he said, a mocking smile dancing on his lips. 'No need to roll out the red carpet for wee old me.'

Kris made a show of ignoring this, and pressed on.

'We're arresting you on suspicion of drug trafficking, conspiracy to commit murder, kidnapping, and GBH. You don't have to say anything, but anything you do say may be noted in evidence.'

Kris produced the cuffs from the waistband of her slacks.

'On your knees,' she said, savouring every word. 'Slowly.'

The Chairman complied. Not that he had a choice,

with five officers pointing guns at him. Kris cuffed his right wrist, brought both of his arms together behind his back, then cuffed his left wrist.

'We've got loads to talk about Mr Guthrie. Or should I call you Mr Chairman?' she said, her voice brimming with grim satisfaction.

'Sure, inspector. Call me whatever you want.' He chuckled drily.

Kris gave him a push in the small of his back, a signal for him to get to his feet.

'I'm looking forward to us getting to know each other better,' she said. 'In fact, I can't wait.'

Somebody had brought one of the ARVs around and parked it in front of the Chairman's driveway.

'Let's go,' Kris said, grabbing him by his upper arm.

The Chairman's smile never faltered as she guided him towards the car and helped him get in.

CHAPTER 20

J onno made a quick stop at the Tesco Extra in the West End Retail Centre — a glorified car park where the Tesco, a Home Bargains, and a Dunelm stood next to each other like the last three soldiers guarding a forgotten outpost — to buy some proper-fitting clothes and a new phone, keeping his hood up and his eyes peeled for CCTV the whole time. He'd have to ditch the car soon, too. That pathetic git would've been missed by now. But before he could head off to Wee Dave's to trade it in for something clean and inconspicuous, he had to finish this business with the Chairman. Do his bit for the team.

He topped up his new phone and tried calling the Chairman several times on both numbers he'd given them, but the calls rang out. Dropping by the luxury office where he liked to play big-shot businessman was out of the question, and not just because a burly six foot-tall bloke with his head half bashed in would look as out of place as a stripper in a cloister. More importantly, the Chairman would be furious at him for daring to go there. And, if he was going to break the bad news about Al, he needed him to be in a receptive mood. So the only other option was to go to the safe house and wait, while trying him on the phone at regular intervals in case he picked up. It wasn't ideal, but it would have to do.

The air was thick with exhaust fumes, and he shut the car windows so he wouldn't have to breathe it in. This was one of the things he'd never get used to about city living. It gave him a fucking headache.

He drove through Strathburgh Way in fits and starts, hitting every single one of the ten million bloody lights that dotted it, until the traffic finally thinned out and he could cruise in fourth gear. Then he signalled left, made the turn, and was greeted by a scene so startling he almost crashed into a parked car.

Correction. A parked *police* car.

The building where the Chairman's safe house was had been cordoned off with white and blue police tape, and uniformed officers were swarming in and out of the main door.

'Jesus,' Jonno muttered through gritted teeth. 'Fuck!'

He was too late. Al must've talked. And the Chairman had either made his getaway and was lying low somewhere far away, or he'd been nicked. Either way, it was over. There was nothing he could do.

These thoughts took a fraction of a second to pass through Jonno's mind. He arranged his facial muscles into a neutral expression, straightened the car, and kept trundling down the avenue at the council-mandated twenty miles per hour, his eyes on the road, his shoulders straight, looking for all intents and purposes like he had every right to drive through.

He turned into the first side road that appeared before him and doubled back, driving as fast as the eejits who'd set the city's speed limits would allow. Half an hour later, he walked into Wee Dave's garage, slumped into one of the peeling faux leather armchairs in the waiting area, and armed sweat off his forehead. He closed his eyes and tried to calm his thoughts.

His next steps were simple. Get a car. Grab some of the money he kept stashed for emergencies. Get the fuck out of Strathburgh until the heat died down. In that order.

He nodded to Wee Dave, who was staring balefully at a black Audi's engine, his grease-stained hands on his hips and what was left of his mousy hair standing in wild tufts. Wee Dave nodded back, growled something inaudible to the mechanic who was standing next to him, then wiped his hands on a cloth that was so filthy Jonno wondered what the point of wiping his hands was.

'Jonno, bud,' he greeted him. 'You're a popular man today!'

He was feigning nonchalance, but his eyes kept darting to the side of Jonno's face, where Al had hit him. It had turned a shade of aubergine.

'Eh?' Jonno said, not getting up from the armchair. 'What do you mean?'

'Harry's been looking for you,' Wee Dave said. 'I took a message.'

He ambled to the reception desk and rummaged around the overstuffed in-tray, muttering softly to himself. Jonno turned the information over in his mind.

Harry'd joined the Company at around the same time as him, but they'd never seen eye to eye. This was partly because they were worlds apart in terms of worldview. Where Jonno had grown up in the relatively sheltered if still oppressive atmosphere of a Catholic boarding school, Harry had already been running amok around the streets of west Strathburgh aged eight, so he'd had more opportunities to carve out a safe space for himself where he could escape the violence of authority figures. But mostly it was because Harry was a flake and a prick. The kind of bloke who'd half-arse a friendly five-a-side but stop playing and take the ball home if he felt his team-mates weren't passing it to him often enough.

What the fuck could the bastard possibly want?

'Here,' Wee Dave said, handing Jonno a dog-eared, formerly white sheet of printer paper.

Jonno reluctantly took it, opened it, and squinted at the contents. It was short and to the point: 'call ASAP' and a mobile number.

'Did he say what this was about?' Jonno asked.

Wee Dave shrugged. Whether it was because he didn't know or didn't care was unclear. Jonno reckoned it was probably both. Wee Dave had figured long ago that the fewer questions he asked, the better.

Could it be the Chairman? Had he managed to escape the police, then? Was he in hiding? Did he have instructions on what to do next?

Jonno balled the piece of paper, got up with a grunt, and headed outside. The Sun was peering sheepishly from behind a cat-shaped cloud, but it wasn't doing a particularly good job of warming the afternoon. He leaned against the concrete wall and stared at the sea of junked cars glinting on Wee Dave's forecourt. Then he scanned the message again and ran through his options.

Should he call? Or just assume the worst, ignore the message, and make his getaway? Put himself first, for once?

But then again, this shitestorm would likely take a fair while to die down, and he couldn't lay low indefinitely, could he? Leaving aside the small matter of money eventually running out, sitting around twiddling his thumbs would give him time to think and reflect. And that would drive him mad.

'Fuck it,' he muttered. 'Let's hear him out.'

He pulled out his new phone and dialled the number. The person on the other end picked up after three rings.

'Who's this?' Jonno asked, confused.

The voice wasn't one he recognised. Or expected.

'Well, hello to you too, Jonno.'

A pause.

'I'm glad you called,' the person continued. 'How are you? I gather you had an eventful evening?'

'How? What? Wh-' Jonno stammered. 'Who *is* this?'

'All in good time, Jonno. All in good time. We'll get acquainted soon enough,' the voice replied. 'But right now, we have work to do. Franco's been nicked, you see. Couldn't be helped, I'm afraid.'

The voice was warm. Friendly. Welcoming, even. And that made it all the more unnerving somehow. Growing up where he had, Jonno had earned a bloody PhD in the perils of faux bonhomie.

'Who did you say this was again?' he said.

The voice on the other end hardened.

'Oh dear. Let's not waste each other's time now Jonno. That wouldn't do, would it?

Jonno gripped the phone tighter.

'Tell me why I shouldn't end this call, right now,' he said.

Another pause.

'Well, I suppose you could,' the voice at the other end replied quietly. 'Sure. Why not?''

There was a faint slurping sound, followed by crockery

— a mug of tea, perhaps? — being placed gently on a wooden surface.

'But I feel like I should warn you,' the voice continued. 'If you're not with us, you're against us.'

Jonno scoffed.

'Scoff all you want,' the voice said with a distinct edge. 'All I'll say is that, if I found you once, I can find you again. Now it's up to you to weigh up the risk.'

Jonno blinked.

'What do you want?'

'You know what I want,' the voice said. 'With Franco out of the picture, somebody's got to take over the reins. I'll need your help to do that. Plus, we have to find your friend Al. Send a message, you understand.'

It was hard to disagree with that. The bastard was responsible for all his aches and pains. And he'd fucking grassed. That was unforgivable.

'Tell me more,' he said.

'Not on the phone. Let's meet.'

CHAPTER 21

'McLeod,' the Chairman repeated for the umpteenth time. 'Where is he?'

He crossed his hands and leaned back in the interview room chair to stress his point. No more talking without his solicitor.

Dressed in grey tracksuit bottoms and an oversize grey jumper in place of his usual tailored suit, he looked different. Diminished, somehow. But his predicament didn't seem to have sunk in yet. At least, not outwardly. His lips were still turned upward at the edges in an arrogant smile.

Sitting across from him at the interview table, Kris could barely contain her glee. The team that had searched the Chairman's safe house had struck gold. They'd found piles of ledgers with transactions dating back years. Files with background research and dirt on associates, business partners, and competitors.

And, most damning of all, hours upon hours of recordings.

Why had he taped his meetings? Kris wondered, as she

sat across the table from him, still unable to believe the whole house of cards had come tumbling down so quickly.

Insurance? Vanity? Hubris? All of the above?

Whatever his reasons, she didn't dare question them too closely. They had earned this. And, magic circle solicitor or not, the Chairman was going away for a long, long time. In fact, it might be fair to say the board was about to remove him.

Kris pressed the rewind button on the tape recorder, then pressed play.

'Get him out of my fucking sight,' the voice on the recording said, audibly winded from the violent and very loud beating the person it belonged to had just administered.

She paused the tape and flashed him her sunniest smile.

'I know you won't listen, but I'll tell you again just in case, Franco,' she said. 'The quicker you level with me, the sooner we can end this pain.'

Guthrie sipped his green tea and studied her with flinty eyes. 'How much do you earn a year, Inspector Hendrie?' he said.

He took another sip, grimaced, and placed the mug on the table.

'That's ghastly,' he said, brushing his thumb against his lips. 'So, £50, £60K a year? Sound about right?'

'You seem to have this wrong,' Kris fired back. '*I* ask the questions.'

The Chairman scoffed.

'Whatever,' he said. 'Let's say £60K.'

He thrust his chin forward.

'I'm willing to bet you that amount I'll never even so much as drive by a prison. Now, for the last time. Where's McLeod?'

'Suit yourself,' Kris replied, unimpressed.

She gathered two files that looked as thick as *War and Peace* off the table and walked out, shutting the door a tad more forcefully than she had to.

'Where's McLeod?' she asked Doug, who was punching in a code on the vending machine in the corridor that connected the custody suite to the bullpen. 'He's made it very clear he's not talking until he gets here.'

'I was just coming to tell you about that,' Doug said.

The vending machine whirred. A packet of Wotsits slid off its shelf, then got stuck.

'Piece of fucking shite!' Doug said good-naturedly.

He grabbed the machine with both hands and shook it. The packet dislodged and dropped into the tray at the bottom.

'He's not coming,' he said.

He opened the packet, crammed a fistful of Wotsits into his mouth and munched on them with the relish of a bloke who hadn't had a decent meal in days. He offered the packet to Kris. She shook her head.

'What do you mean he's not coming?' she said.

'He's not coming,' Doug repeated. 'Says he no longer represents Guthrie.'

'You're serious?' Kris blurted.

'As a heart attack,' Doug said.

He'd wolfed down the whole packet, and now he dropped it into the plastic bin next to the vending machine.

'Somebody's been busy,' Doug continued.

'Aye,' Kris agreed. 'This smells like a move to ensure he's out of the picture for good.'

Kris and Doug both sighed. Fighting the gangs felt like a game of whack-a-mole sometimes. You took somebody down, and up came somebody else, prompt as can be.

Kris shook her head softly and straightened her back. No, they'd worked bloody long and hard on this and they'd landed a huge win. She wasn't about to let this development take the shine off it.

'Come on,' she told Doug. 'Want to see the look on his face when I ask him if he wants us to call legal aid?'

Chapter 22

'And you're sure?' the voice on the phone said. 'Absolutely certain?'

'Aye,' replied the dark figure. 'Somebody's thrown him under the bus. He's not coming out of there. Not even pending trial.'

The line went quiet. For a minute, the dark figure thought the call had dropped. Then he heard the faint rustle of his employer's breath. He scurried across the road, pointedly avoiding the glow of the streetlights, and walked north towards the bridge, taking a large hit off his vape. He held the smoke in, and his lungs soaked up the nicotine gratefully. He blew it out in a thick cloud that coagulated around his head, then dispersed just as quickly into the chill evening air.

'So what now?' he said, unable to take the silence any further.

'Well, this is the fun bit, isn't it? We're going to stir the pot,' the voice on the phone said.

'So we're good to go then?' the dark figure asked.

'Give them a few days,' the voice on the phone said. 'We

don't want to be obvious. Anyway, the Company's new leader is going to want to assert himself, and the Red Hand are going to try and muscle in. It's how these things go. Once they start things off, we give them a little push. Make sure it all goes in the right direction.'

'So what do you need me to do?' the dark figure asked, fetching his keyring from the inside pocket of his jacket.

'Round up the boys,' the voice on the phone said. 'Tell them to get ready to paint the town red.'

PART TWO

FIGHT OR FLIGHT

CHAPTER 23

Al spit the toothpaste into the chipped porcelain sink, rinsed with cold water, and wiped his mouth. The towel felt rough on his skin, but he barely noticed. Over the previous six-odd months, a lot of things he normally wouldn't have put up with had stopped bothering him. And cheap towels were the least of them.

It was funny, really. Humans spend an embarrassing amount of time worrying about what they'd do if they lost what they have, and going to absurd lengths to preserve it. But when something's actually taken from you, it's often not the catastrophe you thought it would be. Turns out, a lot of what we strive for doesn't actually matter. Not the house. Not the fancy clothes. Not the fucking thread count on your hand towels. You adapt. You adjust. It's all relative.

There was a knock on the bathroom door.

'Jack? All good, bud?'

'Aye, Redditch, just a minute. I'm coming.'

That was his new name. Jack Fitzsimmons. Al Edwards was dead. And Detective Inspector Redditch, UK protected persons service officer extraordinaire and the world's biggest stickler for procedure had insisted on calling him it from the minute they'd put the paperwork in.

'You need to get comfortable with it,' he'd say when Al protested. 'It has to become second nature. It's your name, now.'

Al supposed Redditch had a point, but that didn't make it any less weird. It was like wearing clothes that didn't quite fit, even though they were definitely the right size.

'Hurry up then, we have to leave soon.' Redditch prodded from behind the door.

Al folded the hand towel, placed it carefully on the rusty chrome rail, then took a long, hard look in the mirror. That was another thing he didn't think he'd be able to do if he grassed. But here he was. He'd kept up his end of the bargain with the police and hadn't lost a second of sleep. It had been water off a duck's back. Well, bullets ricocheting off steel plate armour, to use a more apt analogy. Maybe he'd have felt worse about throwing the Chairman under the bus if the bloke hadn't tried to have him killed.

Since going into protective custody, he'd let his hair grow out and had some fun with it, styling it into a pompadour. Together with the more prominent cheekbones he'd acquired thanks to a steady diet of salad bags and budget-range tinned beans, his face looked different. More angular. Longer. If it weren't for the fact that his beard was too patchy to do a good job of covering his chib scar, he'd barely recognise himself. Not that his new look would stand the close scrutiny of somebody who knew him well, like, say, one of his former business associates. Or Ma. But it would do just fine where he was headed. A place where nobody had ever seen him before.

Redditch knocked. Louder.

'Keep the head, bud. I said I'm fucking coming,' Al said.

Now that it was time to leave, his stomach was twitching and his heart was beating a tad too fast. He splashed more cold water on his face and sipped some from his cupped hand. Then he blew his cheeks out and took a few deep breaths.

'OK, Jack, bud,' he muttered to his reflection. 'Let's fucking do this. Here's to new beginnings.'

He ran his fingers through his hair a few times, wiped the oily residue from his hands on the towel, and got out of the bathroom.

'That took you long enough,' Redditch said. He was leaning against the living room door, hands folded across his chest, looking at Al appraisingly, but with a half smile playing on his lips. 'Ate a dodgy curry last night, did you?'

'No, it's the shite that passes for food round here,' Al deadpanned.

'Hey, don't look a gift horse in the mouth. You could've been sampling His Majesty's prison service's finest cuisine with your best friend the Chairman. And, tell you what, you'd be greeting for my famous beans on toast.'

'Well I wouldn't be in this position in the first place if you people minded your own fucking business,' Al thought.

'So, you ready to go?' Redditch asked.

'Aye, I suppose so.'

Redditch produced his key ring from the front pocket of his trousers. They made a soft clinking sound in his palm.

'Now, no need for the long face,' he continued. 'I hear Fort Drumblehan has a lovely community hall.'

'Hey, you should visit then,' Al replied. 'We'll drop a

few tabs of blood pressure medicine and go play bingo. Best night out you've ever had.'

Redditch let out a half-snort. They were never going to be bosom buddies, but they'd reached an understanding. You kind of had to when you were forced to live in close quarters with someone you didn't know for an indefinite period.

'All right. Are we going or what?'

Was that a hint of huskiness in Redditch's voice? Perhaps the man had a beating heart, after all.

'Aye, let's go.' Al said gruffly.

He'd never considered himself a sentimental man, either. But it's incredible how easy it is to surprise yourself given the right circumstances, even when you think nothing can touch you anymore.

With growing trepidation, he picked up his luggage from the tatty sofa. It was one, average-sized gym bag, but it was more than big enough to hold the stuff he'd decided to keep from his past life. He gave the house a final look and followed Redditch out the door and into the unknown.

CHAPTER 24

The cork slid out of the Prosecco bottle with a loud pop. Neville poured Kris a glass — more bubbles than drinkable liquid — then poured one for himself.

'Here's to the finest detective inspector in town,' he cheered, glass in the air, holding Jason's arm up with his free hand.

Kris clinked her glass against his and chugged down her Prosecco, but she couldn't suppress a brief flush of embarrassment. She didn't understand why Neville was making all this fuss and she wasn't keen on it. Not one bit.

Aye, the Chairman had been sentenced to twenty-five years for engaging in organised crime, conspiracy to supply drugs, conspiracy to murder, assault, blackmail, bribery, and a whole laundry list of other offences. But, banged up or not, men like him found a way to stay involved if they wanted to. Which was why they were still keeping a close eye on him, to the point of letting him keep an unapproved phone they'd found stashed behind a loose brick in his cell during a routine search and monitoring it covertly. Given

what a long, successful run he'd had, it seemed like a
sensible precaution.

Even if he was really out of action for good, her work
was still far from over. If anything, she was busier than ever.
Instead of quieting down, the violence had escalated. With
the Chairman away, everyone was circling, trying to swoop
in and fill the void.

Then again, she supposed taking down the Chairman
was still worth celebrating. And the win was Neville's as
much as hers. He'd been the one staying home, taking care
of Jason and holding down the fort while she was away for
days at a time. Besides, the Prosecco was going down a treat.
And, if her rumbling stomach was anything to go by, she
couldn't wait to dig into the feast Neville had cooked for
them.

Jason walked to the sofa, humming softly to himself, his
eyes never leaving his iPad, the faint sounds of Mr Tumble
coming through the tinny speakers. Neville refilled her
glass.

'Woah! Take it easy soldier,' she said. 'Are you trying to
get me pissed?'

'Maybe,' Neville said with a half-smile. 'You're not
working today, right?'

He said it playfully, but he wasn't as smooth as he
thought he was. Kris detected a distinct undertone of
reproach which she decided not to dwell on. She had a
growing pile of bodies to worry about, many of them young
men barely out of their teens who had become casualties of
a senseless urban war. But the hours she was putting in were
becoming an increasingly sensitive topic, even now that
Jason had the help he needed at school.

'No, I'm all yours,' she said, drinking more Prosecco.

'Smashing,' Neville said, draining his glass.

They locked eyes and shared a brief smile. Some of the iciness started to thaw, helped in no small measure by the buzz both felt coming on.

She looked at the clock on the mantel. Ten to one.

'Shall we?' she asked Neville.

'Aye, let's. I'm starving.'

Neville opened the oven and pulled out the roast pork. The crackling looked wonderfully crispy, and the smell made Kris' mouth water. Gang war or not, maybe the day off would do her good. She couldn't wait to tuck in.

'Och, that smells incredible, Nev,' she said.

'Aye. I think it came out pretty good, if I say so myself.'

He placed the roasting tray on an aluminium trivet, and pulled the carving knife out of the block.

'Can you get the roasties and the cauli cheese, please?' he said. 'I'll carve this up'

'Aye aye, captain,' she said.

She placed the pan of cauli cheese on the stove, and popped the roasties in the oven for a few minutes to warm them up. Then she transferred both into serving plates which she placed in the middle of the dining table.

'Jason, come on, love. Let's eat.' she called.

Jason was still absorbed in what he was watching and humming softly to himself. She went next to him and touched him gently on the arm. His humming intensified.

'He doesn't like to-' Neville began from behind the breakfast bar.

'Aye, I know,' Kris snapped.

Neville let this pass, not without effort. He was determined they'd have a nice time.

Kris let go of Jason's arm and squatted next to the sofa. Took a breath. Sometimes dealing with her son felt like defusing a bomb. It only took one wrong wire to set the whole thing off. Problem was, she often couldn't tell one wire from the other. On the iPad, Justin Fletcher was telling the weans to wave or cheer when they saw a boat.

'Jase, love. Come eat with us,' she said in her most soothing voice.

He looked up, glanced at her for a fraction of a second, and returned to the iPad.

'What do you say, eh?'

Jason looked up again. This time, his eyes were focused on something in the middle distance, but he nodded and got up. Kris sighed inwardly, then hated herself for feeling relieved that he hadn't blown up. They walked to the table together, the iPad still clutched in Jason's small hand.

Neville had cut up the pork into thick slices, shared them out, and put the plates on the table.

'All good?' he said as he poured two generous glasses of wine and orange squash for Jason.

'All good,' Kris repeated. 'Aren't we, Jase?'

Jason nodded faintly and took his spot at the table.

'Roasties?' Neville asked.

'Aye, thanks,' Kris said, taking the serving plate from him.

She helped herself to several, then tucked into the pork.

It was excellent, and so was the crackling. Crunchy and pleasantly fatty, without being so hard it risked costing you a trip to the dentist.

'You've outdone yourself, Nev,' she said, around a mouthful of cauli cheese.

'Told you all those episodes of MasterChef would pay off in the end,' he said.

'You know, if this writing lark doesn't work out, you could always open a restaurant,' she said. 'I'd come.'

They both laughed good-naturedly, and the ice thawed

some more.

'So how is it going, anyway? With the new book?' Kris asked, 'I thought you'd finished?'

'Aye, the first draft,' Neville said. 'Now the real work starts. Nancy sent me a whole stack of revisions and a twenty thousand-word, blow-by-blow account of what's wrong with it. I'm not sure where to start.'

'You'll do fine,' Kris said, around a mouthful of roast potatoes. 'You always do. Besides, it's only one person's opinion.'

'The editor is always right,' Neville said. 'I think Stephen King said that. And, you know, he's sold a book or two.'

'You're not doing so badly yourself,' Kris said.

Neville's debut novel, *Disciple*, which he'd self-published, had done pretty well on Amazon and got long-listed for a few awards. That had attracted the attention of a few publishers, but the money they'd offered hadn't made sense, and he'd decided to self-publish his next two novels too. The decision had worked out well. They weren't swimming in it, by any means. But writing full-time was financially viable. And between the royalties from his book sales and her detective inspector's salary, they were comfortable.

Neville went off — as he usually did — talking through the intricacies of the plot and how he couldn't figure out how to work in his editor's suggestions without everything falling like a house of cards. Kris tried to stay in the moment, but her mind drifted. To the files on her desk. To the street. To who could possibly have stepped into the Chairman's shoes.

Over the past month alone, there had been five violent murders involving the Company and the Red Hand. In one of them, which had started out as a violent brawl near the

West End Retail Centre, a civilian had been caught in the crossfire. The bloke, a forty-year old electrician, had escaped with his life but without his right eye, which had been squashed to a pulp.

'...of that? Kris?...Kris?'

'Eh, sorry,' Kris said, looking up from her plate. 'I was woolgathering. Say again.'

'I said do you want more?' Neville repeated.

There was an edge to his voice.

'Och, no, I'm full. And I was hoping there'd be pudding.' Kris said.

'You know there is,' he replied.

He got up from the table, cleared the plates, then slid out a homemade lemon meringue from the fridge.

'Och, that looks brilliant,' Kris said.

'Do you want coffee?' Neville asked.

'I'll make it.'

Kris got up and headed to the kitchen. She poured water into the coffee maker, added a generous helping of coffee — it was freshly ground roast, not that sewage they made them drink at the station — and waited for it to boil, leaning against the quartz countertop.

A few minutes later, the coffee began to bubble away, filling the kitchen with its fragrant, slightly floral aroma. She reached for the top cupboard next to the stove and produced two red mugs.

A buzzing sound made itself heard over the bubbling. It took her a second to realise it was her phone.

The move was automatic. Her hand reached for it of its own accord. Her thumb swiped right. And before she knew it, she was speaking to Doug. Neville, who'd been busy slicing the meringue, looked up and a shadow passed over his face.

'Kris, where are you?' Doug asked.

In the background she could hear faint chatter and the distinct sound of clicking. Cameras?

Her spidey senses tingled.

'At home. Where are you?' Kris asked.

'At the old hospital. Something's come up.' Doug said.

'What do you mean?'

Kris shifted the phone from her left ear to the right and walked out into the hallway, where she began to pace in a tight circle.

'There's been another one. Red Hand, this time. I think you'd better come and see for yourself,' Doug said.

As soon as the words 'Red Hand' left Doug's lips, Kris felt the familiar and not unwelcome surge of adrenaline.

'Give me half an hour. I'll be there,' she said.

She ended the call.

'Nev, I'm going to have to-'

'So that's it, is it?' Neville cut her off. 'No more day off?'

'Nev, I'm sorry. I have to. We're in the middle of a gang war and this sounds like-'

'We need you too, Kris, you know? Jason needs you. And so do I.'

He grabbed one of the plates, sat down heavily on a dining chair, and took an angry bite.

'Look, Nev. I have to go. I can't do this now. But we'll talk when I'm back. OK?'

'Aye,' Neville said.

He'd taken out his phone and was scrolling aimlessly, his eyebrows knitted together.

A sharp retort formed on Kris' lips. She bit it back.

'See you later, OK?' she said.

She grabbed her phone and keys and rushed off.

CHAPTER 25

Al and Redditch couldn't have been on the motorway for more than an hour, but Al was already over it. He'd never travelled long distances well, especially by car. But Redditch's driving skills — well, the lack of them — weren't helping matters. They'd been stuck behind a lorry for the best part of twenty minutes and he wouldn't bloody overtake, even though he'd had plenty of opportunities to switch lanes.

'Bud, is this your idea of a Sunday drive?' Al said. 'Because if it is, I can see why you're divorced.'

His right leg was bouncing restlessly up and down, and his hands were starting to itch with frustration.

'Be quiet and let me do the driving,' Redditch said, shifting down from fourth to third gear. 'And enough of that with the leg. I can see it from the corner of my eye and it's making it hard to concentrate.'

'Fine,' Al huffed.

He looked out the window, but there wasn't much in the way of entertainment. In the breakdown lane, a woman in blue jeans and a leopard print blouse was pulling down her toddler's trousers while her harried polo-shirt-and-red-chino-bedecked husband fetched the travel potty from the overflowing trunk of their SUV. An advertisement for the joys of being child-free if there ever was one.

On his right, cars roared past, which reminded Al of how slow they were going and riled him up. In the distance, a power station belched thick clouds of white smoke into the overcast sky. Barely a few feet away, a billboard proclaimed, 'We're working to make your energy cleaner.' And they said irony was dead.

Al spotted a road sign a few yards away.

'Hey Redditch,' he said. 'There's a service area in half a mile. I fancy some scran and a coffee, what do you say?'

'We should keep going,' Redditch said, his eyes never leaving the road. 'I need to drive back tonight. Besides, it wouldn't do if somebody were to see you.'

'Who?' Al said. 'It's a bloody Moto eighty odd miles away from Strathburgh. Come on, lighten up.'

Redditch said nothing. His hands were on the wheel at ten past ten. His gaze fixed on the lorry in front of him.

'Come on, bud. I'll buy the coffee. It's not like we're in a hurry are we?'

'We kind of are,' Redditch said.

'Are we?' Al said. 'Because judging by your driving, it doesn't feel like it.'

Redditch barked a short laugh. Then he relented.

'Sure, OK. I've skipped breakfast so I suppose a sandwich and a coffee would be nice.'

'Good man,' Al said.

Redditch signalled left and took the exit.

The Moto wasn't too busy, but it was chaotic. At WH Smith's the queue snaked from the till all the way out to the newsstand. It was almost as if they were giving away stuff for free, though Al reckoned he wouldn't want anything from that hellhole if they paid him for it. In the food court, three screaming weans were chasing each other around the tables, while their parents stared at their phones like zombies, probably exhausted from being cooped up in their cars with the tiny terrors all day. Two OAPs were seated four tables away, sipping hot drinks, chatting, and shooting the occasional disapproving glance at the weans. A young bloke in a Nike baseball cap was hunched over his laptop with his headphones in.

Redditch and Al headed over to the Burger King counter. Redditch ordered a Whopper. Al ordered an XXL Bacon Double Cheese. His stomach rumbled in anticipation.

The pimply girl at the counter placed their orders on the red plastic tray.

'Enjoy your meal,' she said with faux cheer.

Al lifted the tray, already relishing the taste of the burger, and they made their way towards one of the empty tables. His shoulder bumped into something solid. The impact threw him off balance, and he almost dropped the food.

'Shite,' he said, startled. 'The fuck happened?'

'Hey, watch where you're going fella, you blind?' a nasal growl shot back.

The attitude in the voice turned Al's blood to water. His survival instinct kicked in. He looked up, daggers in his eyes, and saw the voice's owner scowling at him, arms by his side, feet shoulder-width apart as if he were in PE class, about to start warming up.

'What did you just say to me, you prick?' Al said, locking eyes with the bloke, daring him to say something he'd make sure he'd live to regret.

The bloke returned the stare. He was about an inch shorter than Al, but stocky, with broad shoulders, a thin waist, and matchstick legs. The kind of bloke who bragged about never missing a workout, but always skipped leg day. Al sized him up, getting ready to bash his ugly puss in with the food tray, and everything else be damned.

Redditch placed a hand on Al's forearm.

'Sorry mate, don't mind him,' he said quietly to the angry bloke. 'Low blood sugar's messing with his mood.'

'Well he better watch his mouth,' the bloke fired back, his rat-like, unevenly spray-tanned features fixing themselves into a glare.

'I better wha-'

Redditch squeezed Al's forearm, looked evenly at the bloke.

'He will, mate,' he said.

He turned to Al.

'Let's move it along, shall we?'

Redditch practically dragged the seething Al to a corner booth, where the Burger King counter and their new friend would be safely out of sight. They sat down, and Al took a savage bite out of his burger.

'What the fuck do you think you're doing?' he whispered, his eyes fixed on his food.

He couldn't bear to look at Redditch. Why had he not backed him up?

Redditch, a picture of calm, popped two chips in his mouth, chewed methodically, and chased them with a long sip of lemonade.

'Me?' he said, at last. 'What do *you* think you're doing?'

'That fucking bastard,' Al began.

'Tone it down, Jack,' Redditch whispered. 'The last thing you need right now is to bring heat on yourself. Especially here, on our way to, you know. Have you got no bloody common sense?'

Al grabbed a fistful of chips and crammed them into his mouth. His teeth bore down like they were chewing steel nails, not thin slices of deep-fried potato.

'This is the hard part,' Redditch continued. 'You're going to have to shift your mindset, yeah? At the end of the day, it's just some small-time twat trying to get into a dick-measuring contest so he can impress his mates or his girl-friend or whatever. It doesn't matter. What matters is you staying under the radar, or this could all unravel. Do you understand what I'm saying?'

Al sipped his water and helped himself to more chips. His blood had recovered some of its normal consistency. But the anger was still burning a hole in his brain.

'Say you understand,' Redditch pressed, leaning forward and fixing his eyes on Al.

Al looked down and toyed with the few remaining chips in the tray.

'Jack, I'm serious.'

Al blew out his cheeks. 'Aye, OK,' he said half-heartedly. 'Point taken.'

Redditch was right, of course. But, if anything, this annoyed Al even more. In his world, you didn't let rodents with bad spray tans get away with disrespecting you. You crushed them like the vermin they were.

They ate the rest of their meals in silence, then got Americanos to go from Costa and walked towards the car. Al was still stewing. He couldn't let it go. In his mind's eye, he pictured himself ripping the stupid cunt's ears off like they were the wings off a fly. The thought was enough to make him flush with pleasure.

They'd almost reached their parking bay when Al

clocked the twat strutting into the bog. His brow furrowed, and he made a split second decision.

'Hey Redditch, hold my coffee, will you?' he said. 'I've got to go point good old Percy at the porcelain.'

Redditch stopped mid-way into entering the car and sighed in exasperation.

'Couldn't you have gone earlier?' he said.

'Gee sorry Da,' Al said. 'Next time I'll tell my bladder not to fill itself up. Or maybe I'll just magically turn into a camel, how about that eh?'

'Fine. OK. That was out of order,' Redditch conceded.

He shut the driver's side door, placed Al's coffee in the cup holder and sipped his.

'I'll wait in the car. Don't be long.'

Al wiggled his fingers sarcastically as he walked towards the bog.

The pungent smell of stale pish mixed with cheap disinfectant was unmistakable. But, other than that, the facilities were reasonably clean. There were none of the usual puddles of stagnant water, and the tiles still hadn't gone that sickly shade of yellow that seems to be the standard colour palette of every public toilet ever.

Al stopped in the doorway.

'Really, Al?' he thought.

He eyed the empty bathroom.

Aye, really. Nobody had to know. He wouldn't sleep that night if he didn't teach the prick about the perils of running his mouth.

Al spied him from behind the column near the sinks. He was standing in front of the last urinal on Al's right, jeans unbuttoned, not a care in the world. His black baseball cap was pulled down over his eyes, blocking his peripheral vision. Amateur. Al heard the sound of urine hitting porcelain. The bloke sighed.

Al tiptoed right behind him, adrenaline coursing through his body. Ready to strike. He lifted his leg up, centred the sole of his shoe in the middle of the bloke's back. Closed his eyes and steeled himself. Then he gave the bloke a hard shove.

The bloke's head slammed into the wall, and he staggered back. He wasn't done pishing, and the pale liquid splashed everywhere — on the floor, on the urinal's rim, down his left leg, darkening his jeans.

Breathing hard, Al pinned him against the wall with his left shoulder. His hand reached between his legs and squeezed, making mince out of his balls. Mr Bravado emitted a rusty, high-pitched screech and keeled over.

'Ugh,' he said. 'Gggg. Gah'

A few droplets of warm pish landed on Al's hand. He ignored them, and twisted the bloke's ball sack violently, trying to rip it off. The back of the bloke's head banged against the porcelain tiles with a muffled thud. Al floored him with a one-two punch to the solar plexus and the groin.

'Not so cocky now, eh?' Al whispered between rasping breaths.

The bloke moaned incoherently, and tried to get up on all fours. His baseball cap had come askew, revealing a receding hairline beaded with sweat.

Harnessing the last of his anger, Al stretched his right leg all the way back, like a winger about to cross the ball into the box, then drove it forward into the bloke's stomach. The kick landed with a soundless, yielding thud, and the bloke doubled over, dry-retching. Another kick connected with his ribs. The force of it slammed him against the wall and sent him sprawling face first onto the tiled floor. He lay still, moaning softly.

Al unzipped his jeans and aimed a stream of bright yellow pish at the bloke's face. He writhed in disgust, but he was too winded and hurt to move out of range. When the stream dried up, Al zipped himself back up with a flourish and washed his hands, meticulously lathering the hand the prick had pished on. He wiped them dry, then pulled out another wad of paper towels from the dispenser.

He stood over the bloke. His breathing had slowed and the anger had left him. He was calm. Zen. Satisfied with his handiwork. A loser had talked out of turn and he'd put him back in his box. The world was right again.

'Next time, *you* watch where you're fucking going,' he said. 'Fella.'

He threw the wadded paper towels in his face.

'Dry that pish off you, you disgusting, rat-faced prick.'

Al strutted out of the bathroom towards the car, where Redditch was sipping coffee and checking his watch.

'There you are. I was starting to think you got sucked into the toilet and transported to another dimension.'

'Cool it, Redditch. I haven't been five minutes. Told you I really had to go.' Al said, opening the passenger side door.

'Get in, let's hit it,' Redditch said, turning the key in the ignition. 'I'd like to get back home at a decent hour.'

They continued northwards towards Fort Drumblehan, which was a largish town nestled just south of the Cairngorms. The landscape changed, first slowly, then, all of a sudden, the gently rolling hills replaced by jagged peaks interspersed with deep blue water and vast green carpets punctuated by dark brown rocky outcroppings.

It was early afternoon, and traffic was much lighter.

But, for some reason Al couldn't fathom, Redditch insisted on driving in the left lane at forty miles an hour.

'You do realise we could make much better time if you drove the speed limit, right?' Al said.

'Get off my back, will you?' Redditch said tersely.

Al rolled his eyes. He stared out of the window, taking in the view, and what he saw took his breath away. There were none of the chimneys and exhaust-blackened buildings he'd been used to for most of his life. At some point, the novelty would probably wear off. But, for now, it felt like a welcome change.

'So what are you up to next?' Al said, mostly to make conversation. 'Are you taking some time off or heading straight into a new assignment?'

'I'll probably check in at the office to see what's going on. But you shouldn't be asking me that. You know I can't talk about my work.' Redditch replied.

'You're a great conversationalist, Redditch. Has anyone ever told you that?'

'Your Ma tells me all the time,' Redditch shot back.

He signalled left and took the exit.

'Anyway, we're here.'

They drove by a sign that proclaimed Fàilte gu Dùn Druimlean, and, beneath that, Welcome to Fort Drumblehan, Please Drive Carefully. Redditch took a side road off the mediaeval high street. Two turns later, he entered a maze of landscaped avenues in a newly built estate. The rows of semi-detached houses, terraces, and flats all had the same blocky, jarringly clean cookie-cutter architecture and faux brick facades, like they'd been projected whole straight off the assembly line. But it was clean and quiet, if not especially leafy — the trees were young and the leaves hadn't started growing yet. The kind of place you'd raise a family in.

Redditch parked in one of the spots off the kerb and killed the engine, then took the key out of the ignition and opened the driver's side door.

'Let's go in. I'll hand you your papers and walk you through the last few bits and bobs.'

Al got out of the car, stretched his legs, and took it all in. It was quiet. Almost too quiet. After a lifetime of traffic rumbling in the background at all hours, it felt unnatural. He dug his hands into his pockets.

'Come on, Jack,' Redditch said.

Al looked out at the carefully landscaped grounds and the firs in the distance. It was a different world. Might as well have been a different planet.

'Jack?'

Al shook his head and turned round. For a minute he hadn't realised Redditch was calling him.

'Aye, coming.'

He caught up with Redditch, who was waiting for him in the doorway of one of the blocks, a three-storey square dotted with evenly-spaced windows that had modern charcoal-coloured frames.

They walked up a flight of stairs, into a narrow hallway, and stopped in front of a door marked three. So here it was. Al's new home. The start of his new life.

Redditch produced a keyring from his right trouser pocket, and selected the key to the flat. He unlocked the door.

'In you go,' he said, signalling with his left hand.

Al walked into the airy, light-filled hallway. On his right, there were two bedrooms, a storage closet, and the bathroom.

On his left, a short corridor led to a combined living and dining room with a large window overlooking the gardens below. A second door led into what Al assumed must be the kitchen.

It was reasonably spacious, if smaller than his house. And almost completely barren. There was going to be a lot of Ikea assembly in Al's near future. But, then again, it wasn't like he had much else on his schedule.

Redditch walked into the living room, then through the door into the kitchen. He placed his backpack on the pine countertop and pulled out a plastic folder.

'Right,' he said, clearing his throat, suddenly all business. 'Here's two sets of keys — one each for your flat door and the main door downstairs, and two for the storage room in the basement. There's a common storage area and you also have your own lock-up closet.'

He pulled out a stack of documents from the folder.

'This is your new paperwork. Birth certificate, NI number, driver's licence, passport, and a debit card. All in the name of Jack Fitzsimmons. Everything's all set up in the system. So when your driver's licence or passport expires, or if you need a copy of your birth certificate for whatever reason, you just order it online as you'd have done before.'

'Right.' Al said.

'Any issues, email me or call this number. But only if you absolutely have to. The less we're in contact, the better.'

Al sighed and looked over the papers. His throat felt constricted. Over the previous six months, he'd made an effort not to dwell on his predicament. But now that he was in his new home and time was stretching out before him like a 100-mile road to nowhere, dwelling seemed like inevitability.

'They won't find you if you're sensible and stick to the script,' Redditch said, as if he'd just read Al's mind. 'Keep your head down, your nose clean, and try to avoid social media as much as possible. And, for the love of god, no more of that shite you pulled at the Burger King today.'

Al pictured rat-face, lying on the bog floor, covered in pish.

'Aye, bud. I got that the first time,' he said, a tad too forcefully.

'Good. Now, let's go over your story one more time,' Redditch said. 'Tell me, where did you grow up?'

CHAPTER 26

Kris ducked under the police tape and walked towards the old hospital's weathered front steps. The building, an imposing sandstone structure with Ionic columns, large leaded windows, and a metal cupola, hadn't been a working hospital since at least the first world war. During the early 1950s, it had been repurposed into the only public library north-west of the Strath, until funding cuts had shut it down and it was refurbished and converted into flats. But, for some mysterious reason, it had never been able to shake off its original purpose. None of us locals would understand what the hell you were on about if you called it anything but the old hospital.

The place was swarming with forensics people in their trademark white Tyvek suits. Doug was waiting for her next to one of their vans, looking unusually casual in light grey Lonsdale trackies, a red Gap hoodie, and day-old stubble.

'Look at you,' Kris said, unable to suppress a smile, 'You never told me you moonlighted as a ned.'

'Very funny,' he said around a mouthful of chewing

gum. 'I was lounging about on the sofa, minding my own business, when I got the call.'

'So what's going on, that you had to drag me out here on my day off?' she asked him.

'Follow me.' he said.

He spat his chewing gum into a tissue, which he placed in his pocket, then handed her a pair of blue plastic booties and rubber gloves. They donned the protective gear and entered the alley. Ten steps in, it was already noticeably darker, even though it wasn't quite three in the afternoon yet. The air was thick with the ripe smell of rotting garbage. Two skips, most likely the source of the stench, stood side by side like rank sentinels in front of a restaurant's service entrance.

Kris clocked the bodies immediately. Two baby-faced blokes in light grey trackies and black bomber jackets. One of them lay spread-eagled in the middle of the alley, surrounded by a pool of drying blood, his head cracked open like a rotten watermelon. The other bloke had managed to run further away before the killer caught up with him and bashed his head in. He was curled in a foetal position, probably in a fruitless effort to protect himself from the blows raining down on his head and back.

Kris crouched down next to the spread-eagled body to take a closer look.

'Red Hand,' she said, pointing at the crimson sweat-band on his wrist.

'Looks like it,' Doug agreed.

The bloke's eyes were swollen shut. A bluish black bruise started at his left temple and spread across his cheek down to the edges of his jaw. Brain matter had oozed out of the back of his head and dribbled onto the ground, where it was drying in greyish pink lumps like day-old porridge.

Kris noticed the distinctive, evenly spaced marks on his face and neck. Marks that had appeared on every single Red Hand casualty so far.

'Motorcycle chain,' she said, pointing them out to Doug with her index finger.

As if to confirm this, an inch-long piece of silver-coloured metal peered out from behind the victim's left shoulder. Right on cue, a gloved hand appeared over Kris's head and spirited it away so it could be bagged, tagged, and taken into evidence.

Kris frowned.

'Any news from Guthrie?' she said. 'Could they be doing this on his say so?'

Doug unwrapped another stick of chewing gum, popped into his mouth, then shook his head, chewing deliberately.

'Calls his wife and a few friends on the approved phone. Uses the unapproved phone to call his mistress,' he said. 'Nothing to report except a few steamy late-night exchanges.'

'Who could've rallied his troops, then?' she mused, trying to ignore her growing frustration. 'Out of the two highest-ranking lieutenants, one's AWOL and the other's turned. Who the hell has stepped in?'

Doug's silence spoke volumes. Six months and dozens of bodies later, and they had nothing. They stared at the bodies in silence, a sinking feeling in their chests.

'Any witnesses?' Kris asked.

Doug shook his head.

'No. Nobody saw or heard anything.'

It was the answer Kris was expecting.

She stood up and shook her legs to ease the cramping in her calf muscles.

'Do we have the victims' names yet?' she asked.

'Working on it.'

'And maybe that chain might tell us something.'

'Aye. I'll look into that. See if it pans out.'

'Let's have another look around while forensics finish up.' she said. 'Maybe we'll find something else we can work with.'

They walked the length of the alley, scouring it for anything that might look out of place. Another, longer piece of motorcycle chain, perhaps. Maybe even a piece of torn fabric, or some blood. But nothing jumped out at them. A rumpled, grease-stained blanket and an Ikea bag for life were strewn underneath a metal staircase that led up to a service entrance. The bag was overflowing with old clothes, a few tattered paperbacks, and other odds and ends. Remnants of a past life someone couldn't bring themselves to part with. A splash of chunky yellow vomit was drying on the tarmac in front of a graffiti-covered metal door. And, in the distance, the traffic rumbled on, oblivious to the carnage that had just unfolded.

'Well, that's that.' Doug said, extracting another stick of chewing gum from his dwindling supply and slipping it into his mouth. 'Fuck all.'

'Let's canvass the area,' Kris said. 'Maybe somebody has CCTV we could check out.'

'All right.'

They walked out of the alley, slipped off their gloves and booties, and dropped them in the large bin bag next to the forensic vans. The Sun chose that exact moment to peek out from behind a cloud. Kris lifted her face towards it, enjoying the warmth on her face, and took a deep breath.

Exhaust fumes may be bad for you, she thought, but they sure beat the smell of rotting garbage in a dark alley.

She nodded to Doug, and they walked into the Co-Op, fishing out their warrant cards from their pockets.

CHAPTER 27

Al slammed his paperback shut and sighed. The book — a thriller about a failed author who steals another writer's manuscript — was supposed to be a good one. But he couldn't get into it. When Redditch closed the flat door on his way out, the sound had a certain finality to it, like a tomb being sealed. Or, more accurately, a big dose of reality slapping him across the face. Here he was, alone in a place he didn't know, with no idea what was next.

How would he move forward?

And, the biggie: was he safe? Would there ever come a time he'd feel comfortable enough in his new skin to stop looking over his shoulder?

He supposed it depended on whether whoever had taken over from the Chairman would manage to consolidate his power.

Would things stabilise enough for the new boss to have the resources to spare on tracking him down? And would he feel compelled to do it? To make an example out of him? After all, whoever he was wouldn't have ascended the throne if Al — sorry, Jack, the name still felt alien to him — hadn't grassed.

He supposed time would tell. In the meantime, here he was, reading the same sentence over and over, too distracted for its meaning to register.

Except for a white Peugeot SUV, the estate was deserted. It looked like his flat and one of the terraces across the street were the only two occupied dwellings. Exiles in the middle of nowhere. The inside of his new flat made him feel even more despondent. Gone were his comfy sofa, his shelves stacked with books, his 50" smart TV, and his king size bed. Other than a cheap, foldable dining table, an entry-level Ikea chair, and a standard double mattress still wrapped in plastic, the flat was empty. If he spoke out loud, his voice echoed hollowly. The bare magnolia walls, which the developers had probably intended as a blank canvas that would fire up potential buyers' imaginations and make it easier for them to picture living there, just felt stark and impersonal.

He sighed, got up from his chair, and bounced up and down on the balls of his feet. He needed to do something to take his mind off things. It had been barely three hours since Redditch had left and he was already close to driving himself up the fucking wall.

He walked to the kitchen and opened the fridge. Stared at its starkly barren interior. He needed supplies. Something to eat. A trip to the high street was in order. And the walk would clear his head.

He went into the bedroom he'd picked as his own — the one where the vacuum-packed mattress was still lying disconsolately on the floor — pulled on a jacket over his t-shirt, and rushed down the stairs into the brisk evening air. The main road was a single, pothole-riddled two-way lane.

He stopped at the corner and contemplated his next move. Had Redditch taken a left? Or was it a right? Where was the fucking high street? Lush firs extended as far as the eye could see, making one side virtually indistinguishable from the other.

He picked left and set off on the rocky verge, wondering what he'd find at the local convenience. A few staples — bread, pasta, pasta sauce, perhaps a bag of rice and a few tins of tuna — would do to begin with. Then he'd see where the fuck the nearest Asda or Aldi was. But he'd need a car for that. And a job to pay for it. The money wouldn't last forever.

Ach. Fuck.

He shook the thought out of his head and looked up. A grey slate roof peered out from behind a stumpy tree. Thinking he was getting close to the town centre, he walked faster. But what he found wasn't the high street, but a lone, mid-century house with a white pebbledash facade and a gravel driveway. A hand-painted wooden sign proclaimed he'd reached The Mossy Well.

Al glanced at his watch. Ten to six.

Did local conveniences stay open late here in the sticks?

Had he even been walking in the right direction? Should he have turned right instead of left?

He shrugged. Perhaps he could grab something to eat at the pub and leave the familiarisation and shopping to the following day. It would be good to have something to occupy his time. The key right now was to keep moving forward. If you were busy looking ahead, you wouldn't have time to look back.

As soon as he walked through the door, the hum of conversation came to an abrupt halt. Four OAPs sporting sweater vests in increasingly horrible shades of blue — the only punters — looked away from their pints and studied him. It couldn't have lasted for more than two seconds, but it felt like forever. Then they looked away and returned to their hushed conversation. He'd been evaluated, deemed unworthy of further interest, and dismissed.

Al sat at the bar, where a diminutive woman with curly black hair tied in a careless ponytail, and Sailor Jerry tattoos dotting both arms from shoulder to wrist, had her nose buried in a book.

'What can I get you?' she said without looking up.

'Any local IPAs?' Al said.

'Aye. We have Snakes and Ladders. It's nice.'

'Pint of that then, hen.'

She reluctantly put her book down, placing a folded coaster between the pages to mark her spot, served him, then returned to it without a word. Al sipped his beer and looked around, tapping his fingers on the bar.

'Any good?' he said, nodding towards the book.

'Not the best,' she replied.

Al licked his lips. Sipped more beer.

'Is that so?'

'Aye. The plot's a bit far-fetched. But then again, space stories have never done it for me.'

'Och, aye. Fantasy isn't my cup of tea, either,' Al said, clutching at her last remark like a drowning man would hold onto a piece of driftwood.

'It's not fantasy. It's a medical thriller,' she said, putting the book down and giving him an appraising look.

She had intelligent, bright blue eyes and two small dimples on either side of her mouth. A short, square fringe framed her face.

'It's about a group of astronauts on the international space station. There's an alien flesh-eating virus going around, and they have to figure out a way to kill it and get back to Earth before they all get infected and die.'

'That does sound dodgy,' Al said, leaning forward.

'Aye, I don't buy it.'

She returned to her book, flipping a page with one manicured nail.

'So what kinds of books are you usually into, then?' Al asked.

'Honestly? Anything trashy,' she replied with a throaty chuckle. 'I only read when I'm here, to pass the time. So I like stuff that doesn't require me to think too hard. Anything I can follow even if it's noisy or I'm stopping every two sentences to serve the punters.'

'Hey, Al!' a voice shouted from behind him.

Al almost jumped to his feet. Several inches of beer spilled out of his pint glass. His knees bumped painfully against the bar.

'Och, fuck!' he muttered.

'Here, wait,' the barmaid said.

She put her book down and tore several strips of blue tissue paper off a large roll. From the corner of his eye, Al saw a bloke shamble towards the OAPs' table and greet them. He cursed inwardly.

'Sorry, I-'

'Someone's jumpy,' the woman remarked.

'Aye, I. Not sure what the fuck happened, to be honest. The glass slipped,' he said, scrambling to recover his composure.

'Don't worry about it,' she said. 'Here, all done. Do you want another one of those?'

Al drained what remained of his beer, and stared at the dregs for a second.

'Aye sure. Same again, please.'

She picked a glass from under the bar and pulled the pint. Al sat back on the stool, but he couldn't get comfortable. Having his real name called out like that — even if it was an unlucky coincidence — had set him on edge.

The woman set the fresh pint in front of him and he took a long sip. Another bloke walked up to the bar, gave him side-eye, then pointedly ignored him.

'Alright, P?' he said. 'I'll have a lager.' He hesitated. 'And a packet of those pork scratchings.'

He gave Al another look, nodded a greeting, then shifted his weight from one leg to another and whistled tunelessly while he waited. The bloke was obviously going for nonchalance, but there was something about him that felt off to Al.

A few minutes later, the woman apparently called P returned with the bloke's pint and a pack of pork scratchings from a brand Al didn't recognise. The punter stuffed the scratchings into his front jacket pocket, grabbed his pint, and headed towards an empty booth without giving Al a second look.

Al finished his pint in three gulps and ordered a tap water and a packet of Walkers ready salted crisps, thinking it better to keep his wits about him. He sipped his water and munched on a handful of crisps he didn't really want. Any appetite he might have had before entering The Mossy Well had gone.

'Say, eh-'

'One second,' she said, walking the length of the bar, where another customer was waiting.

'Alright, P. Four lagers and two packets of them scratchings, eh?' the punter said.

Had he just tipped her a wink?

P poured the drinks, handed over the pork scratchings,

and took his money. The punter paid and retrieved his change. Then, in an impressive feat, he loaded up all four glasses and both packets of pork scratchings between his hands and duck walked to his table. He got there with minimal spillage.

'Sorry,' she said to Al.

'Och, no problem,' Al said.

A woman entered the pub and walked towards the table where the bloke who'd given him side-eye sat sipping his beer. The bloke got up to greet her. They embraced and left. Al felt himself relax enough to decide another beer wouldn't be the end of the world. He ordered another packet of crisps and some nuts to go with the alcohol.

Over the next few hours, the pub got busier. Al sipped his beer, munched on his snacks, and continued his book chat with P, who had half-bashfully informed him it was short for Paulette.

'So what brings you here, Jack?' she asked during a lull in the service.

Most of the tables were occupied at this point. The punters were in various stages of drunkenness, and the sounds of raucous laughter filled the place.

'Happy accident,' Al replied. 'I was trying to find a convenience store. Instead I found The Mossy Well.'

She smiled, and it lit up her face. Was it the buzz from his three pints or something else that was stirring in his stomach?

'Cheeky,' she said. 'But I meant what brings you around these parts. Fort Drumblehan isn't exactly a tourist hotspot.'

'Och, I live here. In the estate down the road.' Al said, unconsciously pointing in the direction of his flat. 'Just moved in, actually.'

'Is that so?' she said, interested.

A twenty-something woman came up to the bar and ordered a gin and tonic and a packet of pork scratchings. P poured the drink and handed over the scratchings. The woman downed it in two gulps, grabbed her pork scratchings, and shambled outside. She was the sixth punter who'd ordered pork scratchings and acted shifty about it, and Al's nervousness had given way to curiosity. He was starting to put two and two together.

'You were saying?' P prodded.

'Huh?' Al replied, jolted out of his thoughts.

'You were telling me why you moved here.'

'Och, aye.'

Al sipped some more beer to buy himself some time. He and Redditch had gone over his back-story until he'd turned blue in the face, but P's open, receptive look gave him a touch of stage fright. Would a random person buy it? He supposed he was about to find out.

'Promise not to laugh?' he told her, going for sheepish and unsure whether he was succeeding.

'Sure,' she said, smiling.

'I had, I suppose, what you'd call a midlife crisis,' Al continued. 'I was working long hours at a job I didn't particularly care for. Then I turned forty and had a "What the fuck am I doing with my life?" moment. So I picked a town at random and packed it in. I want to take things slow for a while. Daft, right?'

She laughed. A deep, musical sound.

'Hey, you promised not to laugh!' Al said.

'Well, you know,' she replied, her eyes twinkling, 'most guys in your position just buy an obnoxious car.'

'True,' Al said, giving her a bashful look. 'But this is probably cheaper, eh?'

'Right enough.'

They looked at each other. Their eyes locked for a brief minute.

'So what about you?' he said.

'Me?' she said.

'Aye. You. Paulette,' Al said. 'What's your story?'

She placed both elbows on the bar and leaned forward. He caught a faint whiff of floral perfume.

'Och, I'm local. Born and bred. Decided I didn't hate it enough to leave.'

'Well, the landscape's quite beautiful,' he said.

The buzz from the beers had settled in his gut.

'So what's the plan?' she asked.

'The plan?' he repeated.

'Aye. What are you going to do? You know, for work and such? Or are you a man of leisure?'

'Err...'

He sipped more beer, then folded his hands in front of his glass and looked at her, making an effort to seem like he was really considering her question, not getting ready to belt out a canned reply.

'I'm not sure yet,' he said. 'I suppose at some point I'll need to get a job. But I'm going to take it as it comes.'

'Well, nothing much happens around here, I'll tell you that much.'

She sipped cordial from a pint glass she'd produced from under the bar.

'You might get bored sooner than you think.'

'Maybe,' Al said. 'Or maybe not. Tell you what, though,' he lied, 'a spot of boredom sounds pretty smashing right now. Might even do me some good.'

He cringed inwardly, remembering how close he was to ripping his hair out barely four hours earlier.

P gave the bell over the till a vigorous shake. It emitted a loud clanging sound.

'Last call!' she shouted.

'Woah!' Al replied. 'You sure they heard that?'

She laughed.

'Sadly, I think some of them will try to ignore it,' she said.

Al finished his beer while she dealt with a flurry of last orders. A few rounds of beers, the obligatory drams of whisky, a couple of G&Ts, and more pork scratchings.

By now, Al was convinced something was going on. It felt like a scheme. One that could net a tidy income. And his professional interest was really and truly piqued. The question was, how could he broach the subject without putting P's back up? It would take time to earn her trust. Something to look forward to, perhaps.

She'd just finished restocking the fridges and wiping down the bar when he got up from his stool on unsteady legs. He shook them out to get the blood flowing, and reached for his jacket.

'Well, it was good to meet you, Paulette,' he said. 'Top patter.'

She leaned against the wall and gave him another appraising look, her eyes resting for an imperceptible moment on the chib scar snaking up his face. Then she nodded to herself and fired up a joint that seemed to have come out of thin air. The sweet aroma of premium grade skunk filled the room.

'It was good talking to you too, Jack,' she said.

She took a deep drag, held it in, and exhaled a thick cloud of smoke with a sigh of pleasure.

'Want some?' she said, offering him the joint.

Al didn't have to think twice, and not only because this

might provide him with the foot in the door he needed. He liked this woman and had genuinely enjoyed chatting with her. Besides, the alternative — returning to his barren flat and going over the same thoughts with a fine-mesh sieve, like an archaeologist who couldn't accept the dig was a bust — wasn't exactly appealing.

'Sure,' he replied, taking the joint from her gingerly, his fingers brushing tantalisingly against hers. 'Don't mind if I do, ta.'

CHAPTER 28

'How did it go at the motorcycle shop?' Kris asked Doug as he strode into the office. 'Anything come of it?'

She was trying to sound hopeful, but, in truth, she wasn't holding her breath. Despite the frenzied nature of the attacks, the killer — or, more likely killers. These blokes always moved in pairs or packs — rarely left much they could work with behind. So, while they'd had to follow up on the motorcycle chain they'd found on the scene of the double murder at the old hospital, because it was a lead and they had precious few of those, her gut told her it hadn't panned out.

Doug threw his suit jacket carelessly on his desk, which was piled so high with clutter there was barely any free space, sank in his chair, and loosened his tie. He rubbed his eyes wearily and produced a piece of chewing gum.

'Nothing,' he said, confirming her fears.

Kris paused the CCTV file on her laptop and turned towards him. She'd watched the two men in the video cross the road in front of the camera at least a dozen times.

They'd have been completely unremarkable were it not for the fact that they'd produced motorcycle chains and chased the victims — sixteen year-old Henry 'Clippy' Thomson and twenty-five-year old Ritchie Smith — into the alley near the old hospital. Unfortunately, they both wore baggy hoodies with the hoods up, so their faces weren't visible.

'Bog standard roller chain,' Doug continued around a mouthful of gum. 'As generic as they come. Anyone could've bought it from anywhere.'

Kris sighed.

'Well, we knew it was going to be a long shot,' she said.

Her phone pinged.

'Will you be home for dinner tonight?' the notification on her screen said.

She pushed the phone away. If things had been some-what chilly with Neville before, they were solidifying into permafrost since she'd cut their celebratory lunch short. But she didn't want to deal with that now. Better focus on the things she had some semblance of a handle on, like running a criminal investigation.

'It wasn't a total waste of time, though,' Doug said.

She perked up. 'Och?'

He flashed her a half-smile.

'Come on,' she prodded, 'out with it. Don't leave me hanging.'

'So, I'm coming out of the motorcycle shop, feeling pretty deflated, right?' he said. 'And I got a call from HMP Barlinnie.'

'Did you now?' Kris said. 'Regarding what?'

'Well, remember the unapproved phone they found in Guthrie's cell? Seems like our gamble to let him keep it has finally paid off. He got a very interesting phone call.'

Kris shot to her feet.

'Tell me we know who called,' she said.

'Well, no. That would've been too easy, right? But listen to this.'

He dug into the right front pocket of his trousers and produced a memory stick with a flourish. He inserted it into Kris' laptop and opened it. There was a single audio file which he double clicked.

'So how are you enjoying your retirement? Not much fun being on the sidelines is it?' the voice coming out of Kris' laptop speakers said.

It was cartoonishly deep, very obviously manipulated with software. So it was impossible to tell whether it was a man, a woman, or a humanoid from Alpha Centauri.

'I'm disappointed in you,' Guthrie replied. 'Calling to gloat? That's low, even for you.'

'Who's gloating?' the voice boomed. 'I'm checking on you. I'm worried, you know, prison being such a tough place and all. And not any ordinary prison either... the Bar-L!'

Guthrie let out a dry chuckle, like he was bantering with a mate poolside, not banged up with the country's worst offenders. 'Right. I can feel your deep concern.' A pause. 'You've always been too big for your britches. This is going to blow up in your face. You know that, right?'

It was the mystery caller's turn to laugh. The voice manipulation software turned it into an amorphous warble, like a sound effect glitching.

'Now, now Franco. I see prison hasn't done much to dent your arrogance,' the mystery caller said. 'In case you hadn't noticed, I'm here and you're there. So, from where I'm sitting, my britches fit just fine. More than fine.'

'Och, I wouldn't sound the victory bells just yet.

Running a team's a lot harder than it looks. In fact, I heard it's not going that well.'

There was another pause in which the only audible sound was the mystery caller's breathing and something more faint in the background.

'What was that?' Kris interrupted. 'Play it again.'

'He said he knows it's not going that well,' Doug said. 'Clearly, he's got time to read the papers.'

'No, I know that,' Kris said impatiently. 'I meant in the background. Listen.'

She rewound the audio and pressed play. There was a faint rattle and bang, barely discernible over the mystery caller's voice, followed by a short echo.

'It's a door slamming,' Kris said.

'So?'

'So whoever the caller is is confident enough to call from inside a building,' Kris said.

'Aye, but it's probably a burner. I bet there's no way we can trace it.'

'Well, it might be something,' Kris retorted.

They let the audio run.

'You know, Franco,' the mystery caller continued, 'that's always been your problem. You think you're the only one who could possibly run things. But, just because you believe so, it doesn't mean you're right.'

'Projecting our character flaws on others again, are we?' Guthrie said, his voice dripping with venom. 'You've always been great at that.'

'You shouldn't have frozen me out, Franco' the mystery caller hit back, any pretence of civility gone. 'This is mine just as much as it was yours. Now look what's happened.'

Heavy breathing rasped down the line.

'You know what?' Guthrie said. 'Fine. Play cops and robbers if that's what floats your boat. But it's not going to last, and I'm going to love every second I'll spend watching you crash and burn.'

The line went dead.

'Woah,' Kris said, at last. 'Whoever this is, they really got under Guthrie's skin. Did you hear that?'

'Aye. He was seconds away from losing it,' Doug agreed.

'Let's send this over to Kevin, see if he can do something with it.'

'Consider it done,' Doug said.

'Great work.'

'What about CHIS? Anything we can get from them?'

'They're working on it. But it's going to be a while before they establish good enough rapport with somebody who can tell us what the hell's going on.'

'Maybe a wee visit to Guthrie is in order?' Doug suggested.

'We could. But I doubt he'd talk to us. The bloke's as old school as they come.'

'Well, think about it.'

Kris' phone buzzed again.

'You're in demand,' Doug remarked.

'Just Neville checking in,' Kris said. 'Nothing important.'

She stared at the pile of files on her desk. It was growing at an alarming rate — four new cases just in the previous week. The situation was becoming increasingly volatile, and, for the first time in her career, Kris was genuinely scared they might not be able to keep it contained.

She sat back down at her desk, picked one of the files and went through the motions of studying it. This one was the civilian who'd lost an eye. The photos of his bloody socket and the blackness spreading from his temple down to his face screamed accusingly at her.

Her phone screen lit up again. She caught the word 'dinner' from the corner of her eye. Her stomach clenched. She closed the file and tossed it back on the pile.

Doug mumbled something.

'What's that?' she said.

'I said we're back to square one.'

She banged her open palm on her desk. The sound startled them both. An officer looked up from her monitor. Averted her gaze.

'No way,' Kris said. 'Don't you say that. Guthrie's operation is smaller now, and that's a win in my book. We just need to keep working the cases. Eventually, we'll make the connection or they'll trip up.'

'Aye,' Doug said, but he didn't sound convinced.

'Let's reinterview the victims' known associates. Maybe there's some detail we've overlooked. I'll see if we can get a few uniforms to help us out with the legwork.'

'That would be smashing. We could use a few extra pairs of hands.'

Kris looked absently at her phone. Reluctantly, she picked it up, placed it in her handbag, and got up from her chair.

'I'm going to call it a day. I promised Neville I'd get home early. Are you staying?'

'Aye, just an hour or so. I've got some paperwork I need to catch up on.' Doug said.

'Well don't work too late or you'll make me look like a slacker.'

'Somehow I doubt that,' Doug replied.

He popped a fresh piece of gum in his mouth, cracked his knuckles, and double-clicked on one of the Word documents on his overcrowded desktop.

'Well, have a good night.'

'Good night, Kris. I'll see you tomorrow.'

Chapter 29

Kris walked out into the cool evening and made her way to her car. The days were getting longer, and leaving the station while it was still light cheered her up no end. It made a world of difference, especially when you dealt with the actions of people who lived outside the law and their horrible fallout all day long.

Her phone vibrated in her handbag. Feeling her frustration mount, she fished it out without breaking stride and swiped right.

'I'm on my way, Nev,' she said. 'I told you I'd do my best to make it.'

It came out aggressive, and she instantly regretted it.

'Inspector Kris Hendrie?' the voice on the other end of the phone said, bemused.

It was a woman. Her clipped, plummy accent told of an expensive education.

'Och, sorry,' Kris said, taken aback. 'Err, aye. I thought you were... who is this, please?'

'Oh, no no, don't worry,' the caller said, forcing a laugh. 'This is Inspector Fiona McEwan, I'm calling from Kinross police. I was wondering if I could speak with you for a minute?'

'Sure,' Kris said. 'How can I help?'

She rummaged in her handbag for her car key with her free hand.

'I'm investigating a GBH in a service area on the M90, and I was hoping to chat with you about a possible suspect, if you don't mind?'

'Sure. That's way out of my jurisdiction, though, so I doubt I'd have much to contribute to your investigation.'

'Well, that's the thing,' McEwan said. 'So, the victim was attacked in the service area's bathroom. He's in a bad way. Broken ribs, heavy bruising, ruptured testicle. You get the picture. The poor man had to have emergency surgery, and he's still in hospital.'

'Was it an argument that got out of hand, or...?'

'He had a verbal argument while waiting in the queue at Burger King,' McEwan said. 'The suspect ran into him and my victim told him to watch where he was going. The suspect didn't take it well. He followed him into the loo and attacked him. Anyway, the victim took a very good look and helped us come up with a detailed e-fit.'

'OK. But I'm still not sure why you're telling me this, Inspector McEwan,' Kris said.

She eased herself into her car and knitted her eyebrows, puzzled.

'Please, call me Fiona. I'm getting to that,' McEwan said. 'I ran the e-fit through the police national computer and got a hit. One Allan Edwards. Mr Edwards and the man in my e-fit could be twins. Except Mr Edwards was arrested several months ago.'

'Aye,' Kris said.

She was starting to get annoyed at the McEwan

woman's caginess. Al was old news. She had more pressing things to deal with. Like actual dead bodies. And a marriage that would be closer to its terminal stage if she didn't show up for dinner.

'Do you see my problem, Kris?' McEwan said.

'Err... sorry. Your problem?'

'Well, with his record, Mr Edwards should be on remand or house arrest, shouldn't he? So what was he doing in a service area on the M90, over seventy miles away from his last known address?'

Kris paused. Al was history to her, but she needed to tread lightly given he was in witness protection. McEwan wouldn't be able to tell from the computer, but his profile would've been flagged.

'Inspector, are you still there?' McEwan said.

'Aye. Sorry. I was just trying to remember the details but it's been a while, so I'm afraid I can't recall much off the top of my head. Are you absolutely certain Edwards is your man?' Kris said, eyeing her dashboard clock.

'Not 100%, no,' McEwan replied with slight hesitation. 'My suspect has a beard and his hair's different. But they share a distinctive scar. Same shape, same position on the right cheek.'

'Right. Well, I'm not at the station right now, and I'd need to ask the procurator fiscal to find out more. Have you checked the service area's CCTV?'

'I've got the video, yes. But. to be honest with you, we're really short-handed so watching it is still on my to-do list.'

'So, how can I help, Fiona? What are you asking me here?' Kris said.

'Well, em... I was hoping you could help clarify his status, given what I found out.'

'As I said, I'd need to check,' Kris said.

She popped the key in the ignition. Drummed her nails on the steering wheel.

'Maybe I could send over the e-fit and a copy of the video file?' McEwan said smoothly.

The fucking cheek, Kris thought. 'Well, we're slammed here too, so I can't promise anything. But if I have some spare time I can take a look.'

'That would be really helpful, thank you,' McEwan said, way too readily. 'I'll email you a copy just now.'

She'd walked right into that, hadn't she?

'That's fine,' Kris said, pinching the bridge of her nose. 'I can't promise it'll be quick. But I'll take a look as soon as I can and get back in touch.'

CHAPTER 30

'Jack! Hey!'

Al walked down the high street, a bag weighed down with groceries in each hand, checked both sides for oncoming traffic, and crossed. It was a brisk, cloudy day, but the rain had held off and that was fine with him. He'd go home, unpack his shopping, then have a quick shower and go out for a stroll. Kill time until his Ikea delivery arrived. And then, perhaps, he'd treat himself to a second visit to The Mossy Well.

P had enjoyed his company, of that he was sure. She wouldn't have shared the joint with him otherwise, would she? Or spent the better part of two hours chatting with him about this and that after a busy shift. But he didn't want to come across as overeager, even though it was probably obvious to her that he didn't have much going for him at the minute. That would put her back up. And, as much as he hated to admit it, it wasn't just getting in on the action with the pork scratchings that was on his mind. He'd never met somebody who was so easy to talk to.

'Jack!' the voice repeated, louder. 'Hey!'

The words finally pierced through the fog of his thoughts.

Shite, *he* was Jack. He should've responded to his name straight away.

He swung around, trying to go for an uncertain look, like he wasn't sure he was the Jack being called. But the uncertainty gave way to surprise and, then, genuine pleasure when he spotted P waving at him from sixty yards away.

Sitting astride her motorcycle, dressed in jeans and a leather jacket, her curls drifting lazily in the late morning breeze, she was a sight for sore eyes. It wasn't just Al's pace that quickened. His heart did a weird flappy thing in his chest, like he was a teenager in the throes of puppy love.

'Hey,' he said.

'Hey yourself,' P replied. 'I thought you were ignoring me. I hope I didn't talk your ear off last time?'

Al chuckled awkwardly.

'Och, no, no. Of course not. That was... that was fun,' he said. 'I was just lost in my own world, sorry.'

He straightened up and held her gaze.

'And, truth be told, I didn't really expect to have people calling out my name on the high street barely a week into moving to a new town.'

She laughed her throaty laugh. It was genuine. Unforced. Unafraid. Enough to soften the toughest of hearts.

'Say what you will about us,' she said. 'But we're a friendly bunch here in Fort Drumblehan. Too friendly, some might say.'

They looked at each other and he shuffled his feet.

'So,' he said. 'How've you been? Things busy at the pub?'

'Aye. Can't really complain,' she said. 'Then again, it's the only pub in thirty miles. The punters don't really have much of a choice, do they?'

'No, I suppose not,' he said.

'How about you? Settling in?'

'Kind of,' Al said. 'I've been hard at work ordering furniture off the internet. I'm expecting a delivery later today, actually.'

'That sounds like fun,' she said.

'Isn't it just?' Al replied. 'I can't wait to pore over instructions that might as well have been written in hieroglyphics.'

'How's your blood pressure?' she said with a wink.

'Eh?'

'Your blood pressure.'

'Err...'

'Well if it's low, assembling Ikea furniture will do marvels for it,' she deadpanned.

It took Al a few seconds to get it, but when it clicked, he belly-laughed so hard his sides hurt and he couldn't catch his breath. The dopamine hit was delicious. He couldn't remember feeling his uplifted, this free, in... had he ever?

'That's a good one,' he said, shifting the grocery bag in his right hand to his left so he could wipe his eyes with his thumb. 'Where'd you hear that?'

'Promise you won't tell?' she whispered conspiratorially.

'Eh, sure.'

'I read it off the internet and I've been waiting for the right time to tell it for months. So thank you.'

'Glad to be of service.'

He bowed.

She touched her hand to her forehead in a sort of salute. 'Much obliged, sir.'

They studied each other for a brief minute.

'Well,' Al said. 'It was good to see you, but I must be going.'

'Och, sure, of course.' P said. 'And so must I.'

She fired up the motorcycle.

'Say,' she said. 'You live in the estate down from The Mossy Well, don't you?'

'Aye, why?'

'Fancy a lift on the scary motorcycle?' she said.

She opened the rear carrier, fished out a bright blue open face helmet, and handed it to him.

'Sure, that'd be great, cheers,' Al said.

He placed the grocery bags in the carrier, slipped the helmet on, and sat astride the motorcycle.

'OK, hold fast!' P shouted above the engine's rumble.

When he placed his hands around her waist, the twinge in his stomach he'd felt when he'd seen her came back stronger than ever. Much harder to ignore. And as they barrelled down the high street and round the corner towards the estate, he reflected that everything that had happened to him — getting mixed up with the Red Hand, almost getting whacked, grassing — hadn't been the worst things in the world.

No. Not the worst at all. In fact, he thought, he might actually get used to this new life malarkey.

CHAPTER 31

'How is it possible?'

Jonno stared blankly at his new employer, whose name he still didn't know.

'You can call me the CEO,' his new employer had said with an air of magnanimity when Jonno had pressed, the first time they'd met. And that had been that.

Jonno shifted his weight from one leg to another. His throat felt impossibly dry, but he didn't dare touch the glass of water he'd been offered at the start of the meeting. It was better not to take chances. So it lay there, on the coffee table, mocking him. A sweet balm, so tantalisingly close yet so far out of reach.

'Huh?' he replied, at last, unsure what else he could possibly say.

'Huh?' the CEO mocked. 'What's that? Swallowed a fly?'

'No, eh, I-'

'No, really, Jonno. Tell me. I'm genuinely curious. Gobsmacked, actually. How. Is it. Possible?'

The CEO delivered this calmly, from the sofa. A mug of

steaming builders' tea cradled between rough hands. But the relaxed, open posture didn't inspire comfort or confidence. If anything, it charged the atmosphere, giving an uneasy undertone to the proceedings. Like things could take a turn from neutral to very, very negative in an instant.

Six months in, Jonno still had a hard time believing how the person in front of him could be in charge of the Company. But he didn't doubt the ruthlessness that had made this possible for one second. Others had. And see where that had got them.

And then there was the way they'd been going after the Red Hand. No hesitation. No mercy. They weren't conceding an inch. And he respected that. It was high time somebody gave those bastards what was coming to them.

'Jonno, I'm waiting,' the CEO continued. 'How can you have been working on it for six months, and still have nothing to show for it? Explain.'

'Well, er-'

Jonno shifted his weight again. Dug his meaty hands deep into his pockets, as if this would somehow give him a direct line into a well of reassurance.

'Yes?'

'Al's Ma didn't know anything. Insisted the last she'd heard of him was when she was in hospital. And I was very persuasive.'

'Persuasive' was one way to put it. After her encounter with Jonno, poor Jane Edwards had had to return to hospital. This time for an extended stay.

The CEO nodded. 'And our source in the police?'

Jonno swallowed. 'It's very strictly on a need to know basis. The witness protection people aren't involved in investigations. They never mix and chat with the regular polis. And if you need information about somebody in the programme you have to put in a request through the system. So it's impossible to find out who's been with him without raising suspicion. It's-'

The CEO raised a hand to stop him.

'I didn't ask to be educated about the ins and outs of the witness protection programme, Jonno.'

The voice was patient, as if explaining to a three-year old why inserting a fork into a socket was a bad idea.

'What I want to know is, since when are we taking no for an answer? Where's your initiative?'

'Well, I... we've tried turning the screws. But our contact won't budge. Says if they put in a request they need to have a pretext, or it'll be shut down.'

He tugged at his belt buckle.

'And even if they do, and something happens to Al, it's going to point right to them. Look, I can't wait to get my hands on the prick. But our source says there's only one way to find him. And, even if the request gets waved through, it's too much heat.'

Jonno said this last part with a grimace, like it was physically painful. He braced himself for the inevitable explosion. But it never came. The CEO took in the information with equanimity.

'Perhaps we've been looking at this from the wrong angle,' the CEO said, after what felt like an eternity.

'Och?' Jonno said.

'Who was the inspector in charge of the investigation? Hendrie something?'

'Aye,' Jonno said. 'Kris Hendrie.'

'Right.'

The CEO reached for the tea. Sipped it, producing a slurping sound which reminded Jonno of Father Baker eating his soup. It made his stomach churn.

'What do we have on her?' The CEO asked.

'Nothing. Straight arrow,' he replied.

'Hmm.'

The CEO looked straight at him and flashed a smile. It reminded him of a crocodile gliding through the marsh towards its prey. Preparing to strike.

'Family?'

'Husband and a young son.'

'Excellent.'

The smile widened, exposing impossibly white, even teeth.

'She's still in charge of the gang task force, correct?'

'Aye.'

'Perhaps, if our source won't play nice, we might persuade Inspector Hendrie to help us out, Jonno. What do you say?'

CHAPTER 32

W hat a shite fucking day. Christ.

Honestly. I could bloody throttle Phillip.

Remember that business with the company reorganisation? The one he stuck his bloody beak of a nose in?

Well. The client almost went for my plan.

Almost being the operative word.

Then, seconds away from them signing off, the absolute fucking shitehawk had to start mouthing off.

'But what about the international implications, Mr Haig? Is it worth the risk for minimal gain? What about the direction we'd discussed?'

'What direction?' I wanted to say. 'The one where your head ends up your arsehole or the one where your idiocy gets us sued for malpractice?'

But, of course, I said nothing of the sort, since I need this fucking job because, you know, I've got bills to pay. I just sat there, sucking my teeth and clenching every muscle in my body so my eyes wouldn't roll while he undid several months of my good work.

I was pretty sure that, deep down, the clients knew he was talking shite. But what difference does it make? He seeded enough doubt to talk them out of it. So I've worked my arse off and, not only do I have fuck all to show for it, I've been thrown under the bus for my efforts.

I turned around in my chair and drank in the view. Down below me, cars so small they looked like Matchbox toys zipped across the Strathburgh bypass — the motorway that encircled the city — rushing their drivers towards wherever they needed to be. Beyond that, a sea of pine trees were huddled together at the foot of a range of mountains that were still lightly dusted with snow despite it being late March. It was a view that never got old, even though I'd been working from this office, eight hours a day, five days a week, for going on two years. But that afternoon it wasn't doing much for me. I was still seething. Serena would be getting two earfuls at our next therapy session.

'Hey stranger,' a voice behind me said.

I whirled around in my chair. Joan was leaning in the doorway, dressed for success in a deep blue power suit with a crisp white blouse.

'Are you OK?' she said.

'News travels fast,' I replied.

'Aye. You know this office,' she said. 'Word is you were a worrying shade of purple coming out of the meeting.'

She eyed me, smiled wickedly, and stepped inside.

'I did make an effort not to be obvious,' I said. 'But he makes it hard. So bloody hard.'

Joan sighed. Then she stuck out her tongue and crossed her eyes.

'Unfortunately, I know exactly what you mean.'

'But look at you,' I said. 'Important meeting?'

'Aye,' she said. 'I'm on the Shell call. And guess who's tagging along?'

'No,' I said. 'He's sticking his nose in tax now? Lord help us.'

'Well, £10 says he doesn't have the foggiest what's in the file. Or why we're meeting. Too busy, you know...' she made exaggerated snoring noises.

'That's one bet I won't take,' I said, leaning back in my chair and putting my feet up. 'But, tell you what, I'd take lazy Phillip over meddlesome Phillip any day.'

'So what are you working on?' Joan asked, nodding at my laptop.

'You mean besides the whole Carruthers Capital debacle?'

Joan laughed. 'Och, come on, it can't be that bad.'

'It can always be worse, can't it?' I said. 'I could be sitting in prison. On attempted murder charges. Attempted bossicide.'

She laughed and I joined her. The sound of our laughter mingled together made my pulse quicken in spite of myself.

'No, but seriously,' I told her. 'It's a mess. I've got these management accounts I should be doing for a new client, but all I can think about is that bloody meeting so I'm having trouble making sense of them.'

'Why don't I take a look?'

'Sure,' I said, making room for her.

Joan walked to my side of the desk and leaned over to look at my screen. Her thigh brushed against mine, and my stomach did a small somersault, like a gymnast warming up for the main event.

'Woah,' she said, hovering the cursor over a £20,000 transaction tagged sundries. 'What the hell's this?'

I pointed to the pile of bank statements on my desk.

'That's what I've been trying to figure out. It's doing my head in.'

'Who's it been paid to?'

I flipped through the papers strewn about my desk, trying to find the correct document. I usually worked paperlessly, but there was so much to get through I had to print the stuff out, and my desk looked like the epicentre of an explosion.

'Just a minute,' I said, shuffling through a thick sheaf of papers held together with a bulldog clip. 'This says it's been paid to... Superior Foods.'

'Weird.'

'Very weird,' I said.

Superior Foods was a relatively new company, registered just four months earlier. More importantly, why pay a food import and export company £20,000 in sundries? It smelled fishier than the Saturday market at Pike Quay.

'I'm trying to think of a way to broach the subject with our dear leader,' I said to Joan. 'But today isn't the day. For obvious reasons.'

Right on cue, the man himself appeared in the doorway, looking immaculate in a dark blue, herringbone suit, striped white and blue shirt, and red power tie. Platinum cufflinks gleamed from beneath the sleeves of his suit jacket.

'Ah, Ms Strachan, there you are,' he said. 'Mr Haig.'

Was that thinly veiled contempt in his voice? Incompetent twat. Useless bastard.

'Phillip,' I said, keeping my eyes on the paperwork before me.

His phone rang. He swiped left and trousered it without even checking who was calling.

'So are we ready to go, Ms Strachan?' he said with a note of impatience.

'Aye, can't wait,' she said.

The sarcasm went over Phillip's head. It was all I could do not to scoff.

'See you later, Bertie,' Joan said.

Armed with a steaming mug of the blackest, bitterest coffee I could stomach, I sat back down at my desk and tried to make sense of that mess of a set of management accounts. But it was like worrying at a knot, only to find out there were three even tighter knots I'd need to deal with first. By the time Joan knocked at my door two hours later, I hadn't made any headway, which hadn't done much for my mood.

'Well that must've gone swimmingly,' I said.

Joan had her hands on her hips, and she was smiling from ear to ear.

'Can you tell?'

'Smile any wider, and you're going to look like a Canadian on South Park,' I said.

'Ha ha. Very funny, Bertie.'

I dropped the papers I was holding, leaned back in my chair, and drank her in. 'So are you going to tell me about it or what?'

'Sure,' she said. 'How about I do so over a pint?'

My mood brightened. 'How could I say no?' I said.

I turned my laptop off, grabbed my things, and ushered Joan out of my office. We took the lift to the ground floor, and walked out into the brisk evening towards The Grosvenor, a red sandstone building round the corner from the office.

'So what are we celebrating?' I asked, when we'd sat in a

booth with two pints — Guinness for me and an IPA for Joan.

'Vindication.'

'Vindication?' I replied, toying with my beer glass. 'Strong word.'

'Shell loved my idea,' she enthused. 'Not only that. They called it genius. Genius, Bertie.'

She briefly took my hand, and I felt an electric shock going up my arm.

'Phillip barely said a word all meeting,' she continued. 'It was a sight to behold.'

'I bet he was fuming,' I said, relishing the thought. 'But Ms Strachan, are you sure that's the right idea? Surely, the risk's too high.'

Joan giggled and slapped my hand.

'Stop it. My beer almost went up my nose.'

'Bertie! Joan!'

I looked up and saw Shawn from audit waving at us from across the floor. I glanced at Joan and felt a wave of disappointment. I'd been enjoying this, blast him. Then I plastered on my most friendly smile and waved back.

Shawn weaved through the punters, a pint in each hand, and plopped himself next to me with a sigh, spilling an inch of beer from one of the glasses in the process.

'Whoops,' he said mildly, plucking a napkin from the vintage tomato tin they'd repurposed as a cutlery holder.

He wiped the table with a flourish, slurped down what remained of the beer, and emitted a loud burp.

'Classy,' Joan said, wrinkling her nose.

'What can I say? Good digestion,' he said, wiping his mouth with his shirt cuff.

'So how are things? Recovered from your meeting this morning?'

'How could you-' I stammered.

'Bertie actually does a smashing impression of our Phillip,' Joan butted in. 'It's bang on.'

'Does he, now?' he said, looking at me like he'd just found out I was in MENSA.

God, he was a good guy but he really got on my tits sometimes.

'OK well. Let's hear it,' he said, clapping his hands together.

'Umm, I don't know about that.'

I squirmed. Fuck's sake.

'Och, come on now,' he prodded. 'Don't be shy. You know you want to.'

'Pretty please?' Joan said, giving me her winningest smile.

'Fine,' I sighed.

I straightened my back and channelled my inner Phillip. It struck them both as deliciously funny. Joan was in fits and Shawn was laughing his booming laugh, a sound so impossibly deep and loud it almost drowned out the chatter that filled the busy pub.

'Och, you're killing me,' he said. 'Do it again.'

'Nah. If I do it too much it won't be funny anymore,' I said.

'Can you believe this bloke?' he said, clapping me on the back.

We bantered good-naturedly for another half hour or so. But when Shawn offered to get another round, I begged off, wanting to get home at a half-decent hour.

'I'd love to, but I should get going,' I said. 'Long day tomorrow.'

'Well, up yours, party pooper,' Shawn said, shooting me his middle finger.

'The feeling is mutual,' I told him, returning the gesture. 'So long.'

'See you, Bertie,' Joan said.

I gave her a mock salute and we exchanged a secret smile.

CHAPTER 33

Walking off the bus, it occurred to me I hadn't thought about Phillip, Carruthers Capital, or Superior Foods and their dodgy as fuck management accounts for over an hour. Nor was I inclined to resume my ruminations. The brisk air and the good company, helped, no doubt, by the beer, had lifted my mood. And as I walked down the hill towards my building, it felt like my feet were barely touching the ground. I was gliding. Moving along so smoothly I didn't realise I was on a collision course with somebody until I felt my hand connect with a squishy belly and looked up to see deep-set brown eyes shooting daggers at me from beneath bushy black eyebrows.

'You blind, prick?' the bloke growled.

It was enough to make an angry lion shrivel, and I was no lion.

'Sorry,' I squeaked.

I rushed off towards my building as fast as I could without breaking into an all-out run. My heart was still pounding when I reached my landing, and I almost crashed again. This time into Morag. Jesus Christ. Maybe I really was going blind.

'Oh Bertie, just the man I was looking for,' she said.

Of course I was.

'Is that so?' I replied warily. 'What's the matter? Something wrong?'

'Oh, no, no, no. Well, actually yes. I wanted to talk to you about...' she glanced at Graeme's front door. 'Do you mind coming downstairs for a second?'

'Err, I...'

She took me by the arm and attacked the stairs, her walk tentative, but her grip so strong it would leave a bruise just above my elbow. Some people don't take no for an answer. Morag was on a whole other level. She didn't even wait for the answer.

'Morag, I've had a long day. Can't this wait?' I said.

'Oh, this won't take a minute,' she told me, dragging me inside her flat. 'But we really need to discuss this.'

'Discuss what?' I said, fearing I knew what was coming and feeling resentful about it. My good mood was turning sour.

'Let me get you a drink,' she said, hobbling towards the kitchenette.

'No I-'

'Just water,' she called out without turning.

'Right. OK.'

The flat was the same size and had the exact same layout as mine: an entryway with a bathroom to the left, opening on a square studio room. But it was dingy and rundown in comparison. The carpet, which once upon a time must've been a lush cream colour, had turned a sickly shade of beige-grey. The pine kitchen units were chipped in several places. And the smells of reheated pasta and microwave dinners gave the air the faint but unmistakable whiff of loneliness and desperation.

I looked around, unsure what to do with myself. There were no photo frames anywhere in sight. No kids or relatives immortalised for posterity, brightening up the place. The emptiness got to me. It had to be soul-destroying, having all those hours stretching out before you, day in day out, and nothing to fill them with.

Feeling slightly guilty about all the times I'd brushed her off, I softened my tone. 'What's the matter, Morag?' I sighed.

She handed me my water. I took a small sip and placed it on one of her shelves.

'Graeme's motorcycle,' she said.

I groaned.

'What about it?'

'Well, you know how I feel about it,' she said, looking me up and down from behind her glasses.

The lenses were so thick her eyes looked far too large for her face. It gave her a vaguely insect-like quality.

'Aye, you've made your feelings very clear,' I said. 'But you know how he is. The bloke doesn't give two shites what anyone else thinks, so I don't know what you're expecting me to do.'

'I'm not expecting you to do anything,' she retorted. 'I'm saying it's an issue.'

'And you talked to him,' I said. 'And six months later, here we are. The motorcycle's still there. So what's your point?'

'I was thinking of writing a letter to the council. Perhaps if we all signed it, the whole building,' she said, 'it might persuade him.'

She shuffled to the sofa, sat down heavily, and looked up at me expectantly.

'I live across the hall from him, Morag,' I sighed. 'I just want a quiet life. Can't you please just leave me out of it? Please?'

'Well, think about it,' she pressed.

I sighed. 'Fine. I will.'

Thankfully, she didn't press the issue any further, so I scurried out, up the stairs and into my flat, closing the door just in time to narrowly avoid running into Graeme.

'Aye. That's spot on,' he shouted into his phone, in between slamming the door, almost as if he wanted to make sure everyone heard him.

What a prick.

I filtered him out and walked into my living area.

The under-counter light in the kitchenette stopped me in my tracks.

Had I forgotten to turn it off that morning?

I didn't even remember turning it on. But then again, I'd overslept and left for work in a hurry. So maybe I'd turned it on and my caffeine-starved brain had forgotten about it?

God, this was getting ridiculous. If I continued being this preoccupied all the time, I was going to drive myself round the bend.

I crossed the room, fetched the bread from the cupboard over the sink and the butter and ham from the fridge. On the ground floor, I heard indistinct voices and then the sound of Graeme firing up his motorcycle and revving the engine.

I opened the butter and spread it over a slice of bread. But it took me a while to do it, because my hand was trembling.

CHAPTER 34

'No. No. That can't be right,' Al said.

'You think?' P replied, giving him side-eye.

They stood back and looked at their handi-work. P snorted. Al followed. Five seconds later, they were both doubled over, laughing hysterically with tears streaming from their eyes, the sound echoing around the four walls of Al's still mostly barren living room.

The pile of melamine-covered chipboard before them looked nothing like the pictures on the Ikea website or the assembly instructions. For starters, none of the edges matched. But that was the least of their problems. Two of the shelves were laid diagonally, at gravity-defying angles that would make it impossible to use the bookshelf for its intended purpose. And, for some reason, the only drawer they'd managed to assemble wouldn't fit properly. They'd been trying to slot it in for the previous fifteen minutes, but it just wouldn't sit right.

P picked up the assembly instructions from the floor, dusted them off, and studied the diagrams.

'Where did we go wrong?' she mused.

'I think you're asking the wrong question,' Al said. 'It's more like, did we get any part of it right?'

She flipped the pages, her brow furrowed.

'Shite. I think I know why the drawer won't go in,' she said. 'We put the rails on the wrong way.'

'You're serious?' Al said.

He squatted down next to the drawer and ran his eyes over it.

'Aye, see?' P said, pointing at the rail. 'The wheel should face the front.'

'Good thing you've assembled Ikea furniture before, eh?' Al ribbed her.

'Hey, it's your furniture,' P retorted. 'I'm just the help!'

She stuck out her tongue and crossed her eyes. Al gave her the finger. And, just like that, they were doubled over again.

'Have you decided what you'll be doing for work?' she said, when their laughter had subsided from full-on belly busting to sporadic fits.

'Why?' Al said, one of his eyebrows raised.

He'd spent enough time with her to know a punchline was coming, but he wasn't sure when or what it would be.

'Well,' P said, 'I sure hope you're not planning on becoming a joiner. You're terrible at this.'

Al snorted.

'You and me both,' he said. 'Unbelievable.'

'The blind leading the blind,' P agreed.

Al sat down on the floor, his legs crossed. He grabbed a stray shelf and a handful of dowels, and looked at them balefully.

'Fuck's sake. And I've still got the sofa, the wardrobe, the chest of drawers, and the bed to do.'

'That assembly fee isn't looking so expensive now, is it?' P told him.

'I hate it when you're right,' he said.

P sighed, reached for a hand towel, and mopped her brow. It was an easy, unselfconscious gesture, and Al's heart leapt. Whether he'd be able to make this work — and how he'd go about it — were still huge question marks. But right then, it didn't matter. He was too busy savouring every moment. It was everything his past life wasn't. No stress. No pressure. No threats of prison or violence. Not a care in the world.

P glanced at her watch.

'Sadly, I'm going to have to leave you to it,' she said. 'It's opening time soon.'

'Do you have to?' Al said with barely concealed disappointment.

'Afraid so,' P said.

She looked equally regretful.

'I bet that gang of old farts are already lined up outside the door, grumbling about me messing up their routine.'

'Ha, some routine,' Al said. 'It'll do them good to lay off the lager.'

'Tsk tsk,' P said. 'Now don't go telling them that. I can't afford to lose my best customers. A girl's got to eat.'

Al considered bringing up the pork scratchings and whatever they were a front for. He reckoned it was probably weed, given P's proclivities and the fact most of the punters who bought it seemed to be sluggish and had eyes like letterboxes. But he didn't want to risk spoiling the mood.

'Besides, it's going to be busy tonight,' she said, nodding at Al's window.

It was not yet four in the afternoon, but it was so dark they'd had to switch the big light on. The sky was the colour of cast-iron, and the rain hadn't given them any respite all day.

'It's always busy when it's dreich,' she continued. 'Not much to do and nowhere else to go. As you'll learn soon enough if you stick with us.'

'How about I help you?' Al blurted.

He hadn't really considered it, but right then it felt natural. Right.

P scoffed.

'What's funny?' Al said, mildly hurt. 'I'm serious.'

'Do you think you can handle working behind the bar on a busy night?' she said.

'Well,' Al stammered. 'Why not? Besides, it's not like I'm going to be on my own, am I? It'll go smoother if it's two of us.'

P considered this. Seemed to have second thoughts. Ignoring the hammering in his heart, Al pressed on.

'If you're worried about the...' he cleared his throat.

Why was this proving so hard? So what if she got annoyed and left? He barely knew her.

'The thing,' he continued lamely, 'with the packets of pork scratchings.'

'What thing with the packets of pork scratchings?' P said. 'What the hell are you on about, Jack?'

Her brows were knotted. But there was a shadow of a smile dancing on her lips and a wicked look in her eye.

'Och, come on, P,' Al said. 'I've got eyes in my head, in case you haven't noticed. And I've been around, you know.'

His face had turned plum, with the exception of his chib scar, which was a sickly shade of ivory, keloids standing out in stark relief against his patchy beard. P frowned. Al felt his heart sink, and then an unreasonably powerful surge of anger at himself.

'You eejit,' he thought. 'You've fucking gone and blown it.'

'You're adorable when you're nervous. Has anyone ever told you that?' P said.

'Wha-' Al stammered. 'What the hell?'

P chuckled.

'I kind of figured you've been around,' she said, nodding at his scar.

He touched it briefly with the tips of his fingers.

'Well, err, I-'

'It's fine,' she said. 'You can tell me about it when you're ready.'

'Och,' Al said.

The temperature had suddenly gone up several degrees. And he was thirteen again, and completely at a loss for how to navigate his way around the girl who made him feel all sorts of emotions he couldn't understand or control.

'It's fine, Jack, really,' she said. 'Look. Thanks for offering. I could use the help, actually. It's going to be mental tonight. And if you could cover a few shifts I'd be able to have some time off. Live a little.'

'So I'm hired?' he said, tentatively hopeful.

'You're on probation,' she said, but there was an amused note in her voice. 'How does that sound?'

Al gave her his most formal bow.

'I accept the appointment,' he said.

'Good,' P replied, holding out her hand.

He took it. Held on to it briefly, relishing the softness of its touch and the heat emanating from her palm, before giving it a shake. Then they both burst out laughing.

'OK. OK,' P said. 'Now let's get down to business. I'm going to need to explain to you how the scheme works.'

'Aye, aye, boss,' Al said.

She slapped him playfully on the shoulder, then sat down on a clear patch of floor.

'Cut the shite and listen to me.'

CHAPTER 35

'Bud, are you going to serve us or what?'

'Oi, where are my long island ice teas?'

'Hey, bud! Look here! Here! We've been in this bloody queue fifteen fucking minutes!'

'Aye, cool it. I've heard you,' Al snapped. 'Give me a minute. Can't you see I'm busy serving this gentleman, eh?'

Al grabbed three pint glasses from under the bar and slapped them onto the rubber mat near the beer taps. Then he tilted the first one, popped it under the tap marked Tennent's, and let the beer flow into the glass, trying to ignore the bedlam around him. The beer hit the bottom of the glass the wrong way, and the glass filled up with foam.

'Shite,' he muttered, wiping sweat from his brow.

It was getting hot in the pub. Or maybe he just wasn't used to this sort of pressure. He took a deep breath, put the glass in the sink, and tried again with a fresh one. This time, he got the angle right, and the glass filled up with golden, ice-cold liquid.

P had been right. Being behind the bar on a busy night was like going to bloody war. The punters were crowding him on all three sides, shouting in unison like crazed maniacs. He could barely make out half of what they were saying over the din, let alone keep the orders straight in his head.

Who wanted the three pints of lager he was pouring?

Who ordered two G&Ts?

Who was the fucking Philistine who'd asked for ice cubes in their Merlot?

'Och, hiya,' a punter said, deftly slotting himself between a bloke with round-rimmed glasses that made him look like an overgrown, overweight Harry Potter and a redhead who didn't seem too pleased with Mr Potter's attentions.

Al recognised him from his first night at The Mossy Well. He was the bloke who'd bought pork scratchings and waited for his girl at the booth.

'Er, P not in?' the punter said, looking doubtfully at Al and shifting uncomfortably.

'She's in the back,' Al said. 'What can I get you?'

'Err,' he stammered. 'Two lager and... err... can I have a pack of pork scratchings?'

He tipped an exaggerated wink.

'Bloody hell what a clueless cunt,' Al thought. 'Self-awareness of a midge.' Good thing this was a small-time operation in the middle of nowhere, or the place would've been crawling with polis ages ago.

'Aye, I've got you,' he told the punter, hoping his stern look would cut through.

The punter looked satisfied. Al finished the order he'd been working on, then pulled the bloke's two pints and handed them over with a packet of P's special, home-grown pork scratchings.

'That'll be ten quid,' Al said, ringing up the sale.

The punter handed him a £50 note. Al noted with

approval that he'd folded it so it wouldn't catch anybody's attention. An unexpected flash of common sense, after all. He broke the £50 into fives, left £10 in the till, and palmed the rest. £10 went back to the punter as change, and £30 went into a Mason jar under the counter. Nobody had noticed. But if anyone asked, the punter had been so happy with the service he'd tipped extra-generously.

The punter pocketed his change, nodded his thanks, and carried his pints and pork scratchings to the very same corner booth he'd retreated to the previous time. Two shifty-looking blokes were waiting for him, sitting across from each other, hunched over the table.

Al sighed and moved on to the next order. The last time he'd made these same movements, he'd been a naive youngling just coming up in the Chairman's crew. But it hadn't taken long for it all to come back to him. By the fourth punter who'd asked for pork scratchings, he was flying. Operating purely on muscle memory. The movements were coming to him as naturally as if he'd never stopped all those decades before. Just like riding a bike. Well, if riding a bike were the same as dealing drugs.

P walked in, the bottles in the box she was carrying clinking faintly. She placed the box on the floor, and got to work restocking the fridges.

'How's it going?' she asked, raising her voice so he'd hear her over the din.

'Mental!' Al shouted back through gritted teeth.

He was busy trying to pour an old fashioned, but the list of cocktails P had cobbled together for him might as well have been written in a foreign language. He poured bitters into the silver egg cup P used as a measure. Spilled half of it. Tried again. Gave up, poured what was left in the measure, and topped it up straight from the bottle. He'd probably overpoured, but the punter looked plastered. £20 said everything would taste the same to the poor sod.

'Told you it's not for the faint-hearted,' P said.

In the time it had taken him to make the cocktail, she'd finished restocking the fridge. She was now next to him, shoulder to shoulder, pouring a mammoth order of six pints of Tennent's, three G&Ts, and two other drinks he couldn't figure out.

'What are those drinks you're pouring?' Al asked, as he pulled more pints.

'Disaronno and coke,' P said.

'What?' Al asked, certain he'd misunderstood.

'Disaronno and coke.'

'Jesus Christ,' he whispered in P's ear. 'Whoever ordered that deserves prison time.'

P giggled and slapped him on the shoulder.

'Less talking, more working,' she said, trying to look stern but leaning briefly against him in a way that made his heart skip a beat.

Wave after wave of punters kept coming. With the exception of ten minutes in which P left the bar to change a keg, both of them kept at it non-stop. Pouring drink after drink after drink, and serving pork scratchings and other snacks. By the time eleven rolled around, Al was more tired than he'd felt in years.

'I'm wiped,' he grumbled, as he poured what must've been the three hundredth pint of the night.

'Lightweight,' P shot back. 'And here I was going to suggest pizza and a film after we're done.'

'I'd murder a pizza right about now,' Al said. 'But I suspect there's a greater chance of the film watching me than the other way around.'

'I'm sure it'll find it very entertaining,' she said.

'Very funny.'

He walked five steps away from her, to the left, where more punters were waiting for him to ply them with neck oil. He glanced at his watch.

'So does that mean it's time for last call?' he said, pulling the cap off a bottle of pear cider and handing it to a punter together with a packet of pork scratchings and a packet of roasted peanuts.

'It's half an hour too early,' P shouted back.

'And?' Al said.

P handed three pints of beer and two glasses of red wine to a red-faced, older punter, then shrugged.

'Och, what the hell,' she said.

She turned to her left and rang the bell. It was the beauty of owning a business in a place like Fort Drumble-han. The punters may be a bit annoyed at the early night, but the next time they were stuck for somewhere to go, their options would be unchanged. They could greet as much as they liked, but they'd have to go back to The Mossy Well unless they fancied staying home until the weather was more amenable. Or somebody else decided to open another pub.

As soon as P rang the bell and screamed 'Last call,' the wave intensified. People who'd previously been lost in their conversations converged on the bar at lightning speed. And P and Al spent the next forty minutes dealing with an onslaught of punters clamouring for drinks like it was the eve of Prohibition. Once they'd seen the last of the punters off, they restocked the fridges, washed a warehouse's worth of dirty glasses and put them away, mopped the floors, and closed the till. It took them another hour before they were done for the night.

'Fuck, that was intense,' Al said, sinking into a chair with a can of Strongbow.

'Aye,' P said without looking up.

She was leaning over the bar, her attention focused on the joint she was rolling.

'It was unusually busy, to be fair,' she said. 'Good thing you've decided to earn your keep instead of bothering the staff, eh?'

Her eyes looked tired, and the tight ponytail she'd been wearing at the start of the shift had come loose. But Al thought he'd never seen somebody look so effortlessly beautiful. He drained his cider, put the empty can in the overflowing bin bag, and tied the bag up, ready to be taken out back. Then he leaned against the bar across from P.

She took a long drag, passed him the joint, and looked at him. Al held her gaze. With every puff, he felt himself being wrapped in a warm cocoon. His mind blanked. The periphery of his vision blurred. All he could see were P's eyes, swimming around in their orbits. Looking bright and sparkly. He could lose himself in there, and not mind it one bit.

When he handed back the joint, she held on to his hand. And when he leaned over, she met him halfway. The touch of their lips erased every last one of his worries. He was no longer Al, grass on the run, escaping from his troubled past.

For the first time, he felt like a new person. He'd become Jack.

At least temporarily.

CHAPTER 36

Kris parallel parked a block down from her house, killed the engine, and leaned back into the driver's seat, steeling herself. Neville had called her while she was negotiating a roundabout about a mile away, feigning concern. It was over an hour past the time she said she'd be home. Was she OK?

To a casual observer, it would've sounded like a normal conversation between two married people. But she could feel the undertone of accusation dripping from his words. When you scratched beneath the surface, it was very clear they were barely holding it together. The civility was cold. Forced.

She ran her hands through her hair and rubbed her eyes, feeling the exhaustion of a twelve-hour shift wash over her, and wondering how she'd manage three or four hours of walking on eggshells on top of it. Where had they gone wrong? There was a time when they could have entire conversations with a single glance. When they were two jigsaw puzzle pieces who fit together perfectly. Now it was all strife all the time. Almost as if those two teenagers who hit it off in drama class were different people, living a different life.

She got out of the car, shut the door, and pressed the lock button on her key fob. There'd been a collision and traffic had been heavy. So, between the time she'd left the station and parked the car, it had grown dark, and the trees that lined the street were faint silhouettes on a blue-black background.

She fished for her key in her handbag as she walked towards her house. Lost in thought. She didn't notice the figure emerging from behind one of the trees.

'Inspector Hendrie,' the voice growled. 'It's good to finally meet you.'

She pivoted, her eyes searching for the person the voice belonged to. Her fingers curled around her house key, brandishing it like a weapon. She spotted him two doors down from her house, hands crossed, eyeing her like she was a piece of prime beef.

'Jonno Wallace,' she spat, unable to believe her eyes.

The bloke had been the subject of a nationwide manhunt for months and they hadn't had any luck. Not even one reported sighting. And here he was. Right on her bloody doorstep.

'Don't move,' she said.

Her hand slid into her handbag, fumbling for her phone.

'Whatever you're thinking,' Jonno said, 'Don't. You're going to want to hear what I have to say.'

'Do I, now?' she said, staring at him right between the eyes, as if she could shoot him dead with a look.

'Aye,' he said. 'You do.'

He raised his left hand, as if in surrender. Then brought his right hand out from behind his back. It held an A4 envelope which he tossed on the ground between them.

'Take a look, Inspector,' he said, nodding at the envelope. 'I think you'll find it very interesting.'

'What's this, Wallace?' Kris said. 'Your idea of a ruse? Because if it is, it's not going to work.'

Jonno barked a laugh. 'No ruse, Inspector,' he said, a wide but obviously fake smile plastered on his chapped lips. 'Promise.'

He took several steps backwards, almost disappearing into the manicured hedges that lined Kris' neighbours' house.

'There,' he said. 'Am I far away enough?'

Kris sized him up and considered her options. It was tea-time and the street was deserted. But the lights were on in most houses. Lots of families would be gathered together. And her own house was only about fifty yards away. Worst came to worst, she'd scream bloody murder. Somebody was bound to hear her and dial 999.

These calculations took maybe a second. And in that time, her curiosity got the better of her. She edged her way towards the envelope. Inch by inch. She squatted down, her eyes never leaving Jonno. Reached out. Picked it up with her thumb and forefinger, as if it were packed with explosives. Something shifted inside it.

Jonno didn't move. He looked on. Licked his lips. They made a sandpapery rustle that made Kris' stomach turn.

'Very good, Inspector,' he said, when she'd retreated to the safety of a streetlamp's glow. 'See? I stayed put. Just like I promised I would. Not so bad, am I?'

'What do you want, Wallace?' she barked.

'Why don't you take a look inside that envelope?' he said, nodding at it with his non-existent chin.

She inserted her house key beneath the flap, and tore it open. Several glossy four by six inch prints slid out into the palm of her hand. She flipped through them slowly. Deliberately. Her blood had run cold as soon as she'd glimpsed the first one. But she forced herself to keep steady. Focused her brain on sending one, single command to the rest of her body: don't you dare fucking tremble.

'That's just the last forty-eight hours,' Jonno informed her. 'Imagine what else we could do, given more time.'

Jason stared back at her from one of the photos, his tie askew. Sitting on a bench in the school playground. Several other shots of him followed. Three of them close-ups of his face.

The rest of the photos were a whistle-stop tour of a typical day in Neville and Jason's life. Neville guiding Jason into Morrisons. Several shots of Neville putting the shopping in the boot and buckling Jason in his car seat. Neville and Jason in the playground at the back of their house. Jason...

She put the photos back in the envelope and closed her eyes. A wave of nausea gripped her. She swallowed back the acid that was flooding up her throat like dirty water from a burst pipe. Then she looked up at Jonno. Fought to keep her features neutral and her voice even. Ignoring the anger that was burning inside her. And the small, leaden ball of fear at its core.

'What's this supposed to mean?' she said.

'Och. I don't know,' Jonno said, quietly. 'That depends.'

'On what?'

Her fingers had balled themselves around the envelope, and her nails were making small, crescent-shaped tears in the paper.

'We need your help, Inspector,' Jonno said. 'We seem to have lost track of a good friend of ours, and we're worried about him.'

Kris frowned, confused.

'What are you on about, Wallace?'

'Al,' Jonno said. 'You know where he is.' He looked her up and down. Studying her. 'And you're going to tell us,' he finished.

The flames licking at Kris' belly exploded into a blaze.

'That's it. I'm calling the station,' she said. 'Don't move. You're under arrest on suspicion of extortion and participation in an OCG. You don't have to say anything, but anything you do say may be noted in evidence.'

She produced the handcuffs from the waistband of her slacks, and reached into her handbag for her phone so she'd call it in. But her self-control had all but deserted her. Her trembling hands couldn't find the blasted thing amidst the assorted detritus she carried around in there.

'I'd think long and hard about it if I were you, Inspector,' Jonno said, unfazed.

'You people must have lost your minds,' she spat. 'It's the only reasonable explanation for... this.'

She took two steps forward, her eyes blazing. Despite being twice her size, Jonno took an involuntary step back.

'How dare you?' she said, her voice a barely contained whisper. 'How fucking dare you show up on my doorstep and threaten my family.'

'Inspector-'

'No. No. No. No. No. You listen to me, you good-for-nothing oaf,' she said. 'You don't get to threaten my family. Are we clear? Don't you even dare think about going anywhere near them. Or I'll have so many uniforms crawling up your arse your blood will turn blue. Do you understand?'

Jonno returned her gaze, but said nothing. A single tear had collected in the corner of her left eye, but it didn't spill over.

'I said, do you understand?'

'Have it your way, Inspector,' Jonno said. 'But I'd give this some more thought if I were you. Don't say I didn't warn you.'

Kris took another step forward, brandishing the handcuffs.

Jonno laughed.

'Enough with the charade, Inspector,' Jonno said. 'We both know you don't stand a chance against me on your own.'

Kris hesitated. She thought she could take him in a fair fight. But not if he was armed.

'Al, Inspector,' Jonno continued dully. 'Give us Al and we won't need to discuss this again.'

'Don't you ever come here again. Ever.'

Kris heard herself repeating that last word over and over, until it got completely garbled and lost all meaning. But Jonno was already a shadow disappearing into the night.

'Fuck,' Kris muttered under her breath. 'Fuck. Fuck. Fuck. Fuck.'

She reached back into her handbag. Her hands were trembling so badly the phone slipped out of them three times before she managed to pull it out, unlock it, and dial the station.

CHAPTER 37

'We're not going anywhere,' Neville repeated for the fifth time.

Kris shot to her feet, her hands planted palms down on the dinner table. Looked down at him. Behind her, the two uniforms who had responded to her call squirmed. Doug observed the scene from his spot at the breakfast bar, bemused. Jason was fed and safely tucked away in his room.

'Are you mad, Nev?' Kris said.

Two mugs of chamomile tea had done nothing to quell her rage. She was white hot. Thrumming. And, just about then, she was barely able to stop herself from unleashing the full force of it on her goddamn pigheaded twat of a husband. She pointed at the envelope, which was lying on the table in an evidence bag, looking somewhat the worse for wear after its meeting with her nails.

'He had photos, Neville,' she said, her voice hitting a painfully high-pitched note. 'Photos. Of you and Jason.' She lowered her voice to a hiss. 'They were following you around. And you didn't. Even. Notice.'

'Och, so now it's my fault, is it?' Neville fired back, crossing his arms violently across his chest.

Something sparked behind his eyes. His own tinder-box of rage.

'I'm sorry. I didn't get the memo that I was supposed to start looking over my shoulder.'

Kris closed her eyes. Breathed deeply. They could keep shouting at each other and get nowhere. Or she could try and de-escalate. Make him see sense.

'Look, Nev,' she said with a pleading look. 'I'm sorry. OK? It sucks. It really does. But this isn't within my control. They're desperate.'

'No shite.'

'Let me finish,' she said. 'It's just temporary, OK? Until we get them.'

'No,' Neville said.

His voice sounded like a door being slammed shut.

'What do you mean, no?' Kris said, fighting to keep her tone even.

'You're not thinking this through, Kris,' he said.

He ran his hands through his hair and rubbed his eyes. They were red-rimmed. Bruised. The eyes of a man at the end of his rope.

'I'm not messing up Jason's routine. He's doing well. You know how he gets in unfamiliar situations.'

'But-'

'You're not the one who has to deal with the fallout,' he said.

It hit her like a slap in the face. And her rage was back.

'Oh, really? We're going to play that card now, are we?'

She stood back from the table and paced angrily to and fro. A caged lion. Ready and willing to pounce but not quite able to do it.

'Look,' Doug butted in, clearing his throat nervously. He moved towards the table quietly, and straightened his tie. 'How about this? Why don't we arrange for a patrol?'

'I'm not going to be followed around, like some bottom of the barrel celebrity.'

'We'll be discreet, OK? We'll send a patrol round to check on you every few hours. Just to make sure everything's good.'

'Nev,' Kris said. 'Be reasonable.'

Neville bit the inside of his cheek. It was a gesture he did subconsciously, whenever he was working through a tricky problem.

'Nev?'

Neville's shoulders sagged.

'I guess we have to, don't we?' he said. 'Good god, Kris. What have you got us into?'

'Look, I'm sure there's nothing to worry about,' Doug said. 'They bluffed. She called it. No OCG is going to go after a police officer's family. They wouldn't dare. We're just doing this out of an abundance of caution.'

Kris said nothing. Logically, she knew Doug had a point. But this was her family, and she couldn't share his optimism. She felt her rage dissipate, and the familiar guilt creeping in.

'So are we agreed?' Doug prodded.

Neville sighed. 'I suppose we are. But we need to have a serious conversation about this. Because we just can't go on the way we are,' he said, giving Kris a stern look.

'Fine,' she said.

But it wasn't fine. It was the opposite of fine.

CHAPTER 38

Breakfast the following morning was an excruciating affair. Deathly silence, punctuated by clattering crockery. The brief glances they gave each other akin to death stares. You could almost see the lasers beaming out of their pupils and cutting into each other's flesh.

Stepping out of the hallway after a brief peck on the back of Jason's head and a barely-mumbled 'See you later,' Kris felt herself getting physically lighter. Almost as if she'd been carrying a pile of bricks on her back and an invisible hand was unloading them one by one. The air had been just too full of the things they wanted to but couldn't bring themselves to say. Because, what would happen if they did say them? It might lead them to conclusions they weren't ready to accept. Like the fact their marriage might have reached the point of no return.

The buzz of conversation at the station wiped away her sulkiness. She attacked the tower of files on her desk like her life depended on it. Reading reports. Making notes. Tracking down leads. Thinking hard. Trying to connect the dots that were staring her right in the face but, for some reason she couldn't fathom, refused to form the full picture.

By recent standards it was a fairly uneventful day. A rare shift with minimal interruptions, which meant she got loads done.

Then, at 4pm on the dot, all hell broke loose.

Seven blocks northwest of the station, a bloke in a black, full-face helmet, a bolt-action rifle gripped in his right hand and a crimson sweatband peeking out from beneath his black leather jacket, walked into The Sentinel.

Struan, the pub's hapless landlord, looked up to see who'd come in. Before he could even draw breath, the bloke in the helmet cocked the rifle and picked him off with the ease of somebody shooting clay pigeons at the range.

The bullet hit Struan right between the eyes. The back of his head exploded, showering the bottles behind him with black blood, pinkish-grey brain matter, and strands of wispy hair. Struan staggered backwards, hitting the shelves and causing several bottles to crash. Then his body caught up with events, dropping to the floor with a thud that was barely audible in the aftermath of the rifle's deafening whip-crack.

Mel went next. The rifle took away the whole left side of his face, splattering it all over the booth he was sitting in and putting an end to his trolling of people for their questionable fashion choices. He was followed by two eighteen year old blokes, too busy doing shots and confabulating to realise what was going on.

Jimmy, an OAP who'd frequented The Sentinel since before the Company took over its management, gulped down his fifth whiskey of the afternoon and stood up, paralysed. His bladder and bowels unloaded in his trousers, darkening the beige corduroy. A red flower bloomed on his forest green shirt. Spread. Spread. Spread. His hands flew up to the wound and pressed down, trying to stop the flow. But the move achieved nothing except elicit a shock of pain. He groaned and looked at the blood seeping through his fingers, unbelieving. Then went limp and crumpled in a heap on the floor.

Those deaths alone, in a country where mass shootings are unheard of, would have been enough to raise the already simmering temperature of public opinion to boiling point. But matters got worse when the shooter, together with three others also wearing full-face motorcycle helmets, set fire to the pub. It was an uncharacteristically dry afternoon, so the blaze spread quickly. It snaked its way across the grass behind the building. Climbed up a large tree, eating up the leaves as it went. Then it leaped onto the roof of the Co-Op behind The Sentinel, which was packed with students from the high school across the way.

The attack lasted all of five minutes. But the blaze raged on for half an hour, so high it was clearly visible from the other side of town, before the firefighters made it to the scene. It took a further fifteen minutes to get it under control. By the time the last flames were extinguished, it had claimed fifteen people. Seven died, either from rifle wounds or smoke inhalation. Eight were badly hurt, several of them with life-altering injuries.

At the impromptu press conference they'd set up in the station's largest conference room, the press were crowding in like a pack of wild animals. Baying for blood. Shouting questions on top of questions.

'I assure you this won't go unpunished,' DCC Livermore stressed from behind the lectern.

His voice was steel. His lips pressed into such a thin line

they were barely visible. Next to him, Kris stood straight, hands grasped behind her back. Her face was neutral. Her breathing slow and even. But inside, the familiar mixture of fear, outrage, and adrenaline that fuelled her were bleeding into each other. A Molotov cocktail ready to wreak havoc on everything in its wake.

'Inspector Hendrie, my office,' Livermore barked, as soon as the press conference was over.

He marched up two flights of stairs to his glass-panelled, immaculately tidy office. Sat heavily in his chair.

Kris walked into the office, but didn't sit in one of the two PU leather chairs in front of his desk. Instead, she stood up straight with her hands behind her back and waited for his opening gambit.

'Where are we at, Inspector?' the DCC said. 'What do we have?'

'Not much, unfortunately, sir,' Kris said. 'The fire destroyed most of the evidence.'

The DCC looked at her, his eyes blazing with fury.

'So we have nothing?'

'A woman who was getting into her parked car said she saw three motorcycles leaving the scene. But she couldn't tell us the make or model. Just that one of them had a crimson wristband. We're checking CCTV in the area. We...'

'So, Red Hand?' the DCC interrupted, leaning forward and folding his hands on his desk.

'Seems like it from what we know so far, sir. Aye,' Kris said.

'Inspector Hendrie, I'm going to level with you,' the DCC said.

'Sir?' replied Kris.

Her heart hammered in her chest. She had half an idea she knew what was coming.

He opened his desk drawer and produced a blue microfibre cloth from a brown leather glasses case with his initials — FL, for Frederick Livermore — embossed on it in gold lettering. He unfolded the cloth. Slipped his glasses off. Polished the lenses fastidiously, careful not to touch them with his fingers so they wouldn't smudge.

Kris tensed.

Livermore slipped his glasses back on. Folded the cloth slowly. Deliberately. Then he placed it in the glasses case and put everything back in the drawer.

'Inspector Hendrie, I'm this close to losing my patience,' he said, bringing his thumb and forefinger a bawhair away from each other. 'Are you seriously telling me we have nothing? NOTHING?'

He brought his fist down on the heavy mahogany desk. It made a sound like a shotgun blast. Kris winced. Hated herself for doing it.

'You do realise what a disaster this is, don't you, Inspector?' he whispered, absently massaging his hand.

'Sir, I-'

'Children are dead, Inspector. Children.'

A dot of white spittle flew from his lips. Landed on his blotter. He wiped it away with the back of his hand. It left a dark smudge.

'Do you understand how bad the optics are?' he continued. 'What a complete and utter shitstorm this is? The press are going to savage us.'

'Sir, if I may,' Kris pressed on, raising her voice.

She, Doug, and the team had been working round the clock for two fucking years. Leaving no stone unturned to bring down the gangs. And now weans were dead. And the prick was worried about the press? Trying to point the finger? What had he fucking done, except bask in the glory when they made arrests?

Nothing. That's what.

'We're doing everything we can, Sir. But we still can't get a handle on who's running the Company, or why things have escalated so much and so fast between the Company and the Red Hand.'

'Well, find out, Inspector Hendrie,' Livermore said. 'Find out.' His body was relaxed. But his hands were clasping each other in a death grip. 'I want you to round up every single known OCG member. Question them. Threaten the youngers with long prison sentences if needs be. Stop and search anybody wearing gang attire who so much as looks at you the wrong way. Make their lives impossible. Which is what you should have been doing all along. Do I have to tell you how to do your job?'

Kris bristled. 'Sir, we're doing everything we can with the resources we have. We're short-staffed as it is...'

'Don't give me that,' he hissed. 'No more excuses. Make the case your number one priority. I want somebody arrested for it, yesterday. Are we clear?'

Kris said nothing. She was too busy trying to keep her temper in check.

'Are. We. Clear?' Livermore pressed.

'Crystal,' Kris said between gritted teeth.

'Excellent.'

He opened his laptop and started typing without a word. She'd been dismissed.

'Shall I close the door, sir?' Kris asked.

'Yes, please,' the DCC replied without looking up.

It took all her self-control not to slam it.

CHAPTER 39

'How could you have let this happen?' the CEO screamed. 'Why didn't you stop them!'

Something whizzed past Jonno's ear and smashed against the wall opposite. Chunks of glass — what remained of the CEO's mug — landed on the floor.

Jonno blanched and looked down between his legs. Across from him, Harry and the two other Company elders, whom the CEO had also summoned for this performance, were also turning varying shades of white.

The CEO, on the other hand, was purple going on midnight blue. The usual sunny, welcoming facade was nowhere in sight. In its place was a volcano in mid-eruption. And it was terrifying.

'I want you to round up everyone, and raze The Green Lady to the ground.'

'But-' Harry said.

In three steps, the CEO was within kissing distance of Harry. The backhanded slap came out of nowhere, reverberating around the room.

'Don't you say that,' the CEO said, quivering. 'Don't you. Ever. Say that word in front of me again. Are we clear?'

Harry had gone bright red from the tips of his toes to the roots of what was left of his hair. He nodded, reluctantly.

'Say it!' the CEO screamed.

'Aye!' he muttered.

'Lost your voice, have you?' the CEO said. 'I said, are we clear?'

Another slap echoed around the room.

'Aye! Aye!' Harry said.

He was fighting back tears, an extremely disconcerting sight on a tall, gangly bloke with a criminal record twice as long as his arm. Jonno blinked nervously. The two other elders kept their heads down, hoping not to attract the CEO's attention.

'Excellent,' the CEO said, walking out of Harry's personal space and sitting on the sofa.

Harry visibly wilted.

'Now, what was I saying? You've made me lose my train of thought.'

All four elders shuffled their feet. They weren't sure whether the question was genuine or rhetorical. But they were absolutely sure they didn't dare find out. The CEO reached for the mug of tea. Remembered it had ended its life splattered against the wall, just a handful of minutes previously.

'Right. Yes. The Green Lady.'

The even, welcoming tone was back.

'Spare nobody,' the CEO continued. 'Anyone on the premises is fair game. Clear?'

'Aye,' they chorused.

'Excellent.'

The CEO clapped.

'OK. Off you go. I want it done tonight.'

Harry was about to object. They'd be expecting retaliation. Why not wait? The burning in his cheeks stopped him before he could form the words in his throat. Instead, he followed the other elders' lead and shuffled out towards the door.

'Jonno, not you. Wait,' the CEO said.

Jonno stopped. Walked back towards the sofa. An irrational pang of fear struck him in the chest like a body blow. Memories of being summoned to Father Baker's office 'to discuss your moral fibre' threatened to overwhelm him. He swallowed.

'Aye?' he said nervously.

'Al,' the CEO barked. 'What do you have for me? We need to get it sorted. Make sure the message lands loud and clear. Especially now.'

'Well, erm...'

'In fact,' the CEO said, 'I'd say your future in this organisation depends on it. Do you understand?'

Jonno nodded.

'Good. So. What do you have for me?' asked the CEO.

'I spoke to the Inspector. She said no way.'

'And? Is that it? You're going to accept it and roll over?' the CEO sneered. 'You disappoint me Jonno.'

'What would you have me do?' Jonno said.

'That's easy. She called our bluff. We call hers,' the CEO said.

Another pang of fear ran through Jonno. Stronger this time. A fist to the stomach radiating outwards. If the CEO was asking him to do what he thought he was being asked to do, he'd be crossing a line nobody had crossed in a very long time. You didn't mess with the polis, let alone their families. That was the road to unspeakable misery.

'What's the matter Jonno?' the CEO asked. 'You look like somebody just ran over your dog.'

'Well... no, I,' Jonno stammered.

He wasn't sure what to say. What could he say? It didn't matter, because it wouldn't go down well.

'Come on. Out with it. Do you have something to say?'

'No,' Jonno said.

'Are you sure?'

Was he? No. But it was either hold your peace and do as you're told or face the CEO's wrath.

'Aye,' he sighed, hoping it sounded at least a fraction more convincing than he felt.

'Excellent,' the CEO said. 'Off you go then. Now's the time to do it, while the police are distracted.'

Jonno walked towards the door like a bloke walking to his own execution. Whatever happened from here on out, he doubted it would have a happy ending.

CHAPTER 40

They hit The Green Lady that evening at 8:30pm.

Unlike The Sentinel, it was packed to the rafters at the time of the attack. A Blondie cover band was in the middle of a rough and ready rendition of *Hanging on the Telephone* — the band not quite in time, the singer's high notes like the yowling of a cat in heat. The two hundred odd punters who weren't busy heckling the guitarist, who looked like Wallace Shawn, if Wallace Shawn grew a toothbrush moustache, were either too trollied or too busy pogoing in front of the stage to notice the Company blokes streaming in from the front door and the service entrance, wielding motorcycle chains.

The attack quickly turned into a brawl. Several people were seriously injured. An eighteen year-old woman would need five surgeries to repair the damage to her face and neck. And a sixteen year old bloke who'd just joined the Red Hand and had been proudly showing off his crimson sweatband to anyone and everyone would suffer such terrible head injuries he'd end up in a persistent vegetative state.

Then, somebody — in the confusion, it was impossible to tell whether it was a bloke from the Company or the Red Hand — shot a gun.

The display at the back of the bar caved, sending bottles crashing to the floor. Terrified screams reverberated around the pub. And the punters who had either managed to remain unscathed or were well enough to still be on their feet despite having taken their beatings surged in unison towards the front exit. In the ensuing panic, at least twenty people got trampled underfoot. Five of them died.

The mayhem continued in the car park, and then spilled over into the street. The air was pregnant with the sounds of smashing glass, cursing, and screams of pain. A couple who had made the mistake of walking their pug at that exact moment were beaten to a pulp and their dog killed and thrown in a bin. The public order unit had to step in to bring things back under control.

When it was all over, The Green Lady was still standing, but much the worse for wear. Every single bit of glass in the building — bottles, glasses, windowpanes, even the salt and pepper shakers — had been smashed to smithereens. The facade was riddled with bullet holes. Someone had even broken the plumbing, flooding the bogs with a mixture of water and human shite. If public opinion had reached boiling point after the attack on The Sentinel and the damage it had wreaked to the Co-Op and the poor weans who had been inside at the time, it was now molten lava, flowing freely down the streets and burning everything in its wake to cinders. It was all anyone would talk about — at the office, at the pub, in the shops, out in the streets...

Kris' shift became a double, then a triple. She ignored the increasingly frantic texts and calls from Neville, focusing on the work at hand and trying to steer well clear of DCC Livermore, who seemed to have turned a permanent shade of puce.

When she did leave the station, at Doug's insistence, she'd been awake for a full twenty-four hours, in which she'd existed solely on Wotsits and plastic-flavoured instant coffee. Her eyes, bloodshot from the strain of the computer, squinted in the weak morning sunlight. Her right ear burned from all the phone calls. And her body felt as if it would never recover, regardless of how many hours of sleep she managed to get in.

She inserted the key into her front door with a hand that was still trembling slightly from the overdose of caffeine and adrenaline. Her muscles tensed in anticipation of what Neville would say about her disappearing act. But the exhaustion won over and pushed the tension into the background.

'Nev?' she said, pitching her voice so he could hear her even if he was upstairs getting Jason ready for school. 'Jase?'

No answer.

She hung her handbag on one of the wooden pegs lined up next to the front door, and walked into the living room. Toys were lined up next to each other in single files on the carpet. The TV was on standby, the remote strewn among the cushions. The throw was rumpled. Neville's red mug was on the coffee table, empty except for a dark beige film of tea on the bottom.

A flicker of unease licked the base of her stomach. This was uncharacteristically messy. Neville always cleared up and re-arranged the sofa before going to bed. Why hadn't he? Had Jason had an episode?

'Nev? Jase?' she called out.

She cocked her ear and listened intently. Still no answer. Other than the chunky ticks of the grandfather clock — a wedding present from Neville's great grandma, who'd died at the venerable age of 102 and five months — the room was quiet. And so was the house. Too quiet.

She went into the kitchen.

A pot of water was on the stove, ready for boiling. And, on the counter, there were chopped onions, crushed garlic, diced carrots, and a bowl of weighed-out penne.

Kris looked around. A faint alarm bell was ringing at the back of her brain. But she forced herself to stay calm. Perhaps he'd realised they were out of oil or butter and popped out to restock. But the ingredients on the counter were obviously dinner. Wouldn't he have come back, cooked, and cleaned up by now?

Of course he would have. They'd have had dinner at around 7pm. It was eight in the morning.

'Nev!' she called. 'Jase!'

In spite of her efforts to stay calm, her voice had taken on a faint hysterical edge. She looked around for her phone, her exhaustion forgotten. Every sense on high alert. She remembered she'd left it in her handbag. She walked back to the hallway, resisting the urge to break into a run. No, this was nothing. She'd feel incredibly stupid once Neville explained what had happened.

Of course she would.

The screen lit up, revealing several text and missed call notifications. All from Neville. She swiped up. Pressed on one of the text notifications. The message made her legs go weak and watery, and she collapsed into a sitting position on the stairs.

She read it again. Then again. And one more time. Not to make absolutely sure she was reading the message right. But in the hope the letters would move. Form a completely different message.

No. It couldn't be. It wasn't fucking possible. They wouldn't dare. Would they?

Anger and guilt washed over her in alternating waves. Hot and cold. She shivered. Shook her head from side to side. Blew out her cheeks. Looked back at her phone.

'We have your hubby and the wean,' the message read.

The words jumped off the screen. Punched her in the solar plexus. Sucked the air out of her lungs.

'If you want to see them again, you'll tell us what we want to know.'

CHAPTER 41

Kris stared at the message. At some point around the fourth time she'd read it, her body had frozen and her mind had gone blank. The letters were meaningless black squiggles on a white background.

A finger that didn't seem to belong to her pressed the green phone icon. She navigated to her recents. Six missed calls from Neville, starting at 6:39 the previous evening. The last one was at 2am. A call she'd ignored because she'd been too busy running a meeting about the violence at The Green Lady in the incident room. All the top brass had come in, ostensibly to observe, but really to make their displeasure known and pile on the pressure.

She looked up. And, as if the universe were conspiring to bury her under the weight of her guilt, her eyes landed on the array of framed family photos on the console table beneath the pegs in the hallway.

She and Neville on their wedding day, under a rain of confetti. Their smiles so wide every single muscle in their face seemed to be involved. Their eyes twinkling. Their teeth impossibly white.

Her in a hospital gown, looking absolutely knackered but happy, cradling baby Jason in her arms. How old had he been when Neville had taken that? Two hours? Three? She remembered feeling like her heart could burst out of her chest at any second. Little did she know she and Neville had a long and winding journey ahead of them before they eventually got an official diagnosis. PDD. Pervasive Developmental Disorder. The worry, stress, and uncertainty had thrown her marriage into the eye of a category five storm.

She could see them now, in her mind's eye. Jason with his knees touching his chin. His arms curled protectively around himself. Rocking backwards and forwards and humming to himself.

Somebody — probably that oaf Jonno Wallace. That vile bastard — pointing a gun at Neville, threatening to shoot if Jason didn't stop. Neville trying to placate Wallace and calm Jason down. It was enough to break her from her paralysis. Light a fire in her belly.

She pressed the number. Shot up to her feet. Paced frantically around the hallway as the phone rang.

One ring.

Two rings.

Three. Four. Five.

'Answer the bloody call, you evil bastard,' she muttered under her breath.

Ten rings.

Eleven.

Twelve.

Thirteen.

Her heart sank.

What would she do if nobody answered? How would she find them? Where would she even begin? Did any of the neighbours have CCTV? Had they even sent a patrol around like Doug had suggested?

In the aftermath of the attacks on The Sentinel and The Green Lady it had fallen through the cracks. Even she'd forgotten.

Twenty-one rings.

Twenty-two.

She willed somebody to pick up.

'ANSWER!'

Twenty-five.

Twenty-six.

'Inspector Hendrie.'

The voice was cheerful. Like the call was a catchup between two good mates who'd been too busy to chat for a while.

'Cut the shite, Wallace,' she barked. 'What've you done with my family? If you even touch a hair on their heads, I.... I...'

She couldn't finish. Her windpipe had shut off. It was suddenly very hard to breathe.

'Och, they're fine,' Jonno said. 'Lovely wean you have, Inspector. Though a bit... troubled. He got somewhat over-excited, but then we put the telly on. That seems to have done the job. For now.'

She held the phone in a death-grip.

'Don't you even think about laying a finger on them, Wallace,' she croaked, winded from the panic that seemed to have engulfed her.

'Look Inspector,' Jonno said. 'I've no interest in harming your family. You know what I want. What my boss wants. Al's location. Give me it and we'll all live happily ever after.'

He was calm. Infuriatingly reasonable. Like he was

discussing the sale of a box of second-hand clothes, not terms for the release of two human beings. Her human beings. Her family.

Her eyes locked on another one of the framed photos on the console table. Her, Neville, and Jason at the adventure park. Blair Drummond. They were in the car with the windows up. A lion was standing guard over a goat carcass in the background. Jason was looking down. She and Neville were smiling. But, unlike the smiles in their wedding photo, these weren't touching their eyes.

She looked away. Pinched the bridge of her nose with her thumb and forefinger. Took a deep breath, feeling the effects of every single hour she'd been awake. It was impossible to think straight.

'I've already told you what you're asking me to do isn't possible,' she said. 'This won't end well for you. Kidnapping civilians. A police officer's family. Why don't you give your boss up? We can take care of you like we took care of your mate Al.'

She heard a faint click on the other end of the line. It made her frantic. Had he hung up? No. It was hesitation, wasn't it? He was mulling this over.

'You have two days, Inspector,' he growled, cutting through the silence like a butcher's knife. 'If I were you, I'd find a way and make it happen.'

'Wait. Wallace!' she shouted.

Her voice sounded desperate to her. And that increased her panic. She needed every bit of leverage she could get. She couldn't afford to show weakness.

'Where are they? Let me speak to them. Make sure they're safe.'

'Two days,' Jonno repeated.

The line went dead.

The scream seemed to come from the very bowels of her being. It seared her throat and made her ears ring.

She threw her phone like a rugby ball, and it slammed into the wall across the room, leaving a dent in the plaster board. Then she put her hands, palms down, on the console table, and pushed the frames and the vase off it and onto the floor. The vase smashed into six pieces.

She doubled over. Squatted down.

And her chest began heaving with gasping sobs.

CHAPTER 42

'What do you mean sit this out?' Kris snapped. 'How could you possibly expect me to do that?'

She was pacing back and forth around her living room like a raging bull, eyes bloodshot, hair standing up in frizzed-up clumps. Doug eyed her warily, perched on the edge of the sofa. He'd been trying to talk her down for the past hour. But instead of soothing her, he'd only managed to rile her up even more than she'd already been when he'd turned up at her doorstep, still in the rumpled suit he'd been wearing at work the previous evening.

'We'll find them, Kris,' he said emphatically, his face earnest. 'You know we take care of our own.'

She laughed bitterly.

'Fat lot of good that has done us so far. Where was the patrol we were promised?'

'That's not fair, Kris,' Doug said. 'You know exactly what's been going on over the past twenty-four hours. You were there. It's not like we've been twiddling our thumbs.'

Her pacing increased. It was a wonder she hadn't worn out the carpet.

Doug's shoulders sagged. 'Look. I get it, Kris. You feel helpless and you want to do something. But the best thing you can do right now — the only thing you can do — is stay put and let us do our jobs.'

'Stay put?' she spat.

She walked towards him. Looked down at him, her hands gripping her hips to stop them from shaking.

'On what planet is that a reasonable request? How could you even think to ask?'

'You're too close to this, Kris. You can't be involved.'

'I'm already involved!' she cried. 'I couldn't be more involved if I tried!'

Doug got up. Placed a gentle hand on her shoulder. She flinched, but didn't remove it.

'All we need to do is pretend we're going to give Edwards up. Set up an ambush,' she continued.

She'd already floated this idea, and he'd already shot it down. But the more she thought about it, the deeper it took root in her mind. Solidifying as the only feasible next step.

'You're not thinking straight, Kris,' Doug said. 'There's no way the brass would go for it. How would it look if word got out we'd promised an OCG member we'd divulge the location of the witness that put his big boss away? Even if it's just a ruse? Nobody would ever cooperate with us again.'

'So that's it, eh?' Kris said, her eyes welling with hurt. 'I take one for the team?'

Doug sighed in exasperation. 'For Christ's sake. Listen to yourself,' he snapped. He was on the verge of shouting, and he couldn't stop himself. 'Do you realise how it sounds?'

'I'll tell him I'll be alone!' she shot back.

Spittle flew. Some of it landed on Doug, but he stood his ground.

'Use me as bait!' she continued. 'I'll call Wallace up. Tell him I know where Edwards is and that I'll give him the location if he lets my family go. Then you step in and surround him. He won't know what hit him.'

'He'll see right through it,' Doug said.

'Not if I promise to go alone and let him pick the location,' she said.

But it was starting to sound a bit desperate, even to her ears. She was clutching at straws.

Doug spoke slowly. With infuriating calm. 'There's too many ways this could go wrong, Kris, and you know it. Please. Leave it to us. We'll track him down using Neville's phone.'

'That's not good enough, damn it!'

She banged her fist against the wall. The knick-knacks on the sideboard rattled.

'You'll need a warrant. Techs. It'll take ages!'

'We'll get it fast-tracked. You're a police officer,' Doug said.

He was unmoving. There was no persuading him.

'Look. As I said. I understand it's difficult, but you know the drill,' he said. 'Please sit tight and let us get on with it.'

Kris sank into an armchair. There was nothing more she could say. And if they kept going round in circles, rehashing the same arguments over and over, that was time they weren't out there, looking for Neville and Jason.

'We'll move heaven and earth to find them,' Doug stressed. 'I promise you.'

'Fine,' Kris mumbled.

But she wasn't about to sit around at home like the damsel in distress in some cut-rate police procedural. No fucking way.

Before Doug even got to his car, she was already hatching a plan.

CHAPTER 43

'That'll be ten fifty, please' Sunny said, ringing up the sale.

Al double-clicked the home button on his phone, waited for Face ID to authenticate him, and tapped it against the machine. It beeped. Sunny nodded.

'Ta, bud,' he said, picking up his groceries.

He'd just bought some basics for a late breakfast. A loaf of white bread, butter, ham slices, a tin of coffee, a dozen eggs. And Edam cheese. P's favourite.

Sunny, unfailingly laconic, nodded imperceptibly to confirm the payment had gone through. Then he looked at the line and called 'Next please!'

The customer who was queuing behind him — a stout, older woman with a shock of white hair that made her look like Albert Einstein if he hadn't worn a moustache — walked to the till, put her overflowing basket on the counter, and began asking after Sunny's wife and five children. Sunny replied in monosyllables as he painstakingly scanned her shopping, taking his time over each item. There was no rush here. No pressure to scan X number of items per minute, like they did at the Lidl two towns over. And Sunny seemed to make it a point to hammer this home to every customer he served.

Al walked off. P would probably still be asleep after yesterday's gruelling shift. But he'd fallen out of bed at 10am. That's what years of keeping odd hours did to you. It messed with your rhythm for good.

No mind. He'd make a couple of ham and cheese toasties, brew a mug of coffee, and park himself on the sofa with a book until P got up. Or maybe he'd go back to bed, curl up next to her. Or wake her up with his best moves.

That last thought put a spring in his step. He hurried towards the store's exit, keen to get back to the flat as soon as possible. But he spied something with the corner of his eye just as he was about to cross the threshold.

He froze. Looked back.

At the till, Sunny was still ringing up the woman's shopping. Two other customers were waiting in the queue, chatting in hushed tones.

He turned back around.

He almost hadn't recognised the building on the slightly blurry newsprint. Then his eyes had landed on the big, bold, all-capitals headline underneath the picture.

BRAWL AT NOTORIOUS PUB LIKELY RETALI-ATION FOR GANG-RELATED ARSON, POLICE SAY

He stepped closer. Read it again. Picked up a newspaper with a hand that felt leaden.

'*A violent brawl at The Green Lady, a pub in east Strath-burgh, that caused thousands of pounds in damages and left several people seriously injured, including a sixteen year-old boy in critical condition, was likely retaliation for the mass shooting and arson at The Sentinel, this newspaper can reveal.*

'*A reliable source within the Strathburgh police force, speaking on condition of anonymity, told us that the gang task force has strong evidence linking the incident, which happened two nights ago, at 8:30pm, to the organised criminal gang known as The Company. The Green Lady is notorious for being associated with the Red Hand, another local organised crime gang.*

Continued on page 3.'

Al stole a glance at the till. Sunny had just about finished serving the Einstein lookalike, and she was placing her shopping in a yellow bag for life. Behind her, the next in line was waiting his turn. Three other people had joined the queue. But the store seemed quiet, otherwise, considering it was a Sunday morning.

He moved into the aisle, where he couldn't be seen from the till. Then he placed his shopping bag on the floor and, with trepidation, flipped to page three.

'*The brawl is the latest in what our source has described as* "a serious and continuing escalation in the hostilities between the two rival organised crime gangs." *Barely twenty-four hours earlier, The Sentinel, notorious for being a Company hangout, was the scene of a mass shooting that left five people dead. In scenes that wouldn't have been out of place in a Hollywood blockbuster, the infamous pub was then burned to the ground alongside a local Co-Op branch, leaving two more people dead and eight seriously injured, including five students from Craigmoray High School. The incident has provoked widespread outrage and condemnation, with grassroots organisations stepping up their calls for the police to take more drastic action.*

'*Gemma Quigley-Garvey, spokesperson for West Strathburgh Residents against Organised Crime, said:* "*West Strathburgh used to be a safe place, where people could enjoy*

*walks in our beautiful parks without being bothered and chil-
dren played without parents having to worry about whether
they'd be back home safe and sound. It's absolutely
disgraceful that the situation has been allowed to come to this.
It's like the authorities have given up."*

*'When we reached out to the Strathburgh police for
comment, they issued the following statement:*

*"'Organised crime has no place in our local communities,
and the Gang Task Force have been working tirelessly to end
this scourge. Just six months ago, we scored a significant win,
with a twenty-five-year prison sentence for Franco Guthrie, a
prominent figure and leader of the Company. The residents
of Strathburgh can rest assured we'll be doubling down and
ramping up our efforts to bring these criminals to justice and
make Strathburgh safer..."*

The rest of the article rehashed information Al knew all
too well. The long-standing rivalry between the Company
and the Red Hand. The arrest and trial of Franco Guthrie.
And how this had precipitated a war which was now
getting progressively more dangerous and out of hand.

Al put the newspaper back on the newsstand, picked up
his shopping, and strode out onto the bustling high street.
The mild breeze ruffled his hair, but did little to quell his
unease. Because he was in witness protection and had given
evidence privately, his name had never been made public.
Still, it was unnerving, reading about the former high-
ranking gang member whose testimony had brought down
the Chairman in the papers, knowing that they were talking
about him.

It wasn't all bad news, though, he supposed. If the
Company and the Red Hand were still embroiled in an all-
out conflict, whoever had taken over the team would have
his hands full. That was good. With all the Company's

resources and attention devoted to winning the war, there'd be no time to look for and punish the likes of him. He wouldn't be a priority.

The thought made him feel slightly better. He might be safe after all. If he was lucky, the Company and the Red Hand might even wipe each other out. It wouldn't do to let his guard down completely. Not yet. But maybe there was light at the end of the tunnel. Perhaps he could stop looking over his shoulder so much. Get more enjoyment out of the life he was making for himself.

He looked up at the sky. There was grey on the horizon. But, for now, it was clear. Bright blue and cloudless. He'd suggest going for a picnic. When you lived in a place where the weather was so bloody vindictive, you had to make the most of it while it behaved.

The walk to his flat took twenty minutes. When he let himself in, he found P in the living room, staring out of the window with a steaming mug between her hands and one leg tucked under her.

'Hey, you,' she said, turning to greet him.

'Hey,' he said, taking her in.

She was wearing one of his t-shirts and nothing else, her curls tied back in a loose ponytail. His heart fluttered in his chest. But, this time, it wasn't organised criminal gangs, arson, and existential dread that were on his mind.

'Did you sleep well?' he asked, walking towards her, bending down, and giving her a peck on the cheek.

'Aye, as well as I could with a tractor going at it full throttle next to me,' she said, grinning.

'What's that supposed to mean?' Al said in mock outrage. 'You dare accuse me of snoring?'

'No,' she deadpanned. 'I'd never. What's snoring?'

'The more I get to know you, the funnier you get,' Al told her.

She giggled. 'What've you got there?' she said, nodding at the bag.

'Breakfast,' Al replied.

'Och, that sounds nice.'

'I thought we could have some toast and then maybe we could go somewhere? It's pretty nice out. Seems a shame to waste the morning indoors.'

'Aye, sure. There's this spot near the lake I've been meaning to show you,' P said.

'Och, sounds interesting,' Al said. 'Let me brush my teeth and have a quick shower. Then I'll rustle up some scran and you can tell me all about it.'

'Ah, so this smell's your breath, not the drains,' P said.

'Och, admit it. You love morning breath,' Al replied.

He leaned towards her and pretended to blow all over her face. She giggled and slapped him on the shoulder. He dropped the shopping on the sofa, bent down, then put his arms around her waist and buried his face in her neck, making exaggerated growling noises. She squealed.

'Get off me you dirty bastard,' she said.

'Fine, fine,' he said.

He planted a kiss on her forehead, stood back up and winked.

'I'll be right back,' he said. 'Don't get yourself in any trouble while I'm away.'

Aye, he thought to himself as he put his toothbrush back into the cup on the sink, slipped his clothes off, and stepped into the shower. Maybe there was nothing to worry about.

Maybe it was all going to work out for him, after all.

Chapter 44

'Hello, Boaby,' the CEO said. 'It's been a while, hasn't it?'

The contempt was barely disguised, even on the phone.

Kiernan leaned back in his chair and put his feet up on the desk, the black leather of his shoes glistening in the afternoon sunlight. The chair was an Arne Jacobsen, originally designed for Oxford professors, made with premium walnut leather and chrome steel. The desk was an authentic 19th century solid oak leather top. Other than a thin sheaf of papers, neatly stacked at the top right corner, and a brass pen holder with a lone white gold Waterman fountain pen, the desk was completely bare.

He shifted his burner from his right ear to his left.

'So it's you,' he spat. 'You're the CEO. Unbelievable.'

'Does it matter who it is?' the CEO replied. 'This is business, isn't it?'

Kiernan swivelled around in his chair, stared outside at the gothic bell tower of St Kentigern's cathedral, which stood out like a big, exhaust-blackened talon in the heart of

Strathburgh's historic old town. On the other side of the line, the CEO picked up a mug of steaming tea, took a small sip, emitting a slurping sound, and waited.

'What does Franco think about this...?' Kiernan said. He waved his hand about, searching for the right word. 'This?' he finished lamely.

He shifted in his chair. His sciatica was acting up. He was doing too much sitting in offices these days and it was getting on his tits.

'Franco's no longer in the picture,' the CEO said. 'As you well know.'

'Right,' Kiernan sneered. 'You've finally got what you've always wanted, haven't you?'

The conversation stalled. The line went silent except for the rhythmic whistling of Kiernan's outbreaths.

'What do you want? Why are you calling?' Kiernan said when he could no longer take it.

'I think you know exactly why I'm calling.'

'If you don't stop speaking in riddles, I'm going to end the call,' Kiernan said.

There was more tea-slurping. Kiernan's lips drew back in distaste.

'I'd like to propose a truce,' the CEO said.

'A truce,' Kiernan repeated.

It was supposed to be a question, but it came out flat. A statement. He barked laughter.

'And why on earth would I agree to that? You're fed up, so we're all supposed to do as you say? Is that it?' he said. 'I see you haven't changed one bit.'

'Neither have you,' the CEO fired back.

Kiernan sniffed. It blocked his nostril and made the whistling worse. Fuck's sake. Bloody allergies. He dug into the front pocket of his trousers for a packet of tissues. Savagely wiped his nose.

'Enlighten me,' he said when he was done. 'Why should I agree to this... truce?'

'Because you and I are more alike than you care to admit, Boaby,' the CEO said.

The voice had settled into its usual calm, welcoming tone. But it had a predatory undercurrent.

'Is that so?' Kiernan said.

'Yes,' the CEO continued. 'We both understand that what we do is a business. And this thing that's going on between our organisations at the moment... It's not very conducive to business, is it?'

Kiernan stood up, shook his legs, walked to the huge wall-to-ceiling triple-glazed window that took up the whole south-facing side of his office. He looked outside, where a mass of Lilliputians were bustling to wherever it was they were going. He couldn't say he disagreed with what the CEO had just told him. Leaving aside that this war was diverting resources away from the Red Hand's core purpose — making money — it was bringing too much heat. Organised crime was firmly on the agenda. On social media. In the newspapers. On the telly. In the conversations average Joes had while drinking away their miserable existences.

No. It wasn't conducive to business at all.

'So what kind of truce are you proposing?' Kiernan said noncommittally.

'Nothing you wouldn't agree to in advance,' the CEO said.

The reply was perhaps a tad too eager. But Kiernan hadn't noticed. He was too busy eyeing a fire red 1956

Porsche 550 Spyder that was cruising down St Kentigern street.

'OK?' Kiernan prodded.

'How does this sound?' the CEO said. There was more tea-slurping, followed by gentle throat-clearing. 'I'll get my accountant to draw up some paperwork. Something that makes it mutually beneficial for us to keep the peace. The accountant will send it to you to look over, and, assuming you're amenable, we'll make it official.'

Kiernan scoffed.

'It's the sensible thing to do, and you know it,' the CEO continued. 'We can do it somewhere neutral. I have just the place in mind.'

'Of course you do,' Kiernan said.

He walked at a leisurely pace towards the kentia palm next to his desk. Gently rubbed a speck of dust off one of its bright green leaves with the pad of his index finger.

'I was going to suggest that we meet alone. Just me, you, and the accountant. But your people are welcome to inspect the place beforehand. Confirm it's OK to go ahead. Does that sound reasonable to you?'

Kiernan sat back in his office chair. Glanced at his Rolex. He was due his weekly massage in fifteen minutes. Time to end this thing. 'Send over the paperwork,' he said. 'But no promises.'

'Well, think about it,' the CEO said. 'That's all I ask.'

CHAPTER 45

Tick tock. Tick tock. Tick. Fucking. Tock.

Kris sat at the dinner table, hunched over her police laptop, still in the same clothes she'd been in when she'd reached home to discover they'd taken Neville and Jason. Her left leg jumped up and down like it was made of springs. She'd gnawed down her nails to the quick. And, with the exception of two hours here and there, when her body had literally collapsed with exhaustion, she hadn't slept a wink.

She grabbed the mug of triple-strength coffee and gulped some down. It had gone cold, and the taste made her grimace. 3pm, said the clock at the top right of the laptop screen. When had her two-day deadline started running? When she'd spoken to Jonno, or when the bastard had taken Neville and Jason? Did it matter? It was all academic now, wasn't it? Regardless of the starting point, she was running out of time.

With a superhuman effort, she tore her eyes away from the clock and looked at the CCTV video the inspector from Kinross, Fiona McEwan, had sent her what felt like a lifetime ago. She set the playback to 1.5X speed and watched it again as the minutes ticked inexorably by. Cars sped into the service area. People bustled in and out of the Moto. Cars sped out of their parking spots, some stopping by the petrol station to fill up on overpriced fuel. And Allan motherfucking Edwards was nowhere to be seen. He might as well have been a ghost.

'Where are you, Edwards?' Kris kept muttering to herself over and over. 'Where the fuck are you hiding?'

The colours on the screen blurred into each other. The room spun. She was running on the dregs of fumes. This wouldn't be sustainable for much longer. If she didn't catch a bloody break right away, she would have to rest all her hopes on the police. And the police were having rotten luck. When she'd spoken to Doug an hour earlier, he didn't have any news for her. They'd made zero progress. As expected.

She 10Xed the playback speed. Started from 1pm and ran it through a full hour to 2pm. The victim had put the time of the attack at around 1:30pm. So, assuming he'd got it right, Al couldn't have gone into the bog any earlier than 1:25pm, or he'd have lost the element of surprise. But, despite the fact that the car park was half empty, she couldn't seem to spot him. It was like a game of Where's Wally with the difficulty level dialled up to eleven.

'Show yourself, you bastard!'

She rubbed her red eyes. Her phone pinged, and she snatched it. Jumped to her feet. A bundle of nerves. There was a text notification. From Neville.

'Time's running out, Inspector.'

And a photo.

Jason. Staring in the distance, possibly at a TV. The photo was carefully angled, so the background gave nothing away. A sliver of grey sofa fabric. That was all.

Her heart felt like a giant had just grabbed it in his ham-sized fist and squashed it to a pulp. How could she ever have shut herself off? Thrown herself into her work instead of spending time with her family? In the grand scheme of things, it didn't fucking matter one single bit, did it? What had she got out of it, except pain and heartache?

'Gahhhh!' she screamed, banging her fists on the table and making the laptop rattle.

She slapped herself with her open palms. One side. Then the other. Again and again.

Sat back down.

Her eyes burned, but she kept them open. A man in a suit walked towards his fire red Insignia, coffee in hand. Sped off. Two middle aged men stopped by a blue Mokka. Embraced tenderly. Got into the car. A harried-looking woman strong-armed two weans into their car seats.

'Where are you?!'

She ground her teeth. Reached for the mug without thinking. Lifted it to her lips. It slipped and fell on the table.

'Shite! Fuck!'

She shot up from her chair, reached for the kitchen roll. Most of what was left in the mug had spilled on the table. But some of it had landed on the laptop's keyboard. She mopped it up before it could seep in between the keys and damage the circuitry. The last thing she needed was her laptop on the blink. She placed the sopping wet mass of kitchen roll on the table. Stopped in her tracks.

The hair was longer. Styled. The beard was new. But she recognised the walk. It was more accurate to call it a strut. He was at the top left of her screen. Chest thrust out. The timestamp said 1:35pm. He'd probably just beat the shite out of the victim and was feeling pleased with himself. Prick.

Now that she'd spotted him, he was impossible to miss. She watched, transfixed, standing hunched over the table, as he walked towards a silver Ford Focus that was parked in front of the entrance to the Moto. Stopped outside the passenger door. Idly chatting to somebody inside the car? His handler? Then climbed inside. She rewound. Saw him duck-walk back where he'd come from. Then replayed the video forward. Saw him make a beeline to the car.

How had she not bloody seen him?

All those hours, and he'd been right there the whole time.

She sped it up and rewatched it. Slowed it as the car eased out of its parking spot. Paused it.

Where was the bloody pen?

She tossed aside wet kitchen roll and assorted bric-a-brac she'd accumulated while she obsessively watched the video — a half-eaten piece of toast, a cup of Bombay Bad Boy-flavoured Pot Noodle, several plastic wrappers that had contained chocolate-covered rice cakes. Opened her note-book to a random blank page. Jotted down the number plate.

'There you are,' she said. 'I've got you, you bastard.'

She navigated to the ANPR database, keyed in her credentials, then entered the plate number. She homed in on Kinross services, followed it from there.

The sightings stopped somewhere around the Cairn-gorms. But that didn't matter, did it? She didn't need the exact location. Just enough to fool Jonno for long enough to release Neville and Jason. She'd worry about what would happen next when it actually happened.

She snatched the phone. Wiped the coffee off the screen on her blouse. Dialled Neville. The phone rang. She drummed her fingers against her thighs and paced while she waited for Jonno to pick up.

The call rang out.

'God, no. Please,' she whispered.

She was barely functioning as it was. She wouldn't be able to hold it together much longer.

She redialled.

'Answer the bloody phone, you oaf,' she hissed. 'Come on.'

She waited. Eyes closed. She'd crossed her fingers without realising it.

When he picked up, she felt her whole body relax.

'Inspector Hendrie,' Jonno growled.

He sounded breathless.

'I was starting to worry you wouldn't come round.'

'Are they OK?' Kris said. 'Let me speak to Neville.'

'Do you have what we asked for?' Jonno said, pointedly ignoring what she'd just said.

'Let me speak to them, Wallace!' Kris said.

'You will. When you give us what we want,' Jonno repeated.

'OK! OK! I think I know where he is!' she said, fighting not to cry.

'You think? Or you know?'

'I know! OK?' she said.

She let out a shuddering breath.

'Now for fuck's sake. Let them go. Let them go and I'll take you to him.'

'Right,' Jonno said. He chuckled thickly. 'Now, now,

Inspector Hendrie. I expected better from you. You must think I was born yesterday.'

'I'm serious, Wallace. Do you think I'd gamble with my family?' she said.

Silence.

Desperation pricked her heart and spread through her veins. She was dangerously close to being completely overwhelmed. The exhaustion. The fear. The guilt. So much guilt. This had to work. It better, because the alternative didn't bear thinking about.

'Do you?' she prodded.

'I don't know, Inspector. Would you?'

She laughed. A sound like a crazed loon. 'Are you for real? Of course I wouldn't! Look. Tell me where we can meet. Anywhere. Take your pick and I'll be there.'

She listened to the sound of Jonno's heavy breathing while he considered his options. 'You come alone. No polis. Understood?'

She closed her eyes, sagged against the wall.

'Of course not. You can check beforehand,' she said. 'Then, when you confirm I'm alone, you'll let them go and I'll tell you where to find him. Do we have a deal?'

More silence. It was enough to make her want to tear her hair out.

She let herself slide down into a squat. Doubled over. Rubbed her forehead with the palm of her free hand.

'Do we have a deal?' she whispered.

The silence stretched out. She could almost hear the cogs turning in Jonno's brain.

'You better be alone, Inspector,' Jonno warned.

She shook her fist in triumph.

'I get a whiff on anything funny, I blow your little family's brains out. First the wean, so you both can watch. Then your darling hubby. Are we clear?'

She felt hatred engulf her like a heavy black cloak.

'You have my word I'll be alone,' she said.

Her throat clicked.

'I'll text you the location. Be there in an hour.'

CHAPTER 46

K ris splashed her face with ice-cold water, held onto the sink with both hands, and looked in the mirror.

Over the previous two days, she'd aged noticeably. Was that even possible? Her eyes were so red from lack of sleep and the long hours she'd spent in front of her laptop that they looked puffy and inflamed. The worry lines on her forehead had etched themselves deeper into her skin, like canyons. Several strands of hair had turned silver.

She sighed and stepped out of the bathroom. Walked to the kitchen. Poured more coffee into her travel mug, gulped it down and refilled it. Not that she needed it. She was wide awake and wired taut, her hands trembling so badly most of the liquid ended up on the counter.

She grabbed a chef's knife from the block and slipped it in her handbag. Considered briefly.

No. No, it wouldn't do. She needed the knife to be handy, so she could whip it out as soon as the opportunity arose. She rushed up to the bedroom. Secured it to the small of her back with a belt, tightening it as far as she could take it, feeling the leather bite into the delicate skin above her hips. She walked in front of the mirror and turned. Was the bulge noticeable? Barely. But it didn't matter. It's not like she was going to turn her back on that oaf unless he was completely incapacitated.

She raced down the stairs. Grabbed the mug and her handbag. Briefly, ever so briefly, she considered the insanity of what she was about to do. Meeting an OCG member for whom violence came as naturally as breathing. Alone. It was top five — no, probably top three — stupidest things she'd ever done. Shite. Stealing Destiny's Child CDs from Woolworths didn't come close to this. It wasn't even in the same league.

But what else was she supposed to do? Stand still? Do nothing? Hope for the best?

No. She'd done nothing for long enough. It was time to be proactive.

She shut the door. Marched towards her car in the overcast afternoon. Pulled up the location Jonno had sent her on the Maps app and placed her phone on the centre console. Then she took a deep breath, pulled out of her parking spot, and headed towards the city bypass.

Her phone pinged. She touched the screen with one ragged nail. Doug.

'How are you holding up?'

Not good, Doug. Not good. This better bloody work or things would go from horrible to cataclysmic.

Traffic was still light, but it was thickening. The first few stragglers were leaving their offices. Soon, everybody would be on their way home, and the bypass would be packed. This would be over sooner than that, one way or another. Of that she was sure.

She drove five miles, indicated left, and exited onto a

stretch of B road the locals informally called Strathfiodh Way, after the timber mills. Most of the mills had gone the way of the dodo during the industrial revolution. But in the 17th century, they were thriving. And the section of the Strath that snaked its way to the left of the B road Kris was driving on had transported much of the timber the mills had processed.

Another mile ahead, and the thick vegetation gave way to an expanse of built-up terrain, both on her right and on her left across the Strath. Mostly warehouses. Mostly abandoned. Heavily graffitied. The tip of a rusty mountain peeked out over the horizon. The scrapyard where Jonno had told her to meet.

Kris leaned back into the driver's seat. The chef's knife's blade felt cold against the skin of her back. She gripped the steering wheel, trying to get a hold of herself, making the blue veins and tendons bulge.

She indicated left, turned, slowed down. A large chain link fence loomed in front of her. The road turned to gravel, and she stopped. Maps advised her she'd reached her destination. A weathered wood sign confirmed this, announcing she was about to enter Ruxton's Salvage.

She closed her eyes. Took three shuddering breaths. Her heart was beating so fast she half-expected to see her blouse bulge outwards, like in the Pepé Le Pew cartoons. She made herself stare at a spot on the console. Purged her thoughts. Then visualised how she wanted this to play out. A trick she'd learned early on in her police career to quell the jitters before a big arrest.

She saw Jonno in front of her. Appraising her with a menacing stare. He'd insist on Al's location. But that was her only leverage. She'd talk to him calmly. Get him to release Neville and Jason with promises she'd lead him straight to Al. Then she'd get talking. Stretch it out. Get him to lower his guard. And when she got close enough, she'd stab. Not to kill. There was no way she'd let him get off that easily. Just to disable.

She laughed.

It was a terrible, terrible plan. Hopeless. Suicidal. But what else did she have?

She glanced at her watch. Right on time.

Another deep breath, and she drove through the gate.

CHAPTER 47

J onno parked safely out of sight, between a corrugated metal shed that had once been a storage room but was now empty, and the chain link fence that surrounded the scrapyard. In the back seat, Jason was making a godawful humming sound deep in his throat, and it was driving him up the wall. He thought of Father Baker, pacing the classroom, berating him for coughing — 'Is it whooping cough you have? TB? If it's so bad, how about we quarantine you, Wallace?' — and daring him to do it again. Almost felt the unbearable tickling that would seize his throat as soon as the bastard told him to stop it. The thought riled him up. Lit his guts on fire.

'Jesus fucking Christ, does he have to keep doing that?' he snapped, turning around, his eyes boring into Neville.

He absently rubbed the spot on his neck where the little shite had gouged him. It felt tender. He hoped it wasn't infected.

Neville tried to put on a brave face. But it was impossible. Here was a man who kept himself to himself. Who avoided confrontation as much as he could. He was so far outside his comfort zone he wasn't even in the same galaxy anymore.

'He doesn't do well in unfamiliar situations,' he told Jonno, his voice reasonable. 'This is very stressful for him.'

Jonno sneered. 'Do I look like I give a fuck?' he said. 'Shut him up. Or I will.'

He nodded at the roll of duct tape on the passenger seat. Neville's eyes widened. He turned to Jason, started whispering in low, soothing tones, eyeing Jonno warily as he did so. Jason's humming didn't stop, but it lowered in intensity.

Jonno pulled the gun out of the glove compartment. Checked the chamber. He took out a box of bullets. Loaded the gun, inserting the bullets carefully, one by one. Then he snapped the chamber shut, made sure the safety was on, and placed the gun in the waistband of his jeans. He pocketed the rest of the bullets.

He leaned back, checked the cable ties on Neville and Jason's hands. Nice and tight. Nobody was going to cut themselves free and attack him with a shovel today. Not if he had anything to do with it. He opened the driver's side door and eased himself out.

'Don't go anywhere, eh?' he mocked.

He shut the door, locked the car, and looked around. Beyond the shed, there was an expanse of gravel dominated by a huge heap of rusted metal which dwarfed the crane lying abandoned next to it. To his right, the gravel sloped gently upward until it became a hill. This was the main reason he'd chosen this place, aside from it being deserted and outside the city. From this vantage point, he had unobstructed views of the bypass. If that cow tried any funny business, he'd know straight away.

He climbed up slowly, careful not to slip. Looked

through a pair of binoculars. A car drove his way. Stopped at the scrapyard's entrance. Drove in.

He checked his watch. 4:30pm.

'Very good, Inspector Hendrie,' he muttered. 'Very good.'

Kris stopped in front of scrap mountain and got out of the car. She looked around, unsure what to do next. Waited, her fingers tapping nervously against her thighs. She walked in front of the car. Scanned the area in front of her. Wind gusted, and her suit jacket billowed lazily behind her.

Jonno didn't move. He looked through the binoculars and waited.

One minute.

Two.

Neville's phone buzzed in his pocket. Down below, Kris was making a call. He ignored it.

In the distance, the line of cars on the bypass was getting longer. But nobody was headed their way. Why would they come here? Barely visible in the dull afternoon light, a pair of headlights flashed three times from behind a verge. All clear. Or maybe whoever she'd brought with her was staying back. Waiting for the right moment to attempt an ambush.

'Stay alert,' he texted from his own phone. 'Buzz me the second you see anything odd.'

He took another look through the binoculars. Neville's phone rang.

'Inspector Hendrie,' he barked.

'I'm here,' she said.

'So I see,' Jonno said. 'I'm looking at you right now.'

'Where are you?' she hissed. 'Where are my husband and my son?'

She stretched out the last word, as if merely forming it with her tongue caused her unimaginable pain.

'Safe and sound, Inspector. Safe and sound,' Jonno said.

'Let's do this, then,' Kris said.

'Not so fast, Inspector,' Jonno chuckled. 'First, I need to make sure you've lived up to your end of the bargain.'

'I'm alone! I told you I'd come alone!' she said.

'Then I'm sure we can sort this presently,' Jonno said. 'Be right there.'

He ended the call. Scanned the yard.

Right.

Showtime.

Jason's humming was so loud Jonno could hear it even though he was several yards away from the car and the windows were up. He edged between the car and the shed, and walked towards Kris. She spotted him immediately and stood straight, making a show of putting her hands up.

'OK, Wallace,' she said. 'See? I'm alone and unarmed. Let Neville and Jason go, and I'll walk towards you. Then I'll take you to your buddy Edwards. Sound good?'

Jonno cleared his throat. He pulled out his gun and smiled.

'What do you take me for, Inspector?' he said. 'Some bloody daftie?'

He inched two steps forward.

'Here's how this is going to work,' he said. 'You're going to tell me where that prick Al is. And then, if I'm satisfied you're telling the truth, I'll let your hubby and your wean go. Clear?'

'No,' Kris said. 'No. That wasn't the deal.'

'It is now,' Jonno said.

They glared at each other. Kris dropped her hands

limply to her sides. Looked at him with pure loathing. Then she smiled faintly.

'Fine, Wallace. Have it your way,' she said. 'Shoot me.'

She took a step forward.

'You do realise you aren't in a position to call the shots, right, hen?' Jonno growled.

'Och, but I think I am,' Kris said. 'You need me. Or you'll be back to square one, won't you? No info, no Al. And I bet your boss won't be pleased if you go back empty-handed.'

Jonno stood still. Arm outstretched. Gun pointed straight at Kris' chest. His eyes flicked left and right.

'You know what, Inspector? Maybe you're right,' he relented. 'I can't kill you if you don't tell me what you know.'

He began lowering his gun. Kris felt the tension in her stomach ease. She took another tentative step forward. Her hand edged behind her, ready to pull out the knife when she was close enough.

'But you know what?' Jonno continued. 'Killing's overrated.'

The gunshot sounded impossibly loud. Kris felt something tackle her foot. Liquid fire shot up her leg and she crumpled onto the gravel. Jonno moved towards her with surprising speed. Loomed over her.

'Now, let's try again,' he said. 'Where the fuck's that prick?'

The pain was so bad Kris could barely breathe. Her whole leg throbbed. Except her ankle. She couldn't feel anything below her ankle.

'Where?' Jonno repeated.

He fired another shot. The bullet hit the gravel, inches away from Kris. Her face stung and she felt wetness on her cheek. Blood from a wayward speck of gravel mixed with tears of pain.

'I can make this worse if you don't talk, Inspector,' Jonno said. 'Try me.'

'Jason. Neville,' Kris said.

Her eyes were flat, like pieces of flint. She swallowed. It made an audible click in her throat.

'Have you ever been shot in the knee?' Jonno said conversationally. 'Personally, I haven't. But I hear it's very unpleasant.'

He pointed the gun. Kris tried to move out of range but paralysing bolts of pain shot up her leg, digging their metal claws into her hips and gut. She writhed.

'Jason. Neville,' she repeated.

Jonno made an animal noise in his throat. Lunged towards her. Grabbed her by her hair.

'Have it your way,' he growled.

He dragged her through the gravel, towards the shed and the car beyond. The fire in her leg blazed hotly. She screamed.

Jonno threw her violently in front of him. She landed face down, on her nose. Blood gushed out. Her breathing took on a whistling, watery quality. He unlocked the car. Opened the rear left passenger side door. Pointed the gun inside.

'Out, prick,' he screamed. 'Get the fuck out. Both of youse.'

Jason's humming had taken on a piercing note that hurt his ears.

'Kris!' Neville shouted, as he was coming out of the car. 'Kris!'

Jonno grabbed him by the shirt, pulled him out the rest of the way, unbalancing him, and punched him in the solar plexus. The wind rushed out of Neville and he doubled over. Jonno hit his nose with the butt of the gun, sending him crashing to the ground.

'Nev!' Kris shouted.

She'd managed a half-turn. But her leg hurt too much. The tiniest movement sent paralysing jolts of pain coursing through her body. The bottom half of her trouser-leg was soaked and sticky.

Jason's humming had hit a peak. Jonno's stomach churned. His body was boiling hot. Och, those fucking squeals. Jesus Henry Christ.

'Tell me where Al is,' he screamed, waving the gun. 'Or I'm shooting the fucking wean!'

He grabbed Jason from behind. Placed the gun against his temple, pushing so hard it left a round impression in the skin. Jason screamed. Thrashed around, trying to disengage himself. But he was just a wean. Jonno's grip was iron.

'Wait! OK! OK!' Kris shouted.

She was weeping openly. Her face was a mess of snot and blood. Her vision doubled. Trebled. Quadrupled. The weight of the mistake she'd made going there on her own, thinking she could control the situation, was crushing.

'Where?' Jonno said.

Jason had given up thrashing. The shrieks had turned into whimpers that pierced Kris' heart.

'He's somewhere in the Cairngorms,' Kris said.

'Where?' Jonno repeated.

She closed her eyes. Desperately tried to ignore the pain. Not just the physical pain. But also pain that had a more indefinable quality. Looking at Jason's wide eyes. Hearing his whimpers. Seeing Neville lying on the ground, insensible, his face a Halloween mask of blood. Oh fuck. What had she done? What kind of hell had she brought on them?

'WHERE IS HE!" Jonno shouted, pressing the gun harder into Jason's temple. 'You know I'll shoot. Do you, or don't you know where he is?'

'I think I do!' she blurted in between blubbering sobs.

'What's that supposed to mean?'

'The eejit beat the shit out of some bloke at a service area on his way to where he's living now. I tracked the car and narrowed his location down to the Cairngorms. There's a fifty mile radius where....'

Jonno's nostrils flared. A million synapses in his brain exploded all at once.

'So you fucking tricked me, you stupid bitch?' he screamed.

His finger tightened around the trigger.

'No! No!' she said frantically. 'There are maybe thirty settlements in the area, most of them too small for someone like him to be able to blend in. You just need to be methodical. Start from the handful of larger ones. You'll find him.'

Jonno's breathing was becoming more laboured. His eyes narrowed to slits. In his mind's eye, he was crushing her and her prick of a husband and this useless waste of space of a wean to a pulp. How dare she manipulate him like this? Send him on a wild bloody goose chase?

'Let us go now,' Kris said. 'You've got what you wanted. I've told you all I know. It's the closest anyone could get to tracking down his location without tipping off the UKPPS!'

Of course, going back without Al wasn't an option. This was his cock up. He needed to find that grassing prick bastard.

But this bitch.

This fucking bitch. Stringing him along. Treating him like some idiot.

Like she could mess him around.

His finger moved closer and closer towards the trigger.

It was a fraction away.

'Wallace, please,' Kris begged. 'Kill me if you want. But at least let them go.'

A tenth of a fraction.

'Wallace!'

The scream, throat-shreddingly loud, echoed around the scrapyard.

A shot rang out.

PART THREE

RECKONINGS

CHAPTER 48

I t was Al's first Wednesday shift at The Mossy Well, and he'd already decided Wednesday shifts were the bane of his life.

It wasn't that the pub was insanely busy. That would've been exhausting, sure. But also — dared he say it? — kind of fun. That first shift he'd worked, when he and P had been absolutely snowed under, he'd enjoyed the chaos. It gave him the adrenaline rush he was used to. Plus, it had made the time pass more quickly. Much better than Monday evening, when the only punter who had shown up had sat at the bar and stretched the single drink he'd ordered for what felt like an eternity.

No. The problem wasn't the work itself. It was P's brilliant idea to make Wednesdays karaoke nights.

Al wasn't particularly into music. He didn't mind listening to the radio. And he even tolerated Struan's Power Ballad Nights at The Sentinel. But there was a fucking limit. As friendly and welcoming as the denizens of Fort Drumblehan were, their taste in music was absolute shite. And most of them couldn't carry a tune if somebody threatened to drop their entire families into the frozen loch on a January morning. It was barely nine o'clock and he'd already suffered through seven increasingly harrowing renditions of *I'm Gonna Be (500 miles)*. He'd counted.

'Jesus fucking Christ, just listen to him,' he told P, nodding at two blokes who were belting out the chorus so tunelessly they made the sound of a cat being strangled seem like a Grammy award-winning performance. 'How are we going to suffer through two more hours of this?'

One of the blokes on the mic was the punter Al had clocked buying pork scratchings on his first night in Fort Drumblehan. A bloke he now knew was called Marco. Marco had his shirt sleeves rolled up, exposing his hairless, veiny forearms. His unruly fringe was in his eyes. But, rather than disguising the redness born of his predilection for dear old Mary Jane — or, as he liked calling it, The Famous One — his straw blonde hair made it stand in even starker relief.

'Och, admit it,' P said, her eyes twinkling. 'You're loving this, aren't you?'

'Aye, sure,' Al said. 'You've got me.'

She slapped him playfully and smiled. The song ended to a round of extremely rowdy applause.

'Go Marcooooo,' some drunken punter shouted.

Marco and his mate left the stage, replaced by two bikers in double denim, realistic black and grey tattoos covering every square inch of skin from the backs of their hands to the tops of their shoulders. The opening measures of *I Want It That Way* by the Backstreet Boys hit the tannoy, and Al's heart sank.

'Good lord!' he told P. 'What have I done to deserve this?'

The bikers attacked the opening verse. They sounded like walruses in heat.

'They can't be serious,' Al told P.

'Of course not, silly,' she replied. 'It's their idea of a joke.'

Marco headed up to the bar. 'Alright, Jack,' Marco told him. 'Pint of lager and pork scratchings.'

Al tried and failed not to scoff as Marco tipped him an ostentatious wink. Marco, already stoned out of his mind, didn't notice.

'Here you go, bud,' he said, handing him his drink, his pork scratchings, and his change.

Marco headed off to his booth, where his mate and two women that looked like they'd come straight off filming Geordie Shore were perusing the book of song titles, evidently intent on having another go.

'Does he have to wink every time?' Al asked.

P shrugged. 'I suppose it makes him feel dangerous. Not much excitement going on around here if you hadn't noticed.'

'I don't get it,' Al said. 'Someday, he's going to get us in trouble.'

'Och, I wouldn't worry about that,' P said, lifting up the glass rinser tray and sliding it into the washer. 'Nobody's getting hurt or being bothered. So nobody cares.'

Al poured a trio of cocktails. Served them with more pork scratchings.

'Hey, slow down with that,' P said.

'What?'

'We're running low. So strictly regulars only.'

I Want It That Way had given way to *Wannabe* by the Spice Girls, sung by the women who were with Marco and his mate. They weren't bad. Better than the real Spice Girls. Then again, the bar was low.

'When do you restock?' Al asked P.

He'd been wondering how the system worked. Not that he was interested in expanding, mind. This laid back life, where business partners didn't try to kill you over minor disagreements, was starting to grow on him. Especially now that it looked like he might be off the hook. But you could take the OCG member out of Strathburgh but not the OCG out of the man, he supposed. It was how he was wired to think. Just like a solicitor ends up seeing everything as a zero-sum game after practising for a while.

'I'll need to go see Gilby,' she told him, after a pause.

'Gilby?' Al asked.

'Aye. He's quite the character,' P said.

She'd pulled the rinser tray out of the glass washer, and was drying the glasses and placing them back under the counter with practised efficiency.

'More colourful than Marco?' he said, raising an eyebrow and nodding towards him.

He was back. Solo this time. Singing a Craig David song Al couldn't quite place. He sounded like his balls were stuck in a meat grinder.

P chuckled.

'Well, maybe I could meet Gilby some time,' Al said. 'Help out. If you want, that is.'

'Sure,' P said. 'Maybe. If you behave.'

CHAPTER 49

'That's really cool! It sounds exactly like it. Play it again. Play it again!' Frankie enthused.

Jonno obliged, picking out the notes to the intro riff of Coldplay's *Clocks* painstakingly with his index fingers. The poor finger technique meant it didn't sound anywhere as smooth as the original. But you could definitely recognise the tune. And Frankie was bobbing his head and humming along, which made Jonno feel rather pleased with himself.

He'd been obsessed with the song from the first time he'd heard it on the radio. The riff was on a loop in his head all the time when he was stuck in class and the school day felt like it would never end. The ultimate escapist earworm. And he'd been working on it, trying to get the notes and the rhythm just right, for as long as he'd been sneaking up to the wee room on the second floor of the rectory.

He'd discovered the scuffed upright piano while on his way to fetch a fresh bottle of communion wine for Father Michaelson. Ever since, he'd been having a bit of a play whenever he thought he could get away with it. He wouldn't be playing the Royal Albert Hall any time soon — or ever, for that matter. But it made him forget himself for a bit. The walls faded into the background, and the atmosphere didn't seem quite as oppressive. On some days, he even managed to transport himself someplace else.

They fooled around on the piano some more. Jonno banged out what he thought was a pretty decent approximation of *Wonderwall*'s vocal melody. Then Frankie tried to play the chorus melody to *My Heart Will Go On*. He'd never been anywhere near a piano before, so he mangled it. But it was enough to set them off.

'Stop it, you stupid twat,' Jonno giggled.

Frankie played it again, humming along with an appropriately sombre look on his face. It sounded like somebody had dropped the piano down a flight of stairs. They doubled up, hands holding their bellies, tears streaming down their faces.

'Och, stop it. I can't breathe,' Jonno said.

'Aye, right. You don't have to pretend with me, bud. I know you secretly love Celine Dion. I bet you know all the lyrics by hea-.'

'What do you boys think you're doing in here?'

The voice behind them hit them like a flash of lightning on a sunny day. It cut their laughter off instantly. A flick of a switch. They spun around, their hearts already racing.

'You know you're not supposed to be here,' Father Baker said flatly.

His Belfast accent became thicker the angrier he got. 'Know' came out 'noy'. The 'Rs' sounded like a high-powered engine revving.

'You're supposed to be in your rooms, doing your homework and taking some time for quiet reflection,' he continued. 'So why are you here? Who gave you permission?'

The vein in the middle of his forehead throbbed. That was very bad. Very bad.

'Er Father, I...' Frankie began, but he couldn't continue.

Fear had overcome him the second he'd seen Father Baker looming in the doorway, hands crossed, his face pinched into an ominous scowl. He was close to tears.

Father Baker stepped into the room, which was really no more than a utility closet, long and narrow. His eyes went from one boy to the other.

'We were just having some fun,' Jonno said.

His heart was in his throat. But he was damned if he was going to take this lying down. What the fuck had they done wrong? Since when was it a crime to play the piano? They weren't hurting anyone, goddamnit.

'You were just having some fun,' Father Baker said tonelessly.

His voice had gone quiet. If looks could kill, both Jonno and Frankie would've been corpses. He took another step forward. Stopped. Seemed to consider what to do next.

Jonno saw stars. In less than half a second, Father Baker had closed the distance and backhanded him across the face.

'You. Were. Just. Having. Some. Fun,' he repeated.

Every word was punctuated with a slap and a grunt of satisfaction. Of pleasure. Like this was a much-needed release.

'We didn't think we were doing anything wrong!' Jonno protested, but weakly.

Father Baker had really put his back into the slaps and Jonno's cheeks were on fire. But the stinging pain was nothing compared to the shame burning inside his chest and warming the tips of his ears.

'You're out of bounds without permission,' Father Baker roared, his attempt at quiet menace all but forgotten. 'Your instructions were to stay in your room and do your homework.'

He slapped him viciously. One forehand, one backhand.

'Have you finished your homework? No, scratch that. Have you even started it?'

'No, Father,' Frankie moaned.

'No,' Jonno said tonelessly, his eyes downcast, the tips of his fingers trembling.

'I thought as much.'

Frankie's head was bowed, and silent tears were trickling down his face. Jonno's whole head felt like it was on fire. Another slap rocked him off-balance. The sound of flesh hitting flesh was enormous in the small room.

Slap.

The room spun, its four corners twisting to form a shape he couldn't quite recognise.

Slap.

His back slammed against the piano. The keys tinkled.

Slap. Slap. Slap.

Father Baker was no longer punishing him. This was pure unadulterated rage. At eleven years old, he was too young to comprehend that, whatever Father Baker was angry about, it was bigger than him. That he was simply a convenient scapegoat. But he was old enough to know the priest's self-control was slipping. That he might even lose it completely and do something with permanent consequences. He opened his mouth to scream, but nothing came out. His throat was paralysed. His body thrashed from side to side, trying to twist away from the blows raining down on him.

Then he opened his eyes. His consciousness flooded back, but his body refused to respond to his brain's orders.

Panic gripped him. He fought to move. Straining every brain cell. Then the feeling came back to his legs and slowly coursed up the rest of the body.

He shot up into a sitting position, the bedsheets pooling around his waist. Cold sweat trickled down his spine.

Where was he?

He wiped his face with the bedsheets. They came back moist, the formerly white fabric a pale yellow. Fumbled for the light switch. The room was so tiny the foot of the bed almost touched the wall, which was painted a bright shade of lime green that might've been fashionable at some point in the late nineties. A twenty-two-inch TV hung from a bracket on top of a cheap wardrobe covered in faux pine laminate. Next to it, the door, a set of crumpled fire emergency procedures stapled to it.

He was ok. He'd left St Patrick's the minute he'd turned eighteen, vowing never to return. To put it all behind him for good. Remember?

Except the memories hadn't left, had they? They were like a nasty case of herpes. He'd do well for a while. And then they'd be back, unbidden. Attaching themselves to his brain like parasites whose lives depended on sucking out the faintest hint of joy.

No, not St. Patrick's, but a B&B in a small village in the Cairngorms. More like a wide space in the road, really. As good a place as any to stop for the night after a day of fruitless enquiries.

Nobody'd recognised his long lost mate. Not the pimply girl with the septum piercing and a luxurious moustache at the FatFace counter. Not the barrel-chested bloke with the ridiculously high-pitched voice who was manning the local Co-Op's only till. Not the punters at the pub. Not the old couple crossing the road towards a hiking trail.

Nobody. Nothing. Nada. Not a flicker of recognition when he showed them the picture of him and that prick — he couldn't bear to say his name — all smiles, posing with a Darts trophy at The Sentinel.

He padded to the bathroom, dressed only in his socks, took a long pish, and drank water straight from the tap. He hadn't shaved in several days and his scruff was starting to look unruly. Coupled with the dark circles under his eyes, the overall effect wasn't doing much for him in the approachability department. He'd seen the old couple's eyes widen in fear when he approached them. And while the FatFace girl and Co-Op bloke seemed unfazed by their hulking interlocutor, they hadn't exactly fallen over themselves to help him.

He sat down heavily on the bed. The lumpy mattress creaked in protest. He launched his Maps app. Zoomed on the area of his search.

He'd only been looking for one day, but he felt like he'd covered a reasonable amount of ground. The lack of progress was discouraging. No. Frustrating. Really, really frustrating. It was a needle in a fucking haystack.

That bloody cow. He'd fallen for her story hook, line, and sinker.

His mind flashed back to her snot-and-blood-covered face. How it had crumpled as she begged him to release the wean. And how the wean's moaning had filled his head. Blotting out everything else. Transporting him back. So familiar. So much like Frankie's. As if any such sounds could ever elicit any pity from that devil of a priest.

His eyes drifted southwest, from the blue dot that

pinpointed his location, to the grounds he knew all too well.

What if he went there? Had a heart to heart with that evil bastard?

He stared at the lime green wall until the floaters in his eyes coagulated into two large black spots with a red centre. He blinked them away.

Was there a chance it might make him feel better?

Help him close the chapter? Get rid of the dreams once and for all?

Because, clearly, trying to lock it up hadn't done the trick.

It wasn't strictly within the area where he was supposed to be looking for that grassing prick. But it wasn't too much of a detour either. He could be there in an hour and a half, tops. Make a day of it. Then get back to looking.

Call it a mini-break.

Physical therapy.

Ha. That made him chuckle in spite of himself.

He stood up. There was no way he could go back to sleep. So he grabbed his shaving kit and headed back to the bathroom. The day wouldn't dawn for another two hours. But he might as well get ready. Give himself a head start. Besides, he wanted to make sure he looked his absolute best if he was going to have a reunion with dear, old Father Baker. Aye. What a long heart-to-heart they were going to have!

He lathered up his head and face.

As the blade made its first run across the stubble, he began humming the *Clocks* piano riff under his breath.

CHAPTER 50

'I still can't get over this,' Al told P, his voice full of wonder, as they dismounted her motorcycle and unbuckled their helmets.

'What can't you get over?' P said, amused.

'Just...'

Al opened the carrier at the back of the motorcycle, placed his helmet inside it, closed it, and waved his hand about. He snapped his fingers, trying to find the right words.

'It's fucking brilliant, isn't it?' he said. 'Dealing out of a convent.'

'It's not a convent, it's a manse,' P corrected him, still with the same look of amusement on her face.

'Och. Convent. Manse. That's not the point,' Al said.

'So what is it?' she replied.

'Nobody'd suspect it, eh? It's the last place I would've thought of.'

'Well, then I hope you can keep a secret,' she said.

Al made a zipping motion across his lips, then mimed turning a key and throwing it away.

They'd spent the morning lounging about in bed, watching daytime telly and chatting about this and that. Basking in each other's company. She couldn't believe how they'd become inseparable so quickly. How easy. How effortless it all was.

When she'd mentioned she had to get to Gilby's to restock before the weekend rush, and he'd suggested tagging along, it felt natural. Her misgivings swept aside by the glow of contentment. So they'd headed off in the unusually glorious weather, taking a scenic route on B roads that cut through a seemingly endless expanse of highland wilderness. And now here they were, him taking it all in with a look on his face like a wean in a sweet shop, which she found adorable but also kind of unsettling.

Their hands had slipped into each other, the fingers interlocking. They walked up a narrow path in between large firs with elephant-like trunks, P's boots and Al's Converse trainers crunching on the gravel.

They ducked under a stone arch, walked down a short flight of steps, and stopped in front of a heavy black door with a brass knocker shaped like a lion's head. P knocked three times. They waited, Al staring at the mountain peaks in the distance, and marvelling at the thickness of the forest below them.

He was so lost in thought Gilby's voice startled him.

'Alright, P,' he said. 'How are you doing?'

He looked at Al, then at P questioningly.

'This is Jack. He's err...'

She wasn't sure what to say. Lover felt frivolous. Boyfriend felt a bit too much. And also sort of juvenile.

Friend with benefits?

No. More than that. And it wasn't the kind of thing

you'd say to your weed supplier, was it? Not in front of the actual person.

'He's...'

'I'm a friend. And I'm working at The Mossy Well,' Al said, smoothing things out.

'Alright, Jack,' Gilby said, friendly as can be. 'Good to meet you, bud.'

He wiped his callus-hardened hands on his paint-splattered overalls and offered his right. Al took it, and they shook. Briefly but firmly.

'So what do you have for me?' P asked.

'A new shipment just came in,' Gilby said. 'Braw stuff. White widow. Just finished packing a stash for you, ready to go.'

'Is that the same one as last time?' P asked. 'That went down well.'

'Och, this is better,' Gilby said. 'More uplifting. No paranoia. Come on in, I'll sort you out.'

Gilby's quarters were dark, even though the Sun was shining at full blast. Al and P walked around a rusty rake and a mud-caked shovel into the main room, a square expanse of exposed brick and weathered wood flooring with a country-style L-shaped kitchen and a heavy oak table. Tucked away in a nook, just out of sight, there was a steel bed frame with rumpled covers, the pillow folded in two and lying at an angle.

Gilby grabbed two patterned mugs from the open shelf that ran along one side of the kitchen and switched on the kettle.

'Tea? Coffee?' he asked.

'Aye, tea please,' P said.

'And you, Jack?'

'Sure. OK, ta,' Al replied.

Gilby made the tea and plonked the two steaming mugs on the table.

'I'll be five minutes,' he said, and disappeared into another room.

Al sipped his tea, which was so weak and milky it could barely be called that. He spat it back into the mug.

'Good god, it tastes like dirty dishwater,' he said, pitching his voice low so Gilby wouldn't hear. 'What'd he do, pass the teabag in front of the mug and considered the job done?'

P laughed and took a sip of her own tea.

'Agreed.'

They shared a look and smiled at each other. The silence was comfortable. There was no pressure. No need to say anything.

'So how does this work?' Al asked. 'Packs it himself, does he?'

'Aye,' P said. 'I don't ask too much, to be honest.'

'Why so?'

P shrugged. 'The less I know, the better, I suppose,' she said. 'It's quality stuff. Nobody's ever complained. That's good enough for me.'

'OK,' Al said.

It was a completely different mentality. There was a complacency that was alien to him. But not in a bad way. For as long as he could remember, his life had been about forward motion. Making enough money to get out from under Ma's thumb. Then moving up the ranks. Earning respect. Being feared. Making more money. Having enough to indulge his whims. P wasn't like that. She was happy with her lot in life. Savoured what she had. It was an outlook he found refreshing.

His hand automatically reached out for the mug of tea. He absently took another sip. Grimaced. P snorted.

'What?' he said.

'Just the look on your face. It's not *that* bad.'

'What isn't?' Gilby asked, walking into the room with a black gym bag.

'Eh, hard to explain,' Al said.

P kicked him under the table.

'Ow!' Al said.

Gilby looked at them. Shook his head. 'Anyway,' he said. 'Here you go. Ten ounces of special pork scratchings coming up.'

He dropped the bag. P took out a wad of cash from the hip pocket of her jeans. Placed it on the table.

'Thank you, kind sir,' she said.

Gilby took the money, making a show of not counting it, and tucked it into the back pocket of his overalls. He pulled out a chair and sat at the table.

'One for the road? On me?' he asked, spreading out three Rizlas, joining two of them together to make a larger rolling paper, and sticking a third one beneath them for support.

Al and P looked at each other. Shrugged.

'We have time, don't we?' Al said. 'We won't open for a few more hours.'

'Aye, sure. Why not?' P said. 'Roll away.'

CHAPTER 51

D riving through St Patrick's wrought iron gate and onto the paved courtyard filled Jonno with a weird sense of déjà-vu. The square stone arch, painted white with St. Patrick's spelled out in black, gothic lettering, the landscaping, and the heavy oak double doors were exactly as he remembered them. It was like time had stood still. Even the atmosphere had the same quality. It was quiet. Idyllic. But not in a good way. There was an underlying sense of something not quite right that you couldn't put your finger on. Like it was too perfect to be real.

He remembered his first day, almost twenty-five years earlier. God, had it been that long? How afraid he'd been of this unfamiliar, secluded place where he'd been dropped off without warning. He hadn't believed Da would make good on his threat and send him away. But then he did. At some point — he never could figure out when and why, even though it had kept him up most nights for a long time — it had gone from being empty words, something Da said in anger, to becoming his reality.

At first, he'd concluded it wasn't so bad after all. Not as

terrible as Da had made it out to be in hopes of scaring him straight, anyway. Then it had started.

The unreasonable demands. The screaming. The beatings.

When he'd left, with £50 to his name and so few possessions they fit in a single plastic shopping bag, it had felt like a weight had been lifted. Except the weight had been too heavy, and had borne down on him for too long to leave him unscathed. And the parts of him that had broken under it had never managed to heal properly.

He shuddered and pushed the thought away. The priests had always taught them there'd be a day of reckoning. A balancing of the scales, where the good would be rewarded and the evil would be punished for eternity. Hellfire and brimstone. He'd never bought the idea of an angry, vengeful god. But it didn't matter. Whether a higher power existed or not, Father Baker was going to get his just desserts.

Of that he'd make fucking sure.

He parked in an empty space and walked into the reception area, unsure how he'd play this. As soon as he passed through the polished oak double doors, the weight returned. Crushing him. His resolve wavered. Maybe this was a bad idea. A terrible one, actually. Was St Patrick's even still operating as a home for troubled boys? Was Father Baker still here? He supposed he'd find out soon.

The reception area was empty. The painting of our lady of sorrows that had given him nightmares as a wean was still there, dominating the room, hung across from the door so it would be the first thing anyone who came in would see. Jesus was half-naked, nailed to the cross. His ribs were pushing out of his stretched skin and his face was contorted in pain. The virgin Mary was on her knees, a look of absolute devastation on her face, surrounded by cherubs with wings on their bare backs. Nobody in their right might would've looked at it and not be creeped out. But here it had pride of place.

Only the headshot of the Pope looked different. Had the German bloke died? In the intervening years, he'd been otherwise occupied. No time to keep up with the goings on at the Vatican.

The reception led to another set of double doors. As soon as he walked through them into the large hall beyond, more memories hit him like a kick in the balls. The smells of soup, boiled chicken, and incense assaulted his nostrils. The subdued murmurs and shuffling of feet as weans lined up, single file, like underage soldiers going into battle, filled his ears. So did the shrill sound of the whistle. One, called the first sign, to stand straight. And another — the second sign — to be quiet, or else. Half a word was a serious enough offence for you to spend the evening in your room copying out bible verses instead of eating your meagre tea.

Across from the double doors, there was the alcove where he'd hide when he got kicked out of class. How much time had he spent there, his back pressed to the cold wall, wondering how he'd be punished? Too much time. Too fucking much.

He walked aimlessly about, taking it all in. If time travel existed, this was what it would feel like. You'd be obviously out of place but, at the same time, operating on muscle memory. Everything strange but also oddly familiar.

'Can I help you, sir?' a voice asked from behind him.

Jonno turned around. A man in grey trousers and black shirt, a silver crucifix pinned to the breast pocket — the standard priest's uniform — peered at him from behind thick glasses. He was so young his hairless chin was still covered in angry pimples. But he'd already affected that fake humble, sickeningly self-righteous air they all had. It was their stock in trade.

'Och, aye,' Jonno said, mustering all the politeness he could manage. 'I'm looking for Father Baker?'

'Father Baker?' the priest asked.

'Err, aye. He's the English teacher?' Jonno said. 'Well, he was, twenty-odd years ago. Tall guy? Dark hair? Belfast accent?'

'Och, you mean Father Peter?'

'Och, I suppose so,' Jonno said. 'We always called him Father Baker, but aye. I believe that's his name.'

'You were a student here?' the priest said, perking up.

'Aye. I happened to be passing through, and thought I'd drop by,' Jonno said. 'Have a friendly chat.'

'Well, I'm sure he'd be delighted to see an old boy,' the priest said, cracking a smile that made him look all of twelve years old.

'Och, I'm sure he would, the prick,' Jonno thought.

'Unfortunately,' the priest continued, oblivious to the shadow that had passed over Jonno's face, I'm afraid he's not here anymore.'

'How so?' Jonno asked.

Had the prick kicked the bucket?

'He had a stroke a few months back,' the priest said. 'He's better now, praise god, but it was touch and go for a bit.'

The prick joined his hands in prayer, casting his eyes towards the ceiling as he said this. Jonno's face clouded over. So he wasn't dead, but mortally sick? Did a stroke hurt? He hoped it did. He hoped the pain was fucking unbearable.

'I'm very sorry to hear that,' he said in his best solemn voice. 'Is he still in the hospital?'

'Och, no. No,' the priest said, shaking his head as he did so. 'He got discharged some time ago. But he's living at St Mary's now.'

'I see,' Jonno said. 'Where's that?'

He had to see this for himself. Make sure the bastard was really getting a fat old dose of the retribution he liked to dole out.

'Do you think I'd be able to visit?' he blurted.

'It's not too far from here, actually,' the priest replied. 'About an hour's drive. He tires easily these days, though, so you wouldn't be able to stay long.'

'Och, no, no,' Jonno said. 'As I said. Just a friendly chat. It's not every day I pass by.'

This seemed to please the sod, because he put on his best empathetic smile. It looked as fake as they came. Jonno's stomach clenched. His hand twitched.

'I'm sure he'd be pleased to see you,' the priest said. 'He's very fond of all the boys that have been under his care.'

'Aye, fond of beating the shite out of them because he was pissed off he couldn't get laid,' Jonno thought.

He could feel the familiar red mist descending. Getting harder to control. He'd better wrap this up before he lost it.

'How do I get to St Mary's?' he asked the priest.

'Aye so, turn left out of the gate, and keep going straight,' the priest said, making hand-gestures to show him in which direction he had to go. 'It's a bit twisty at some points, but you pretty much follow the road. Can't go too far wrong.'

'Sure. I should find it on my Maps app anyway, right?'

'Och, aye, right enough,' the priest replied. 'Of course.'

'Well it was good to meet you, Father,' Jonno said, taking a step towards the reception's double doors.

'Brother. Brother Fergus.'

'Right, Brother Fergus,' Jonno repeated.

So the prick wasn't even a real priest.

'I'll get going then. You have a good day now, eh,' Jonno said.

'Peace be with you, son,' Brother Fergus said. 'Och, I don't think I got your name?'

But Jonno was already barrelling through the reception area, pulling his phone out of his pocket and typing St Mary's into the search bar.

CHAPTER 52

The first thirty-odd miles of the trip to St Mary's were a pleasant drive on reasonably straight, well-maintained roads that cut through a vast expanse of pasture. Cattle and sheep milled about, grazing or basking in the Sun. A narrow river meandered through part of it, before disappearing into a thicket of spruce.

It was peaceful. Serene. But Jonno barely noticed any of it. He drove in silence, hands gripping the wheel, his mind the theatre of an increasingly bitter civil war between diametrically opposed emotions.

So the bastard was sick. Maybe even critically so.

No more strutting about the classroom for him, spouting his vitriol and taking out his frustrations on others. So what was the point of confronting him then? Why face a man who'd brought him nothing but misery, when that man had already got what was coming to him? And who, even now, had the power to rob him of sleep. To make his heart beat faster, and his throat clench.

But had he suffered enough?

Did Father Baker comprehend what his actions had taken from him? Had his illness brought this home?

Jonno didn't think so. The magnitude, the enormity of it, was just on a different scale. If he thought back to his childhood, there were very few memories he'd consider happy. And even those were tainted. When Father Baker wasn't slapping him or whipping him with his belt, he chipped away at him in a million other ways. Always with a snide comment at the ready. Constantly reminding him of his inadequacy. Of how bad he was. So bad his own parents couldn't control him and had to hand him over to St Patrick's.

The maze of sharp bends, blind corners, and dead ends that made up the last part of the route to St Mary's interrupted his train of thought. He had to retrace his steps twice, cursing his Maps app, his phone, Steve Jobs, and whoever maintained these roads. Eventually, after having to double back several miles, he took the correct turn, and St Mary's appeared on the horizon, a lone outpost in a sea of densely-packed evergreens.

The building was much smaller and far less impressive than St Patrick's — a bog standard, perfectly rectangular 18th century brick manse. But it sat on a hill with panoramic views of the loch, spruce forests, and mountain peaks beyond. Taking in the views, Jonno couldn't help but feel his bitterness solidify.

So he got recurring nightmares, and that bastard got to while away his final years here. It was enough to drive anyone mad.

His heart was still playing paradiddles in his chest. But, looking at the place had turned his resolve to iron. Oh, he was going to have a wonderful catchup with his old friend Father Baker. One of those chats for the ages.

He grabbed his gun from the glove compartment, tucked it in the waistband of his jeans, and covered it with his jacket. Then he looked in the rear view mirror, nodded to himself, and walked towards the manse's front door.

This time round, when he walked into the reception area, he was greeted by a sixty-something lady with a perfectly sculpted, blue-grey hairdo and an impressively large bosom.

'Hiya, can I help you at all?' she said in a cheerful contralto.

'Alright? Aye, I've just driven from St Patrick's. I was hoping to visit Father Bak, err Father Peter? I understand he's living here?'

'Och, and who is it who'd like to visit him?' she said, smiling.

'Ach, err, it's um Frankie Drummond. I was a student at St Patrick's many years ago. I was passing through and thought I'd stop by for a visit. But the person I spoke to at St Patrick's — Brother Fergus? — said Father Peter's here full-time now?'

'Och, it's lovely of you to think of visiting,' she said. 'I'm sure Father Peter will be delighted. He hasn't been the same since he had his stroke, the poor dear.'

Jonno nodded and gave her what he hoped was an appropriately solemn look. The lady, who told him she was called Isa and had been working here since her husband died of lung cancer two years previously, led him through a warren of corridors as tackily decorated as a Travelodge in some arsehole town off the motorway.

They made a right turn, then went up a flight of stairs and passed through another narrow corridor with maroon, funky-smelling carpet. Isa chattered away the whole time. About the order's quirks. About how she'd never be able to live that kind of life, but enjoyed working for them. About that bastard's routine.

Jonno mostly filtered her out. But the last bit was interesting. It sounded like he wasn't having a great time of it. The thought made his lips curl into a surreptitious smile that was more like a snarl.

They stopped in front of a door marked 213, and she knocked lightly.

'Father Peter,' she said in a sing-songy, high-pitched voice. 'You have a visitor.'

She cracked the door open, and Jonno was assaulted by the sickroom smell. Broth. Unguents. Medicine. All tied together by a ripe undertone of putridity.

Death was already here. Biding its time. But stepping over the threshold still felt like crossing a rickety bridge ten feet over a raging current. Suddenly, he was no longer an adult with access to a gun and no qualms beating the shite out of some random bloke for utilitarian reasons. He was a scared, defenceless wean.

He took a deep breath and walked in.

The room was a sparsely-furnished single that looked more like a prison cell than an old man's bedroom. Actually, no. That wasn't fair. Jonno reckoned his lodgings had been better the last time he'd done a stretch.

Given the beauty of the surroundings, the austerity of the room was jarring. The walls, which at one point were probably white, were cracked in places and in desperate need of a fresh coat of paint. A single bed with a steel frame and a thin, lumpy mattress took up most of the space, the obligatory crucifix hanging on the wall over the headboard, and a bare night stand next to it. A small desk was tucked away in the corner against the wall, opposite the bed.

At first, Jonno almost turned to Isa to tell her this was a

mistake. It had to be. The husk in the chair next to the window, enveloped in a cloud of dried sweat and stale pish, couldn't be Father Baker. The thick black hair was gone, replaced by thin white wisps that lay on his liver-spotted head like the maggot-infested remnants of a dead animal's pelt. His skin was pale and doughy, with deep-set wrinkles. And, instead of the military posture that struck fear into so many weans' hearts, this man was slouched in his chair, too weak to hold himself up straight.

But the worst thing about him was the look on his face. The right side was limp and droopy, the lips curled downwards in a half-frown. The left side was slack-jawed and listless. His eyes were glassy, staring fixedly in the distance at nothing in particular.

And then he saw the mole on the top right of the temple, standing out in the middle of a nest of liver spots. The horny hands with their long fingers. Fingers that had left deep red impressions on his face more times than he cared to count. And that prominent vein, all too often a warning that a beating was coming and there was nothing he could do except wait for it to be over.

'I'll let you two catch up,' Isa, who Jonno had completely forgotten about, told him. 'I'll be back in around half an hour to take him to the chapel for afternoon prayers.'

'Sure, thank you,' Jonno said.

He barely noticed her leaving. Barely heard the door close. Here was the man who beat him, tormented him, robbed him of anything that introduced even a sliver of joy into his childhood and then made sure he'd never forget about it by haunting his dreams. Except he was a ghost. A shadow. A helpless invalid. Not the monster he remembered.

Jonno squatted down to eye level and gave Father Baker a cold, hard look.

'Anyone home?' he growled. 'Do you recognise me, you prick? It's me. Jonno Wallace?'

But the rage in his voice felt hollow. There was no reaction. Father Baker was completely motionless, staring unblinkingly out of the window. There wasn't a flicker of recognition in his eyes. Just emptiness.

He felt a stab of... what was it? Was it pity?

No. That couldn't be. He hadn't taken this detour so Father Baker would make him feel sorry for him. The piece of shite didn't deserve his or anyone's pity.

Jonno placed his hand on Father Baker's thigh. It felt thin and impossibly bony, but he found the fleshiest bit, grabbed it between his thumb and forefinger, and twisted hard. Viciously. Projecting all his anger into it. A soft moan escaped Father Baker's closed mouth. More like a gurgle. But his reflexes didn't respond. He remained motionless. Expressionless.

Jonno stared at him, desperately hoping he was in there, fully aware of what was going on and unable to communicate it. Trapped. Watching this happen to him as if it were a film, unable to have any control. And scared of what might happen next. But the vacant look in his eyes told a different story. Father Baker wasn't there. Not really. Whatever it was that had made him the despicable prick Jonno knew as a wean had checked out and left the building. What remained was an empty shell. Proof there was no soul. No god. That what makes us who we are is just a random collection of grey cells burning off energy. Something so fragile an arterial blockage is enough to wipe it out of existence.

As if to hammer the point home, Jonno heard the

squelching of shite. A sulphurous, sewery aroma filled the small room.

'What a sorry end,' Jonno said. 'Who's mediocre now, eh? Your god hasn't saved you. You're sitting in your own pish and shite until somebody can be arsed to clean you up.'

The tears took him by surprise. He hadn't been able to cry in over a decade. But now they were running freely down his cheeks. Tears of anger and hate. But also tears of deep, deep sadness. For the memories he'd been saddled with. For the childhood he'd never get back.

He was never going to get a do-over was he? A second chance? And even though he knew it was unreasonable — irrational — to be angry about this, the thought opened a bottomless well of despair.

How might things have been different, if the man who was supposed to take care of him had actually done so, instead of taking every opportunity to make him feel small?

No, it wouldn't do for him to dwell on this. That way lay madness.

His hand moved towards the waistband of his jeans. This was what he'd come for. To watch this bastard die in front of him. To exact his pound of flesh.

He pulled the gun out. Flicked off the safety. Aimed at Father Baker's unmoving head. His arm was unsteady. Trembling. The tears were dripping from his jaw and onto his chest. He closed his eyes. Steadied his hand. Curled his finger around the trigger.

And then a thought struck him. His hand dropped limply back to his side.

'You know, you useless piece of shite,' he said in a choked voice, 'I've fantasised about this moment for years. I've imagined every little detail. Played it out in slow motion in my head, hundreds of times. How I'd beat the living shite out of you, like you used to do to me for no reason other than because you could. How I'd let you beg for your life. How I'd give you the faintest glimmer of hope that I'd let you live, then blow your brains out, see them splatter everywhere.'

He paused. Licked his lips. In spite of the tears raining down, they were dry and cracked.

'But, it turns out,' he continued when he'd regained some semblance of control, 'you taught me one useful thing after all. There are worse things than death.'

He moved towards the window, and looked outside at the grounds. A trio — two men and a woman, were strolling along a tree-lined pathway, deep in conversation.

'I'm going to go, now, Father,' Jonno said without turning. 'And from now on,' he said, 'when I'm feeling a bit maudlin, I'm going to think of you, in this sorry excuse for a room, sitting in your own shite and unable to do anything about it. And it's going to cheer me up no end.'

His hand balled into a fist. It was itching to connect with Father Baker's solar plexus. Or crunch into his nose. Or maybe he'd just backhand him a few times across the face, like he had liked to do.

But what was the use? He was getting his comeuppance. That's what he used to preach during Mass, wasn't it? That the evil you put out in the world is returned to you? Well, have a load of this, you prick.

He looked at the grounds, savouring the moment. The tears had stopped and he felt better. Lighter. Clean. More level-headed than he'd been in years. He took a deep breath, not minding the aroma of shite that wafted up with it one bit. If anything, he relished it. It was the smell of victory.

And perhaps the shite would irritate Father Baker's fragile old man's skin so much it would cause painful sores.

Outside, the trio had stopped in a clearing. They were chatting animatedly, the woman waving her hands about. But it seemed relaxed and friendly. She said something, and one of the men — a bloke in paint-splattered overalls, laughed heartily. He could hear the faint echoes ringing out against the sash window's panes.

The second bloke replied to the woman's comment, and Jonno's ears pricked up. His brow furrowed. There was something familiar about him.

The way he carried himself?

He looked him over. Studied the hair, which was swept back from the forehead in an oily pompadour. The patchy beard. Skinny jeans. Converse trainers. A paisley shirt peeking out from under his light jacket.

Jonno did a double-take, unable to believe his eyes and sheer, dumb luck. The longer hair and the beard had changed the shape of his face. But the beard was so patchy it didn't do an especially good job of covering his cheeks. So he could see the scar he'd got when they'd beat the shite out of a bunch of wannabes one drunken night in town — fuck, that had been five years ago — as clear as day.

And then there was that ridiculous shirt.

How many times had they ribbed him about it?

He'd recognise it from a hundred miles away.

CHAPTER 53

It was him, one hundred percent.

That fucking rat bastard. Gallivanting about like he owned the place.

Once Jonno had looked beyond the hair and the beard, it was patently obvious. No way there was somebody else who had that same scar in the exact same place. And the same ghastly taste in shirts.

Jonno looked out of the window, frozen in place, as Al put an arm around the woman's waist. She leaned into him, placing her head on his shoulder briefly. He kissed the top of her head, then uttered something he couldn't make out. She smiled and the bloke in the paint-splattered overalls bellowed more laughter.

So this was it, was it? Grass, create a complete shitestorm, and ride away into the sunset, while those like him, who had managed to somehow escape the fallout, were left holding the bag?

It wasn't fair. It wasn't fair at all. And this made the familiar rage rise up in his chest. It was overwhelming, but also oddly comforting. He knew exactly what to do with anger. With sorrow, not so much.

His first instinct was to barrel out of Father Baker's room, and out of St Mary's. To head to the clearing where Al and his little friends were chatting away, whip out his gun, and shoot all three of them, right then and there.

But that slippery bastard had already bested him once. And he wasn't alone. Jonno might have the element of surprise and the gun, but things could get messy. And this time round failure wasn't an option. He didn't even want to think about what would happen if he made a mess of things again.

No, the best course of action was to bide his time. Watch him. Study his habits. And then strike when he'd least expect it.

Worried they'd leave before he could follow them, Jonno lifted the window sash and looked outside. There was a sturdy looking tree branch he could grab onto and use to shimmy his way down. But he feared it might not bear his weight and he'd fall down flat on his arse, giving himself away.

He left the room without giving Father Baker a second glance. He was ancient history. Done and dusted. He took the stairs two at a time, and rushed towards the reception.

Mercifully, Isa wasn't there to trap him with more mind-numbing chit-chat. He sprinted out the main door, turned right, then ducked behind the hedges and edged towards the clearing as silently as he possibly could.

'You should join us. It'll be fun,' Al said.

'Nah, no way. I'm not the outdoorsy type,' replied the man in the overalls.

'What the hell are they on about?' Jonno wondered as

he peered at them through a small break in the thick shrubbery.

'Och, but we wouldn't be roughing it out,' Al said. 'There's showers, heating, comfy beds. All the mod cons.'

'Well what's the bloody point then, eh?' said the bloke in overalls.

'Ha, that's what I told him,' the woman said. 'Where's the fun in it if you don't shower in a bucket and shite under the stars?'

Al and his mates chatted for another few minutes, with an ease that made Jonno's blood boil. His hand reached for the gun all by itself, and he had to make an effort to stop it.

Patience, bud. Patience. This time he'd fucking get him. But he had to wait for the right opportunity.

The woman looked at her watch.

'We need to get going, or the punters are going to be annoyed at us,' the woman said.

'Aye, aye boss,' Al replied.

She giggled and slapped him playfully.

Jonno's stomach turned. What a prick. What a bastard. Acting like nothing happened. Completely at ease and comfortable in his own skin.

They said their goodbyes and began walking towards the road. Jonno edged his way back through the shrubbery, stumbling twice and scratching his cheek against a wayward holly bush. He cursed and wiped his hand on the seat of his jeans, not caring that it would leave a smear. He peered over the hedge, saw Al and the woman put helmets on.

He moved as fast as he could, tiptoeing his way back to the main entrance and reaching his car in a crouch, so they wouldn't spot him. Then he got into the car and waited.

The woman sat astride the motorcycle and kick-started it to life. Jonno turned the key in the ignition. The motorcycle was so loud he could barely hear his car's engine turn over. When they left in a cloud of exhaust, Al riding pillion, he put the car into second gear and inched his way after them, keeping his distance. Waiting for them to turn corners before he drove forward so they wouldn't notice him, and hoping they didn't disappear unexpectedly through a concealed exit.

He took a deep breath, and realised he felt good.

Better than good.

Father Baker could no longer hurt him. He was a shell of a man fading out of existence.

And Al.

Well, Al was going to get what was coming to him. With interest.

CHAPTER 54

Sitting on a stool with his back to the bar, sipping an ice-cold Stella, Al felt tired but content. It had been an exceptionally busy Friday. His brain was fuzzy, and his feet ached from standing up for hours dealing with the onslaught of punters. But it was a good tiredness. The kind that made you feel like you'd earned your beer and your rest.

He and P passed a joint back and forth, chatting idly about their plans for the night.

'Why don't we watch Ben Hur?' she said. 'Ever heard of it?'

'Isn't that a three-hour long film?' Al replied.

'It's a classic!'

This was a new thing for them. P loved old films, and she was trying to turn Al onto them. Al protested, but it was mostly in jest. In truth, he didn't really mind what they did as long as it didn't involve physical effort

P puffed on the joint, and handed it over. He brought it to his lips and took a long drag. Gilby had been right. This was top stuff. Every inhale was making him feel more relaxed. And as he looked out at the sea of empty tables and chairs, he could feel a warm glow spreading across his body.

'Right, I'm going to take those bad boys out to the bins,' P said, nodding at two huge white plastic bags overflowing with the night's detritus. 'Want to lock up, and I'll meet you outside?'

'Your wish is my command,' Al said.

She blew him a raspberry, grabbed the bin bags, and headed out towards the service entrance. Al finished his beer, popped the glass in the washer, then locked the pub's front door. One deadbolt. Two large brass bolts. It felt like overkill. Every night, P emptied the till, counted the takings, and locked them in a safe. And even if somebody fancied themselves a hotshot safecracker, it was unlikely they'd get away with it. Everybody knew everybody in Fort Drumblehan. Word would spread. But he did it anyway. Force of habit. Where he was from, you didn't take any chances.

He gave the bar one final look to make sure everything was in order. The chairs were all upside down on the tables. The fridges restocked. The till lying open and empty. He nodded, satisfied, shrugged on his coat, and patted down the pockets for his house keys as he walked around the bar and towards the back door.

'Well, look who's here.'

The spring in Al's step died as soon as he heard that voice.

'Alright Al. Surprised to see me, eh?' Jonno said. 'Or should I call you Jack?'

The bin bags were lying on the floor, assorted cans, straws, bits of blue roll, and other rubbish spilling out of them. Jonno was standing next to them, his hairy left arm wrapped around P's shoulders, his right arm hidden behind her back.

The tableau hit him like a cold shower. The pleasant fogginess he'd been relishing vanished, and he was suddenly stone cold sober. His hands curled into fists. His biceps tensed.

The room, which was small to begin with, was packed with beer kegs, crates of cider, and boxes of whisky, gin, vodka, and assorted liqueurs. There was so much stuff there was barely any room to move. Behind Al, the only door led back behind the bar and to the pub beyond. He was trapped. Boxed in. P and him both were. This time, he didn't have his hands tied behind his back. But neither was he carrying a razor blade in his shirt cuff. He'd dispensed with that, without giving it much thought, in the days after reading the newspaper article about the gang war in Strathburgh.

Stupid mistake.

'Jonno. How the fuck did you find me?' Al seethed.

Jonno laughed. It was a disconcertingly high-pitched, humourless sound that made Al's skin crawl.

'Let's just say an old friend came through for me,' Jonno said.

'Jack?' P pleaded. 'What the hell's going on?'

She squirmed, almost slipping from Jonno's grasp. He tightened his grip on her. The tendons in his forearms bulged.

'Who's this bloke?' she continued. 'Why's he calling you Al?

A cruel smile teased Jonno's lips.

'So she doesn't know, does she?' he said. 'This is going to be more fun than I thought.'

'What? What don't I know?' P said.

Her face was flushed, her eyes wide. But she also had an air of grim determination.

'That's enough. Shut the fuck up, hen,' Jonno snapped. He nodded to Al.

'Get back inside, bud or I'm going to shoot your missus right here.'

'Jonno, this is between us,' Al said. 'Leave her out of it.'

'Jack?'

'Let her go,' Al said.

'Enough!' Jonno roared. 'I said, get back inside.'

Al raised his hands. He walked backwards through the bar area and into the pub's main space. Jonno and P followed, inching their way forward awkwardly, like dance partners who were still getting used to each other.

'Grab a chair,' Jonno said.

His gun hand dug into the small of P's back.

'Don't move or I shoot. Understood?' he whispered in her ear.

P nodded calmly. He slowly let go of her. Fished a hunk of rope from his jacket pocket. Handed it to her.

'Tie him up,' he said.

P scanned the room. She looked at Al, at a loose chair on one of the tables, then back at Jonno. Al looked at her quizzically. Jonno pushed her forward. Impatient.

'Move,' he said.

P edged towards Al. Slowly and deliberately. Her eyes fixed in front of her. Her expression unreadable.

'I said move it, you stupid fucking cow,' Jonno said, waving his gun. 'I don't have all night.'

P pivoted. A chair flew towards Jonno's head. Instinctively, Jonno lifted his hands towards his face to protect himself. The gun clattered to the floor and went off.

The sound was deafening in the enclosed space. Al felt his cheek smart. He touched it with the tips of his fingers and they came away bloody. P lunged for the chair. Raised it over her head. It connected with Jonno's wrists with a dull thud. Jonno screamed with pain and rage.

It was now or never.

Al sprang to his feet. Rushed Jonno. Jonno crashed into the bar, and Al kicked him in the balls. Jonno groaned and doubled up, seething with fury. No, the prick wasn't going to best him again. No fucking way.

He lunged forward with a roar, but it was clumsy and shambling. Al kicked him in the face. There was a crunch of teeth. Blood dripped out of Jonno's mouth and onto the pub's freshly mopped floor.

'Och, you fucking rat bastard,' Jonno growled. 'You're DEAD! YOU HEAR ME?'

He swung wildly at Al's head with his balled up fist. Al ducked. His heart was racing. But his tiredness, the weed, and the beer were also making themselves felt. He wasn't sure how long he could keep this up. He had to neutralise Jonno, now. Or he was done for.

Jonno's fist connected with his cheek and his jaw exploded with pain. Jonno peeled back his bloody lips in a ghastly approximation of a smile.

'This time you're not getting away you prick,' he said.

Jonno moved forward, pressing his advantage. The backs of Al's thighs connected with one of the tables and a chair tipped over, clattering to the floor. There were other tables on each side, and Jonno was kissing distance. He had nowhere to go.

He saw P from the corner of his eye, sneaking up on Jonno. There was a click. Jonno felt cold metal pressing on the back of his skull.

'That's enough,' P said, quietly.

Jonno lowered his hands.

P backed away, her eyes never leaving Jonno. The gun trained on his face.

'On your knees,' she said. 'Do it, or I'll blow your head off.'

Jonno did as he was told.

She nodded at the hunk of rope Jonno had given her to tie Al with. It was lying forgotten on the floor.

'Tie him up,' she told Al, all business.

Al picked up the rope, tied Jonno's arms behind his back, pulling the rope tight.

'Fuck,' Jonno growled as the rough material bit into his forearms.

'Shut up,' Al told him.

When he was done, he pushed Jonno into a chair. Then he used what was left of the rope to tie Jonno's bound hands to the chair's back. He nodded grimly. His cheek still stung from whatever had grazed it — a bullet or a wayward splinter. But he'd managed to best the oaf yet again. Thanks to P.

'That was some quick thinking,' he told her. 'Thank you. I couldn't have kept it up much longer.'

P said nothing.

He began walking towards her.

She swivelled her arm, pointed the gun at him. Al froze.

'P, what the-'

'Stay where you are,' P said, in a no-nonsense voice he could barely recognise.

Her eyes had gone dull. She looked at him like she'd never seen him before. Like they hadn't spent entire mornings in bed chatting about this and that while the world went by around them.

'P?' Al said.

'Go on. Move back.'

Reluctantly, hating the sinking feeling in his stomach, he obliged.

'Now, one of you,' P said, moving the gun from Jonno to Al and back again, 'I don't care who, is going to tell me what's going on. Or I'm going to fucking shoot you both. Am I clear?'

'So you've been lying to me all along, then?' P said, prowling in front of Jonno and Al. 'You've been feeding me one lie after the other, day in, day out, with a straight face. Is that it, Jack? Or is it Al?'

The name was made up of just two letters. But forming the sounds felt like chewing hunks of rotten meat. She'd listened to Al's story — how he'd got involved with the Red Hand because of Ma Edwards' debt, how the Chairman had tried to have him killed, how he'd had to grass to save himself, which meant he'd had to assume a new identity and move away from Strathburgh — with a blank expression. Not giving away anything. And then she'd gone silent. Mulling over what she'd learned.

But now, betrayal was written all over her face. In the way her eyes avoided him when she spoke. How her lips were drawn. The set of her jaw.

Al felt an unexpected stab of pain. But he was so inured to hiding any emotion that might be perceived as a sign of weakness that he pushed it back down where it belonged with both fucking hands.

'The only things I ever lied about were my name and what brought me here. Nothing else,' Al said. 'And only because I had to. To protect my cover.'

P scoffed.

'Sure. So you've never given me any specifics about your "past life",' she fired back. 'But lying by omission's still lying. You do know that, right?'

He lifted his hands, then let them drop by his sides. What *could* he say? Hadn't he made it clear that it was come here or get shot and buried in a shallow grave in an anonymous stretch of green belt? And that he was secretly glad he'd taken the first option, because being here, with her, had started changing his perspective? Showing him a different life — a happier life — was possible, even for somebody like him?

He tried again.

'P, listen,' he began.

She raised her hand to shut him up. Turned her face away.

'You have one hour to sort out whatever your business is with your buddy here,' she said, her eyes fixed on a point in front of her. 'One. And then we're done. Get the fuck out of my pub and my life. Understood?'

'P-'

Her throat worked.

How dare he? How fucking dare he?

She had trusted him. Let him in. Involved him in her fucking business. And he'd been stringing her along. They'd been actors in a play she didn't even know she was a part of.

'Did you even care?' P said, her voice so bitter he felt physically stung. 'Or did you pretend to like me just so you'd have a piece of my business?'

Al felt something in him break. 'Of course I do care!' he said. 'P, I-'

'Save it,' she said.

She put the safety on and threw the gun onto a free table like it was covered in poison. Turned towards the bar and the back door beyond.

Al looked at her, unsure whether to go after her, reach out, or let her go. What was he expected to do? He'd told her the truth. He really did care, and this was uncharted territory for him. He'd never cared before.

'One hour,' P repeated without turning. 'Don't be here when I'm back.'

CHAPTER 56

Al watched P disappear behind the bar. Heard the rear door slam shut with a metallic clang. Why did this happen? Why did everyone leave? How had it all gone so wrong, so fast?

He stood there, unable to move, staring at the empty space between the arches that led to the back room. His fists clenched and unclenched, as if he were a robot that had short-circuited.

'Looks like someone's in love,' came the sarcastic growl from behind him.

The words barely registered. But the tone, dripping with contempt, enraged him. Brought him back to the moment. There would be time for him to be maudlin. After he'd squashed this freakishly large insect and dumped him off the edge of a cliff.

He grabbed the steel rod they used to prop the rear door open, gripping it in his right hand like a cricket bat, so tight his knuckles turned white.

'How did you find me?' Al said.

He walked towards Jonno's chair, bumping the rod

rhythmically against the side of his thigh. It made a muffled, thunking sound.

Thunk.

Thunk.

Thunk.

Jonno looked up at him, with thunder in his eyes. 'I'm not telling you shite, rat,' he said.

He made a gurgling sound deep in his throat and spat a gob of greenish-yellow phlegm. Part of it splattered against the white toecap of Al's right trainer.

'I think you are,' Al said.

He swung the rod behind his shoulder with both hands. Drove it into Jonno's stomach. Jonno ground his teeth and tried to breathe through it, but the wind had rushed out of him. He felt acid rising up his throat and swallowed it down.

'Let's try again,' Al said, when Jonno had brought his breathing back under control. 'How. Did. You find me?'

Jonno gave him a defiant look. Closed his mouth. Behind him, his fingers tried to worry at the knot that bound his wrists together. But Al had tied him too tightly. He had barely any range of motion and his fingers were going numb.

'Tell me!' Al shouted in Jonno's face. 'Tell me, you piece of shite! Spit it out!'

Jonno didn't flinch.

Al ground his teeth. He could feel his blood pressure rising and he mashed the rod across Jonno's jaw. When it connected, making more blood spout out of Jonno's already injured mouth, he felt something loosen inside him. A deeply satisfying release.

'You know what?' Al said. 'Fine. There are other ways to make you talk.'

He cast the metal rod away. Reached for the gun and aimed it at him.

Jonno laughed.

'You haven't got the balls,' he sneered.

Al flicked the safety off.

'Try me.'

Jonno lifted his head, stared right back at him.

'Go on, you prick,' he said. 'Let's see what you're made of.'

The shot rang out near-instantly. The force of the bullet slammed Jonno against the chair.

'How does that feel?' Al said, cocking the gun, a grim smile on his lips. 'Want another demonstration? Because I'm happy to oblige.'

The bullet had hit Jonno in the fleshy part where his right arm connected with his shoulder. He'd live. But the pain was delicious. So excruciating he felt lightheaded. Sweat beaded his temples.

'So?' Al prodded. 'What is it going to be?'

He put the gun down, picked up the rod. Rammed it into Jonno's bullet wound.

Jonno screamed. A strangled, childlike sound.

'How'd you find me?' Al said again.

His face was inches from Jonno's, and he was screaming. Showering him with spittle. The red mist had infiltrated every neuron in his brain. He was seconds away from losing control, and then he didn't know what would happen.

'Tell me! Tell me! Tell me!' he kept shouting, over and over in Jonno's face. 'Tell me or I'll fucking kneecap you. I swear to god.'

Jonno's eyes had gone wide and his skin papery white. Partly from the pain. But mostly because he'd been through this before. The bloke shouting at him now wasn't a priest. Nor did he have a Belfast accent. But it didn't matter. It was so close. So fucking close. Oh fuck, wasn't he supposed to be wasting away in a manse in the countryside? Hadn't he seen this for himself just two days before? How had Father Baker come back? How was he here? How had he regained his strength?

Al stepped back. Pressed the rod lightly against the wound. Jonno emitted a pathetic whimper.

'Inspector Hendrie,' he whispered, so softly Al could barely hear him.

'What?' Al said. 'Say that again.'

'It was Inspector Hendrie,' Jonno repeated, louder.

His lips were trembling and the confidence had drained from his eyes. There were large sweat patches under his arms, deep blue pools on an expanse of lighter fabric.

'What? How?' Al said.

He stopped. Stared at him, confused. Was he winding him up?

'Don't you lie to me,' he said, lifting the rod over his head.

'I'M NOT! I'M NOT!' Jonno pleaded.

'Explain,' Al said.

'That bloke you roughed up at the service station talked to the polis. We leaned on Hendrie, and she used the info to track you down.'

Al wasn't sure he understood what Jonno was on about. Then his mind flashed back to the rat-faced prick writhing on the bathroom floor at the Moto, and he cursed himself.

Of course. Of fucking course.

His hand let go of the rod. What a daft fucking cunt. Why hadn't he listened to Redditch? Why hadn't he let it go? Now look at this mess. Everything had been ruined because he had to show some random eejit who was top dog.

'Who's we?' he sighed. 'Did Guthrie send you? Is that it? Is he still running things from inside?'

Jonno leaned back in his chair. His skin had taken on a waxy colour. Sweat had pooled under his fleshy chin and darkened his shirt collar.

'Guthrie's finished,' he said in between rasping breaths. 'Living dead.'

'Then who's in charge now?' Al snapped back.

'The CEO.'

The CEO. Who the fuck was that? Who had taken over? This was getting worse by the minute. Not only was his cover probably blown. But the polis would be after him too if that rat-faced bastard had grassed.

That last word, 'grassed', made him laugh. If you could call the sharp, humourless sound that came out of his throat a laugh. It was almost poetic. He was the punchline in a cosmic joke.

'What does the CEO want?' Al growled.

'What do you think?' Jonno clapped back.

Right. Of course. The CEO would want to send a message to cement his authority, even if he'd benefitted from Guthrie being sidelined. You grass, you die. It was all politics. Theatre.

The next step felt scary. Stupid. But also right. If he stayed here he'd be a sitting duck, ready to be plucked by whoever came for him first — the polis or the CEO's next henchman. He had to get in front of this.

Al dropped the rod to the floor with a clank. Wiped Jonno's blood off his hands with a wad of blue roll. Then he looked up at him.

'It's your lucky day,' he told Jonno, whose breathing, whistly even on a good day, sounded like a boiling kettle.

Jonno raised his head.

'Is that so?' he told Al in a hushed whisper.

'You get to live. For now.'

Al walked behind Jonno, crouched down, and untied the rope from the back of the chair, making sure Jonno's hands were still trussed up tightly. Not that he could do much in his state. He was going into shock.

'Get up,' Al commanded.

Jonno tried to stand up, but he couldn't make it. His legs were too wobbly. He tried again, and managed with Al's help.

'Let's go,' Al said.

'Where?'

'Strathburgh,' Al said. 'You're going to introduce me to the CEO, and we're going to straighten this whole thing out.'

CHAPTER 57

That Friday, as Al's past caught up with him, I was sitting in The Grosvenor, sipping a pint of Guinness and aimlessly scrolling my news feed. It had been a tiring day — well, week, actually — but in a good way. Productive. Phillip had barricaded himself in his office, working on something top secret. And that meant the rest of us could actually get stuff done instead of wasting our energy managing his whims. I'd even smoothed out the Carruthers Capital thing.

'Fine, fine, Mr Haig,' Phillip had told me, in a surprisingly dismissive tone, when I'd tried to tell him about a compromise position I'd come up with. 'Do what you think's best.'

He'd barely even glanced up from his laptop. This was so unusual, so anticlimactic, after all that palaver, that I was about to protest. But he practically shooed me out of his office before I could open my mouth. Whatever it was he was working on, it must've been pretty important.

'Penny for your thoughts?'

I looked up and saw Joan smiling at me, a cocktail glass full of orange-coloured liquid in her hand.

'Hey,' I said, returning the smile.

My mood, already upbeat, brightened even more.

'I see you've started without me?'

She pursed her lips and dropped her jaw. 'That won't do now, Mr Haig. Will it?'

She'd honed her Phillip impression to the point where it was much better than mine. I laughed out loud. She sat at the table across from me and sipped her drink.

'What's that you're having?' I asked. 'Looks very fancy.'

I lifted the beer to my lips and drained half of it. The condensation had pooled on the cardboard coaster, making it soggy and sticking it to the bottom of the glass.

'Tequila sunrise,' she said.

'Bringing out the big guns tonight!'

'It's Friday and I am *over* this week.'

'That bad, eh?'

'You know how it is. Clients gonna client,' Joan said.

'Well, on the bright side, no Phillip,' I replied. 'He's been conspicuous by his absence, hasn't he?'

'Och, aye,' she told me. 'And thank fuck for that.'

She leaned in towards me conspiratorially.

'What's that about? What's he doing in that office of his, do you think? He even answered his bloody phone! He never does that.'

I took another sip of beer and shrugged.

'Fuck knows. Whatever it is, though, I hope it keeps him busy for a long time.'

'I'll drink to that,' Joan agreed.

We clinked glasses and drank.

'He's a menace,' I said. 'I don't know why the other

partners haven't forced him out. I bet they've got an area in the filing room just for staff complaints about him.'

'Och, no. He's harmless,' Joan said. 'I mean, a bit eccentric, endlessly frustrating, and fucking laaaazzzzyyyyyy. But I suppose I'd be weird and lazy too if I'd never had to put in any effort because Daddy left me a successful financial consultancy.'

Maybe she was right. I looked up to tell her so, but she was doubled over, sniffling.

'Hey, what's wrong?' I asked, alarmed, thinking she'd burst into tears. 'What happened?'

She lifted her head. To my relief the tears streaming down her face weren't sad tears. They were tears of laughter. Her face was bright red, and she was laughing so hard she was beside herself.

'What?' I said, confused. 'What's going on?'

'Och, no... I'm just-' she said.

She waited for the laughter to subside. Sipped her cocktail. Wiped her eyes.

'Sorry... I just flashed back to the last time Phillip had a top secret project,' she said.

'Och?'

'So this was around five or six months ago, I think,' she started. 'Actually, I can't believe I haven't told you this before. It's way too juicy. The thing with the spreadsheet?'

'Eh, no? What spreadsheet?' I said, unsure where this was going.

'So he gave me a list of businesses and told me to put together a spreadsheet. Date of registration. Registered address. Shareholders. Turnover. That sort of thing.'

'What? Why didn't he give that to one of the juniors?' I said, feeling outraged on Joan's behalf.

Joan nodded. 'I know! But he looked very solemn. So I

said you know what? If it gets him off my back for a few days, it'll be worth it. So I put together the info and emailed it. Job done. Forgot about it.'

'Right.'

She was overcome by another fit of laughter.

'Och, god, sorry, I-' she gasped, holding her hands up in surrender. 'It's just too much.'

I waited for her to get herself under control, intrigued. What could be so funny?

'Sorry,' she said, wiping more tears from her eyes. 'So, I was saying. For a day or so, it does the trick. Phillip's shut away in his office and barely comes out. Not even at lunchtime. Then, the next day, he summons me, absolutely livid. "Ms Strachan, what do you think you're playing at?" he says, his face turning purple. So I manage to calm him down somehow and ask him what's wrong. And get this.'

She brayed more laughter.

'He's spent I don't know how many hours working on this bloody spreadsheet, right? And then he goes home, comes back to the office the next day, and finds that all his work's gone. Nothing's been saved. So he's all flushed pink, accusing me of tampering with his spreadsheet and telling me to put it back like it was.'

'Are you going to say what I think you are?' I said.

'No. Worse.'

She giggled.

'Believe it or not, he actually remembered to save the document. But somehow, he managed to switch it to read only. So he thought he was saving when he wasn't.'

'Och, what an eejit.' I said, spurting Guinness from my nose.

'To be fair to him, he's improved,' Joan said. 'I remember a few years back we were working with this

American company. Sensitive industry, lots of security, so he needed a password to access their documents. I set it up for him, picked one he'd remember, and wrote it down. But he said he didn't need it. "If I forget it I'll get in by trial and error, Ms Strachan." Aye, except the system locked him out after three failed attempts. We had to have a conference call with their IT department to sort it. And then legal got involved. A whole shitestorm.'

I shook my head. 'But look at us,' I told Joan. 'Why are we talking about Phillip on a Friday, anyway?'

'Stockholm Syndrome?' Joan suggested.

'Well,' I chuckled, 'whatever his top secret project is, long may it continue.'

'Amen to that,' Joan said, raising her glass and draining it.

'Do you want another one of those?' asked, pointing at her empty cocktail glass.

'Aye, sure, thank you,' she said.

I got up. The room spun and I sat back down with a thump.

'Something wrong?' Joan asked.

'Och, no. Just a dizzy spell. I must've stood up too fast.'

I tried again, more slowly. This time the room stayed put, and I walked to the bar without incident.

CHAPTER 58

'You're doing amazing!' Jillian DeVoss proclaimed through the laptop's tinny speakers.

Her soft, breathy voice and Valley Girl accent grated on Morag's nerves. But the workouts were great — challenging enough to get the blood flowing, but also easy to follow and not so demanding that you felt wiped afterwards.

'Now gently clasp your shins and bend your knees inwards, into your chest, timing it with your outbreath.'

Morag brought her knees to her chest gradually, working through the tightness in her hamstrings. She was probably going to regret this later. But, as she breathed out, she really did feel the tightness ease and a sense of wellbeing wash over her.

As if her body wanted to confirm this was, in fact, the case, a loud fart trumpeted out of her ample arse. She sighed. Bliss. Shame that arrogant prick's face wasn't in the vicinity. It would've made it all the more satisfying.

She cackled and let another fart rip. It came out with

such force she felt friction against her arse cheeks, a sensation like she'd been rolling around in gravel pants-free.

'Focus on your belly,' Jillian continued, oblivious to the strident sounds and sulphurous smells in Morag's flat. 'Feel it pressing against your legs with every inhale. And then it moves out, slowly, as you release your outbreath, and presses against your legs again with your next inhale.'

Morag's hamstrings were burning, and she loosened her grip. There was a lot to be said for the benefits of yoga, but it was never going to be something she looked forward to. She constantly had to remind herself of how much better she'd feel afterwards. And how important it was that she stay fit.

Now more than ever.

She rolled onto her stomach, lifted her arse up in the air, and placed her forehead on her yoga mat. The muscles in her calves and shoulders stretched, which felt uncomfortable but not exactly unpleasant. She held the pose, breathing in and out slowly, feeling the tension ease. Then Jillian urged her to like the video and subscribe to her YouTube channel, breaking the spell.

Morag shut her laptop, got up from the yoga mat, and shook the residual tension out of her limbs. The clock on the mantel said 7pm. It was almost time. She sipped water, wiped the sweat off her face and under her arms with a towel, and applied some roll-on deodorant. There was no time for a shower. But that was neither here nor there. They might get a whiff of body odour. Turn up their nose at it. And she'd still get her way.

The yoga class had made her feel much more calm and centred. But there was still an elusive thread of nervousness weaving its way around her body. She needed this to go perfectly. She picked a jumper — a teal number to go with her deep blue slacks — put her glasses back on, and peered out of the window. The street was deserted. Everyone would be inside for tea and telly.

Her phone was on the small folding dining table. She picked it up. No texts or missed calls. Damn the man. Where had he gone? He'd said he'd be here. The thread of nervousness thickened into a string. Well, it was too late. The wheels were in motion. If she cancelled, she'd lose her window. It had to happen that night, with or without him.

She dialled the first number in her recents. Waited for that insufferable prick to answer. The phone rang out. She closed her eyes, waited for her frustration to subside.

'Stay calm,' she said. 'Serene. Swans. A lake with a surface so still and clear it seems like a piece of glass.'

She visualised it in her head. Smelled the lavender's sweet aromas, and felt the Sun through her jumper. Heard the birds' plaintive cries as they glided across a beautifully clear blue sky.

Yes, that was better. Much better.

She redialled. This time, he picked up on the fifth ring.

'Where the hell were you?' she hissed. 'I've been trying to reach you.'

'Sorry,' he replied. 'Phone was in the other room.'

She bit her lip.

'Any news about our mutual friend at The Grosvenor?'

'Aye. The package's been delivered. Bloke's had his pint and he's in the process of getting completely slaughtered. By the end of the night he won't know his own Ma if she shouts his middle name.'

'Wonderful. Now keep your phone next to you and be on standby. I'm going to need you later tonight. Got it?'

CHAPTER 59

'One Guinness and a tequila surmise, please,' I mumbled to the barman, a short bloke in a black muscle shirt and biceps the size of rugby balls.

'Tequila what, bud?' he shot back.

'Surmise.'

'Eh?'

What the fuck was I saying? Why wasn't it coming out right?

'Surprise... err sunrise,' I finally managed, with some effort.

The barman looked at me impassively and got to work pouring the drinks.

'That'll be £15,' he said.

I fumbled out my phone. For some reason, my hands were shaking, and I couldn't double click the button well enough to launch the wallet app. The bloody thing slipped and fell on the sticky pub floor. Fuck's sake. I bent down to retrieve it. Almost got stabbed in the eye with a six-inch stiletto heel.

Never mind. Fuck shortcuts. I unlocked my phone and launched the wallet app the old school way — by pressing it. The barman was waiting, card machine in his outstretched hand, shaking his head, which made me feel unreasonably annoyed. I paid and navigated back to our table, feeling decidedly worse for wear and not sure why. Perhaps the week had caught up with me. I certainly hadn't had enough to drink to justify being in this state. I placed the drinks on the table. Saw Shawn sitting across from me.

'Didn't see you coming in,' I said.

'Aye, that's me. I'm a sneaky ninja eh,' Shawn said.

He leaned back in his chair and spread out, draping his left arm expansively across the back of Joan's chair. I lifted my pint and drank deep. Half of it dribbled down my chin and onto my shirt.

'Fuck's sake!' I slurred.

'It's cool, Bertie, chill,' Shawn said.

He handed me a napkin.

'Here. We can do the beer-drinking basics lesson when you're less irritable, eh?'

He elbowed Joan and winked. They held each other's gazes and chuckled, and I felt an irrational pang of jealousy. He drained his beer and let out a mighty burp.

'Good lord, Shawn. That smells like something died in your mouth,' Joan said, holding her nose.

Whatever moment had passed between them, the spell was broken. Whew.

'So, are you coming for a run with me this Sunday, or what?' Shawn asked me.

When he'd first joined the firm, about a year back, I'd agreed to go because he'd caught me on the back foot and I didn't know how to get out of it. To my horror, he'd never let me forget that one moment of weakness. He'd been on my case about making it a regular thing ever since.

'No, not after last time, bud,' I said. 'I almost had a bloody heart attack.'

'That's because you're out of shape. You stick with me, you'll be fighting fit in no time. You could even run the Strathburgh marathon.'

'The what?'

'The Strathburgh marathon. It's in September. Five months' time, which is plenty.'

He put his palm to his forehead, like a man who was either suffering from a monster headache or had just had the most brilliant idea ever.

'Actually, you know what? We should all do it!' he said.

'Are you daft? How long's a marathon?' Joan asked, looking horrified.

'Twenty six miles.'

'What?' I said.

I looked at Joan.

'Is he serious? He is, isn't he? Thirty-six miles. Bloody hell.'

'Twenty-six, bud,' Shawn said. 'It's very doable, you know. Last one I ran there were older runners, a blind bloke with his cane... you've no excuses.'

Shawn went off, laying out his training plan, the finer points of race-day pacing, how to choose the right running shoes. Even his smoothie recipes and the merits of different brands of protein powder.

At some point between pint two and pint three, his voice took on a gurgly quality, like he was talking underwater.

The last thing I remember about that night is that I

tried to shake it off, but it just kept getting worse, so I tuned him out.

Pint three became pint four. Pint four became pint five.

As I'm sure you'll understand, my memory went from somewhat fuzzy to nonexistent after that. I've no clue what happened from here on out.

CHAPTER 60

Morag picked the bottle of Macallan and three tumblers off her kitchen counter, careful not to touch their rims, and walked towards the hallway. A look through the peephole confirmed the coast was clear, so she got out of her flat and climbed up the stairs as quickly as she could without abandoning her hobbling walk completely. Judging by the silence enveloping the building, it was unlikely she'd run into anyone. Even Graeme's voice — perennially speaking to somebody on the phone — was conspicuous by its absence. But she didn't want to risk it. That would give the game away.

When she stepped onto the landing, she shifted the whisky bottle to the crook of her arm. Then she selected the skeleton key from her ring and let herself inside Bertie's flat. The smell of slightly burnt toast hit her straight away. She wrinkled her nose and cracked open a window to air out the smell. This was another strike against him. Not only was he rude to her, like he thought he was doing her some sort of favour by giving her the time of day. He couldn't cook to save his life. Shame he thought he was some sort of master chef, judging by all the fancy recipes he tried out. But she supposed that was the way of the world. The mediocre always overestimated their abilities, while those with real potential thought too little of themselves. At least he was neat and she didn't have too much tidying up to do. That was just as well, because her phone rang.

'Yes,' she said into the phone.

'Ms Stevenson, hello. How are you?'

She rolled her eyes. The prick thought making needless small talk was quaint. She ignored the question.

'Mr McAllister, have you arrived?' she said.

'Yes. We're downstairs,' Phillip sniffed.

'Very well. And I'm assuming you're all good to come up?'

'Ye-es,' Phillip said testily. 'Mr Kiernan's satisfied it's OK to do so.'

'Very well. I'll buzz you up.'

Kiernan led the way, looking dapper in a custom-made tux and red bowtie, his Rolex peeking out of his shirt cuff in a way that was meant to look accidental, but which was actually — Morag was willing to bet good money on this, even though she loathed gambling — a considered move on his part. A way for him to show off. His iron grey pompadour gleamed in the light of the studio room's single fixture. Phillip trailed behind him. His dark blue suit was probably just as expensive as Kiernan's tux, but much more understated. The choice of somebody comfortable enough in his wealth not to feel compelled to scream 'Look at me!' all the time. His face was pinched like somebody had pooed under his nose. His combover covered his scalp unevenly, revealing the pink pate underneath. The few times she'd met him, Morag had always wondered why he went through the trouble of concealing what was patently obvious to anyone with half an eye. But she supposed you could never underestimate the power of denial.

'Good evening, gentlemen,' Morag said, ushering them in. 'Make yourselves at home. Please.'

Kiernan didn't need any cajoling. He plopped himself on the sofa with a satisfied grunt, crossed his legs, and spread his arms wide, resting them on the cushions on either side of him like he owned the place. Phillip grabbed a chair from the dining area and wiped it fussily with a powder blue handkerchief. Then he sat down, balanced his brown leather briefcase on his lap, and pulled out a thick sheaf of papers.

'So here we are,' Kiernan sneered. 'Enjoying this, are you, Gretchen?'

'Don't call me that!' Morag was about to say.

She caught herself just in time. It wouldn't do to rise to the bait. Let him have his fun.

'Och sorry. Do you prefer to be called Madam CEO these days?' Kiernan continued, grinning mockingly. 'How does your brother feel about that?'

Morag visualised what she had planned for the prick. It had the same effect on her as if she'd just spent fifteen minutes watching videos of frolicking kittens on YouTube.

'Whatever you're comfortable with, Boaby dear,' she said.

The patronising note in Morag's voice seemed to go over Kiernan's head, because he didn't react. He checked his Rolex, straightened his bow tie, leaned back into the sofa.

'Can I offer you a drink, Boaby?' Morag said. 'I've got a lovely forty-year old Macallan. Unless it's too early for you?'

She wasn't sure he'd need convincing. But she reckoned some reverse psychology wouldn't hurt. Men like him relished being contrarian, even when it was against their best interests.

'Aye, I'll have a dram,' Kiernan said.

'Phillip?' she said, secretly hoping he'd say no.

If he wanted one, it might complicate things. But it wouldn't seem right not to offer.

Thankfully, he didn't disappoint. 'Err, no, thank you,' he replied.

'Can I get you something else? A glass of water perhaps?' Morag insisted.

'No, that won't be necessary. I'm fine, thank you,' Phillip said, not looking up from the papers resting on his lap.

Morag walked to the kitchenette, feeling pleased with herself, poured a generous measure of whisky for Kiernan and a smaller one for herself. She handed Kiernan his tumbler.

'Cheers,' Kiernan said, draining half the glass in a single gulp. 'Och, that's gooood. Liquid silk.'

He smacked his lips.

'Cheers to you,' Morag said smugly.

She took the smallest sip she could get away with, and placed the glass on the coffee table. Phillip cleared his throat, and looked first at Morag and then at Kiernan with a pained expression.

'Mr Kiernan. Ms Stevenson. Shall we begin?' he said.

Kiernan looked on expectantly, sipping the remains of his whisky.

'Go on then,' he said.

'I have two copies of the documents setting up the trust, here,' Phillip said, handing them each a sheaf of papers held together with black bulldog clips.

'If you turn over to page one,' he continued, 'you'll see this is a conditional trust that will come into being when-'

'Can't you just give us a brief summary?' Kiernan butted in. 'I've got to get to the theatre soon. We'll take your word for it that you've taken your duty as an impartial third party seriously. As I'm sure you have, right?'

Kiernan arched his right eyebrow as he said this. The hidden threat wasn't lost on Phillip, who kept his gaze fixed downwards and fidgeted with the papers in his lap. The poor man looked like he'd rather be getting a colonoscopy without anaesthetic. But if this act was meant to impress and intimidate Morag, it wasn't working in the slightest. It had been this way since he was a wean. He gave himself all these airs, but deep down he was just an insecure little boy from the estate who thought that, because he now wore bespoke suits, drove a Mercedes, and went to the theatre, his poo didn't stink anymore.

'I have to make sure you both understand what you're signing up to,' Phillip insisted. 'But, sure, I'll keep it short and give you the highlights if you're in a rush.'

'Sounds excellent to me,' Kiernan said.

Morag said nothing. Sometimes the best thing you could do was let events run their course.

'So, this is a conditional trust, which means it's only triggered in the specific circumstances set out in the constituting document. Do you both understand?'

Kiernan and Morag nodded.

'I'll not go through the finer details, since Mr Kiernan is pushed for time. But please review the document and get back to me if you have any questions. We can also make tweaks if there's anything you aren't completely happy with.'

Kiernan nodded again, impatiently.

'Let's get this over with,' he said.

'To confirm, the trust kicks in in the event of the suspicious death of one of the parties. Those parties being Mr Robert Kiernan and Ms Morag Stevenson. Should the circumstances surrounding said death point to the involvement of the surviving party, the entirety of said surviving party's business interests will be put in trust for the sole benefit of the decedent's heirs.'

'What the fuck does that even mean? Can't you say it in English?' Kiernan said.

'Och, why do you have to be like this?' Morag said.

She made an effort to keep her tone even, but her exasperation came through. He was showing off and they all knew it. He wouldn't have showed up if he hadn't had okayed every last detail in advance.

'You know exactly what it means, it's what we agreed. You get me killed, your territory, your routes, and your distribution are transferred to my organisation. I get you killed, the same happens — you get my business. We don't try to kill each other, we both live happily ever after. Literally and figuratively. Sounds about right, Phillip?'

Phillip gave Morag a brief, grateful look. He cleared his throat and continued.

'From the date of signature, both parties also agree that any and all claims by one party against the other respective party are hereby dismissed.'

'That means no more fighting,' Morag interjected before Kiernan could flex again. 'In case you're wondering.'

'And no motorcycle chains, eh?' he retorted.

'I've already told you,' Morag said. 'That wasn't us.'

Kiernan huffed. 'Then who?' he said.

He made as if to get up, but couldn't quite manage. Morag raised her palms in a placating gesture.

'Fine, don't get all twisted up about it,' she said. 'Look, let's agree to disagree so we can go back to doing business. It's better. For both our sakes, eh?

'Fine,' Kiernan said, draining the last of his whisky with a sigh. 'Ach, this is really good stuff.'

'Would you like another dram?' Morag said.

She almost regretted it. Had she asked too quickly? Sounded too eager? But, once again, Kiernan hadn't seemed to notice. He glanced at his watch and shrugged.

'Sure, why not?' he said. 'Just a wee one, though. I don't want to have to get up for a pish in the middle of the play.'

Charmingly put. Morag poured him another dram. He took a healthy gulp, and she relaxed. This was almost too easy. The great Robert Kiernan had grown complacent.

Phillip cleared his throat, but some of the awkwardness had left his face. He too had been worried. But both Kiernan and Morag seemed to be on the same page, and he was relieved. He rummaged about his briefcase. Produced a Parker pen. Clicked it and handed it deferentially to Kiernan.

Kiernan, who was absently rubbing his bicep and flexing his hand, took it.

'Well,' Phillip said, 'If you're both satisfied, there are three copies for you to sign. One for each of you, for your records, and one I'll retain in my office for safekeeping.'

He flipped through the pages of the document, pointed next to a yellow sticker with SIGN HERE in bright red letters. 'There. Signature, initials, and today's date, please.'

Kiernan leaned over the coffee table and scrawled his name with a flourish. He passed the documents and pen back to Phillip, who passed them to Morag. Then he sighed and leaned back into the sofa, his right leg jumping restlessly.

'Are you OK?' Morag asked.

'I'm fine,' Kiernan snapped. 'It's just...'

He glanced at his Rolex. His watch hand was shaking ever so slightly.

'I'm in a rush,' he finished.

Morag sat at the other end of the sofa, signed her name, and handed everything back to Phillip, who checked the signatures with a studied meticulousness that seemed unwarranted. He put one of the contracts and the pen back in his briefcase. Gave Morag and Kiernan a copy each.

Kiernan was huffing and rubbing his right thigh so hard he was giving himself a friction burn. He snatched the sheaf of papers out of Phillip's outstretched hand.

'Right,' he said. 'So that's that, eh? Are we all set? Good to go?'

'All set,' Phillip said.

'Wonderful,' Morag chimed in.

They all stood up, Kiernan with a marked effort. Morag shook hands with Phillip. Offered her hand to Kiernan. He looked at her as if she'd just suggested that he put his hands down an unflushed toilet. His right eyelid twitched.

'Are you sure you're OK?' Morag said. 'You look pale.'

In actual fact, Kiernan was more than pale. He was whiter than a sheet that had been left to soak in bleach all day. His lips and the skin under his eyes had taken on a bluish tint. His forehead was beaded with sweat.

'I'm...' he trailed off.

His eyes bulged. His arms shook violently. Whitish froth bubbled out of the corners of his mouth in thick, ropey strands.

Phillip dropped his briefcase and recoiled. He stepped

backwards until he bumped into the bookcase that divided the studio's living area from the sleeping nook.

Kiernan staggered forward, making choked gagging sounds. He tried to claw at his throat with shaky fingers, but they couldn't quite reach it. His muscles were too tense. Morag stepped out of the way. She could feel herself smile and made no effort to hide it. More foam bubbled out of Kiernan's mouth. His eyeballs were bulging so far out of their sockets they looked like they were about to pop.

'What's going on with him?' Phillip asked in a high falsetto. 'Do something, Ms Stevenson, for the love of Christ! Can't you see the man's distressed!'

'Take a breath and shut up, Phillip, why don't you?' Morag snapped.

She wasn't about to let him ruin the moment for her by behaving like a silly little boy.

Kiernan looked around him like a rat in a cage, hyper-ventilating, trying to look everywhere at once. He rushed towards Morag, two clumsy, drunken lunges. Morag side-stepped with ease, letting her leg trail behind her. Kiernan tripped, landing flat on his back on the bed. His left leg, dangling over the edge of the mattress, twitched jerkily, swishing against the bed covers. More gagging sounds gurgled out of his throat. Froth dribbled down his chin. He swiped at his shirt collar, but weakly. So weakly his hand barely made it halfway.

It was over just as quickly as it had started.

His lungs made one last-ditch gasp for air, but his chest seemed unable to expand. His fingers twitched. Both legs jerked. Violent, uncontrollable spasms. Then his bulging eyes went glassy and opaque, and his body relaxed with a long, guttural groan.

He was gone.

And good goddamn riddance, Morag thought.

Phillip slumped in his chair, trembling all over. His shaky breathing punctuated the silence.

'What have you done?' he said, his voice breaking. 'Oh dear god. What have you done, Morag?'

It was a measure of how upset he was that he'd ditched the formalities and called her by her first name.

'Is the briefcase unlocked?' she asked him.

Phillip sat up straight, with his hands palms downwards on his thighs. He'd have looked like a sphinx were it not for the juddery rise and fall of his chest.

'Is it unlocked?' Morag repeated.

He nodded absently.

She reached out. Opened it. Pulled out his copy of the trust document and picked up Kiernan's copy from the floor, where he'd dropped it. She placed them both in a pile on the coffee table. She'd get somebody to burn them later. Leave no trace.

'I'll take care of these documents, so you don't have to worry about them,' Morag said. 'Did anyone see you together?'

Phillip was too busy trying to get himself under control to speak.

'Just nod for yes, shake your head for no,' Morag said. 'Did anyone see him pick you up?'

He shook his head vigorously.

'Good. Does anyone else know about this meeting?'

Another vigorous shake.

'Wonderful,' Morag said. 'This meeting never happened. Are we clear?'

Phillip's eyes had gone vacant. The shock of what he'd just seen was settling in.

'Don't zone out on me,' Morag said.

She slapped him, palm open. Then backhanded him.

'Phillip,' she commanded. 'Look at me.'

Another slap. He looked up at her.

'I said, are we clear?'

'Yes! Yes!' he said. 'Absolutely.'

'Wonderful,' Morag said, smiling. 'Now, I suggest you get out of here and put this behind you. Why don't you go for a nice dinner, or whatever it is you do to relax? Somewhere public, where lots of people can see you. Do you understand me?'

Phillip hesitated.

'Do you understand me?'

He nodded shakily.

'Very well,' she said. 'I'll be in touch about settling your bill. Now, come on. Off you go.'

She clapped at him, like a schoolteacher summoning unruly kids.

The sharp, whip-like sound roused him from his shock-induced torpor. He snatched his briefcase and shot out of the flat so fast his patent leather shoes barely touched the floor.

CHAPTER 61

The call rang out.

Morag looked at her phone as if it were a dead rattlesnake, and felt something curdle inside her. She'd specifically told him to be on standby. Where the devil was he?

She closed her eyes. Redialled. This time he picked up on the second ring. His voice, she noted with displeasure, was thick and slightly out of breath.

'Where are you, Harry?' she said with barely concealed annoyance. 'I told you I'd be calling.'

'At home,' Harry replied.

The slur was slight, but noticeable.

'You've been drinking, haven't you?' she said.

'No, boss. No.'

'No, of course not,' she thought acidly.

She pushed the issue aside. They'd revisit it. Have a heart-to-heart about how his performance was failing to meet her expectations. But, first, to the more important task at hand.

'How soon can you get here?'

Harry considered. 'An hour?'

She glanced at the clock on the bedside table. 9:30pm. They were cutting it too fine for her liking, even if Bertie was out of commission.

'Forty-five minutes,' Morag snapped. 'And don't ring the buzzer. Call me on the burner. Understood?'

'Aye.'

'I hope so, Harry. I really do.'

She ended the call. Scanned the flat.

If it weren't for Kiernan's body lying supine on the bed, there was little evidence of what had happened. Three glasses — two on the coffee table, one on the kitchen counter next to the half-full bottle of Macallan. A misplaced dining chair. And the copies of the trust document.

She washed the glasses, dried them, and placed them and the whisky bottle in the hallway, so she wouldn't forget to take them away with her. She put the chair back where it belonged, in the small dining area. Plumped and straightened the sofa cushions. Then she turned around and surveyed the scene on the bed.

The telltale bluish tint had left Kiernan's skin, making it look as if he'd simply fallen asleep. It was almost as if he hadn't spent the better part of fifteen minutes gagging, fighting off muscle cramps, and struggling to breathe. A bad death for a bad bastard. A toxicology report would reveal traces of arsenic in his system. But an autopsy wasn't on the cards. He was going to vanish into thin air. That would create more uncertainty. More chaos. All the better for her to take complete control.

She glanced at the clock. 9:45pm. Half an hour.

'Move it, Harry,' she thought. 'Get your skinny bum over here.'

With nothing else to do, she tried Jonno. The call rang out and went to voicemail.

'Jonno! Where are you?' she hissed into her phone. 'You should be back by now, for god's sake. I want an update. Call me at once!'

She slammed the phone down on the dining table in frustration. Paced in a tight circle in the small space between the bed and the sofa. Waiting. Waiting for Harry to turn up.

Fifteen minutes became half an hour, then an hour. And still no Harry. Blast it. So she paced and paced. And just as her annoyance was on the brink of becoming anger, her phone buzzed.

She took the call without looking at the screen.

'Harry, what's taking so long?' she hissed.

'Sorry boss. There was an accident and I got stuck,' he said.

Morag thought this rather unlikely. More like he took his sweet time. Never mind. What was important was that he was here.

'I'll buzz you in,' she said, and ended the call.

Harry looked like he'd been startled out of a deep sleep. His eyes were red-rimmed, and his black trackies had a large tear in the seam of the right leg. He caught her disapproving stare.

'Sorry, boss,' he said. 'I didn't have time to change. You said to come over as fast as I could.'

She waved at him to shut up and led the way to the main room.

'There,' she said, pointing at Kiernan. 'Get him out of here. Make him disappear.'

'Is that-' Harry couldn't continue.

She'd shown nothing but ruthlessness since that idiot

brother of hers had let himself get put away. But the lengths to which she'd go still surprised her underlings. This pleased her. People craved predictability, because it made them feel comfortable. But when people got comfortable, it gave them time to reflect. Time in which they could get ideas above their station. And that wouldn't do. No, it wouldn't do at all.

'Less talking, more doing,' she snapped at Harry. 'Come on. Let's get this over and done with.'

CHAPTER 62

Something was wrong.

The dark figure was sure of it.

Ever since Kiernan and the other bloke — the one that looked like he'd had a very big stick rammed up his arse — had rocked up to the building in their tailored suits, he'd been waiting for them to come back out so he could inform his employer and they could put their plan in motion.

So far. So simple to follow instructions.

But then the bloke with the stick up his arse had run out of the building sans Kiernan, flying across the tarmac like an Olympic sprinter trying to set a new record. He'd waited and waited and waited for Kiernan to come out behind him. But he hadn't. And then another bloke — a tall gangly guy he knew was involved in the Company — had turned up and gone inside.

The dark figure paced in the underbrush and looked longingly at the vape. It was late. The street was deserted. Even the traffic that usually hummed away in the distance was barely discernible. Surely, one small puff wouldn't give him away.

He shook his head.

No. He couldn't risk it.

He turned his attention to his phone. Checked the time. 10:30pm. Nodded to himself. Dialled the only number on his contact list.

'Aye,' his employer replied, answering on the first ring. 'Any change?'

'No. Still no sign of Kiernan,' the dark figure admitted. 'But some bloke just went up. I've seen him before. He's with the Company. Something happened.'

The dark figure's employer went silent. In the background, the dark figure heard the low hum of chatter. The kind of good-natured sounds you'd hear in a restaurant or a pub. He looked at his surroundings, felt the tiredness in his feet, the silent screams emanating from his nicotine centre. A thought started forming in his head, and he crushed it before it came together.

'What should I do?' he prodded.

The dark figure's employer considered this.

'Stick to the plan,' he said slowly. 'For now, we wait. If they went in, they have to come back out at some point. Let me know once they're out and follow them. We'll play it by ear.'

The dark figure stretched. Nodded. Saw something from the corner of his eye and lifted his gaze.

'Boss?' he said, uncertainly.

'What now?'

The shadow he'd seen walking up to the building moved closer. And when it was illuminated by the street-light, the dark figure recognised who it belonged to immediately.

Except, the bloke wasn't really walking. He was staggering forward. Shambling. A clumsy, uncoordinated mass of limbs that only barely approximated a human gait.

'What?' the dark figure's employer repeated.

'This is going completely off the rails. The bloke who's flat they're in. He's back. This is going to blow up.'

On the phone, a sigh of exasperation.

'Boss,' the dark figure pressed. 'I think we need to change tack. Or it's going to ruin our plans.'

'Stay put,' the dark figure's employer said. 'Keep me posted. I'll get there as soon as I can.'

CHAPTER 63

Harry placed his hands under Kiernan's armpits. Half-lifted him off the bed with a grunt. Despite being somewhat gangly, Harry's arms were ropey with muscle. But Kiernan's dead weight still took him by surprise.

He dropped him. Stretched. Steeled himself. Stepped forward and placed his hands more firmly under Kiernan's armpits. Took a deep breath.

'Shhh! Enough!' Morag hissed.

'What the-' Harry started.

Morag signalled him to shut up.

'Can you hear it?' she whispered.

He cocked his ear.

At first he wasn't sure what she was on about. Then he heard it. A jangle of keys, followed by the faint scratching of metal on metal, as if whoever it was couldn't quite find the keyhole. It was coming from the hallway. Somebody was at the front door.

Morag lifted her index finger to her lips and gave Harry

a stern look. She walked towards the hallway. Signalled him to follow her.

She inched towards the peephole, peeked out, and felt her stomach drop. On the other side of the door, Bertie, his face scrunched up like he was trying to work out a particularly tricky maths problem, his eyes two slits, was attempting to insert the key into the lock. The key wasn't quite making it. He was too out of it to aim straight. But that was beside the point. He was here.

She waved her hand at Harry. Pointed to a shadowy corner of the doorway. They pressed their backs against the wall, Morag shaking with fury.

How had the idiot come back already? He should've stayed over at one of his little friends'. Maybe with that tart he pined for. Or passed out in an alley. Why had that useless twat let him get home? Hadn't she been clear when she said he shouldn't let him get out of his sight? And why had this useless bastard next to her come late? Bertie was going to come in and see the body. And then this would get hopelessly messy.

For another interminable minute, the sound of scraping filled her ears. Then the key found the lock. The door clicked open. Bertie staggered in, smelling like he'd been standing in the way when a beer vat had exploded, mumbling to himself.

He threw his house key in the general direction of the bowl on his shoe rack, missing by an inch. The keys jangled to the floor. He shrugged his coat off, first one arm and then the other, as the mumbling intensified. Then Morag realised he wasn't mumbling. The stupid, stupid excuse for a human being was humming a tune. He was HAPPY. HE WAS ENJOYING HIMSELF.

She stared through the hallway at the main room

beyond. Thought of Kiernan on the bed. The fury coursing through her body was all-consuming. Melting her insides. Why was it so difficult to find competent help? Why did nobody behave like they were supposed to? Like she needed them to?

Bertie removed his right shoe with his left instep. Bent over to pick it up. He unbalanced. Stumbled forward. Almost regained his balance. Lost it. Careened towards the floor.

Harry pounced. Bertie never hit the floor. Instead, he gasped in surprise. Panicked. Tried to shake Harry off. But he was too far gone on the GHB and all the beer he'd drunk on top of it to put up much of a struggle. They moved side to side, writhing together like two contortionists practising a new routine. It didn't take long for Harry to get the upper hand. He grabbed Bertie in a chokehold.

The pressure cut the supply of oxygen to Bertie's brain. He crumpled into a heap on the floor, senseless, but Harry didn't let go. He kept the pressure, panting with effort, sweat beading his temples.

'Enough, for god's sake,' Morag whispered. 'What do you think you're doing? The last thing we need right now is a missing neighbour!'

Harry let go. Bertie thumped limply onto the floor.

'Put him to bed,' she told Harry. 'He won't know what hit him tomorrow morning.'

'But, boss,' Harry began. 'What if he-'

'We'll deal with it,' she shot back. 'But let's try and avoid it. I don't want the police asking questions about him, unless it's because they think *he's* involved in a crime.'

'OK.'

Harry lifted Bertie up and over, onto his shoulder like a

sack of potatoes. Morag pulled back the bed covers, and he dumped him on the bed.

Working quickly, they undressed him. This would work best if he woke up as normal. Thought he'd undressed himself but had been too out of it to remember. Which, to be fair, was more or less adjacent to the truth. Morag took off his left shoe, then grabbed his right shoe off the floor and placed them both in the shoe rack next to each other. They placed the clothes in a neat pile next to his bed. Tucked him in.

By the time they were finished, Bertie was snoring lightly, none the wiser.

'All right. Move it, Harry,' Morag said. 'Let's get Kiernan out of here.'

Harry walked towards the body.

SMASH!

He froze in his tracks.

'What the hell was that?' he said, turning around.

The sound had been deafening. A grinding crash of metal and glass. This was followed by a door opening, then another. Voices. A commotion.

'What's going.... OH MY GOD ARE YOU OK?!'

Blair from flat two. Her voice, initially querulous and thick with sleep, had risen to a fever pitch in ten seconds flat.

'My bloody hand slipped. I rolled the throttle instead of the brake.'

When she heard that voice, Morag's blood bubbled like molten lava.

That bastard.

That stupid, stupid, stupid, entitled piece of cat excrement.

She'd been sounding the alarm for months. Of course he'd time an accident for maximum inconvenience.

Careful to stay in the shadows, Morag peered out of the studio room's big window. There was a gaggle of people around the building's front door. In the middle of them stood Graeme, his helmet under his arm, his hand holding the back of his skull in a sheepish gesture, as if to say, 'Aww shucks.' The blasted motorcycle was lying on its side. It had smashed through the aluminium door, breaking the glass and tearing it half off its hinges.

It was maddening.

'Are you sure you're alright?' another concerned voice she couldn't place said. 'Shall I call an ambulance?'

'Och, no. I'm fine,' Graeme said. 'Just a few cuts and bruises. The door took the worst of it.'

'You should get checked anyway'

A third concerned voice.

'Boss?'

It took a minute for Morag to register that this was directed at her.

She turned to Harry, her face a mask of hatred. Harry recoiled, shocked by the naked emotion he saw on her face.

'What?' she snapped.

'We have to go,' he said.

'What?' Morag shot back. 'And leave him here?'

She nodded at Kiernan, who was still lying on his back on the bed, next to the obliviously sleeping Bertie.

'We've no choice, boss,' Harry insisted.

Right on cue, another voice — that busybody Lizzie from the terrace across the street, damn her ridiculous harem trousers — joined the chorus of concern.

'I'm calling the emergency door repair service just now,'

she said, her voice calm and in control. 'Are you absolutely sure you don't want an ambulance, Graeme?'

Morag relented. For once in his life, Harry was right.

'He'll probably still be out of it by the time all this gets sorted,' Harry said, nodding towards Bertie, as if he'd read Morag's mind. 'And Kiernan, well... he's not going anywhere.'

'You don't say,' Morag said acidly, unable to help herself. 'I don't suppose he'll come back from the dead and leg it, will he?'

Harry said nothing. He'd learned the hard way it was better not to when she was in this mood. Morag risked another look out the window.

The voices were getting louder. Someone — Blair, by the sounds of it — was complaining that Lizzie shouldn't have booked the repair service without discussing it with everyone.

'Why do you always have to be difficult?' Lizzie shot back, incensed. 'I'm just trying to help. Show some gratitude.'

Blair fired back with a tirade about how Lizzie should take lessons in minding her own business. Morag couldn't say she blamed her.

'Boss?' Harry repeated.

'Fine,' Morag said, reluctantly. 'Let's go.'

She didn't like this. Not one bit. But it was true. There was nothing they could do now. Between waiting for the emergency door repair people to arrive and the argument that had erupted, they could be out there for hours. In fact, she probably should make an appearance.

Harry cracked the door open, peered out. The building was silent. All the action was outside. Graeme sounded like he was complaining. But the sound didn't carry as well as it did from Bertie's studio room window and they couldn't quite make out the words.

Morag locked Bertie's front door. They tiptoed downstairs as quickly as they could. Safely inside her flat, she slammed her fist against the wall, barely feeling the jolt of pain that shot up her forearm on impact.

This was a complete disaster.

A catastrophe of cosmic proportions.

Kiernan was supposed to have disappeared. Gone without a trace some place nobody would ever find him. But instead he was still there. In Bertie's flat. With Bertie sleeping next to him. A complication she could've done without.

Blast.

Damn it.

Damn them all.

Damn Boaby Kiernan.

Damn Harry.

Damn Bertie.

And damn Graeme and that goddamn motorcycle. She should've got somebody to set fire to it when she'd had the chance.

PART FOUR

NOW

CHAPTER 64

'I won't repeat myself, bud,' the plumber says.

He tenses his gun hand and knots his eyebrows, which makes him look even meaner.

'What the fuck did you do with Boaby Kiernan?'

I'm confused. At this point, I'm still not clued up on the events that led up to this moment. But, in what's probably one of the worst ideas I've ever had while in the throes of panic — and there have been many. Far too many, believe me — I vaguely think my confusion isn't such a bad thing. If the bloke can see I'm genuine, he'll realise I'm just an innocent bystander in all of this, and he'll let me go.

He has to, doesn't he? It's the rules. Even deranged plumbers who brandish guns at their clients have to see reason eventually, don't they?

Except, this guy probably isn't a plumber.

No, scratch that probably. He certainly isn't. He's obviously much more than that. Much, much more. And he doesn't play by the rules, does he? He's made that abundantly clear.

Oh god.

Oh fuck.

What am I going to do?

'Where. Is he?' he prods.

'Boaby Kiernan?' I mumble weakly.

The plumber

(Harry. His name's Harry.)

puffs out his chest. Cocks his gun.

'Cut the shite,' he says, pointing it just under my breast-bone, where a bullet would tear through countless organs and inflict maximum damage. 'I know for a fact there was a dead body in your bed. I saw him with my own two eyes yesterday evening. What have you done with him?'

'What? *You* put him there?'

I realise too late that I've admitted knowledge of the body by implication. But the admission's the least of my concerns right now. The events of this morning have taken on a whole new significance, and my mind reels.

'There was no leak coming from my bathroom, was there?' I ask.

It's more of a statement than a question. I'm quite positive I already know the answer. Harry shakes his head, confirming my suspicions.

'And Morag? Did you hurt her? What've you done with-'

A stunning succession of thoughts hit me mid-sentence.

How is it that the plumber who turned up to fix my leak happens to know about the body in my bed? That, by his own admission, he was here yesterday evening, when the bloke was apparently already dead?

More to the point, though, isn't it quite the coincidence that the leak was discovered on this specific morning?

When said body was in my bed? And that the person who alerted me to the leak, the person who called said plumber...

Christ alive.

What if?

No, it can't be.

Can it?

She's a frail old lady with too much time on her hands. Surely, she wouldn't be mixed up in a fucking murder? Why would she? How would it even work?

'Wait,' I tell Harry.

I can't help myself. I have to ask. Gun or no gun. I have to *know*.

'Is Morag? Is she in on this?'

'You ask way too many fucking questions, bud. Anyone ever told you that?' he growls. 'It's not good for your health.'

He hesitates before saying this. It's ever so slight, but it's there. Impossible to ignore.

Good lord.

Morag.

Morag killed a man in my flat. And now her henchman's holding me at gunpoint. My panic-addled mind spins itself into the stratosphere.

Harry cocks his gun.

'Last chance, bud. Or I'll turn you into a human colander. Where is he?'

His finger curls around the trigger. Slowly, and inexorably, the distance between his finger and the trigger decreases. Fraction by fraction.

'You have five seconds,' he says.

I close my eyes. Feel myself trembling all over.

'Five. Four. Three. Two-'

'OK! OK! Please don't shoot me!' I say. 'Please. God. No.'

At some point between the first OK and the No I start to cry. I hate myself for it, but I can't help myself. I'm scared out of my fucking mind. Not just by the gun, but by the predicament. By the fact that this is happening in my home. That Morag's most likely in on it. And that this fucking bloke is so relaxed. It's his equivalent of a fucking client presentation. Except instead of Excel or PowerPoint his tool of choice is a loaded pistol.

'He's under the bed,' I continue. 'I moved him before you got here. After M-M-M...'

I can't finish.

'Show me,' he says, unmoved.

He jerks his head towards the bed.

'Pull him out of there.'

I take a tentative step forward. I still have my hands up, so I look like I'm tip-toeing my way around a puddle instead of simply crossing the small rectangular room that makes up the bulk of my studio's floorspace. When I get to the bed, I turn around, raise my hands a wee bit higher. I want to reassure him, beyond reasonable doubt, that I'm not doing anything untoward. The last thing I want to do is give him ideas. A reason to shoot. No, please. Not yet.

'I need to bend down, OK?' I say. 'I stuffed him under there, and put the storage boxes in front of him, so he'd be hidden properly.'

He nods imperceptibly.

I crouch down, lift the duvet, and get to work pulling out the storage boxes. Dust fills my nostrils, and I sneeze violently. Three times. In between them, I hear a faint buzzing sound. My phone. Still on the floor where I dropped it what seems like aeons ago.

'There,' I say, sniffling. 'There he is.'

The body — Boaby Kiernan — is still as dead as he was this morning. The only change is the dust bunnies that have stuck to his pomaded hair.

'So, are you coming to see for yourself?' I say.

Harry is upon me before I can finish. His hand closes on my throat, his grip iron. The world swims in and out of focus.

'Quit trying to be cute,' he spits. 'I'm running out of patience, and I didn't have much of it to begin with.'

I smell onions, coffee, and something else on his breath. Something rancid. My bladder lets go, warming up my leg. My bowels feel like they could go next. I clench my arse cheeks tight. I'm not going to shite myself in front of this bloke. I refuse to do so.

'From here on out, you're going to shut the fuck up and do as I say,' he growls. 'Understood?'

I manage a shaky approximation of a nod.

He lets go, and I fall to the floor, doubled over.

'Och. Fuck,' I say, gasping to catch my breath.

'MOVE IT!' Harry roars.

I scrabble onto all fours, scurry towards the bed, and get to work retrieving Kiernan. My neck feels bruised and it hurts to breathe. But Harry's attack has also had a sobering effect on me, kicking my survival instinct into high gear. This guy's not only willing, but more than happy to go all the way. To hurt me badly. Or end me. One false move and I'm dead.

I grab Kiernan under the arms and drag him out. Faintly, I hear the phone buzz again, just as Kiernan's upper half emerges from beneath the bed.

'Good,' Harry says, moving closer, his gun still trained on me.

'Now wrap him up.'

'With what?' I say. 'With a rug? I don't have one, as you can see.'

I point to the expanse of wood flooring that covers my studio.

Harry's eyes turn to slits. He takes two steps forward.

'What did I say about back talk?' he tells me. 'Grab your duvet off the bed and wrap him in that.'

I'm about to protest that I won't have anything to sleep in tonight. Then it dawns on me that it probably isn't going to matter. I've seen his face. I know he and Morag killed a man. I'm that most clichéd of clichés. A loose end.

Unbidden, my life flashes before me. What the fuck have I been doing? Why have I never asked Joan if she'd like to have dinner sometime, just us? Why have I stuck around at Kinnock, Fraser, and McAllister Financial, under Phillip, even though I can't stand him? Why have I never taken that trip to South America?

Why? Why? So many whys. And not one single fucking answer.

I grab the duvet off the bed and spread it on the floor, then drag Kiernan onto it, my brain in overdrive. Harry's a big guy with a gun and no conscience. I'm an out-of-shape accountant who last threw a punch in high school. But that doesn't matter.

I need to fight back. I have to. I must.

CHAPTER 65

'So you're saying you want out, then?' Kris says. 'You're quitting on us?'

She jerks into a sitting position without thinking. It sends a shot of pain up the stump where her foot used to be before Jonno turned it into so much gravel in a sock.

'Kris, you're not hearing me,' Neville replies.

Standing next to her hospital bed, his hands on his hips, his voice unnervingly calm, he looks and sounds like a stranger, not her husband of fifteen years.

'At no point did I say I'm quitting on us,' he continues.

He clears his throat. Runs a weary hand across his face. His three-day stubble rasps under his palm.

'You do understand where I'm coming from, don't you?' he says more quietly. 'Jason still isn't himself.'

At the mention of Jason, Kris' mind flashes back to the scrapyard. She sees Jonno pressing the gun against Jason's temple, so hard it will leave a bluish black bruise that will linger for days before starting to fade. She sees his finger closing in on the trigger. How time had stood still. How distinct every single heartbeat had sounded in her ears. She remembers the high-pitched ringing that had drowned out everything else after the shot rang out. The overwhelming pain. Not from her injured leg. But a pain deep in her soul. Because she'd thought Jason was gone. That Jonno had shot him. Because of her.

And then Jason had barrelled into her. That bastard had fired in the air, as a diversion, shoved him, and sped off. Oh how she had cried then. How they'd all cried. Long and hard. Tears and snot streaming down their faces in thick runnels, until the police and the ambulance arrived.

But then the dust had settled. She'd gone into surgery and Neville had had time to think. And now their marriage is no longer in its terminal phase. It's on life support. And Neville's terms for attempting resuscitation aren't up for negotiation.

'Look,' he continues, 'I know you love your job. And, honestly, I can live with the long hours and all the other BS that comes with it. Where I draw the line is Jason being put in harm's way.'

'That was a fluke. A one-in-a-million thing. It's never going to happen again,' Kris insists, red-faced.

'You can't know that,' Neville says. 'What if it *does* happen again?'

'Well, what if you get run over by a car? Does that mean you're never leaving the house again?'

'Och, come on now. It's not the same and you know it.'

'Of course it's the bloody same! Everything's a risk.'

Neville scoffs.

'Fine. Have it your way. But I've been very clear and I'm not changing my mind.'

'Nev,' Kris says, struggling to keep her voice even. 'I've been doing this job for almost as long as we've known each other. How many times did something like this happen? No, really. Answer me.'

'Kris, please be reasonable. A gangster barged into our home, abducted us at gunpoint, and shot you in front of us. *He held a gun to our son's head.* What would you have me do? Act like nothing happened?'

'So you're asking me to choose, then. Is that it?' Kris says.

'I'm asking you to please bear in mind that what you do affects your family, and to not do things that could blow back on us.'

'Same bloody difference.'

'Look, for all our problems, I love you, Kris. God knows I do. And I want you to be happy and have a fulfilling career. But Jason and I can't be around you if there's a risk that what you do could put us in danger. I won't have Jason go through that again.'

Kris' mouth opens, and she snaps it shut with an audible click before she can say something that pushes them further past the point of no return.

'Just think about it, Kris,' Neville insists. 'Will you do that, at least?'

'What's there to think about, Nev? You seem adamant. Your way or the highway.'

It's Neville's turn to stay silent.

There's a rap on the partition and Doug's head appears from behind the blue hospital curtain.

'Och, sorry,' Doug says.

He looks at Kris, then at Neville, and the tips of his ears go red.

'Shall I come back?' he stammers.

'No, don't worry,' Neville says. 'I was just leaving.'

He picks up his jacket from the armchair. Gives Kris one last, lingering look.

'Think about it. OK?' he says before walking out.

'Sorry, I-' Kris says.

She puts her face in her hands.

'Ah. Shite,' she says.

Doug walks to the armchair, takes a seat, and carefully unwraps a stick of gum while he waits for her to compose herself. He's obviously overheard a fair bit of the conversation, but he's doing a bang up job of pretending he hasn't. And Kris loves him for it.

'How are you feeling?' he asks, when she looks up at him, keen to steer the conversation away from any awkwardness.

'Good. Well, as good as having half your leg chopped off can be, I suppose,' she replies.

She shifts in bed to get the blood flowing back into her numb arse, and the movement sends another shot of pain up her stump.

'Do you know when you're getting out of here?' he asks.

'I'm not sure. The leg needs to heal. Then I have to start rehab,' she replies. 'They tell me it'll be tough, but I can't bloody wait. I need to get out of this place. It's doing my head in.'

For the past four days, the cubicle next to hers was occupied by a bloke related to one of the nurses who works on the ward. This somehow gave him the impression he had the run of the place. Visitors were coming in at all hours and making a godawful racket, which pushed her patience dangerously close to its limits. If the nurse hadn't told him he was lucky to be alive before he left, she might've told him so herself.

They looked at each other, neither of them comfortable bringing up the reason Kris had ended up in hospital so they can clear the air.

'Do you have something for me?' Kris asks when she's unable to contain herself any longer.

'What was I supposed to bring?' Doug says, faking an innocent look.

'Come on, Doug, don't play dumb,' she replies. 'Did the request you sent the NCA come back? What did they say?'

'You know I can't tell you, Kris.'

'Och for fuck's sake. Edwards was my collar. And they kidnapped my family over him. Fuck, I gave up my foot for this case.'

Doug squirms.

'Come on Doug. Throw me a bone here. I need something to keep me occupied or I'm going to drive myself up the wall.'

Doug glances at his watch. Shifts in his seat. Chews down harder on his gum.

'So?' Kris asks.

He drops his voice to a whisper.

'Look, you didn't hear this from me, OK?'

'My lips are sealed,' Kris says.

'We tracked Wallace part of the way down the A9, and then he must've ditched the car. But, given the location, I think it's safe to assume he's either looking for Edwards or he's managed to find him.'

'And Edwards?'

'Goes by Jack Fitzsimmons now. His girlfriend — well, former girlfriend, judging by her tone — says he upped and left without telling her where he was going and why.'

Doug fingers his watch.

'But I don't buy it.'

'What makes you say so?' Kris asks.

'Gut feeling. Something felt off, like she was holding back. But the local police agreed to us being in on the interview as a courtesy and strictly as observers, so I couldn't push her.'

'Who is she?' Kris asks.

'Paulette Murricane. Local woman. Runs the only pub in town. I did some digging and there's talk she sells pot on the side. If that's true, she's got good reasons for not wanting us to look too closely at her.'

'So what are you planning to do next?'

'Look, Kris, I've said more than enough.' Doug says. 'You really should rest. Focus on getting better.'

'Fine,' she says, deciding not to press the issue. 'I appreciate you telling me all this.'

The conversation drifts towards office gossip. Who's getting into whose pants, who got bollocked for messing up, whose bootlicking finally paid dividends... But while Kris is careful to stay tuned in enough to grunt noncommittally in the right places, her eyes take on a faraway look. Where's Al gone? Has Jonno found him? Where are they now? A voice in the back of her head keeps nagging her. Telling her that, if she tracks Al down, she'll find Jonno. And then he can pay for what he's done to her family. For how he's probably been the proverbial straw that will break her marriage.

The largely one-sided conversation flags, and Doug gets up and makes his goodbyes, promising to visit again as soon as he has can.

'Hand me my bag before you go, will you?' Kris asks.

Doug knows her laptop's in there and he's loath to encourage her. But he also knows that if he doesn't hand it over, she'll ask a nurse. He picks it up and gives it to her, reluctantly.

'Try to take it easy, OK?' he tells her half-heartedly, before he walks out of the cubicle. 'We'll get Wallace, I promise. Him and whoever's behind all this. You don't need to worry.'

Kris considers telling him that, had she not taken the initiative, Neville and Jason would most probably be dead. But she grits her teeth and smiles obligingly.

Doug has barely reached the ward door when she opens her laptop and fires up Google. With nothing to do but stare at the wall and brood about her life or brave the spotty hospital WiFi and try to watch something on Netflix, she reckons that, even if she doesn't make any headway on Jonno's location, she'll at least kill the few hours until it's time for her next dose of painkillers. But who is she kidding? Missing leg or no missing leg, she wants to be the one to find him. She wants to look him in the eye as he's being dragged, kicking and screaming, into the custody suite.

She navigates to SID — the Scottish police's nationwide intelligence database — retrieves the details of the car Jonno was last seen driving and keys them into the ANPR system. But there are no further sightings after the last time he was spotted on the A9. Of course there wouldn't be. The car was too hot by that point. He'd have ditched it. Or stuck to secondary roads.

She changes tack and googles Jack Fitzsimmons, then runs him through 192.com for good measure. There are only the bare essentials: name and approximate age. He may have no compunction about beating the living shite out of a random bloke in a service area bog, but he's very careful about his online footprint.

She doesn't get much further with Paulette Murricane. Tall, slim, tattooed, with long hair, high cheekbones, and a strong nose, she smiles at Kris from a photo on the Fort Drumblehan Courier's website. In the photo, she's posing next to her pub, The Mossy Well, a historic building which, the article says, she lovingly restored after having bought it at auction in a dilapidated state.

'Where did you go, Edwards?' she thinks to herself as she browses the three photos Paulette Murricane's restricted Facebook profile allows her to see — two of which are of a customised motorcycle. 'Did you leave because you no longer felt safe? Or did Wallace find you?'

She stares at the hospital curtain, absently doodling on her notepad. On the surface, her mind's blank. But, deeper in the recesses of her brain, the wheels are turning. Mulling things over. Making the connections her conscious has missed.

On a whim, she logs on to Companies House. Keys in Franco Guthrie into the search tool. It returns two pages worth of all the businesses Guthrie has been involved in. Many of them legitimate. Some of them probably fronts he used to funnel his dirty money. She hunts around her laptop for the spreadsheet they'd put together at the start of the investigation. Maybe she can cross-reference it to the Companies House data in case something jumps out at her. But she can't seem to find it.

'Fuck,' she mutters. 'Why can't I keep anything organised?'

She fires up her email app. Perhaps the list is attached to an email thread. She scrolls through a blur of unread emails. Pointless circulars. Memos from the brass. Two new autopsy reports. A collection for a uniform who was about to retire. Well wishes from colleagues.

And then she sees it. A reply to an email that, in the craziness she's been caught up in, she forgot she'd even sent.

That recording of Guthrie and his mystery caller. Has Kevin managed to get somewhere with it?

Feeling the familiar trepidation creep into her chest, she opens it.

'*Hey Kris,*

Sorry for the delay.

I made a few calls and my contact at O2 came through. They confirmed the call was made on their network and we've been able to triangulate an approximate location.

Unfortunately, because it's a recording of a call made from a burner phone, and the caller's voice is disguised, it's not as accurate as I'd have liked. We've narrowed it down to a 200 metre radius, give or take.

I realise that's a fairly wide area, but it's the best I could do.

I hope it at least helps you focus your search.

Cheers,

Kev'

Kris opens the attachment — a map of west Strathburgh with an area circled in red — and she almost can't believe her eyes.

She logs on to Google Maps, zooms in on the area, and switches to street view, because she needs to make absolutely sure.

Kev's right. 200 metres is a lot, especially when the area's mostly made up of terraces that could've come off an assembly line. But, among the sea of sameness, there's one building that immediately draws her eye. It's just as boring and nondescript as the rest of the street. But she remembers it very clearly, because it's where Guthrie held court. Right under their noses. And where he'd kept stacks upon stacks of evidence that, together with Al's testimony, had helped nail him to the wall.

So it was somebody here. In this building. A place they wouldn't look at again because it was compromised. And nobody in their right mind would engage in criminal activity in a place that was already known to the police? Right?

Jesus Christ. Whoever the CEO was, he was thumbing his nose at them.

Feeling energised, Kris reaches for her phone.

'Doug, where are you?' she says.

She can hear the sound of his car in motion.

'I'm heading towards the station. Why? What's going on?'

'Turn back. There's something you have to see.'

CHAPTER 66

'It's her,' Kris says. 'It has to be.'

Doug sits on the edge of the hospital bed and leans in, stares at the laptop. At the name glaring back at them from the screen.

Morag Stevenson. Fifty-eight. Strathburgh born and bred.

Except that isn't her real name.

For the first twenty-three years of her life, she lived as Gretchen Guthrie. Daughter of one Albert James Guthrie and Elaine Guthrie. Elder sister of one Francis Guthrie.

'God, how did we miss this?' Doug says.

'It's nobody's fault,' Kris replies. 'She hid herself well. We'd have never made the connection if we hadn't managed to get a location on the call.'

She says this for her benefit as much as his, because right now she's disgusted with herself. All those lives lost in this senseless gang war. They could've prevented them if they'd looked at this sooner. But they'd been too busy chasing shadows to consider the bleeding obvious.

The first thing Kris did after calling Doug was phone

up the Land Registry to get a list of the flats' owners. Then she began the painstaking work of cross-referencing the names for a possible connection to Guthrie. That was three hours ago, and they'd drawn several blanks.

Until they'd had the idea of looking into Guthrie's relatives.

Once they found out that Gretchen Guthrie fell off the face of the earth in 1988 — and that the reason for that was that she now went by Morag Stevenson — everything fell into place at frightening speed.

There she was, involved in several of Guthrie's former companies. Not as a director or shareholder. No. Never that simple. As a shareholder of a corporate shareholder of a corporate shareholder. Always several degrees removed. Deeper than most people would ever think to dig.

'Christ, this woman's slippery,' Doug says, around a mouthful of gum.

They stare at her passport photo, in which she looks much older. Seventy at least. Mostly because of the way she carries herself. Her choice of clothes. The glasses.

It has to be intentional. An act.

'What are we going to do?' Doug asks. 'The connection's pretty tenuous. Any solicitor worth their hourly will throw out the call. Say there's no way we can convincingly prove it's her.'

'I think it's worth bringing her in anyway. Asking her a few questions,' Kris says.

'About what?' Doug asks.

'Well, it's a fact she's related to Guthrie. She can't deny that.'

'But being related to a criminal isn't a crime,' Doug fires back.

'No. But we can still question her as a witness. Pretend

we want to pick her brain about who the person on the recording might be. It'll give us an opportunity to size her up.'

Doug shakes his head imperceptibly.

Kris blows out her cheeks, exasperated.

'Do you have a better idea, then? Because, if so, let's hear it.'

Doug genuinely makes an effort. He thinks hard. 'No,' he replies, simply. 'No. I don't.'

CHAPTER 67

Morag paces across the living room floor. Her head down. Her fists clenched. Breath blasting out of her flared nostrils like steam from a train. Her mind is stuffed full of worst case scenarios. And the din of power tools from downstairs, isn't helping one bit. Every screech of the multitool, every whine of the drill, makes her want to scream.

What the hell is Harry playing at? Why hasn't he called? Has he found the body yet?

And what are they going to do with that interfering imbecile?

How has this become so complicated?

Damn it. She's so, so close.

She looks at the clock. Contemplates going upstairs to see what's going on for herself. But what would that achieve? Isn't it better to stay in the shadows? Especially now that her plan is almost complete?

The flat, small to begin with, shrinks around her. It feels microscopic. Oppressive. The walls are closing in.

Squeezing her until she's as flat as a cardboard cutout. She can't stay here and wait around any longer. She needs something to do.

She peers out the window. Watches the tradesman at work, the crack of his arse peeking out of his grime-stained Authentic Apparel boxers. Blair looks on. And Graeme and his motorcycle are, of course, nowhere to be seen. Typical. He drops a grenade and watches it explode from a distance.

Thinking of him makes her mood worse.

Perhaps she should go downstairs. Pretend to be interested in what's going on. They'll expect her to show up at some point, anyway. It's the reputation she's built for herself, for good reason. Nobody minds the old lady, especially if she's a busybody. If anything, they're only too happy to ignore her in the hope she'll go away.

Yes. That's what she'll do. Go downstairs. Maybe even walk to the Caffè Nero up the street. Have a cup of tea and a flapjack. And if that lazy moron doesn't update her by then, she'll go up. Sort it out herself. She never wanted it to come to this. But needs must.

She hobbles down the stairs, step by painstaking step.

'Hello,' she says, her voice full of fake cheer.

'Hi,' Blair says.

But she can tell Blair isn't pleased to see her. The cow. Her shoulders have slumped. Her eyes are downcast. She's crossed her arms defensively beneath her breasts.

The repairman grunts. Selects a Phillips screwdriver from his voluminous toolbag. Screws in a new hinge.

'Big damage?' Morag says.

'It wasn't in good shape to begin with, eh,' the tradesman grunts. 'You should've changed it a long time ago. Could've been much worse.'

He finishes screwing in the hinge.

'There,' he remarks, wiping his hands on the front of his grease-and-dust-stained shirt. 'All done. Good to go.'

Morag and Blair look on in silence as he packs up his tools. She racks her brain for an inoffensive topic of conversation.

No. She can't do this. Not today.

Her nails have dug crescent-shaped divots in her palms. She makes herself stop. Says her goodbyes. Starts walking up the street.

It's a grey day. It will probably rain soon. But the temperature is mild, and she doesn't mind walking, even in her mock arthritic hobble.

Yes, this is what she needs. It'll clear her head. Staying inside and brooding isn't healthy at all.

She focuses on her steps. One foot at a time, giving each one her full concentration. She barely notices the goings on around her. Lizzie, head down, trimming her hedges. The flash of blue across the street.

When the hand closes on her forearm, gripping it tight, and the round object that feels suspiciously like the business end of a gun presses into her left kidney, she freezes. But there's also no surprise. It's almost as if she's been expecting this. Things have gone so wrong it seems only natural. What's the saying? It never rains, it pours.

'Hiya, you must be Morag,' the voice whispers in her ear.

She doesn't recognise him. Which is fair enough, because she's never met him in person even though he's been on her mind a fair bit.

He's before her time. A mythical shadow she's been chasing in the hope of cementing her position. Of proving she's worthy of striking fear into the hearts of her underlings and enemies alike.

He doesn't hold her in suspense.

'I don't think we've been formally introduced,' he says, the scar snaking up his cheek moving in time with his lips.

'I'm Al. And I believe you've been looking for me.'

CHAPTER 68

For such a simple task, it takes me an unreasonably long time to get the duvet off my bed and lay it out straight on the floor. My breathing's too shaky. And the uncontrollable trembling in my hands isn't helping. The duvet slips. Twists. Tangles. Contorts itself into all sorts of fantastical shapes. It's near-impossible for me to straighten it and lay it out flat. I'm as uncoordinated as a drunk ninety-five year-old.

In my defence, these are perfectly normal reactions when, you know, somebody's been pointing a gun at you and implying they're seriously considering shooting you dead.

But that's cold comfort. It doesn't change the nature of my predicament. Or put me any further away from shiteing myself.

Trying to talk him down is out of the question. I think we're beyond threats now. If I open my mouth, I fear he'll shoot for real. As for lunging at him, I might as well jump out the window for all the good it would do me. He's placed himself strategically behind the dining table, where he can aim and shoot comfortably, while being safely out of my reach.

What's left to me — the only play I can think of — is to stretch this task out for as long as I can. Stretch it out and hope. For what, I don't know.

I grab Kiernan under the shoulders and drag him halfway onto the duvet. The edges curl up, and I have to stop and rearrange them before I continue.

I finish the job and look at Harry expectantly.

He stares back at me, his expression blank.

'What's wrong, bud?' he says. 'Are you waiting for a pat on the back or something? Wrap him up.'

I fold the bottom of the duvet over Kiernan's legs and pull the short side over him, tucking its edge underneath his body. Then I roll him over until I've used the whole width of the duvet, wrapping him as tightly as I can.

He's starting to look a bit green around the gills, and his eyes are sinking into his sockets. His face, vulpine to begin with, is looking more angular. His nose sharper, more blade-like. Like he's turning into Nosferatu. So when he's all covered up — the rancid filling of the world's biggest, most gruesome burrito — I feel a weight lift. Even though my situation has, if anything, become more precarious.

'Now what?' I tell Harry.

He glances outside. It's just half a second. But I presume it's enough for him to confirm the coast is clear. The grinding of power tools stopped some time ago. The sky has darkened too, even though it's only half-past noon. It's dreich as dreich can be. Seems fitting, given the circumstances.

'Pick him up,' he tells me. 'Let's go. We're going to get him out of here.'

I look at the wrapped up duvet. Human shaped, but

vaguely so. Would anyone notice? Given the weather, I doubt anyone will be around to notice. I have a feeling everyone's fixing to cosy up in front of the telly to while away the afternoon.

When I don't move, Harry clears his throat and makes a menacing gesture with his gun hand.

'What's the hold up? Let's go.'

Inspiration strikes. For what I don't know. But my gut tells me to go with it, so I do.

'So you're not going to help me?' I say.

'Help you?' He snorts. 'Can you believe this bloke?'

'He's heavy,' I insist. 'We'll work much faster if we share the load. The longer this takes, the greater the risk that somebody will see us.'

He considers this.

He has to know I have a point. The guy's dead weight, and I'm not a big bloke. The question is, does he think he has a good enough handle on the situation to go along with my suggestion?

His lips move. His mouth opens and closes.

'Eh,' he mumbles.

'I can't lift him. I'll have to drag him,' I say. 'It's going to make an awful lot of noise.'

That does it.

'Fine,' he snaps. 'But I go down the stairs first, so don't go thinking of trying anything funny.'

'You're the boss,' I say.

To underscore the point, I raise my hands and give him my meekest look.

He slides out from behind the dining table, the gun trained on me, and edges his way towards the body, being careful to keep his distance.

'Lift him by the legs,' he says, nodding towards them.

I squat down. Grab the duvet with both hands. Kiernan's calves are rock hard.

'What the fuck do you think you're doing, bud?' Harry says.

'Lifting him,' I reply. 'Like you said.'

'Check the hall first,' he tells me. 'Look through the peephole, then open the door. Make sure there's no-one around.'

'Right.'

Clearly, I don't have much of an aptitude for crime, even if I weren't feeling as if 75,000 volts are coursing through my body.

I walk into the hallway. Harry's right behind me, his gun boring a hole in my back. I look through the peephole, then crack the door open and peer outside. Across the hall, it's dead silence. Downstairs, Gandalf is telling Frodo he'd better leave the Shire double-quick. His admonitions are punctuated by Ally McCoist enthusing about the Hibees' pressing in midfield.

'I think we're good,' I tell Harry.

'You think or you're certain,' he says.

'Well, that's what it *sounds* like,' I say. 'Aye. We should be OK.'

'I'll hold you to it. You're wrong, you and whoever pokes their nose into our business dies. Are we clear?'

I nod.

'Off you go, then.'

Harry waits for me to lift my side of the body. Then he lifts him by the shoulders, and we carry him towards the front door. The shared load makes the job much easier. We make quick work of it.

Harry duck-walks out onto the landing and attacks the stairs. I stop. Reach for the doorknob.

'What the fuck do you think you're doing?' he hisses. 'Keep going.'

'I need to close the door, don't I?' I say.

'Just keep fucking moving,' he replies. 'Let's get the fuck out of here as fast as we can.'

Harry takes the first step down, pulling the body aggressively towards him. I move as slowly as I think I can get away with.

What's the plan here? I don't know. I don't fucking know. Do I risk calling for help? See if somebody comes out? Do I push him? Do I wait?

There's two floors. One hundred and ten steps to go. I've counted them a few times. One hundred and ten steps to come up with something.

'Move,' Harry growls, pulling the duvet.

I take a step forward. Then another. And another.

I see it seconds before Harry steps on it. A wet patch on the edge of the stair. Harry's trainer slips. He clutches the duvet, pulling it towards him, and I lose my footing. I can feel myself about to unbalance. Without thinking, I work with the momentum instead of pulling back.

Harry topples down the last three stairs onto the half-landing, and falls flat on his arse.

I let go. Run down the stairs. Leap over Harry, using the railing as leverage. He lifts his hand. Tries to grab the leg of my jeans to stop me.

I make it, barely. His fingers close on empty air. I careen down the remaining stairs at top speed and crash into the main door, breathing heavily.

My hands are slick with sweat. Partly it's the warmth of the duvet. Mostly it's because, on a scale of one to ten, my anxiety is a solid twenty-five. The doorknob slips through my fingers. Behind me, Harry gets to his feet. Swears. Storms down the stairs two at a time.

Oh fuck.

Oh shite.

What the fuck was I thinking? Now I'm really going to end up dead.

I wipe my palms on the seat of my jeans. The wetness in my crotch has made it stick to me uncomfortably. But I barely feel it. I'm laser-focused on turning the doorknob.

I grab it. Mercifully, my hands don't slip. I turn it to the right, as far as it can go. Something in my knuckle cracks. But the bloody door's stuck. It won't budge.

Gah!

Fuck!

Open up!

I slam into it with my shoulder. Blam. Blam. Blam.

Behind me, Harry thunders down the stairs.

A door opens.

'What the. Hey! Hey, you bastard!'

Come on. Come on. Come on.

I slam into the door, violently. My entire skeleton shudders with the impact. The aluminium jerks itself out of the frame, spitting me out, hands outstretched. I collide with the ground at top speed. Two shocks of pain shoot up my forearms, but I'm too frantic to notice. I get up. Barrel out into the street.

Hearing Harry's footfalls getting closer, I hazard a look back. He's running in slow, shambling strides, his face twisted with rage, but he's almost at arm's length and gaining.

I pat down my pockets. It's useless. I already know my

phone isn't on me. It's on the floor, in my flat. Where I left it before this all kicked off.

Shite.

I keep running as fast as I can, legs pushing forward, arms pumping. If I can make it to a busy street, he'll have to stop chasing me. Or, if he doesn't, somebody will intervene. Somebody has to, right?

My fondness for second helpings and lounging about at every available opportunity are starting to catch up with me. My lungs are on fire. I haven't had a stitch this bad since the one and only time I went running with Shawn.

Something whizzes past me. There's a stinging pain in my temple. Warm wetness drips down behind my ear. I lift my fingers to my head. They come away sticky and red with blood.

Fuck. Fuck. Fuck. Fuck. Fuck.

The bastard is fucking shooting at me.

I'm struggling. Gasping for air but not quite managing to fill my lungs. My calves are as tight as violin strings. I'm light-headed. Yesterday's beers, my lunch — fuck, breakfast, lunch, and dinner from two days ago. They're all coming back the way they went down. I can't keep this up.

Another bullet whizzes past me. I look ahead. The main road appears on the horizon. Tantalisingly close. A car trundles by, and I've never, ever seen such a beautiful sight in my life.

Blessed civilisation. I'm going to make it.

I dig deep into my rapidly depleting reservoir of energy. I pump my arms harder. But, despite my best efforts, I can't seem to run fast enough. It's like a giant has wrapped their arms around me, and is holding me in place.

There's an enormous blast. I feel like I've been punched

in the shoulder. A high-pitched whine like a dentist's drill fills my head.

I trip. Lose my balance.

And as my body meets the ground, everything goes dark.

CHAPTER 69

Al spots the car — a black Vauxhall Insignia — as soon as he emerges from Shoregate, the three-mile underwater tunnel that connects the northern and southern parts of the city at the Strath's narrowest point.

In the back seat, Jonno, whose bullet wound is showing the first signs of infection, is lying back with his eyes closed, drenched in sweat and breathing heavily. Morag sits quietly next to him, looking out the window, her hands tied behind her back. She doesn't know what she's going to do yet. But if experience has taught her anything, it's that good things come to those who wait. You just need to recognise the opportunity when it presents itself. So she ignores the nervousness gripping her, and tries to keep her mind focused on the moment. Something will come up. She has to believe that.

At first, Al gives the Insignia no mind. It's just another vehicle among the thousands driving around the city on any given Saturday afternoon. But when he exits the bypass onto the B6372 — which snakes through the sprawl of commuter towns south of Strathburgh and will lead them to an abandoned field where he's going to end this once and for all — and the Insignia is still behind him, his gut tells him to stay alert.

He drops the speed from sixty miles per hour to forty, and peers into the rear view mirror to see what happens. Right on cue, the Insignia slows down too, putting several feet of distance between them.

This doesn't help Al relax. If anything, it makes him more nervous. But the road is a two-way single carriageway with not much room for manoeuvre. So he doesn't attempt a sudden U-turn, which he reckons will make matters worse. Instead, he fishes out Jonno's gun from the glove compartment, drops it in his lap, and drives on, his left leg bouncing restlessly. There's nothing else he can do for now.

The next two miles are uneventful. Al drives on, the sound of Jonno's heavy breathing and the muted purr of the car's engine punctuating the silence. His gaze flits from the road to the rear view mirror, and from the rear view mirror back to the road. The Insignia maintains its respectful distance, making no move to catch up.

Is he imagining this? He begins to wonder.

Ever since he walked on Jonno holding P at gunpoint, he's been extra cautious. He knows people are out to get him. But this doesn't feel like a case of hypervigilance. The Insignia has been following him for far too long for it to be a coincidence.

He glances at the gun in his lap. Scans both sides of the road for a concealed exit he could turn into at a moment's notice. Gets so distracted he almost doesn't see the pothole, a gaping two inch-wide crater in the middle of the carriageway.

He swerves right to avoid it. At the same time, the

Insignia accelerates. He hears the crack of safety glass behind him.

'What the-'

There's no time to finish the sentence. He hears more cracking glass, followed by a muted thump. The car's left side sags as air escapes the rear tyre. Then he hits another pothole and loses control.

Al steers to the right, then to the left. But it's hopeless. The car careens off the road, propelling all three of them forward. It crashes into the rocky verge, so violently the airbags deploy. The car rebounds. Then it lurches forward once more. Metal crunches. The wheels spin. The engine revs alarmingly. Sputters. Dies.

Dazed but somehow unhurt, Al looks behind him, the seatbelt eating into the soft flesh of his neck. Jonno's glazed eyes stare sightlessly back at him. The left side of his head, where the bullet exited before lodging itself into the windscreen, is a ruin. Blood mixed with blobs of greyish-pink brain matter soak the front passenger seat's headrest.

Crushed under Jonno, unable to move, Morag makes frantic animal noises. All semblance of calm and control has left her. Violence isn't new to her. But she's always experienced it with detachment. It's something she inflicts on others. People like her aren't supposed to be in danger of being on the receiving end. And now that she's in the thick of it for the first time, the fear is overwhelming. Her legs are numb. Her belly is on fire. Her brain is in pure flight mode. She needs to run. To get away from here as fast as she can. Her life depends on it. But Jonno's dead weight has pinned her down in the back seat of a stolen Vauxhall Mokka. And with her hands tied behind her back, she has no leverage. She's trapped.

The high-pitched ringing in Al's ears is so loud he

doesn't hear her. He fumbles with the buckle of his seat-belt, but it's stuck. He presses down on the release button, and it won't budge. From the corner of his eye, he sees two figures emerge from the Insignia, brandishing guns.

Time stretches. Bends. Freezes. The figures, and Al's hand on the seatbelt, move in slow motion, to the sound of his heavy breathing. He presses down on the button, so hard he feels a jolt of pain shoot up his thumb. Nothing happens. He grits his teeth. Tugs at the seatbelt with his free hand. Pushes. His movements get more frantic by the second. Unless he can disengage the seatbelt and get out of the car, he'll follow Jonno into eternal nothingness.

When the seatbelt releases, time speeds back up to normal. Adrenaline floods his bloodstream, and he's on autopilot. He reaches for the gun, which fell in the passenger side footwell when the car hit the verge. The ringing in his ears subsides. He hears Morag, whimpering like a mauled animal that knows it's done for.

Putting his shoulder into it, Al opens the door. It flies open. He lands on the tarmac, arms outstretched in front of him to break his fall. He scrambles to his feet. Runs. To where he doesn't know. He hazards a look behind him. The figures have opened the left rear door of the Mokka, dragged Jonno out and thrown him onto the tarmac. One of them, clad in blue jeans, a black jacket, and a scarf that covers most of his face, reaches inside. Drags Morag out of the car by her hair. The other figure, also in blue jeans, black jacket, and a scarf around his face, grabs her legs.

Morag writhes and squirms like a rabid snake. But it's no contest. Her hands are tied and her interlocutors are big and strong. They easily overpower her. One of them hits her over the head with the butt of his gun, and she goes limp. They bundle her into the back of the Insignia and peel off with a screech of rubber.

Al stares at the scene transfixed, on legs that feel like jelly.

There's no thought of Morag. Whether he's the one to kill her isn't important, as long as she's out of the picture. But the sight of Jonno disturbs him. Fills him with a depth of sadness he didn't think he had the capacity for. Here lies a man who gave the team his unconditional, unquestioning loyalty. And look what he got for his pains. His short life ended with him discarded at the side of the road like a stray bit of rubbish.

His thoughts turn to the life that, for the briefest of moments, was his. And of the person that made him believe it was possible.

Of P.

He turns away from the wreck of the Mokka. Begins to walk. Towards somewhere he can find another car, so he can drive up to Fort Drumblehan.

Can he make amends?

Will P forgive him?

Will she agree to follow him somewhere neither his past nor the polis can get to him?

He doesn't know.

But the urge to ask her, to do his best to persuade her to give him another chance, is overwhelming.

It fills every fibre of his being.

He has to try.

He will try his very best.

CHAPTER 70

At first, I can't get my bearings. The dirty ceiling, the blue curtain, and the high-pitched sounds that are pinging in time with my pulse are like pieces of a puzzle that you know should go together but don't quite fit.

Where the fuck am I?

What are these weird sights and sounds?

And why does my head feel like somebody inserted several cases of C4 inside it and detonated them all at once?

I vaguely remember waking up hungover, with very little recollection of what had happened the night before. Images flash briefly before my eyes. A middle-aged bloke in a tux. Something about a leak. A gun.

Holy fuck!

I jolt upright. It sets off an explosion of pain inside my head. I see stars. Lay back down on the... bed?

I see a wire snaking out of the crook of my arm. A display of numbers on a monitor next to me. The source of this infernal pinging.

And then it all comes flooding back.

Waking up with a dead body in my bed. Getting threatened at gunpoint. Legging it. Getting shot at.

So what happened? Is this the afterlife? Am I in some sort of holding bay where they cure you of whatever killed you before they break the news and reveal what's in store for the rest of eternity?

No. There's no way I'm dead. My head hurts too much for that.

Everything fucking hurts.

I turn left and right. Slowly. Gingerly. Spot the buzzer. Press it. My throat's parched. What did that bastard do to me? I think he shot me. And seeing as I'm in a hospital bed, he must have hit. Hard enough to maim but not kill.

'Ah, good morning, sunshine,' a rail-thin nurse with steel-grey hair tied back in a bun tells me.

'What's going on?' I try to say.

But the sound that comes out is a strangled croak.

'Take it easy,' the nurse says. 'Here, have some water.'

She picks up a plastic cup from the side table, and places the straw in my mouth. It's blessedly cold. Revitalising. Every cell in my body soaks it up greedily.

'What happened?' I try again.

'The doctor's doing the rounds,' the nurse says. 'She'll come and speak to you. But the gist of it is that you're very lucky.'

She points at my temple.

'A couple of inches to the left, and we wouldn't be having this conversation,' she says.

I let this sink in.

'It's just a graze,' the nurse continues, probably because she's seen my eyes widen in alarm. 'But you've also suffered a concussion. The doctor wants to keep you under observation. As I said, she'll explain everything.'

I look at the nurse, dumbstruck. It's hard to fathom what she just told me. You spend your life trying not to think about death, because the end of everything's too scary to contemplate. Except nothing you can possibly imagine about it even comes close to how it plays out in the real world. I could've been gone, in a second. And I'd have had no idea.

None at all.

I shiver.

'Are you alright?' the nurse says. 'Do you need another blanket?'

'Erm, no. No I'm fine,' I say.

But am I, really?

What she's just told me. Everything that's catching up with me. It's. A LOT.

'Well buzz if you need anything,' she says. 'I'm afraid you've missed lunch. But there's the menu for tonight on your side table and we can make you a toast in the meantime, if you want.'

Food's the last thing on my mind. God. I'm sick to my stomach just thinking about it.

'I'm OK for now,' I say. 'I think.'

'That's fine,' the nurse says.

She bustles out of my cubicle.

I should feel happy to be alive. Angry at the plumber. Harry whatshisface. At Morag, for dragging me into her drama. Because she's involved in all this, isn't she? That cock and bull story about the leak.

Or maybe I should be re-evaluating my life choices. Isn't that what people do after a near-death experience?

But I'm just. Numb.

I lean back into the pillows, feeling the coarse fabric

through the bandage on my head. Stare at the blue curtain, my mind blank.

At some point, I must've drifted off. When I wake up again, there's a bloke in a rumpled suit standing at the curtain, looking at me appraisingly and chewing gum. Behind him are two uniformed officers.

'Hello, Mr Haig,' the bloke says. 'I'm Inspector Doug Lennox.'

He flashes his warrant card. I give it a cursory glance, barely registering what I see.

'May I sit down?' he asks me.

'Err... aye sure,' I stammer.

He comes in. Sits in the institutional grey armchair next to my hospital bed. Folds his hands in his lap. The two uniforms stay put near the curtain, shuffling their feet.

'How are you feeling?' he asks.

The concern on his face looks genuine.

'Honestly?' I tell him. 'I'm not sure. In pain. Confused. Kind of numb.'

'Do you remember what happened at all?' he asks.

'Bits and bobs,' I say. 'There was... there was a dead body. And then my downstairs neighbour sent a plumber up, something about a leak. And next thing I know he pulled a gun on me.'

Doug nods.

'The plumber's name is Harry McVeigh,' he says. 'And he's as much a plumber as I'm the King of England. In fact, if you'll pardon my French...'

He leans forward, and I get a whiff of his aftershave and another smell I can't quite place. Berry?

'...he wouldn't know the business end of a wrench if you shoved it up his arse,' he finishes.

He sits back in the armchair. Chuckles at his own wit.

Then his features rearrange themselves. He's all business again.

'You're very lucky we got there when we did, Mr Haig,' he says.

'So I'm told,' I say wearily.

'McVeigh. Your neighbour Morag Stevenson. It looks like you got yourself mixed up with some very bad people,' he says.

'So she's involved?' I say.

'In charge,' Doug replies.

'Fuck.'

Over the next half hour, I recount my version of events. I tell the inspector how I don't remember much about last night. How I woke up this morning to find this bloke I'd never seen before in my life in my bed, stone cold dead. How Harry pulled a gun on me. I probably shouldn't have told him I decided to hide the body, but I held nothing back. In my state, it's not like I could've thought things through. Got my story straight. Whatever that means.

He seems very understanding, though. Compassionate. He tells me that they've arrested Harry but can't find Morag. About her rise to power, including Al's role in it. And he gives me the scoop about her gang-related activities. Apparently, unbeknownst to me, my flat was doubling as her private office. Which goes a long way towards explaining how I ended up with a dead body in my bed, as well as all the other weird stuff that's been happening. Like finding lights I was sure I'd switched off turned on.

'Right,' I say. 'So this Kiernan is the boss of the Big Hand, and Morag—'

'Red Hand,' he corrects me.

'Red Hand. Right,' I say.

I stare in the distance. Shake my head.

'Morag. An organised crime mastermind. Jesus fucking Christ.'

'We'll need you to come down to the station and make a formal statement,' Doug says, standing up. 'When you feel up to it.'

'Right. Err, sure. Of course.'

'Bertie! Oh my god!'

I look up. Joan's standing at the curtain, in between the two uniforms. My spirits lift instantly.

'Joan. How did you? How did...?'

'I saw it online,' she says, walking in. 'They said there was a shooting, and I recognised your address.'

The fact she remembers where I live, even though I've mentioned it maybe once, in passing, makes me extraordinarily happy. I could almost consider this whole ordeal worthwhile. Almost.

'I tried to call you, and when you didn't answer, I got worried,' she continues. 'So I drove down and there was police tape everywhere, and blood, and... god I'm so glad you're OK.'

The inspector clears his throat.

'I'll leave you to it, Mr Haig,' he says.

He hands me his card.

'Give me a call when you feel up to it. No rush.'

'Err, aye.'

He walks out, the two uniforms flanking him like bodyguards.

Joan sits in his place. Leans forward. Takes my hand in hers.

We chat late into the afternoon, laughing out loud and making plans for dinner when I get out of this place. Sans Shawn.

And we don't mention work or Phillip a single time.

EPILOGUE

Could you imagine waking up one morning, and finding a random dead bloke in your bed?

'Fucking hell,' Doug thinks as he walks out of the hospital and into the dreary afternoon. 'Poor sod.'

The weather has lived up to its promise. The dark clouds that bore over the city the whole morning have finally unclenched, releasing fine droplets that look more like mist than rain.

But Doug doesn't hurry.

He waves goodbye to the uniforms, who walk to their squad car. Then, when he's sure he's on his own, he discards his chewing gum, retrieves the vape from his trouser pocket and takes a long drag, holding it in his lungs for a full thirty seconds before exhaling an enormous cloud of smoke.

With the exhale, his lips curve into an involuntary smile. Fuck chewing gum. What a poor substitute it is for the real thing. Smoking is a filthy, filthy habit. One day it'll kill him, he's sure. But god it feels so good. You could be having the worst day ever, and a single puff instantly puts the world back to rights. Without fail.

He strolls towards his car, barely feeling the rain in his nicotine-induced euphoria, unlocks it, and gets in. He's putting his seatbelt on when his phone buzzes into life.

He checks the caller ID. It's the call he's been expecting.

'Inspector Lennox,' he says.

'Hello Inspector,' the voice on the other end — a voice that sounds pained and overworked — says. 'It's Tom. Harries. The duty sergeant. How far are you from the links?'

'I'm around fifteen minutes away. Why?' Doug says.

'We received a call about a body out near the lake,' Harries says. 'Older female.'

'I see. And any reason in particular you're calling me about it?' Doug says. 'My shift's almost over. Can't somebody else attend the scene?'

'I know, Inspector. But the uniforms say it looks gang-related.'

'Gang-related?' Doug says, feigning surprise. 'The links aren't gang territory.'

'I believe it's how she's been killed, sir,' Harries says. 'It would really be best if you saw for yourself. I wouldn't know from here.'

'Right,' Doug says. 'I'm on my way.'

He ends the call. Sits back in the car. Cracks a window open. Indulges in several more puffs from his vape. He wouldn't usually vape in the car, but he thinks he's earned this.

To a job well done.

He retrieves the other phone from the glove compartment. Dials.

'Aye,' his employer says.

'They've found her,' Doug says. 'It's over. The bitch is dead.'

There's a brief pause, pregnant with meaning.

'Good job. Good job.'

'Now what?' Doug says. 'Are we done?'

His employer considers.

'Almost,' he says. 'Now we watch the bottom-feeders destroy each other. There'll be nothing left of either of them in no time.'

On the other side of the line, Doug's employer sits astride his motorcycle looking from a distance at the bedlam surrounding the building he's called home for four years. Almost as long as he's been planning this.

The police have just bagged Boaby Kiernan and taken him away. That was a stroke of luck. He'd never have believed she'd be so foolhardy. So stupid. To kill Kiernan. And to do it on her own bloody doorstep. As his Da was fond of saying in his more lucid periods, before the drugs destroyed everything about what made him, well, him, you don't shite where you eat.

But who was he to complain?

She'd made his job much easier. Sped up the plan that had begun to form in his mind the first time they'd crossed paths on the landing as he was walking up to his flat, minding his own business. The plan to destroy the Guthrie family. And indeed, the bloody gangs of west Strathburgh. The gangs that destroyed his Da, his family, and his childhood.

The rain peters out.

Graeme breathes deeply, inhaling the scent of petrichor.

It's a pure smell. Cleansing. Just as his plan, now in its endgame, will cleanse west Strathburgh once and for all.

The thing these people don't understand is that power is relative.

Impermanent.

Every dog has its day.

And, for one particular dog, today is a very fine day indeed.

THE END

1 August 2022, Newton Stewart —
20 November 2023, Edinburgh

Afterword

On a dreich Friday afternoon in January 2021, I stumbled across a list of writing prompts online.

At the time, I was starting to think that maybe I didn't have it in me to write a novel, an ambition I've had since I was at least 8 years old. I'd tried (and failed) to write one several times over the years. And, now, I had nothing. Not even the seed of an idea.

But one of the prompts — what if you woke up next to a dead stranger? — stirred something in me. I jotted the idea down in my Notes app so I wouldn't forget it. And then I promptly forgot about it and went on with my life. As you do.

Then, in 2022, my friend Penny Brazier told me about #2badpagesaday — a Twitter (I refuse to call it X) challenge, where you write 2 pages of something, anything, every day from 1 August until the end of the year. The idea is that, by the time December rolls around, you should have a draft that, while very messy, is a foundation you can build on.

#2badpagesaday was the kick up the arse I needed.

'It's two bad *pages a day. So it doesn't matter if it's shite. It kind of has to be, right?* I'd tell myself on days when staring at the document made my heart race (in a bad way), and writing felt like pulling teeth.

It worked.

The voice in my head shouting at me that I couldn't do this and should stop wasting my time gradually quieted down, and the words started coming more easily. Within six weeks, I'd finished the first draft of the book you're holding in your hands.

Penny also read the first draft and gave me invaluable feedback which greatly improved the story.

My friends Craig Wright, Louise Shanahan, Dee Primett, and Jo Aaron also read the first draft. Their comments and suggestions were invariably on point, and this novel is all the better because of them. Thank you.

PC Sam Davison answered my questions about the ins and outs of Scottish police procedure. Thank him for everything I got right. Blame me for any howlers.

Rebecca Millar, my developmental editor, gently but firmly dished the brutal truth about my manuscript's shortcomings. Her recommendations unlocked the narrative, and it's no exaggeration to say they took my story to another level.

Kieran Devaney did a fantastic job on the line edit. He made me sound like a much better writer, and put forward several suggestions that improved the narrative flow.

Designer Adam Hay understood what I wanted even though I had no clue myself. Thank you for your patience and the brilliant cover design.

Last, but most definitely first, my wife Analise has been incredibly supportive throughout. She gave me the space to write, read my manuscript (twice), and cheered me on every step of the way. You're the best. There's no-one else I'd rather be taking on this adventure called life with.

And to my daughters Alicia and Adelaide, thank you for being who you are. I hope that, in some small way, I've inspired you to forge your own paths.

About the Author

André Spiteri was born in Malta in 1982. He lives in Edinburgh with his wife, their two daughters, and two cats. *Back From The Dead* is his first novel.

Stay up to date on andrespiteri.com

Printed in Great Britain
by Amazon

41126811R00253